FAIRER THAN *Morning*

Book One

THE SADDLER'S LEGACY

ROSSLYN ELLIOTT

Blessings to you,
Rosslyn Elliott

THOMAS NELSON
Since 1798

NASHVILLE DALLAS MEXICO CITY RIO DE JANEIRO

For all those who never find freedom in this world

but will find it in the next

Published in Nashville, Tennessee, by Thomas Nelson. Thomas Nelson is a registered trademark of Thomas Nelson, Inc.

Published in association with the literary agency of WordServe Literary Group, Ltd., 10152 S. Knoll Circle, Highlands Ranch, CO 80130. www.wordserveliterary.com.

Scripture quotations are taken from the KING JAMES VERSION.

Thomas Nelson, Inc., titles may be purchased in bulk for educational, business, fundraising, or sales promotional use. For information, please e-mail SpecialMarkets@ ThomasNelson.com.

Publisher's Note: This novel is a work of fiction. Names, characters, places, and incidents are either products of the author's imagination or used fictitiously.

Library of Congress Cataloging-in-Publication Data

Elliott, Rosslyn.
    Fairer than morning / Rosslyn Elliott.
       p. cm.— (The saddler's legacy ; bk. 1)
    Includes bibliographical references and index.
    ISBN 978-1-59554-785-9 (trade pbk.)
    1. Indentured servants—Fiction. 2. Fugitive slaves—Fiction. 3. Abolitionists—Fiction. 4. Underground Railroad—Fiction. 5. Pittsburgh (Pa.)—History—19th century—Fiction. I. Title.
    PS3605.L4498F35 2011
    813'.6—dc22   2011001782

Printed in the United States of America

11 12 13 14 15 RRD 5 4 3 2 1

One

PROPOSALS OF MARRIAGE SHOULD NOT CAUSE PANIC. That much she knew.

Eli knelt before her on the riverbank. His cheekbones paled into marble above his high collar. Behind him, the water rushed in silver eddies, dashed itself against the bank, and spiraled onward out of sight. If only she could melt into the water and tumble away with it down the narrow valley.

She clutched the folds of her satin skirt, as the answer she wanted to give him slid away in her jumbled thoughts.

Afternoon light burnished his blond hair to gold. "Must I beg for you? Then I shall." He smiled. "You know I have a verse for every occasion. 'Is it thy will thy image should keep open, My heavy eyelids to the weary night? Dost thou desire my slumbers should be broken, While shadows like to thee do mock my sight?'"

The silence lengthened. His smile faded.

"No." The single word was all Ann could muster. It sliced the air between them with its awkward sharpness.

He faltered. "You refuse me?"

"I must."

He released her hand, his eyes wide, his lips parted. After a pause, he closed his mouth and swallowed visibly. "But why?" Hurt flowered in his face.

"We're too young." The words sounded tinny and false even to her.

"You've said that youth is no barrier to true love. And I'm nineteen." He rose to his feet, buttoning his cobalt cutaway coat.

"But I'm only fifteen." Again Ann failed to disguise her hollowness.

She had never imagined a proposal so soon, always assuming it years away, at a safe distance. She should never have told him how she loved the story of Romeo and Juliet. Only a week ago she had called young marriage romantic, as she and Eli sat close to one another on that very riverbank, reading the parts of the lovers in low voices.

"There is some other reason." In his mounting indignation, he resembled a blond avenging angel. "What is it? Is it because I did not ask your father first?"

"You should have asked him, but even so, he would not have consented. Father will not permit me to marry until I am eighteen."

"Eighteen? Three years?" His eyes were the blue at the center of a candle flame. "Then you must change his mind. I cannot wait." He slid his hands behind her elbows and pulled her close. His touch aligned all her senses to him like nails cleaving to a magnet. With an effort, she twisted from his grasp and shook her head.

His brow creased and he looked away as if he could not bear

the sight of her. "I think it very callous of you to refuse me without the slightest attempt to persuade your father."

"I do not think he will change his mind. He has been very clear."

"Then perhaps you should have been—clearer—yourself." His faint sarcasm stung her, as if a bee had crawled beneath the lace of her bodice.

He dropped his gaze. "You would not give up so easily if you cared. You have deceived me, Ann."

He turned and walked up the riverbank, the white lining flashing from the gore of his coat over his boot tops. Before she could even call out, he topped the ridge and disappeared from view.

She stared blankly after him. She was so certain that the Lord had intended Eli to be her husband. But that once-distant future had arrived too early, and now it lay in ruins.

Numb, she collected the history and rhetoric books that she had dropped on the grass. She must change her father's mind, as Eli had said. If she did not, all was lost.

She clutched the books to her like a shield and began the long walk home.

In front of the farmhouse, her two young sisters crouched in the grass in their flowered frocks. Mabel pointed her chubby little finger at an insect on the ground. Susan brushed back wispy strands of light-brown hair and peered at it.

"Have you seen Father?" Ann asked them.

Their soft faces turned toward her.

"He's in the workshop." Mabel's voice was high and pure

and still held a trace of her baby lisp. She turned back to inspect the grass.

"He said he is writing a sermon and please not to disturb him," Susan added with the panache of an eight-year-old giving orders.

Without comment, Ann angled toward the barn, which held the horses and also a workshop for her father's saddle and harness business. Like most circuit riders, he did not earn his living from his ministry, and so he crafted sermons and saddles at the same workbench.

He glanced up when the wooden door slapped against its frame behind her.

"Ann." His clean-shaven face showed the wear of his forty years, though his posture was vigorous and his constitution strong from hours of riding and farm work. "I asked Susan to let you know I was writing." There was no blame in his voice. He had always been gentle with them, and even more so since their mother had passed away.

"She did. But I must speak with you."

"You seem perturbed." He laid down his quill and turned around in his chair. "Will you sit down?"

"No, thank you." She clasped her hands in front of her and pressed them against her wide sash to steady herself as she took a quick breath. "Eli Bowen proposed to me today."

"Without asking my blessing?" A small line appeared between his brows. "And what did you tell him?"

"That I cannot marry until I am eighteen. That you have forbidden it."

"That is true. I have good reason to ask you to wait." He regarded her steadily.

She summoned restraint with effort. "What reason? I am

young, I know, but he is nineteen. He can make his way in the world. He wishes to go to medical school."

"I don't doubt that Mr. Bowen is a fine young man." Her father's reply was calm. "But I do not think your mother would have let you marry so young."

"Dora Sumner married last year, and she was only sixteen." She paced across the room, casting her eyes on the floor, on the walls, anywhere but on him. He must not refuse, he must not. He did not understand.

"I am not Dora's father." His voice was flat, unyielding. He turned to his table and gently closed his Bible. When he faced her again, his demeanor softened. "Your mother almost married another man when she was your age. She told me it would have been a terrible match. She was glad she waited until she was eighteen." He looked at her mother's tiny portrait in its oval ivory frame on the table. "She said that by the time she met me, she knew her own mind and wasn't quite as silly."

"I am not silly. I know how I feel. And he is not a terrible match." Her voice grew quieter as her throat tightened.

"I am sorry, Ann. I must do what I think is right." He was sober and sad.

Or what is convenient. For who else would care for my sisters, if not me?

But such thoughts wronged her father, for she had never known him to act from self-interest.

"But how can he wait for me? He is older than I am. He will want to marry before three years are out." She did not try to keep the pleading from her voice, though her face tingled.

He paused, then leaned forward, as steady and quiet as when he comforted a bereaved widow. "Then he does not deserve you."

"No, you are simply mistaken. And cruel."

He stood up and walked to the back of the barn.

Clutching her skirt, she whirled around, pushed through the door, and ran for the house.

She would not give way to tears. She must stay calm. She slowed to a walk so her sisters would not be startled and passed them without a word.

Her bedroom beckoned her down the dark hallway.

She did not throw herself on the bed, as she had so often that first year after the loss of her mother.

Instead, she went to her desk, lifted the top, and fished out her diary. Her skirts sent up a puff of air as she flounced into the seat and began writing feverishly. After some time, the even curves of her handwriting mesmerized her, and her quill slowed. She lifted it from the page of the book and gazed ahead at the dark oaken wall.

What if he does not wait for me?

She must not doubt him so. Eli would regain his good humor and understand. He had told her many times that she was his perfect match, that he would never find another girl so admirable and with such uncommon interest in the life of the mind.

Besides, she had been praying to someday find a husband of like interests and kind heart, and God had provided. Eli loved poetry and appreciated fine art, but he was nonetheless a man's man who liked to ride and hunt. And of course, he was every village girl's dream, with his aristocratic face. No other young man in Rushville could compare.

She doodled on the bottom of the page. First she wrote her own name.

Ann Miller.

Then she wrote his. Then she wrote her name with his.

Ann Bowen.

Ann Bowen.

Ann Bowen.

She smiled, pushed the diary aside, and pillowed her head on her arm to daydream of white bridal gowns and orange blossoms.

Two

PENNSYLVANIA
18th July 1823

IF A YOUNG MAN HAD TO SIGN AWAY HIS FREEDOM FOR five whole years, surely this was the best way to do it. Will pulled the heavy window cloth aside and leaned forward to look out the carriage window.

"Not yet, boy," Master Good said.

What a kind voice Will's future master had. It was smooth as oiled leather, befitting a man with a calm brow and a steady gaze. Master Good's hair was uncommonly dark for a man of middle age, his light blue eyes ageless under the rim of his fine black hat. He lifted his hand with fluid grace to gesture at the window. "See that hill?"

"Yes, sir." The carriage drove alongside a huge mound that obscured their view. All Will could see was a tapestry of grass rolling past the window at a rapid rate. The foot-tall growth on the hillside was mostly green, but here and there threads of dry straw whispered of colder days to come.

"The city won't come into view until we round the hill."

Master Good lifted his leather satchel into his lap. Unbuckling the clasp, he drew out several pieces of ivory parchment and thrust them in Will's direction. "Look, boy."

Will let the cloth fall back over the window and wiped his hand on his pants before taking the papers.

His master leaned back against the leather seat. "We'll be stopping soon to sign this and have it witnessed by my neighbor. Best to read through it now so we can be quick."

Will was grateful his father had taught him to read so well. Father would be proud now, if he could see how Will had secured such a good future for himself.

The threat of tears prickled in his eyes. He fought them off. It had been six years since he lost his parents. The boy of ten who wept every night that year was now almost a young man. He would behave like one, especially in front of his soon-to-be master.

Holding the documents in one hand, Will pressed his thin knapsack with the other and reassured himself that his folded packet of letters was still in there. Those letters and the little silver locket were all he had left of his mother and father.

He stared at the papers Master Good had given him. The letters stood out in thick flourishes, stark and black against the purity of the paper.

County of Allegheny

To wit

Mr. Jacob Good Came this Day in the presence of witness, to receive William Hanby as an Apprentice for the period of five years, to learn the art or trade of

Saddlery and perform sundry duties to support his Master's trade. During the whole of this period said Apprentice will be in His Master's Service and will not work for Hire for any other person; he will be obedient to his Master's command and diligent in his Employment. To his Master he will grant all Sovereignty over his person and his whereabouts for the duration of his Apprenticeship; his Master shall provide him with bed and board. Upon the successful completion of the Term, his Master shall furnish him with a set of tools of the trade, one new coat, and one pair of new shoes.

Signed, dated, and countersigned,

"You see that all is in order," Master Good said. He adjusted his hat and opened his hand for the papers.

"Yes, sir. Thank you, sir." Will gave back the indenture agreement with care.

The driver on top of the carriage whistled to the horses in their traces; the whip cracked. The jostling increased, and Will's shoulder rammed into the wooden doorframe on his left. Wincing, he leaned again to the window and pulled the small curtain aside.

The city of Pittsburgh! The coach had topped the hill. In the valley below, three rivers joined and a jumbled maze of dark buildings spread out between them. Smoke drifted over the city like thick fog. He smelled something unpleasant, like burning refuse. *No matter. Naturally, where there's industry and wealth, there will be smoke.* Nothing could quell his excitement.

All he had known was life on a farm. When he was seven, his parents and his two sisters had developed a consumption that gave them first a cough, then fever and pains throughout the body. On a doctor's advice, his father had indentured Will and his still-healthy brother, Johnny, to two separate farming families, in order to save them from infection. Over the course of two years, one letter after another informed Will that first his sisters and then his father and mother had succumbed to virulent infection of the blood, an effect of consumption no doctor could heal.

With the Quaker farmer, Will's work had been hard, though the farmer was fair and honest. Will had longed to see more than barns and horses—he wanted to read books, see ships, talk to travelers. When his farm indenture expired last month, he had jumped at the chance for a Pittsburgh apprenticeship. He could hardly wait for the larger world that lay before him.

At the bottom of the hill, the coach entered a labyrinth of streets dense with buildings. First was a two-story mercantile, then a livery stable. Next came a brick warehouse with "Rifles and Munitions" painted in white across its side. Pedestrians clotted the road. The coach clattered past doctors' establishments with gilt signs, and offices for attorneys-at-law.

"Master Good, look. Another saddler." Will pointed to a sign with a saddle and two crossed whips.

"Yes, I have plenty of would-be rivals." His master did not seem curious about the sights, but instead picked up a newspaper that lay on the seat beside him and scanned the advertisements. Outside the window, the crowd thinned and wider plots of land girdled genteel residences.

The carriage slowed and shuddered to a stop as the driver yelled, "Whoa there!" Boots thumped on the ground outside and the driver opened the door for them, his hat and whiskers covered with dust.

Will's master stooped to exit the carriage, and then it was Will's turn. He slung his knapsack over his shoulder with care. He would not let it out of his sight until he had a safe place for the letters and the locket in the little drawstring pouch.

When Will climbed down from the coach, his master was already striding toward a two-story white home, graceful amid green lawns. Will had never seen such a large dwelling; he tried not to let his eyes pop like a bumpkin's.

He quickened his step to catch up with his master, who rapped with a brass knocker on the blue double door. After a brief wait, the door opened to reveal a young woman in a gray dress and white apron, her hair bound in a net.

"Hello, Mary," Master Good said. "I need to speak with the doctor, if you please."

She bobbed her head and ushered them in, then disappeared into the recesses of the home.

The foyer had a high ceiling, marble floor, and a banister-lined staircase curving up and back to the left. A painting in muted tones depicted a dark valley, relieved only by rays of light breaking through massed clouds above.

"Good afternoon to you, Jacob." A deep voice issued from the man who stepped through the arched doorway on the far side of the foyer. He was of average height and wore a black frock coat; his hair was pure white and his shoulders straight as a soldier's. As he crossed the room to offer a hand to Will's master, he shot Will a quick glance. Will wished his own coat and trousers were not so threadbare and shabby.

"Dr. Loftin." Master Good shook the doctor's hand briefly, then clasped Will's shoulder. "This is my new apprentice, William Hanby."

The doctor nodded at Will.

"He is entering his term of apprenticeship today. We need a witness for his papers of indenture." Master Good stepped over to a small mahogany table against the wall, placed his satchel on it, and removed the papers. "Would you serve as our witness?"

The doctor hesitated. His bright green eyes were set in crow's feet; his gaze lingered on Will's face. "William." He did not take his eyes off Will even as he extended his hand for the papers. "Are you aware of the significance of this contract?"

"Yes, sir."

The doctor's expression was grave. "You realize you will be irrevocably bound to your master for five years? You understand that?"

"Yes, sir. I'm grateful for the opportunity Master Good is providing for me."

The doctor looked over the papers. At last he spoke, a furrow creasing his brow. "Very well. The last time I witnessed an indenture document was twenty years ago, and it was for a grown Irishman, not a boy. But if you are certain, William, I suppose we will need a quill."

It was the work of a moment to call the maid for a quill and inkhorn. Good signed first, writing "Jacob Good" in a jagged hand like an insect's trail. Will scrawled his name beneath, then the doctor signed "Robert Loftin, MD" at the very bottom.

"Well, it's done," the doctor said. "And I pray God will watch over this indenture." He spoke quietly, almost to himself.

"I'm sure he will," Master Good said, and shaking the doctor's hand once more, bid him good day.

Master Good's household lay just a short walk beyond the doctor's home. Will trailed his master as they headed down a winding path past the doctor's animal pens. A fine white sow and her piglets rooted in their trough. His little brother, Johnny, loved feeding piglets and hearing them squeal. Will hoped his brother would get along all right in Beallsville.

A two-story home loomed ahead of them, not as large as the doctor's, but sturdily built of whitewashed planks. Master Good must have been very industrious to be blessed with such a home, as well as a large barn and fenced-in land. The master walked up to his front door without ceremony and let himself in. Will ran behind and barely caught the door with his elbow before it closed.

They stood in a dim, large room. To the left, stiff maroon chairs posed in front of a fireplace. To the right was a kitchen with a large hearth and stone floor. Pots and pans hung from the imposing central beam of the kitchen ceiling. There was a damp smell, as if the bones of the house were old and in need of air.

"Jane!" Master Good's unexpected shout made Will jump.

Something thudded to the floor upstairs. Feet pattered on the staircase next to them, and down the lower flight of steps rushed a rail-thin, middle-aged woman with mousy hair pulled tightly back from her forehead. She stopped, poised like a heron about to take flight. "Jacob," she said. "Welcome to you."

He brushed past her and into the kitchen. "Come over here, boy," he said over his shoulder. Will hurried after him to the hearth.

"Jane, where is Tom?" Without waiting for an answer, the master bellowed, "Tom! Tom Reece!"

The kitchen door flew open and a tangle of limbs fell

through, sorting itself into the figure of a slight boy with dark hair and a grimy face. He appeared younger than Will—perhaps a year or two. His cheekbones were sharp, his elbows so skinny they looked as if they would snap at the slightest pressure.

"Tom, this is your new fellow apprentice, Will Hanby. Explain to him our rules."

"Yes, sir," Tom said faintly.

Good removed his hat. The skinny woman scurried over and took it, then retreated back against the wall. "Well?" Good said to Tom.

Tom spoke in a quick monotone as if reciting a lesson learned by heart. "In this house, Master Good, you are the head and your word law. Your authority covers Mistress Good"—the boy turned his head toward the bird-like woman—"and she has your authority over me as well."

Jane Good hunched her shoulders at the mention of her name. She clutched her husband's hat, her face pale.

"Will, you shall learn from Tom what is expected of you." Master Good's tone was controlled. "You will gather wood, do washing, prepare leather for me, and anything else I desire. You will be instantly obedient, not wasting my time in dithering, nor slouching, nor remaining in bed like a sluggard. I expect you to have already risen and stoked the fire by the time I arrive downstairs. You will sleep in the hayloft with Tom, as we cannot have two servant boys here in the house with us."

The hayloft. We will freeze to death in winter. Will tried to keep his face blank, but a cascade of cold shock poured over him.

"In your best interest, I will instill discipline in you." Master Good walked past the hearth and plucked with his long fingers a thin cane that leaned in the corner. "I am sure you agree that it is a master's duty to ensure his apprentice has the qualities to do well in the world." He flexed the cane in his fingers, then set it back against the wall. "Tom, show Will where the dirty crockery is and how to take it for washing at the pump."

Tom scuttled to the hutch and opened the wooden door, a visible tremor in his outstretched arm. He removed a small stack of bowls, tucked the bowls in the crook of one arm, and closed the hutch. As he turned toward the kitchen door, the stack of bowls shifted, and the top bowl teetered. It eluded Tom's desperate grab and tumbled to the floor, its green curve shattering with a loud crash. Shards littered the stone floor.

Breathless silence fell. Jane Good's white face froze in a hard mask. Tom blinked and cowered behind his forelock of dark hair, his arms curled around the remaining bowls.

"You clumsy boy," Master Good said. "Put down those bowls on the table before you drop another."

Tom did so, his eyes glued to Master Good, who bent to the floor to gather a few shards. He straightened up and walked over to Tom at the table, placing the broken pieces gently beside the other bowls. Without any warning, the master drew back his arm and struck Tom with great force on the temple. The boy lost his footing, slammed sidelong into the wall, and fell to the ground.

"I would request that you pick up the rest of this mess, Tom," Master Good said. "But I'm afraid that for such a clumsy boy, these sharp pieces might be dangerous."

Tears etched white streaks in the grime on Tom's face.

Moved, Will spoke up. "Master, surely it was an accident."

An icy light kindled in the depths of Master Good's eyes.

"Oh, you disagree with my discipline of the boy? I can see that you and I will need to have a long talk."

Hairs lifted on the back of Will's neck.

"Get out to the barn, Tom, and make yourself presentable," Good said, his mouth twisting in disgust. "And show him the pump, as I told you. You, boy." He indicated Will. "Take the bowls."

Tom pushed himself to his feet and staggered out the door.

The last thing Will wanted was to approach Master Good, but he had to pass by him in order to get the bowls.

Will stepped to the table. As he reached for the dishes, his master grabbed him by the shoulder and hooked one finger under the strap of his knapsack. "What's in here, boy? I need to make sure you're bringing nothing indecent into the home."

His stomach turned at the master's touch, but he dared not move.

Master Good yanked the knapsack off his shoulder and emptied it on the floor. "Underdrawers? And what's this?" Snatching the doeskin bag, he picked at its tight drawstrings and pulled out the letters from Will's mother.

Frowning, he perused them. "Worthless. Sentimental. You'll need to learn to avoid sentiment if you're to be worth anything. To start, we'll toss these in the rubbish." He handed the letters to Mistress Good, who crumpled them in her fist.

The gesture knocked the wind from Will's lungs. In his airless state, he could not manage a protest.

Master Good pulled out the locket with his father's portrait and fingered it. "Pretty, but also of no value. Mistress Good may keep it or sell it as she pleases." His master dropped the locket back in the sack and tossed it at his wife. It hit her in the chest and fell at her feet, but she snatched it up and scurried away toward the stairs.

"Now, my boy," and he sounded, if anything, even kinder than before. "Go with Tom. He will tell you about some other lessons—the ones you may wish to avoid."

Three

RUSHVILLE
Christmas 1823

IF ONLY SHE COULD AVOID SEEING ELI TODAY. IN THE corner of the general store, Ann bowed her head and prayed for a quick escape from the public eye.

Rushville was a small town, and the store rarely saw more than one customer at a time. But today was the Saturday before Christmas, and several ladies puttered about the shelves or stood in line between the heaped sacks and barrels.

Ann clutched her embroidered handbag. Her pin money would buy gifts for her father and her sisters. Such holiday luxuries were a benefit of life in a family of only four, she supposed. But she would have given anything and everything they owned to have her mother still with them. This would be their seventh Christmas without her.

She kept a sharp eye on her sisters, who roamed around poking at jointed puppets and picture books.

"Ann, may I have some candy?" Susan appealed to Ann

with her best china doll face. She pursed her lips together and widened her blue eyes—the same shade as their mother's eyes.

"No, Susan. Christmas is coming in three days. You'll get plenty of sweets then."

Susan wrinkled her forehead and pouted until even the ribbon in her light-brown hair seemed to wilt. When Ann would not relent, she drifted off to poke her nose over the side of the candy bin, vying for space with her sister Mabel.

Which candy was attracting such glinty-eyed interest? The maple sugar.

"Susan, Mabel, there are too many people in here. You need to go outside to clear some room."

"But I want to look around!" Susan said over her shoulder, entranced by the fair hair of a doll sitting on a barrel.

"You heard me," Ann said.

Behind the counter, Mrs. Sumner met Ann's gaze and smiled. Susan and Mabel were probably not the first little girls to be sent out of the store that day because it was "too crowded."

Susan sighed, took Mabel's hand, and dragged her out the door.

Through the storefront window, Ann saw her sisters greet their playmate Hattie Anderson in silent pantomime. The three girls crouched down to pry pebbles out of the frost-hardened dirt road. At least this cold would keep their mittens clean.

Her view of the girls was blocked as the store window framed a young man and his girl, looking like a happy portrait in their holiday finest. Ann's breath caught.

It was Eli. He strolled toward the door of Sumner's General, lean and fair, with the gracious turn of head that always made her think some forgotten duke lurked in his family line. Phoebe

Vanderlick held his arm and sauntered next to him. He smiled and removed his hat as if he himself had invented the courtesy just for Phoebe. The black-haired girl patted his sleeve.

Ann wanted to run, but there was only one door. The bell tinkled and the couple walked in. Eli guided Phoebe past the line of customers and cordially begged their pardon.

Then he noticed Ann. He stiffened; his smile faded. His complexion took a subtle pink cast, and Phoebe's lively dark eyes lost their warmth. Ann assumed what she hoped was a mask of indifference.

"Good morning." Mrs. Sumner broke the hush with loud cheer as she bustled behind the counter. She addressed herself to Mrs. Anderson, who had wandered over to a shelf full of spices. "Would you like some eggs today, Rebecca?"

Ann still could not move from where she stood or take her eyes from the couple.

Phoebe tucked her curly black hair behind her ear and stood closer to Eli, tightening her grip on his arm. "Eli, I think I have forgotten my shopping list at home. Would you mind terribly if we went back to get it?"

"Not at all," he said, plainly glad for any excuse. They wheeled around like a finely matched pair of carriage horses and fled.

While Mrs. Sumner finished measuring dry goods for Mrs. Anderson, the heat died down in Ann's face and her breathing steadied. How could Eli smile at Phoebe that way and hold her so close to his side, when only a few months ago he had sworn his devotion to Ann?

But no one else knew about his proposal, and no one ever would.

Mrs. Anderson bundled her packages and gave Ann a friendly nod on her way out.

"What can I get you, Ann?" Mrs. Sumner asked.

Ann cleared her throat so she could speak past the lump in it. "Mrs. Sumner, did a delivery come in for us? From Pittsburgh?"

"Let's see . . . Miller, Miller . . ." Mrs. Sumner dabbed vaguely at a floury spot on her dark blue dress. "Oh yes, the big barrel. How could I forget?" She turned to the corner where a large pine barrel sat in its iron hoops. "It's from Pittsburgh, all right. But how will you get it back home?" She tipped the barrel to check its weight.

"I brought the wagon."

Mrs. Sumner wiped her hands on her apron. Her sun-spatter of freckles gave her a constant cheerful air, but now her face was sober. "You're a credit to your house, young lady. I don't know many other girls who manage as well, and care for two little girls too."

Yes, and other girls are free to marry their sweethearts. Ann schooled her tone to mildness despite the hurt. "Thank you."

"George," Mrs. Sumner called back through the shop curtain. "Can you come help Ann Miller with this barrel?"

Mr. Sumner lumbered past the curtain, tucking his spectacles in his shirt pocket before thinking better of it and handing them to his wife. A man of burly stature, he merely nodded to Ann before hoisting the barrel in his arms.

Ann hastened to open the door for him. Her father's wagon and their bay mare stood next to a hitching post just a few yards down the street. Mr. Sumner took a fresh grip on the barrel and set off with the sidelong crab walk of a man carrying a bulky load. Susan and Mabel skipped behind him.

While he loaded it, Ann stepped back inside to ask Mrs. Sumner for some toys and candy for the girls. For her father, she chose a small writing book with blank pages. He always needed a place to scribble sermon ideas that came to him as he worked on his fine saddles.

When all the parcels were wrapped up and hidden from curious little investigators, Ann handed over a few coins. "Thank you very much, Mrs. Sumner. God bless you this Christmas."

"You and your family, as well." Mrs. Sumner handed Ann the parcels and touched her lightly on the shoulder in farewell.

Outside, Ann herded the girls into the back of the wagon and climbed up into the driver's seat. When she looked back to assure herself that the barrel was secure, something caught her eye.

The word *sugar* had been painted out, and instead, an address wobbled in black ink around the knots in the pine: *From Saddler Jacob Good of Pittsburgh to Saddler Samuel Miller of Rushville, Ohio.*

She did not know why, but something about that spidery handwriting unsettled her. She gazed at it for a long moment.

"Why are we waiting?" Susan rubbed her hands together.

"We're cold." Mabel pretended exaggerated shivers where they sat in the back. They both giggled.

Ann slapped the reins and clucked to the mare. She had to get her sisters home.

The temperature was dropping, and on the way back to the farm, the girls' breath floated in misty plumes before their mouths. Susan and Mabel amused themselves by seeing who could make more mouth-steam. The trees stood bare and stark against the gray sky, not a bird or an animal in sight the whole way home.

The girls' chatter ran off Ann's silent thoughts without

touching her, like water from a tin roof. She lost herself in memories of Eli, the day he showed her Shakespeare's sonnet and touched her cheek as she bent over the book, saying, "Let me not to the marriage of true minds admit impediments." His promise that in only another two years he would have saved enough to go on to university, or to train in medicine, if his father's friend in Cincinnati would take him on as an assistant. The moment he asked her to marry him.

Ann pulled up the wagon at the door of the empty farmhouse. "Girls, go inside and stoke the fire. Warm up."

Mabel and Susan piled off the back of the wagon and hurried through the doorway, closing the dark door behind them quickly as they had been taught.

Before Ann could go in the house, she had to tend to their mare, Bayberry. She had raised the horse from a foal, and now that Bayberry was full grown at four, Ann took pains to care for her properly. Nothing comforted Ann as much as the touch of the mare's velvety nostrils against her palm or the look of peace in her dark eyes.

Ann led the horse into her stall. Her gloves made it harder to unbuckle the harness, but she was determined not to take them off until she was in the house. Her fingers were numb with cold even with the gloves on.

When she had laid the harness aside, she put her arm around Bayberry's neck, buried her face in the mare's black mane, and closed her eyes. The picture of Phoebe and Eli together would not fade; her throat burned. She breathed deeply, grateful for the icy air that brought an ache to her lungs to distract her from the one in her heart. Eli had forgotten her so quickly. Why could he not wait?

She must think of any blessing she could find in his faith-lessness, or she would cry.

At least she could remain with her sisters here at the farm. She could not let them grow up without a motherly presence. She could not leave them to struggle through the beginnings of young womanhood alone, as she had.

Over six years ago, in the bedroom, her mother's life had seeped away while Ann held in her hands a squirming newborn Mabel. Her father had not returned from his ministry for two days. Like an automaton, Ann had scrubbed the blood from the floor as best as she could, burned the bed linens that would never be white again. And she had spent two days in the house with her mother's cool, rigid body with its awful staring eyes. She had not known to close them immediately; by the time she tried, it was too late.

Now a shameful fear consumed her every time her father left the farm, a dread that something terrible would happen, just as it had that day when she lost her mother and no one was there to help.

No one knew what she had seen, not even her father. She buried the awful memories in the darkness beneath Bayberry's mane, letting the warmth of living flesh against her cheek call her back from what was cold and dead.

The barrel from Pittsburgh. She had better take it inside the house.

Latching the stall behind her, she left the barn and went back to the wagon in the yard. She lowered the buckboard and wrestled the barrel out, moving her toes out of the way as it dropped with a thump on the frozen ground. She knew what was inside; it would not suffer from a thumping.

She dragged the barrel over the threshold. Warmth tingled on her cold nose and ears. Susan was becoming expert at stoking the fire. In a few years she would be even more help around the house.

The girls rushed over to see what was in the barrel, but the lid was wedged in place and would not budge.

"Mabel, will you bring me the fire iron? No, don't skip," Ann said as Mabel bobbed up and down, her ringlets tumbling over the shoulders of her white pinafore. "It's not safe to skip with a poker in your hand, and it's not proper in the house, anyway."

Mabel restrained herself to a tiptoe walk, still waving the black hook of the poker wildly so Ann had to grab it to avoid a poke in the gut.

Ann pried off the lid. A gorgeous red-brown cowhide, tanned and oiled, lay tucked in a spiral inside the barrel. Ann would let her father take it out and examine it in two days, when he came home from his current preaching trip. Her father was a master saddler, and only his experienced eye would determine whether this leather was fine enough. The customer had insisted on sending it all the way from Pittsburgh, to be returned when her father had shaped it into a sidesaddle.

Her sisters ran off to their bedroom to play hide and seek. They were bored by the sight of yet another piece of leather, to them just like every other tanned hide in the barn. Ann lifted the lid from the floor to set it back on the barrel.

But something else caught her eye, in the bottom, almost hidden by the coiled hide. Was that just rubbish or scrap paper? Curious, she tilted the barrel over on its side and reached in to her shoulder until she could snatch the crumpled papers and pull them out. She smoothed all six sheets and set them on the floor next to the hearth.

The light of the fire fell on the pages. She leaned over the nearest and read: *My dear Will.*

A letter. It wasn't right to read someone else's letters, but how could she return them if she didn't know whose they were? She would read just enough to figure it out.

30th July 1817

My Dear Will,

I wish I could be with you on this special day, your tenth birthday. I love to remember when God brought you into the world, blessing us with our firstborn. That morning that you opened your eyes and looked at me, what unspeakable joy and love I felt! The years since you and your sisters and brother were born have been the happiest years of my life, especially this past year in my sickness. I only hope that you will know what joy you have brought me, and keep it in your heart always.

Your father says perhaps we may be able to come home by autumn. We miss you terribly, but we cannot risk passing the consumption to you and Johnny. Be good and trust in the Lord to bring us through this time.

Your Loving Mother

The familiar ache of loss sharpened. How she would have treasured a letter like this from her own mother. But she and her mother had never been separated while her mother lived, and so there had been no occasion to write letters.

Surely this was not the kind of letter someone would throw away. Why had it been tossed in the bottom of a shipping barrel? She must get these letters back to whoever had lost them— probably someone in Pittsburgh. She could discuss it with her father, but he might say it was none of their concern. Or the mention of a sick mother in the letter might trigger one of his dark moods that could last for weeks.

Troubled, she collected each of the letters and folded them together. She must think on this. She would put the letters in a safe place where no one else would see them, until she could decide what to do.

Four

RUSHVILLE

22nd February 1826

ANN DIPPED HER QUILL IN THE INK AND SCRATCHED
on the page:

> *My Dearest Eli,*
>
> *It has been over two years now since you asked me to be your wife. You once told me that none should bar the marriage of true minds, and yet you yourself have done so without a backward glance. How could you turn from me with no further questions, as if choosing a new horse at market?*
>
> *You keep company with Phoebe Vanderlick. Does she share your love of letters? I have observed no such interest in her, for she never spoke of our studies in school but only of ribbons, games, and parties.*

Her hand trembled as she wrote the words, and an ugly stain blotted the page of her diary. She strained to read what she had written, but the cold light from her bedroom window failed to reach her desk. If only she could write to Eli of what was really in her heart—her abiding and passionate conviction that God had destined her to be Eli's wife, that there could be no other spouse for either of them. But she did not know how he would respond, so the words stayed trapped in the pages of her diary.

"Ann! Where are you?" her father called from the kitchen.

She snapped the little book shut, heedless of the likely smearing, and knelt down beside her bed to shove it under the loose floorboard. She kept the diary there with the wrinkled letters from the boy Will's mother, which she had read again and again until they were like letters from her own mother.

"Are you ready?" her father asked from the hall. He came to the door of her room, the gray in his hair belied by his clean-shaven face and vigorous bearing.

He closed his mouth in a firm line. "You aren't dressed."

"No, Father. I don't wish to go to the dance."

"You can't mew yourself up in here like a convent girl. You're eighteen years old. It's time for you to get out, meet young men." He avoided her eyes.

"I don't wish to meet any young men."

"That's not what your mother would have wished." He shook his head. "She would not want you to spend your life with me on our farm. I am to blame; I have not raised you as she would have—" He broke off. Perhaps he was thinking of the forbidden betrothal. His face grew overcast, the brows heavier, forecasting the coming gloom.

Ann sighed. "Very well, I'll go." The dance would be torture, with Eli and Phoebe certain to be in attendance, but it would be worse to see her father enter the shadows of his grief for her mother. When he did, Ann would be forced to put on an air of artificial lightness in the presence of her sisters, to keep the farm from sliding into full-scale mourning. She would rather bear up under two hours of chatter and dance invitations than two weeks of false gaiety.

"And wear the good dress I brought you from Pittsburgh," he said. "Your old ones don't fit as well, now that you're growing up." He looked away in embarrassment. "You too seldom make the most of your appearance. If your mother were here, she would urge you to tend to your hair as the other girls do. You're a very pretty girl, when you make up your mind to groom yourself and dress properly."

It doesn't matter now. "Yes, Father." She failed to keep the impatience from her voice. He withdrew from the doorway.

She was sorry when she was abrupt with him in that way. He had done what he thought best about Eli's proposal, and he was a good-hearted man. Still, his attempt at matchmaking now grated on her like a washboard against raw knuckles. She walked to the wardrobe and jerked open the door with ill will.

The dark red dress hung in satiny folds, taking up almost half the wardrobe. She snatched it without ceremony and tossed it on her bed. After she had divested herself of her everyday work dress, she laced her stays a little tighter and slipped the new dress over her head. The high neck with its ruffles across the shoulders was becoming and modest enough for an eighteen-year-old. The dress fit close around the middle before sweeping out over her petticoats. As her father had said—so mortifyingly for both of them—she had been growing more womanly. The satin against her skin did make her feel prettier, but she had no one to charm. The dress would only earn her more unwanted dance requests from James Murdoch and David Crawford, who were fine enough boys but not well spoken or interested in much beyond their farms.

When she had dressed and twisted her chestnut hair into something resembling the fashionable upswept style, she joined her father in the kitchen. He lifted his head from the volume of sermons he had open on the table and regarded her with approval.

"Beautiful, my girl." He stood and gave her a clumsy, one-armed embrace around her shoulders. "You'll have a fine time with the other young folk, you'll see."

Mabel rushed into the kitchen through the screen door, grubby from an adventure in the mud behind the barn. Her lips were blue; the wind bit sharp in late February, even in the absence of snow.

"You're a princess!" She clapped her hands and bounced, which brought some color back to her face.

"Just going to a dance, my sweet," Ann said. "You need to come in from the cold. Go tell Susan to come in too." She turned to retrieve her own cape from the stand and wrapped its woolen length around her arms. It was no match for her dress, but practicality trumped fashion. She would never ask her father to waste their money on a fine coat that would be ruined the first time she wore it to clean stalls or feed pigs.

Mabel twisted one yellow curl around her finger. "I want to go to the dance! May I?"

"When you're older you may go," Ann said. "You wouldn't like it."

"Oh." Mabel grabbed a tin cup from the shelf on the wall. "I need to finish one thing outside." She darted out before Ann could say another word.

Ann's father walked to the door and held it open for her. She walked out, holding her skirts away from the doorframe.

Across the yard, the girls were in heated conference as Mabel gestured with cup in hand. Susan, a head taller, gave half-audible instructions to her little sister about the water pump and a dirt pile.

"Girls! Go in the house this minute," Ann called. "You aren't to come back out until we return. There's sweeping to do, and, Susan, mind the fire, if you please."

With slumped shoulders, the girls obeyed. Ann smiled at their crestfallen expressions. She was glad they were still so interested in play. Susan was about the same age as Ann had been when their mother died. Ann had not been so carefree.

She didn't usually need help into the wagon, but her father had to boost her by the elbow because of her voluminous skirt. When she was settled, he took the driver's position and picked up the reins, clucking to Bayberry. The wagon lurched and rolled out of the yard, startling some of the chickens in the coop into squawks and flurries. It was gray and gloomy. The trees of the woods stood like paupers with their bare arms outstretched for alms.

Her father turned his face toward her. "I will have to go to Pittsburgh again next week."

The familiar frisson of dread ran through her. "Why?"

"Mrs. O'Hara wants me to make a new saddle for her and personally check its fit while I am there."

"I can't imagine the money that family has, to be able to pay you for such journeys."

"Well, for the heir to Pittsburgh's greatest fortune, such things are not as significant."

"But I would be alone here! What if something happens to you while you're gone?"

He sighed. "We cannot fight this battle again. I must go. The money for the O'Hara saddles runs our farm for a year. We must trust God to protect all of us when we are apart."

She did try to trust in Providence, and she did find some solace in the psalms during the nights her father was gone. But God had not protected the life of her mother, and Ann was still afraid.

With her father, however, she must take a less painful line of reasoning. "Why do the O'Haras choose you? Why can't they hire the man who does the leather?"

"I don't know. Perhaps because when I lived in Pittsburgh, he supplied the leather and I did the work."

"But why does it matter so much? There must be saddlers in Pittsburgh who could do it."

"I don't know. Sentiment, I suppose. Mrs. O'Hara didn't commission me when I first moved out here. Not until after her husband died."

"Please," Ann said. "Let me come with you this time."

Her father raised his eyebrows. "And what will we do with the girls?"

"Bring them along."

"That will be arduous," her father said. "You think we can bring such young girls by stage and by steamboat for days?"

"I will assume responsibility. I can entertain them."

"And who will care for the farm?"

Ann thought quickly. "James Murdoch. He has enough brothers—his father could spare him. We could pay him from your profit; he would be glad of the money. And really, he would only have to look after the animals. There won't be much more to do until the thaw."

Her father fell silent and stared ahead at Bayberry's haunches. When he glanced sidelong at Ann, his eyebrows resumed their natural position. "Very well then. Perhaps just this once. On one condition."

"What is that?"

"You must do your best to enjoy yourself and to be sociable to any appropriate young men we meet. I will undertake the expense of this trip in part out of hope that you will be more amenable to the social pursuits of a large city."

"I will try." That was the best she could do. The city would not offer a better man than Eli.

But then the thought of the journey brought a rush of exhilaration, and she put her hand through the crook of her father's arm. "Thank you, Father."

He smiled.

She could hardly believe it. Soon she would see the city and its fine buildings, scores of shops, steamboats crowding the rivers—all the things her father had described to her. Her spirits lifted as the wagon jostled along the road. A journey to Pittsburgh was enough to take her mind off lost love.

Enough, that is, until Eli walked into the Murdochs' barn, where couples were already whirling and skipping through the steps of a country dance. Ann perched quietly on one of the chairs that circled the edge of the barn, her burgundy skirt pooling in stiff folds where it touched the floor. She had already danced once with James Murdoch to satisfy her father, but then politely declined a second dance. She held a warm glass of cider and watched the others.

Eli and Phoebe lingered in the open double door, glowing with fun and good health in the cool afternoon light. Eli put a gentle hand on Phoebe's shoulder, and Ann fought to keep her expression unruffled. That should have been *her* shoulder.

He caught Ann's eye and they exchanged a long look. Was he glad to see her? Phoebe must have noticed their mutual glances, for though she didn't acknowledge Ann's presence, she tugged at Eli's arm like a coy little girl. He grinned at her in reply and they stepped out into the cleared space where others were dancing. Phoebe was the center of attention, for her dancing was so lively it made a girl want to get up and dance just for the sheer joy of it. Her black hair flew and her mouth opened in laughter as she nimbly cut the steps across the floor at Eli's side. God had made Phoebe to dance.

He apparently had not made Ann to dance; at least, she had never taken the obvious pleasure in it that Phoebe did. Ann always felt as if she moved like a courtier of the last century compared to some of her carefree friends. Perhaps if she danced with Eli her feet would be lighter.

The fiddler launched into a frenzy of bowing—this dance would be ending shortly and a new one would begin. David Crawford approached from the refreshment table and held out his hand. "Will you dance with me?" He smiled his crooked smile, brown hair flopping in his eyes. "The floor is not the same without your grace, Ann."

I would rather dance with joy than grace. Ann set her cider down and rose to her feet to take his hand. "Thank you, David."

They moved to a place at the side of the floor to wait their turn as the fiddler struck up something slower. A quadrille. Ann loved this dance. It had been around the Continent for a number of years, or so her Welsh schoolmaster had said when he taught the young people the quadrille. He had taught them after school a few years ago. Not all the children were permitted to dance by their parents, and he would not have dared teach it during school hours. Nonetheless, most of the Rushville youth had learned it. It was a stern parent who would forbid even the pleasure of dancing, out here where there was little else by way of entertainment.

Ann counted eight couples in the barn. She and David stood on the opposite side of the room from Eli and Phoebe, but to her dismay, several of the couples left the floor at the sound of the quadrille. Only four couples remained, which meant that she and David would have to dance in the same figure as Eli and Phoebe. Worse, they were standing on the diagonal from them, and thus they would dance with them immediately. It was too late to stand down without creating a scene. Eli supported Phoebe's arm, but his attention to his partner was too rapt to be natural. He also must have realized that he and Ann were about to cross paths in the figures of the quadrille.

When Ann and Phoebe stepped forward and interlaced their arms, circling each other as required by the first pattern, Phoebe's eyes were like a dark wall, her arm stiff, an artificial smile plastered on her lips. Ann was immensely relieved when they finished that odd stalking circle. But what followed was even more trying: she had to place her hand on Eli's shoulder as he rested his hand against her side where her dress fitted her closest. They circled each other. After a few seconds, she braved a glance up at his face.

"You look beautiful." He spoke quietly, under his breath. Shocked, she dropped her eyes and released her grip. Fortunately, it was the appropriate moment in the dance to go back to her place by David. She wasn't sure she could maintain her composure, so she stared fixedly at the other pair of couples who were now dancing together in the center. They parted to reveal Eli on the other side. He was still watching her. Heat pulsed up the back of her neck and burned in her cheeks.

The dance ended. Pleading over-warmth, she asked David to walk with her in the cool air outside. But when she went alone to retrieve her cape from a pile on a trestle table, Eli stood next to it, his fair head still, his gaze intent as he watched her approach.

"You're leaving?" he asked, again barely audible.

"Not just yet. Soon."

"I wish we could sit awhile and talk."

"But you're here with Phoebe."

"That doesn't preclude talking."

"Oh, you mean sit together with you and Phoebe and talk?" She heard faint derision in her own voice.

He winced. "No. Some other time, I hope?"

"I'm leaving for Pittsburgh next week. I'll be away for some time."

The wrinkle she loved appeared at the bridge of his nose. "Why?"

"My father has a very important saddling commission. Now, if you'll excuse me . . ."

She took some satisfaction in leaving him standing there as she plucked her cape from the table. She swept off to walk with David, whose expression called to mind the proverbial cat with the canary.

During their walk, she remained quiet and let David chatter on about horses. Perhaps there was something to the new dress after all. But, if she left for Pittsburgh now, Eli might very well be betrothed to Phoebe by the time she returned. The thought dampened her pleasure, but what else could she do? He had not waited for her. His words tonight might be only a whim on his part. She would not give up this journey with her father for a mere wisp of a chance.

Five

PITTSBURGH
24th February 1826

THE DUST OF CRUSHED BONE CLUNG TO HIS CLOTHES
long after he left the hill. No doubt that was why Master Good
had sent Will here every week for over two years. The master
wished to remind him of how much worse things could yet be.

This hill rose half a mile northwest of the city, where the
smoke from the river foundries still drifted on windy days.
Will climbed a rickety wooden stairway cut into the hillside,
clutching the frayed edges of his coat. The buttons had given
up their tenuous hold months ago. He could hardly choose
which was worse: freezing his hands in the air, or shoving them
in his pockets and leaving his coat to flap open and freeze his
chest. For now, he chose to hold the coat closed with numb
hands.

He reached the door of the poorhouse. With an effort, he
curled one hand into a fist and pounded it against the dark
brown wood.

"Oakum!" he yelled. The oakum he had brought, tarred

rope from the docks, provided labor for those in the poorhouse, who had to untwist it by hand.

The door opened and an old woman peeked out, her face like a wizened apple in its ruffled bonnet, her back hunched. "You the oakum boy?"

"Yes, ma'am. I cannot bring the handcart up the hill. The able-bodied men will have to help." He did not remember this woman from his previous trips to the poorhouse, but that was not unusual. The residents moved in and out, sometimes on their own feet, other times in the county hearse. Will was not permitted to walk the grounds without first speaking to whichever old crone happened to be answering the door.

"You'll have to go 'round the side and tell them," the woman said and shut the door in his face.

He trudged around the end of the ugly square building, counting his steps. At least he could find some kind of warmth in the work shed, though the wooden-slatted sides of the building looked thin and temporary. He stepped up to the dark door-way and pushed open the door—really more like a gate, with its primitive hinges and flimsy boards.

"Shut the door!" a hoarse voice called out.

"Shut it, ye dolt!"

"It's freezin' already in here!"

Will slammed the gate, standing still while his eyes adjusted to the darkness. The smell of rot was overpowering. The forms of a dozen men and boys took shape. They bent over the long stone troughs, their shoulders tight. Some had paused with their iron bars raised to ogle the stranger.

"Don't stop, ye laggards!" The man with the hoarse voice was the overseer of the poorhouse, portly Mr. Fogarty.

The men began to beat their bars against the trough again. The white bones in the trough bounced, cracked, and powdered under the onslaught. Even from his place by the gate, Will could see the shreds of rotten horseflesh and dogflesh that still clung to some of the bones, causing the terrible stench. A coal fire guttered in a makeshift hearth between the two troughs, its rancid smoke thickening the soupy air.

"Oakum boy, ain't ye?" said Mr. Fogarty, rubbing his sidewhiskers and giving a great snort as if to clear his nose. "I guess the men'll be needing to go down and get it."

"Yes, sir." Will breathed through his mouth to avoid nausea. His frozen fingers tingled with a first premonition of pain as they thawed. "It's in the cart at the bottom of the hill."

Fogarty scrutinized Will. "You take an armful to the women in the main house, you hear?" The overseer pointed at one of the men. "You there! And you on the first trough! Go pick up the tarred rope this one brought. He can show you where it is."

The men looked up, their gray faces weary. They dropped their bars with a clang into the trough as they staggered to their feet. One man furtively picked a shred of meat from the ground and popped it in his mouth, making a terrible face as he chewed. Will's gorge rose, and he turned and fumbled for the gate.

He emerged gasping into the open air and light, stepping quickly away from the shack in the hope that the odor would fade. After him the men shuffled like ghouls over the dead grass, all still bent from labor. One stumped on a wooden leg; another had a torn sleeve that dangled empty by his side.

Somehow they all made it down the hill. Even the bitter cold was better than the awful scene of the workhouse. The crippled men and three younger ones—about Will's age—hefted the lengths of tarred rope. They did not speak, just turned and made their grim, bent way back up the hill. Will scooped up the last ropes and began the arduous climb for what he hoped was the last time. He was getting tired; his breath came in shorter puffs and his legs felt the strain of every stair.

Of course, there would be no penny for this delivery. There never was. Master Good received the credit for his public-spirited munificence in picking up the oakum from the dock and delivering it to the poorhouse, and Will received nothing but chilblains.

When he made his way back to the main building, the same old woman came to let him in. She opened the door wider and beckoned him through with a palsied arm.

In the long hallway, only one candle flickered in a wall sconce to light their way. The old woman led him down to the far end and into a large room.

Five or six women sat at tables, already picking oakum. The orange light of the fire revealed half of each woman's face, leaving the other half in shadow. Their movements were slow and their cheeks sagged with bitterness and pain.

"Put the oakum over there," the old woman said, pointing to a large basket half full of oakum close to the fire. Will walked over and without ceremony cast the oakum in his arms down into the basket. He turned to go.

Sitting at the end of the table closest to him was a girl of about his own age. Even in the eerie half-light, her face was not ugly with suffering like the others, though she was terribly thin. She looked up at Will from under a fringe of light hair that escaped the edges of her grimy bonnet.

"Good day," he said.

She did not reply, but nodded slightly.

The old woman snickered. "Don't be a-courtin' our girls, young man."

Will hesitated. This girl shouldn't be in this grim place, but he knew of no way to help. He raised his voice to answer the crone. "I'm just bringing them some more work, ma'am." Bending to the basket, he selected a piece of oakum and moved a few steps to hand it to the girl.

She reached for the length of twisted rope, revealing fingers blistered and torn from her work. Pity sliced through Will and he searched for anything he might say. "God bless you and take you away from here soon."

Both of their hands held the rope, and for a moment it was as if he looked from the deck of a ship and saw a soul tossed on the waves. He held on to the rope, wishing he could take her with him, feeling the gentle pull of her hand on the other end. But he had nowhere to take her.

"Stop dawdling!" The old woman's voice was harsher. Will let go of the oakum and walked away. He didn't look back for fear he would be moved to do something foolish.

When he finally walked in the kitchen door of the Good home, Jane Good was standing over a chunk of spitted meat, turning it with a handle over the fire. She did not look up.

"I need some water," she said.

Will bit his lip, turned, and scooped the bucket from the porch. He could not feel the handle cutting into his palm, and in his cold-weakened state, he found he had to use both hands. Stumbling across the yard, he threw the bucket down under the pump and grabbed the handle, working it hard. The faster he finished, the sooner he would get inside. He dreaded the pain that always came with thawing his fingers, but he had to warm them up soon. He knew boys who had lost fingers to the cold.

The barn door opened and Tom came out, eyes shadowed, his coat as thin as Will's, and only a rag around his neck to keep out the wind. "Are you getting back inside?" Tom asked, when he was close enough not to be overheard by anyone in the house or barn.

"Just the water now," Will said. After two years together under Master Good, they hardly needed words to communicate.

Tom eyed Will's hands. "Go ahead. I'll get it."

"It's not worth it." Will hoisted the full bucket and turned toward the house. They both knew that if Tom came with the water instead of Will, Mistress Good might report it to the master.

Once inside, Will deposited the bucket carefully on the hearth and retreated to the kitchen table. Tom followed close behind and collapsed next to Will on the bench. The boys always ate there, while the Goods took their supper at the formal dining table around the corner at the far end of the room.

The front door opened and closed, and boots trod heavily in the entry. The master. He emerged into the open great room and scanned it.

"Loitering at the table, boys? Isn't there enough work to do?"

Will despised the word *boys*, at least when the master said it. Will was eighteen and Tom sixteen—old enough for more respect. But that was why Master Good did it, of course.

"Will just returned from the workhouse and Tom from the

barn," Mistress Jane said. "They'll need a minute to warm up if we want them to tend the pigs later."

That was the way of the mistress. No kindness, just ruthless practicality.

Frowning, Master Good shrugged out of his coat. Jane hurried to take it for him and disappeared into the hall. The master always walked right past the coat pegs and still expected his wife to take his coat and go back to hang it up for him.

"Supper is ready," Jane said as she came back to the hearth. Her long, thin arms moved like a windmill as she removed the spit from the fire, picked a fork from its wall hook, and pushed the meat onto a platter.

Will tried not to think of how that roast beef would taste as the aroma sent pangs through his empty belly. He and Tom would not be eating that meat. A pot of watery broth hung on the hook over the fire. The mistress usually boiled the inedible parts of the cow for the apprentices, threw in some old potatoes, and called it stew.

"I have news," Master Good said to his wife. "The saddler from Rushville is coming to town." He looked at her significantly. "He will be staying with Dr. Loftin while he completes the commission."

"Indeed?" Jane asked. "It's beyond me why the O'Hara woman wants that man to do the work, when she could have yours instead. And yours is so superior."

"It's an insult," the master said.

Jane slopped some stew in the bowls, then thrust them in front of the boys at the table. She never allowed them to serve themselves—she said they would take more than their share.

The master turned toward Will. "While the other saddler is

here, I have a task for you." He cracked his knuckles. "You must gain every scrap of knowledge about how he works the leather and attempt to learn his style. I'm determined that we will take any future O'Hara commissions from him. Appeal to his heart, make him pity you, so he holds back nothing."

Will was silent. Bad as it was to go cold and hungry much of the time, it was worse to be subject to this man's every command.

"What's that? I didn't hear your answer. Look sharp." The master spoke evenly, but he moved a step closer to the corner where the whip leaned.

"Yes, sir." Will didn't know whom he hated more at that moment—his master, or himself.

Six

CINCINNATI

1st March 1826

THEY WERE BEING FOLLOWED; ANN WAS CERTAIN OF it. The man with the beaver hat pulled down over his brow—she had seen him three or four times now as they made their way through Cincinnati's streets to the dock. On each occasion, he slipped behind buildings or into open doorways as soon as she caught sight of him. She would never even have noticed him among the crowds were it not for his furtive manner.

But immediately she chided herself. Who would pursue them all the way from Rushville to Cincinnati by stagecoach? No one could possibly have such interest in their little family, nor would anyone know to seek them here on the busy wharf at the steamboat packet office.

As her father finished with the clerk and turned back to the girls, tickets in hand, a cry rang out from the edge of the waterfront.

"Packet a-comin'! All passengers to dock!" A mustached man in a red uniform held his head high and bellowed his summons with satisfaction.

The steamboat loomed behind him on the river, jaunty minstrel music drifting down from a piano buried somewhere in her towering decks. Steam gushed from her escape valves with a giant sigh; she glided inch by inch toward the dock. Black smoke billowed from twin chimneys, and an iron bell clanged from the pilot house.

"Stop her! Stop her! Stabboard reverse! Labboard reverse!"

The paddlewheels in back ceased, then began a slow backward revolution. At the bow and stern, two deckhands threw ropes to the waiting dockmen.

Ann had never seen a three-deck boat before. The lowest deck teemed with rough-clad men running this way and that, untying freight, carrying wood, shouting commands. Under the protected veranda of the middle deck, fashionable cabin passengers crowded to the ornately carved guardrails. A couple of young ladies in fur coats waved gaily to the Miller girls.

Mabel tugged at her father's sleeve without taking her eyes from the steamer *Emissary*. "Look, look, Father!"

"Can we go aboard now?" Susan asked at his other elbow.

"Be patient," he said. "They must unload the freight first." He smiled, his new top hat distinguished among the hats on the dock. The other hats flocked together like different species of birds. Over there were flat woolen caps on working men. Here, a bright bevy of fine ladies' hats fluttered on the passengers who could pay higher prices for cabin passage. Though a few top hats stood proudly with their fair companions, a much larger number hobnobbed together in masculine solidarity behind the women. Their owners variously smoked pipes, stamped feet, and nodded to one another as they watched the boat with anticipation.

"I'd better whistle up a stevedore," her father said, lifting his arm in the air. Across the wharf, a line of men marched like soldiers, back and forth, carrying boxes, bales, and baggage. Ten yards away, a light-brown man cast his crate on the dock with a thud. He noticed Ann's father, raised a hand in return, and made his way through the steady stream of waterfront traffic.

"Yessir?" he said. "You need these moved to the *Emissary*, sir?"

"Yes." Her father fished in his waistcoat and came up with a coin.

The man took it and stuffed it in his pocket. "She'll be lowering her gangplank soon."

Even as he spoke, the wide gangplank dropped into place, and a stream of men poured off it—some carrying freight, others yelling boisterously to one another or simply hurrying up the levee to disappear into the bustling streets. Down the boat's front staircase came six or seven of the more refined passengers, followed by crew members toting their belongings. As the cabin passengers disembarked, they nodded and smiled at their peers who were waiting to board.

"She's fast as the best of 'em," one gentleman proclaimed, tipping his hat to the ladies as he stepped from the gangplank to solid ground.

"Beautiful," one lady said to Ann, as if confiding a secret. "You will enjoy it."

A bearded man in a blue coat with brass buttons stepped to the curlicued railing, resting one hand on the white top rail. "Welcome, ladies," he said to the small cluster of women. "I'm Captain Pruitt. If you care to follow me, I will escort you to your cabin."

As four or five ladies gathered their skirts in hand and followed the captain, Ann glanced at her father. "We'll travel separately?"

"Yes," he said. "I'll go to the men's staterooms at the bow.

You'll be in your own staterooms at the stern, by the ladies' salon. But we'll meet on the promenade, and at meals." He handed her three of the tickets.

"Very well," she said. "Girls, come with me. Mind your step."

She started up the gentle incline, the heels of her boots clicking on the wood. When she turned to ensure that Susan and Mabel were following safely, she glanced over their heads at the wharf. Again, there was that man in the beaver hat, standing with the deck passengers, head still lowered, face obscured. A ripple of unease passed through her.

But of course he was going to board the boat. That would be the most likely reason why he had stuck so close to them on their way here. She was being very silly, and if she did not pay attention, she would step right off the gangplank into the cloudy Ohio River.

Captain Pruitt led them up the staircase at the bow, then along the veranda to the far end of the middle deck. He opened the heavy white door with obvious pride. "The ladies' salon."

The ladies filed in, Ann and her sisters bringing up the rear. The white salon glittered with gold lacquer. Fine upholstered chairs discreetly bolted to the deck promised a comfortable voyage. Ann added her murmur of admiration to the compliments of the other ladies. The captain pointed out the doors to their staterooms and withdrew with a bow.

"But which stateroom is ours?" a young lady of about Ann's age asked. She wore a silk day dress under her dark fur cape; her voice was smooth and rich as molasses.

"I suppose we'll have to confer with our new friends," an older woman said in a similar drawl. She extended a gloved hand to Ann. "I hope you'll forgive my manners, but it appears we must introduce ourselves. I am Mrs. Philip Holmes of Nashville, and this is my daughter, Miss Amelia Holmes." Both of the Holmes women were vivacious, their prominent chins framed by broad-brimmed hats.

"So pleased to meet you." Ann took the other woman's hand and marshaled her best etiquette from her classes with the Welsh schoolmaster. "I'm Miss Ann Miller, and these are my sisters, Miss Susan and Miss Mabel." When Mrs. Holmes cocked an eyebrow, Ann hastily added, "We're traveling with our father, Mr. Samuel Miller of Rushville."

Mrs. Holmes smiled and squeezed Ann's hand gently before releasing it. "Such a charming family."

Mrs. Holmes turned to greet the other two women who stood by. They wore tailored walking dresses in muted good taste, only their scarlet- and blue-feathered hats hinting at prosperity. The elderly woman in the dark blue dress took Mrs. Holmes's proffered hand with some reticence, but apparent good will. "I'm Mrs. Lewis Burbridge of Pittsburgh, and this is my granddaughter, Miss Louisa Burbridge."

Louisa Burbridge, fair-haired and retiring, turned striking gray eyes to Ann before dropping her gaze to the floor. Ann took pity on the girl's shyness and spoke warmly to her. "We're headed for Pittsburgh. How wonderful to have traveling companions who can tell us about the city."

"We're also going to Pittsburgh," Amelia Holmes said. "Papa is going to look for a runaway slave, so we thought we'd tour the North while he plays the hunter." She giggled.

Mrs. Holmes shot her daughter a forbidding look. "Amelia! Hardly a subject for polite company."

Amelia fell silent, which left a brief hush. Louisa Burbridge was pink, and Mrs. Burbridge fiddled with the strings of her handbag. Perhaps they were abolitionists. The Millers did not approve of slavery either.

Mrs. Holmes cheerfully addressed Ann as if Amelia had not spoken. "Miss Miller, what takes you to Pittsburgh?"

Ann didn't know if she should tell them her father was a saddler. Something told her the Burbridges and Holmeses might not be accustomed to associating with craftsmen—not even master craftsmen. It would be a long voyage if they decided the Millers were not genteel companions. But honesty above all. "My father has business there with the O'Hara family," she said. "He has been commissioned to make a saddle for Mrs. O'Hara."

Mrs. Holmes made no response, but lifted her chin ever so slightly, which gave the unfortunate impression that she was looking down her nose. Then she averted her posture from Ann to address Mrs. Burbridge. "Rather dry weather for March, isn't it? Not much snow this year," she said.

The weather. One couldn't choose a more obvious conversational snub. Slow warmth spread across Ann's cheekbones. Over Mrs. Holmes's rounded shoulders, Amelia eyed Ann, her expression bland as milk.

"Mrs. Burbridge," Mrs. Holmes said sweetly, "I believe I know of the Burbridges of Pittsburgh. Wasn't there a Burbridge who acquitted himself bravely in our struggle for independence? At Yorktown, perhaps?"

"Why, yes, that was my husband's father." Mrs. Burbridge smiled. "I'm so pleased that someone remembers our heroes. Colonel Burbridge is gone these twenty years, but we still miss him sorely."

Ann stood at a loss, holding her sisters' hands, while Mrs.

Holmes nattered on with her back to them about her love for Revolutionary history and her own father's part in the victory at King Mountain.

Louisa Burbridge stepped around the Holmes women, pulling aside her heavy green skirt so as not to brush them in passing. "Your father must be a master of his craft," she said to Ann. "The O'Haras are a fine family. We were so sorry to lose Captain O'Hara. He did a great deal for our city. Will you be staying with them?"

Louisa now stood with her back to the Holmeses, transforming their snub into a mere parting of ways in the conversation. Ann's father had told her that steamboats were usually floating islands of social democracy, and perhaps that was true. Or perhaps Louisa was simply more tolerant than the others.

"No, we won't stay at the O'Hara home." Ann's relief made her words tumble over one another until she made a conscious effort to slow down. "We will board with Dr. Robert Loftin, a friend of the O'Hara family. He is neighbor to another saddler who will assist my father in his work."

As she finished her sentence, Ann realized that the stevedores were still clustered outside the ladies' cabin with their luggage and trunks. She pointed them out to Louisa. "I see that the men need to place our belongings somewhere."

"Perhaps we should decide on our rooms?" Louisa leaned around Mrs. Holmes to repeat her suggestion to the rest of the ladies, who agreed.

They chose a stateroom for each family and directed the dockmen to deposit their burdens in the appropriate cabins. Ann found an additional coin for her stevedore to compensate him for his patience. She noticed Louisa Burbridge doing the same, though the Holmeses were chatting too loudly with each other to notice.

Ann left Susan and Mabel bouncing on the rather hard beds of the cabin and went in search of her father. He must have conceived the same plan, for she encountered him on the veranda, heading in her direction.

"The accommodations are very pleasant, Father. We've seen our room and met the other ladies."

"Good." He seemed distracted, looking past her and over the railing at the main deck below them. When she followed his gaze, however, she saw nothing unusual.

"What are you watching?"

"Just the men on the deck." He turned back to her. "They're rough, but that's to be expected. Flatboat men, mostly." He glanced in the direction of the ladies' salon. "Where are the girls?"

"Safe in the stateroom," she said. "I wouldn't leave them anywhere else. They know they're not to roam without me."

"Of course." He offered his arm. "Now, let me show you where I'm lodging, in case you have need of me." She took hold of his elbow and they walked toward the bow.

Hurrying workmen left the veranda as gentlemen emerged from their staterooms to gather at the rail for the departure. Two men in top hats and frock coats were so engrossed in their conversation that they almost collided with Ann and her father.

"I beg your pardon," the younger man said to Ann, putting out a hand instinctively to steady her. She recognized those gray eyes.

"Not at all." Her father smiled. "Mr. Allan Burbridge, this is my daughter, Miss Miller."

"A pleasure." The young man removed his hat and bowed with military precision.

"Mr. Burbridge, I believe I've just met your family." Ann returned his smile.

"Have you? Then you may have also met the fair companions of my new acquaintance." He indicated the older man with him, who was short and had removed his hat to reveal a head of graying hair. "Mr. Miller, Miss Miller, this is Mr. Philip Holmes."

"Charmed." The older man spoke with one hand placed artfully at the lapel of his striped waistcoat.

Her father shook hands with Mr. Holmes. "Mr. Burbridge and I are sharing a stateroom—that one there, the Connecticut Room." He gestured to a cabin door a few feet past them, emblazoned with a state sign.

This revelation both pleased and disturbed Ann. She hoped her father would not disturb Allan Burbridge by snoring in the night, as he did occasionally at home.

Mr. Holmes made an odd and repellent sound in his throat, as if blasting everything in his breathing apparatus upward with a rattling honk. "Shall we go meet the other ladies?" His drawl emanated from his nose. "I'm sure they will enjoy witnessing the boat's departure."

After that honk, Ann was not so concerned about her father's snoring.

"Splendid idea," Allan Burbridge said. When Ann's father nodded, they all strolled back toward the stern. The deck was solid beneath them. Here, in the lee of the dock, the waves were mere lines traced in the water.

Ann made a detour to fetch her sisters from the stateroom. She rejoined the party just as the gentlemen met the women at the starboard rail near the stern. As they exchanged further introductions, the Holmes women lavished Allan Burbridge with pretty speeches but barely acknowledged Ann's father. She hoped her father would not notice, but even a man could not miss the deliberate one-sidedness of the conversation. Finally, Allan and Louisa turned away from the Holmes women to speak with the Millers.

"Miss Miller's father is a master saddler," Louisa said to her brother, nodding to Ann in her friendly, subdued way. "Is that not intriguing?"

"I suspected as much when he told me he was under contract with the O'Hara family," Allan said. "But of course he was far too modest to go into detail."

"I believe we're about to depart." Ann was anxious for a change of subject. The Holmes's behavior would not improve with any reminder of her father's status, no matter how kind the Burbridges might be.

The wharf beside them still crawled with men, but all the dockworkers had left the boat, leaving only the passengers and crew on the engine deck. The steam whistled out of the gauge cocks; the bell rang again. Louisa and Ann stood in companionable silence while Allan talked to Mabel and Susan with enthusiasm, pointing out parts of the ship and explaining how it worked in terms a child could understand. Ann liked the crinkles at the corners of his eyes when he laughed at some precocious comment from Mabel.

"Ann, they're casting off!" Susan pointed to the wharf.

Two men were untying the mooring ropes. Looping them in their hands, they jumped across the gap to the boat with practiced ease. Ann could tell from Mabel's alert posture that she wanted to try that daring jump herself. She had always been nimble, like Ann. There wasn't a tree on the farm that Mabel hadn't scaled. Ann would have to make sure her littlest sister did not try any adventurous feats on the packet boat. Fortunately Susan was more cautious and ladylike and would not do anything to jeopardize her new grown-up demeanor, now that she was all of eleven years old.

The deck hummed beneath their feet. The great wheels began to turn, churning the water, pulling the massive vessel away from the dock. Bystanders on the docks cheered and waved their farewells to the passengers on board. In the icy wind off the river, the ladies nestled in their furs and the men shoved their hands in the pockets of their greatcoats.

Below on the engine deck, men still carried wood by the armload to the bow. Men without such tasks sat on the nearest available box or pallet of goods. Ann saw cards and dice in two of the groups. Several audible curses flew up from one card game; she blushed and darted a glance at Allan Burbridge. She thought he had heard, but he gave the impression of deafness and deep concentration on what Susan was saying. That was considerate of him.

A man stood apart from the card players, his back to Ann. She marked his beaver hat.

Her father was staring with furrowed brow at the same man.

When her father noticed her attention, he looked away and made a show of fumbling in his breast pocket for his watch.

Perhaps she had reason for concern after all.

Seven

SHIP TIME WAS PRECISE, BUT LITTLE GIRLS WERE NOT.
Ann hurried toward the dining room, holding fast to the hands
of Susan and Mabel, both of whom were out of breath from
their rush to dress for supper. It had been ten minutes since the
black iron bell called them to the supper hour. She feared they
would keep the company waiting.

When she stepped over the sill of the dining room door,
she saw to her mortification that the cabin passengers were
already standing behind their chairs. An awkward hush pre-
vailed as she led the girls to the seats at the end of the long
table, where her father waited for them. His face was expressionless, but she could tell he was displeased. The girls took
the two places next to him. Ann kept her head down and
crossed to the other side of the table, where she stood next to
Allan Burbridge.

She wanted to apologize to the company, but she did not
know if doing so might violate the etiquette of a shipboard meal.
The captain stood in commanding silence at the head of the
table. A cavalcade of covered dishes marched from his end to
where Ann stood. What a quantity of tureens and platters; there

were only thirty-odd cabin passengers, and she was sure there must be a serving dish for each of them.

"Will it please the company to be seated?" the captain said.

Chairs scraped against the deck. Allan Burbridge whispered, "Good evening," and pulled her heavy oaken chair back for her. She seated herself as gracefully as possible; she was unaccustomed to having a man's assistance with the task. Rushville was not known for its society suppers and formal manners. But across the table, her father acquitted himself well in seating Louisa Burbridge, and a low buzz of conversation began.

Allan leaned toward her to speak quietly. "I'm glad they allow us to converse at meals on this boat."

"You mean some do not?"

"I've traveled on several where the captain kept us silent as the grave."

"Whatever for?"

"Excessive propriety."

She smiled, her taut nerves untwisting themselves in the ambiance of his wry humor. He removed the lid of the dish between them and poked at its contents with a fork. "Would you care for congealed chicken? I suspect it was not congealed thirty minutes ago, but it has developed a fine aspic now."

She inspected the chicken. The other passengers were deep in conversation, so she could speak freely if she kept her voice down. "It is rather gelatinous." She smiled up at him.

"They serve a fine array of foods on board packet boats, but none of them remain hot." He cut a chunk from the mass of chicken and placed it on her plate.

"Well, I imagine that would be a challenge with the limitations of a galley kitchen. We can't be too choosy." The merriness of her own reply took her by surprise. She could not remember the last time she felt so light of heart.

"True." He took his own portion of chicken and replaced the lid. "I admire your simple fortitude. It's refreshing." His words were casual, but his sideward glance at her lingered long enough to tie her tongue.

His grandmother spoke up from across the table where she sat next to Louisa. "Allan, are you planning to monopolize the conversation of the lovely Miss Miller for the rest of the evening, or may we hear from her as well?"

"You may hear from her only while I pause to nourish myself." He grinned and removed the lid of a tureen.

Amelia Holmes interrupted from her seat at Allan's left. "Mrs. Burbridge, I do so wish to hear about your city. You must know it very well."

"Yes." Amelia's mother brightened across the table. "Why—I have an idea! It would be so lovely to have your son show us the city for a day. I don't suppose you could spare the time, Mr. Burbridge?"

Allan paused. Perhaps he merely had to swallow a bite of chicken, for he sounded perfectly agreeable when he replied. "Of course, I would be delighted."

"Oh, how kind of you!" Amelia sounded as pleased as if he had made the suggestion himself.

Mrs. Holmes echoed her daughter's sentiment and said without pausing, "Mrs. Burbridge, will you tell us about Fort Pitt during the war? It must have been so exciting to see the troops coming and going."

But Mrs. Burbridge did not respond to Mrs. Holmes with her earlier enthusiasm on the subject of the war. "I grew up in

Boston, Mrs. Holmes, and only moved to Pittsburgh upon marriage." The old woman turned her attention back to Ann. "Tell me what you are reading these days, young lady."

Ann was no more accustomed to discussing her reading with strangers than to having a handsome young man seat her at a dinner party. But at least she was an avid reader, in her few private moments on the farm, and she knew what the Burbridges would probably have read. "I greatly enjoyed *The Pioneers.*"

"Oh yes." Mrs. Burbridge's wrinkled face came alive with interest, though her voice quavered with age. "Cooper is one of my favorites. Isn't it wonderful that the English love him as well? It's time an American wrote of our real life here."

"Quite." Ann's father leaned in, waxing enthusiastic. "And he writes so well of the natural beauties of our country. The English did read Brockden Brown also, but I'm afraid he didn't represent the best we have to offer."

"I wholeheartedly agree with you, Mr. Miller," Mrs. Burbridge said, watching Louisa pour tea into her teacup.

"Who is Brockden Brown?" Ann hoped she wasn't betraying some unforgivable ignorance.

"The author of a ghastly novel. It's quite right for you never to have heard of it." Mrs. Burbridge pressed her lips together.

Ann's father nodded. He had strong opinions of what was and was not good literature. He had, in fact, strong opinions on a number of issues. Ann hoped he would not raise any of them here tonight.

"Mrs. Burbridge, I wonder if you've heard of the doings of William Ellery Channing in Boston." He waved his fork at his plate, growing more animated by the moment.

At least if he had to choose something controversial, it was religion and not slavery. The Holmeses were busy chatting to the captain at the far end of the table, but Ann would not want her father to spark a debate at supper.

Mrs. Burbridge's eyes sparkled. "Indeed, Mr. Miller, I have heard about Channing. And I don't like it one bit."

Ann thought she heard a groan from Allan, but it was so soft that she couldn't be sure. Mrs. Burbridge and Ann's father proceeded in a lively discussion of the dangers of Unitarianism, while poor Louisa sat silent between them.

Allan turned to Ann again, murmuring, "Your father has found a way to make himself very popular with my grandmother."

"Well, she's endearing herself to him as well. He's usually quite reasonable, but Unitarianism is his pet hobby horse." Ann smiled at Allan's chagrin.

"The only advantage that will come from this conversation," he said as if consoling her, "is that she's sure to invite him— and you—to our home when we arrive in Pittsburgh, so they can continue railing against Channing. But I promise you that I will provide for you and your sisters a more diverting time. Pittsburgh is not Philadelphia, but we have social pleasures of our own."

Ann didn't know how to reply—she did not think it was quite proper to discuss a visit to his home if a formal invitation had not been issued—but even as she hesitated, she heard Mrs. Burbridge inviting her father to call on them, just as Allan had predicted. She couldn't help but giggle and tried to hide it with a napkin in front of her face. Allan chuckled too, taking a sip of wine to hide his amusement. Ann's father squinted his eyes at her in mild suspicion but accepted Mrs. Burbridge's invitation.

"My parents would be delighted to meet you, were they in

town," Allan said. "They are admirers of simplicity and sincerity as much as I."

She couldn't tell from the glint in his eye if he was flirtatious or in earnest, but her face warmed.

"Alas, they are gone to New York, so my father may produce more money and my mother may spend it." His affectionate tone took any real sting out of his quip. "And what of your mother?" he asked. "Did she not wish to travel in winter?"

"She passed away nine years ago," Ann said.

"Oh." He stared at his plate. "I'm so sorry for your loss."

On the few occasions when she had met young men since her mother died, this was always the way of things. When the subject of mothers came up and she had to tell them, they did not know what to say, making it even more awful.

"Tell me," she said with forced cheer. "Do you plan to make a great name for yourself, as every young man dreams these days?"

"I don't know about that," he said, smiling. "I'll probably assist my father in his business for some time. In his absence, I must supervise the daily operations of the firm. But I would like to invent something, perhaps. Something wonderful, like a steamboat."

"It is quite wonderful."

"Your sisters are taken with it. They are charming girls."

"Thank you." Try as she might, she could not summon the effervescence of their earlier exchange.

When the captain thanked his passengers for joining him and pushed back his chair, the company rose to leave.

"Let's go look at the stars," Mabel said.

She and Susan had behaved so well at the meal, both quiet

and polite. They should be rewarded. A brief walk on the deck under the stars could not hurt.

"I would gladly take you, Mabel," Ann said. "But I left my cape behind in the cabin."

"Suppose you go fetch it while I take the girls to the promenade." Allan offered his hands to Susan and Mabel. "Louisa, would you like to join us?"

His sister agreed, and then the Holmeses expressed their enthusiasm for a stargazing party. All three families decided to go up together, with the exception of Mrs. Burbridge, who was not keen on the cold, and Ann's father, who said he was suffering from fatigue and would retire.

As the men helped the women and girls into their coats, Ann walked down the veranda to retrieve her cape, wrapping her arms around herself in a vain effort to stay warm in the clear, frosty night.

The light of her cabin's lamp revealed her dark fur cape lying atop the coverlet of the bed. She was grateful that her father had insisted they buy a more formal cape for her in Cincinnati. She would have felt out of place among the other women in her old woolen farm cape, practical or not.

When she lifted the fur and flung it over her shoulders, her matching fur bag tumbled to the floor by her feet.

She picked it up, loosening the drawstring. Inside were the letters she had saved these two years. She had brought them on the faint chance that she might be able to return them to their owner. They had come to her, after all, from the barrel sent by Jacob Good to her father, and now they would be staying with Jacob Good's neighbor. If she were ever to find the boy, this was her opportunity.

She withdrew one of the letters and unfolded it. It was the last of them, the one she loved most.

29th October 1817

My Darling Will,

I don't know if I shall be able to celebrate Christmas with you this year. The doctor tells me that I am worse, and your father is still too ill to converse. I do not give up the hope that God may bless us with a full recovery, in time.

In the event that it takes longer than I had hoped for us to see one another again, I wanted to share some reflections that have been constantly with me of late.

The first is that I love you and your brother deeply, and I pray that you will always remember that love, no matter where life may take you.

I also want you to be a strong and brave boy, and to do what is right, even when it is difficult. Take care of your brother. I know that you must live on different farms, but please make every effort to see him when you can. He is too young to remember, and you must help him.

Finally, do not be angry at God for our illness. He has His own ways and His providence is beyond our knowledge. The loss of your sisters was bitter to us, and we grieve them deeply, but they are beyond suffering now, as we all shall be some day. That is the promise in which I trust, and in which you must trust.

There are many more things I would write, but I tire too easily this month. I will write again as soon as I am able.

Your loving mother

In the wake of telling Allan that her mother was gone, the letter struck her as powerfully as it had the first time she read it. She wanted to meet this boy. She would understand him, and he her. She would tell him how she had saved the letters for him. He would not be uncomfortable or wordless. He had known the same loss she had known in that terrible year of 1817.

The deck was completely dark and empty when she emerged from her stateroom. She carefully made her way toward the stairs to the promenade. Below on the engine deck, hoots and shouts arose from card games. The hum of the boiler traveled through the deck and vibrated under her feet.

As she passed the midpoint of the ship, she walked closer to the railing, drawn toward the inky skies pricked by countless points of light. It would be a good night for stargazing.

A muffled thud rose from the engine deck where it stretched out to the side and below her. There, two men stood very close to one another in the gloom. She could barely make them out.

The first man pressed the second against the wall of the boiler room. He muttered something. The other man responded in an angry half whisper and broke away from the first man's hold, walking quickly toward the bow. As he passed under the lamp in the wall sconce, she saw with shock that it was her father. After a moment, the other man slunk in the opposite direction. The moonlight behind him traced the silhouette of his beaver hat.

Eight

WILL STOOD BETWEEN THE ARMS OF THE HANDCART and pulled like a beast of burden, bracing his feet against the frozen ruts of the road. The cart would not budge. He did not know if he had grown weaker or the load heavier since he hauled it from the wharf yesterday. Two weeks had passed since he last hauled the oakum to the poorhouse, but the arrival of March had failed to ease February's bitter chill.

Tom stood in the yard eyeing him skeptically. "You should let me try."

"Don't be a fool. You're half my size."

Tom stood up straight, squaring his thin shoulders. "Then I'll push." He moved to the back of the cart and set his shoulder to it. "Ready, steady . . ."

Will heaved forward and the cart followed, Tom stumbling in its wake.

"Just don't stop!" Tom said, panting as he caught up with Will's steady, quick pace.

"Easier said than done." Will's breath billowed behind him.

"I should come with you to help if you get stuck."

"It's too far for you without a real coat and gloves," Will said.

"I can barely stand it even in this rag. Besides, the master'll have your hide if you don't finish with the pigs."

Tom fell back out of sight, and Will couldn't look back and risk losing his momentum. He soldiered on. It seemed an eternity before he made it past the Good property and Dr. Loftin's stately home. His thoughts grew vague and slowed to nothingness, his full concentration simply on placing one foot in front of the next.

A rattle and a jingle drew his attention to the road ahead. Rounding the corner from the hill was a town coach with blue trim—Dr. Loftin's. The two grays drawing the carriage trotted briskly toward him. Will moved farther to the side of the road. The carriage and team were wide; there was barely space to pass even if it pulled off the path.

When the coach was only a few yards away, he saw with surprise that the man riding postilion on the nearer of the grays was Dr. Loftin himself. Usually he had a man in that saddle for him.

"Hello there, Will!" the doctor called. He pulled onto the dead winter grass, reining his horses to a halt, which caused the carriage to rock gently.

"Good afternoon, Dr. Loftin," Will said. He had to stop his cart now, out of respect, and he prayed the road was smooth enough here to allow him to continue in a minute. He touched the brim of his cap and nodded his head.

"Where are you going on this frigid day?" The doctor's penetrating gaze took in Will's flimsy excuse for a coat, his raw, gloveless hands.

Will would have blushed in shame, but he was bloodless from cold. "I'm taking Master Good's donation to the poorhouse."

"Oakum," the doctor said wryly. "How kind of him."

Will felt one corner of his mouth pulling up into a grin. He ducked his head to hide it.

"I see you've forgotten your gloves," the doctor said. "Take mine. I'm nearly home."

"Oh no, sir, I couldn't."

"You most certainly can. Here you are." The doctor stripped off his gloves and handed them down. As Will approached and reached up for them, the curtain of the coach twitched, and a pair of blue eyes looked out at him from a china doll face.

"Susan!" he heard a girl's voice whisper. Behind the little girl sat an older girl, her face framed in a dark fur hood. She was pink at the cheekbones; whether from embarrassment or the warmth of the carriage, he couldn't tell. The curtain fell back into place, though it did not block the sounds of high-pitched giggling and shushing.

He was too glad of the gloves to care what they said about him for now. Later, he knew he would mind. "Thank you, Doctor," he said stiffly, fumbling to draw the gloves over his fingers.

"My passengers are Mr. Samuel Miller and his young daughters," the doctor said with a note of apology, as if to explain the laughter. "You will be meeting them soon, as Mr. Miller will be working with your master."

"Very good, sir. And thank you again."

The doctor nodded and clucked to the horses, and the carriage moved on toward the Loftin house.

The gloves were leather and lined with fur. He could not believe their luxurious softness and warmth. He flexed his fingers and hoisted the bars of the cart once more. It was like a blessing from God himself how the gloves cushioned the strain on his hands. His face might still freeze, but the gift would ease the pain of the journey.

As he trudged on, he remembered the last time Dr. Loftin had encountered him, by the pigsty that lay on the boundary between the two properties. The doctor had given him an orange, offhandedly, as if he always carried such things in his pockets for half-starved young men. Will hid it in his feed sack, sneaking it back to the barn where he and Tom tore it apart and ate it carefully, piece by precious piece. Will had to stop Tom from eating the peel, knowing that its bitterness would bring up the gorge and waste the sweetness of the orange in retching. He had tried it once himself.

Will buried the orange pips and peel so Master Good would not know that the doctor had given them food. His master's moods were unpredictable, which meant Will would have to find a very good hiding place for the gloves. But perhaps the doctor had intended to lend them, not give them. Will would return them as soon as he finished this errand.

The base of the hill loomed ahead. What of the yellow-haired girl whom he had seen on his last trip to the poorhouse? Was she still there? He almost hoped he would not see her, as there was nothing he could do. He couldn't even help Tom or himself. If they went hungry and cold, he had no business thinking of himself as a rescuer. For some reason, God had ordained that the girl, Will, and Tom be subject to the whims of others in this harsh world. He did not understand why it should be so. He tried to be a good person, as his mother would have wanted, but his master owned him by law, body and soul, for another year and a half. If he tried to break his indenture, the master would set the law on him and he would be recaptured. And even if he escaped, there would be no one left to protect Tom from the full force of Master Good's brutality.

Just the thought of the master churned sour anger in his stomach. The other day the master had knocked him down for what he called an impudent stare. Perhaps it was impudent— Will hoped it was. He didn't see how he could contain himself at all times in the situation at the Good house. He wasn't a boy any longer, but a young man of eighteen.

As he drew the cart to a stop at the foot of the hill and climbed the steps, the anger in his gut hardened into cool determination. He would help that girl, though he didn't know how just yet. He was sick to death of doing nothing for himself or Tom, imprisoned by the parchment he had signed. Even if he could not stand up for his own nonexistent rights, he might be able to do something for this young girl who was not legally bound to anyone.

When he arrived at the poorhouse door, his gloves muffled the thud of his knock. There was no answer. He pounded again, harder. Perhaps they could not hear.

But the door opened, and to his surprise, it was not the old woman but the same young girl he had met before. She regarded him with equal surprise, her eyes shadowed by her bonnet, her fair hair twisting down in locks over her shoulders. "You have a delivery?" she asked.

"Yes," he said. This was his opportunity to talk to her alone. "What's your name?"

"Emmie. Emmie Flynn."

"I'm Will Hanby." They stared at each other. The faint smudges of exhaustion under her eyes emphasized her fragile beauty, the drooping grace of a flower blighted by frost.

"Where's the old woman?" Will asked, afraid the crone would scream from the hallway at any moment.

"Dead," Emmie said. "Yesterday."

Will could not say he was sorry. Without the old woman's sharp tongue to drive him away, perhaps he could figure out a means to help the girl.

"But the new overseer for the women will come soon," Emmie said.

He moved closer and lowered his voice. "Why are you here? Can I assist you in some way?"

Her expression grew distant. She brushed away a truant lock of hair from in front of her face. "No, there's nothing you can do." She turned away.

"Wait." He put his hand on the door for fear she would try to close it. "I know a man who knows the owner of a glass factory. Would it be possible for you to work there?" He had no idea whether Dr. Loftin would even agree to ask Mrs. O'Hara such a thing, but it was his only recourse.

She looked over her shoulder at him. "But I would have nowhere to live."

"There are boarding houses near the factories. It would be better than . . . here."

She turned back to face him, lips parted as if to say something, but wordless, just searching his face. "All right then," she whispered, and fled down the hall.

When Will returned from the almshouse, he pulled the cart up beside the pigsty and walked back to Dr. Loftin's home. The white back door set into the white brick was discreet; he would not disturb anyone if he passed the borrowed gloves to Dr. Loftin's maid.

But for the second time that day, a door opened to reveal someone he did not expect. It was not Mary in her uniform. Instead, a chestnut-haired young woman in a red dress stood on Dr. Loftin's threshold. "I'm sorry," she said, her voice gentle, her words clear. "I should not have answered on Dr. Loftin's behalf. I was just passing by when you knocked. Would you like to speak with him?"

"Yes." He was painfully aware of the mud streaking his trousers, his hair that Jane Good had hacked into unkempt waves with blunt scissors. Compared to this dainty girl in her fine dress, he was a crude, dirty savage.

Just then, Mary the maid walked up behind the young lady. "Miss Miller, don't trouble yourself. I'll get the doctor," she said, and was gone as soon as she had come.

Miss Miller. This was the saddler's eldest daughter, then. They stood awkwardly regarding each other. He noticed that her eyes were deep brown and fringed with dark, thick lashes. Eyes that looked sad and kept secrets.

"You work for the saddler?" she asked.

"I'm his apprentice. One of them."

"Then perhaps you and my father will work together."

"My master has told me so," Will said, the taste of self-loathing bitter in his mouth.

She shrank back a step. What could he expect her to do, face-to-face with a foul-smelling youth who spent his days in pig slop and his nights in a barn with animals?

Now the doctor came to the door and stepped in front of her with a polite, "Miss Miller." She retreated down the hallway;

Will watched until her straight back and the dull gleam of her skirt disappeared from his view.

"Yes?" the doctor asked.

"Your gloves, Doctor," Will said, offering them to him. "Thank you."

"Oh no, I intended for you to keep them." The doctor's brow wrinkled in puzzlement. "Do you not need them?"

"Sir—Doctor—I could not keep such a pair of gloves," Will said, searching for an excuse. "They aren't suited to my work."

The doctor paused. "Are you certain?" he asked.

"Yes, sir."

"But I think you may need them for your journeys to the poorhouse, at least," the doctor said. "Keep them. I have others."

Will nodded and tucked them under his arm. "Doctor . . ." He did not know quite how to proceed, but waded into the matter. "There's someone at the poorhouse whom I wish to help. I was hoping you might have some influence with an employer. To get her a position . . . perhaps in a factory."

Dr. Loftin crossed his arms and raised one hand to stroke his white close-cropped beard. "I don't often ask my friends for that variety of favor."

Will's heart sank.

"How old is this woman?"

"She's just a young girl, about my age, Doctor."

"And you have some reason to believe that she's a hard worker, not a drinker or an immoral woman?"

"I believe in my heart she's a good girl, sir. And I know she works hard, her hands were blistered." He had another thought and blurted it out. "If she was immoral, she wouldn't be in the poorhouse. There's plenty a house with its doors open to loose women in this city." Will could not believe he had said such a thing. He kicked at the ground with the worn toe of his boot.

"A good point." The doctor smiled faintly. "I'll see what I can do."

"Thank you, sir!" He wanted to shake the doctor's hand, but he should not overstep his bounds. He kept his arms rigid at his side instead.

"I'm pleased that you wish to help someone in need. I know God will bless your compassionate heart." The doctor cleared his throat. "Good day to you."

Will turned to go, ashamed. The doctor might not think him so compassionate if he knew of his black, violent hatred for his master.

"And, Will—"

He looked back at the doctor.

"Would you tell your master that Mr. Miller, the saddler, wishes to meet him at his convenience? Perhaps later today."

"Yes, Doctor."

"Thank you."

Will started back toward the Good house. He heard a click behind him as the doctor closed the door on that other world, where people spoke in soft voices and thanked apprentices—a world of satin and rosewater.

As he crossed the Loftin grounds and drew level with the doctor's large stable, something moved at the edge of his vision. He looked over by the barn to see a man watching him. The man said nothing but slipped out of sight around the whitewashed corner of the building. Strange. Dr. Loftin's grooms were usually either in uniform or dressed in work clothes, but the man by the barn was in a greatcoat and hat. Perhaps it was Mr. Miller, the saddler. If so, he was not very friendly to give such a piercing look to Will but make no greeting and disappear like a specter.

No matter. If Mr. Miller was cold or odd, it would make it less abhorrent to follow Master Good's order to try to steal his business. It was a sickening prospect, but Will had no choice. At least he would have the consolation of knowing he had not stolen from a kind and honest man.

Nine

Ann, a note came for us!" Susan hurried into the bedroom, her light-blue dress rippling like water and bringing out the sparkle in her eyes. She clutched a large ivory card in both hands like a bouquet. "It's from the Burbridges."

Ann took it in one hand while she smoothed her skirt to one side in order to sit on the fainting chair. Not that she felt faint. The thought made her smile. She liked Allan Burbridge very well, and of course, he was attractive. But he was not the kind of man whose words could be stored up and treasured. His compliments had clearly caressed the ears of many young women in Pittsburgh and were not to be compared to Eli's passionate, soulful declarations. Of course, it was over two years since Eli had made such statements to her . . .

She could not dispel her hope that, in the end, God might still intend her to be Eli's wife. There was a romance between them that she knew she would never feel with another man. It heightened all of her senses. His thoughts on poetry, or indeed any intellectual topic, drew out the best from her own mind. They would never want for stimulating conversation. And surely that was the most a woman could ask of any match: a true romance and a meeting of the minds. His words to her at the dance renewed her hope. Painful as it had been to witness Eli's courtship of Phoebe, he was a young man, and she could forgive him for losing heart under the circumstances.

"Ann, will you read it?" Susan looked at her with undisguised impatience over the top of the card.

Ann scanned the perfect calligraphy. "To Mr. Samuel Miller and the Misses Miller. Mrs. Lewis Burbridge requests the pleasure of your company for dinner on Wednesday the eighth of March at half past five o' clock."

"Tomorrow! I wonder what kind of house they live in." Susan sidled around to peer over Ann's shoulder at the gilt-edged note card.

Mabel poked her head in the doorway. "What is that?" She came to look.

"We're going to the Burbridges' home for dinner. Do you think it will be a very large house?" Susan asked. "A mansion?"

"Perhaps they have gold plates and forks," Mabel said.

"Let's not speculate on such things," Ann said. "It's not polite. Yes, the Burbridges are well established, but what matters is that they are kind enough to offer us hospitality."

"And that their plates are solid gold!" Mabel giggled and poked Susan, who brushed away her hand as if it were an annoying fly.

"Don't be so silly." Susan used her grown-up voice as she picked up a newspaper from the marble table beside Ann's chair. "Listen to Ann. You need to learn to be a lady." She rolled up the newspaper. "You mustn't embarrass us. Not even when you drink from the ruby and emerald glasses." She swatted Mabel on the head. Mabel shrieked and grabbed for the paper. A struggle ensued, punctuated by laughter.

"Girls!" Ann said. "You won't be allowed to go at all if you insist on acting like wild animals." Mabel had just succeeded in snatching the newspaper from Susan. At this most dire of threats from Ann, they froze and recovered their innocent expressions. Mabel replaced the newspaper on the table, patting it down where it curled at the edges from its mistreatment.

"We'll be good," she said.

"We'll be young ladies," Susan echoed. As if by mutual agreement, they walked out the door in genteel fashion, but as soon as they were out of sight, Ann heard loud whispering and the patter of their running feet down the stairs.

She couldn't help but love them with all her heart—even more when they were mischievous. But she winced at the memory of their laughter when they encountered that poor young man on the road today with his cart. She didn't know anyone in Rushville who was so thin, or so poorly dressed. When he came to the door just now, he seemed angry when she mentioned the possibility that he might work with her father. Perhaps he thought that her father would not give him anything for his work. But he frightened her a little. He looked like someone who had seen his share of fights—all sinew and bone and warning. He would be good-looking, with his square jaw and deep-set eyes, were it not for the painful thinness and the—yes, the smell. As a farm girl, she was not one to turn up her nose at animals or hard work, but if a man worked with pigs, it was very important that he wash and change his clothes. Perhaps this young man had no other clothes.

A man's heavy step approached in the hall. Her father appeared in the doorway.

"Come in, Father." This was her opportunity. She had not been alone with him since that frightening scene on the boat.

"The girls made me aware that we have received an invitation." He grinned, his hands behind his back, neat in his waistcoat and tie. "It seems you have made an impression on young Mr. Burbridge."

"Or perhaps it is *Mrs.* Burbridge who loves your conversation," Ann said tartly.

He chuckled. "I believe we need to go on a shopping expedition. We will spend only within reason, but we must outfit you and the girls appropriately. The girls will be presentable in their best dresses, if you air them out. And the doctor has kindly offered to lend you some of his late wife's clothing, for he thinks you were close enough in size. But all three of you will need evening gloves."

"Father, you're acting like an old maid trying to marry off an aging cousin." Her comment was light, without the resentment it might have held before. After all, Eli might not be lost.

After an uncertain pause, he smiled. "No matter how you may protest, I know you will enjoy dressing for the dinner."

Now was the time to ask about the other matter, while they were alone. Ann took a deep breath, stood, and crossed to the door of the room. She eased it closed so no little eavesdroppers could listen and pivoted to stand with her back to it. "I'm grateful for your care for me, Father, but I must ask you about something."

"What's that?" He crossed his arms.

"An incident that disturbed me while we were on the boat."

"Which was?" His expression was guarded.

She approached him, and spoke softly in the hope he would

see her honest love and concern. "A man accosted you on the freight deck. I saw you. He took hold of you, and the two of you had words."

He was silent.

"Do you know him?" she asked. "Why did he dare treat you so?"

He still made no reply, his brows knitted, his head turned aside.

"Why didn't you report him to the captain?" she asked. "Does he have some hold over you?"

At that, her father broke away and walked to the door. He jerked it open and turned back to face her. "It's none of your affair." He shoved his hands in his trouser pockets, his eyes dark with disapproval. "Don't speak to me on the subject again. We will have a pleasant time here, if you will do your part to make it so."

He walked out, shoulders stiff.

Ann stood still, aghast. It must be serious, indeed, for him to behave so harshly and refuse to say a word. What wrong had her father done that he could not be frank with her?

Not long afterward, Susan returned, already wearing her coat. "Ann, Father says you must come. The doctor is taking us to meet the other saddler."

Donning her fur cape again, Ann followed her sister down the curved stairs and into the spacious marble foyer. Dr. Loftin and her father waited there with Mabel.

"Shall we walk over to meet Master Jacob Good?" the doctor asked. He opened the front door and held it for them.

Ann took Susan's and Mabel's hands and they descended the front stoop. The road was embedded with pieces of gravel, and remnants of the last snowfall frosted the hillocks of the roadside.

Her father and the doctor conversed a few yards behind her as they walked the thirty or forty yards to the next house. Her father sounded as if not a thing in the world troubled his conscience. But she saw no way to excuse the evidence that he must be deceiving them in some way. No one would be manhandled by a stranger on a boat and then hide the reason why, unless he had a guilty conscience. Yet, for the life of her, she could not figure out what he might have done. He was a part-time minister, a man of simple tastes who avoided drink and gambling.

And yet—did she really have any way of knowing what her father did in those days when he was absent from the farm? She had never met his congregants, scattered far and wide as they were across southern Ohio. How did she know that they really existed? Perhaps not every venture away from the farm was for virtuous purposes. He was a man living without a wife, after all. But now she disgusted herself, and she refused to entertain that train of thought any further. She stole a glance back at her father, where he chatted with blithe goodwill. Was it possible that the contours of that face so familiar to her might someday shift to reveal someone she did not know?

At the Goods' front door, Dr. Loftin knocked on their behalf. The door opened to reveal a sallow, gawky woman in a plain dress and apron.

"Mistress Good, I've brought Mr. Samuel Miller and his family to introduce to you and your husband."

"Why thank you, Dr. Loftin." The syrupy way that Mistress Good spoke reminded Ann of overly sweet tea. It did not match her thin bony face. "I'll just be getting Master Good."

In a moment, the man who must be her husband came to the door and walked down the steps to greet them. He was shorter than the doctor or her father, distinguished by his striking dark hair and light eyes. He was powerfully built through the shoulders and well dressed in a new black coat and trousers. A gold watch chain dangled from the pocket of his waistcoat.

He took her father's hand first, as the two men murmured civil greetings, then bowed over her hand. She did not know why, but she was relieved when he did not kiss it. The idea bothered her, even though her hand was gloved.

Master Good took them around the side of his home and back to the large barn.

"We built this addition some years ago," he said, indicating the one-story structure that jutted out beside the tall barn. "Especially to house the saddlery."

"Very nice," her father said.

Good led them in. Ann was surprised that it was slightly warmer inside, then remembered no saddler would let his leather freeze, lest it become too stiff. A small iron firebox stood in the center of the room—there must be coals smoldering within.

The walls were studded with half a dozen saddles in various stages of completion—brown, black, red, one just a bare tree with the padding stitched on. On the stitching horse at the center of the room, a saddle was propped on its pommel, its cantle supported by the wooden post that protruded from the bench to allow for clamping and stitching.

Her father walked over to the saddle. "Fine finish here, Master Good." He ran his finger over the invisible seam on the cantle, then traced the neat line of stitches on the pommel. Fine stitching was a hallmark of a master craftsman; he had taught Ann as much.

"Thank you, Master Miller," the saddler said, with a hint of smugness.

Dr. Loftin admired the saddle for a moment. "Samuel," he said—he and her father were already on a first-name basis— "I'm sure Jacob would like to see your work as well. Perhaps we can send one of the apprentices for the saddle at my home."

"You brought a saddle with you?" Jacob Good raised his brows at her father. "I thought you were building the new O'Hara saddle from tree to finish in my workshop."

"I am," her father said. "The one Dr. Loftin refers to is a saddle I made two years ago, from that fine piece of leather you sent. Mrs. O'Hara's groom brought it over to serve as a size model for the new one. It's for the same mount, so I can use its measurements."

"I see." Good turned toward the barn and raised his voice. "Boy!"

Through the door to the barn came the apprentice Ann had seen earlier, along with an invisible cloud of odor. She was embarrassed to see Mabel wrinkling her nose.

"Boy, we need Master Miller's saddle from the doctor's house. Go get it, quick now."

It did not seem right for him to call the young man "boy," as if he were a child. Ann noticed the contrast between the apprentice's clothes, so ragged and worn that they had no real color, and the crisp new tailoring of Master Good's coat. She began to dislike the saddler.

The apprentice went out, expressionless.

"Then the new saddle will be similar?" Master Good asked her father.

"They're both sidesaddles, but she wishes me to lower the pommel horn, as increasing age has made it difficult to mount."

They discussed the design of sidesaddles then moved to harnesses and the merits of rounded leatherwork versus the traditional flat-stitched pieces. Ann and the girls stood aside while the doctor waited patiently, asking an occasional question about any unfamiliar words he heard from the saddlers.

The apprentice came back, bearing the saddle over his arms as carefully as if it were glass. His head was down, his attention riveted on the gorgeous floral patterns worked into the red-brown leather of the saddle flaps. Ann wanted to smile. She was convinced that her father hand-tooled leather better than anyone else in the country, though he denied that compliment. Obviously, Good's apprentice knew the quality of the work he cradled before him.

Master Good saw it too, but instead of displaying the subdued awe of his apprentice, his face tightened. "You did this work?"

"Yes," her father said. She sensed the discomfort behind his simple response. Anyone could see that Good was not overwhelmed by collegial respect, but instead was subtly hostile.

"Admirable," Good said without warmth. "Place it on one of the racks."

The apprentice obeyed, still treating the saddle with great care, and turned to go.

"Wait," his master said. The young man froze, face averted.

"Master Miller, I will be too busy to assist you in your work,"

Good said. "But this boy will give you any aid that you require, including any tools you may need."

"That's very generous of you, Master Good," her father said. "And, young man, as we are to work together, I would like to know your name."

The apprentice remained silent, but looked at his master.

Good answered for him. "This is Will Hanby."

"I am glad of your assistance, Will," Ann's father said. "If your stitching is half as fine as your master's, I may enlist your help in that area."

Will. The letters . . .

"Will . . ." Ann was horrified to realize she had said it aloud in the shock of discovery. "Will you excuse us? It's getting too cold for the girls."

What a sad excuse for a subterfuge. She was almost as embarrassed by the stupidity of her recovery as by the mistake itself. Master Good, her father, and the apprentice stared at her. Her cheeks flamed under their scrutiny; she was sure she was crimson.

"Of course, you must go warm up," Good said, opening the door. "I'll show you and the doctor out while Mr. Miller speaks to the boy about the necessary supplies."

As they filed out of the saddlery room, the apprentice regarded them quizzically, apparently unaware of the line of dirt that ran along his strong jawline.

His glance lingered on her. She looked away in discomfort, but when she glanced back at him, he was still looking at her, his dark eyes questioning. She hurried out without looking back.

She had this young man's letters—his mother's precious

words. She must find a way to be alone with him soon, so she could give them to him. He might be angry with her for reading them, but the letters would still be of comfort.

She did not think she had ever seen a young man so clearly in need of comfort.

Ten

8th March 1826

THE PIGS HAD ESCAPED AGAIN. FROM INSIDE THE BARN, Will heard the telltale snorting and squealing punctuated by shouts from Master Good and others in the yard.

He latched the horse's stall and ran out the door. Dr. Loftin attempted to herd the white sow back through his gate, but she would not leave her eight piglets, which had scattered across the Goods' property in all directions. Master Good stalked along his property line with the puffed-up, false geniality that promised bad things to come, later, when the doctor was not present.

The back door of Dr. Loftin's house flew open, and the two little Miller girls ran out, faces lit with the excitement of the chase.

"We'll help you, Doctor!" the older one said, while the little one laughed and ran past her. They rushed after the little piglets, trotting in complex spirals, darting behind barrels and tools, enjoying the game.

"That's quite all right, girls!" Dr. Loftin shouted to catch their attention through the chaos. "Let the piglets settle down."

But the middle sister was intent on reaching for a fleeing piglet only inches ahead of her, and the littlest sister had actually caught one by the hind leg and was holding on for dear life as it kicked to free itself.

Will hurried over to the little girl and grabbed the pig, picking it up despite its struggles. As he turned to bring it back to the doctor's property, the oldest Miller girl came out of the Loftin house, her face dismayed. She hoisted her red skirts to run toward her sisters, wisps of brown hair flying around her face. "Susan! Mabel!" she called.

Will kept a straight face as he passed her with the piglet grunting in his arms. He dumped it in the doctor's pig run, which was secure. The doctor let his pigs run free sometimes, which was why they escaped through his property fence. But Will was glad the doctor let them run free. It was better than the nasty sty where Master Good penned his pigs.

"Loo-cy!" the doctor called, making a clucking noise with his tongue. The white sow raised her head and looked at him. Her little tail wagged like a dog's. She was a very smart pig and a valuable brood sow. But she would not leave her piglets, even for her owner.

Skirt billowing, Miss Miller ran across the freezing yard toward the middle sister, who had her piglet pinned down and was holding it with fierce determination. "Let go, Susan!" the pretty young woman said.

"But he'll get away!"

Miss Miller hesitated, then knelt down, her skirt crunching into folds. She reached for the piglet.

"Miss Miller! Your dress!" Dr. Loftin called out, raising a hand as if to stop her.

She ignored him, seized the piglet in a truss-hold by both

pairs of legs, and whisked it upside down. She marched to the doctor, who took it from her with a wry grimace as it expelled a blob from its nether parts.

Another piglet stood at bay against the barn. Will scooped it up and walked toward the pig run. The doctor called Lucy again, and this time the sow peered over at the three piglets on the Loftin side of the fence. She walked back through the gate and headed for the run, and one by one, the other five piglets swiveled their little heads and trotted nimbly after their mother.

"My apologies, Master Good," Dr. Loftin said. "We'll find that hole and fix it before I let them out again."

"I'd be much obliged, Doctor," the master said, with a bizarre death's-head grin that made Will want to smash his teeth in. He could not abide the way the master ranted on at length in private about the doctor's pigs but was all ingratiating smiles to the doctor's face. He knew his master was jealous of the doctor's pigs—their fine breeding, the prolific sow, the way people came even from across the river to admire them and talk to the doctor about the piglets. Most of all, his master hated the doctor's "soft" treatment of the animals.

Will himself quite liked the doctor's pigs and stopped to scratch their jowls and stroke the piglets when he thought he could do so unobserved by his master or mistress. The white pigs were much better tempered than his master's pigs, which were surly and restless from their confinement in their own filth.

The Miller girls walked back to the doctor's property, the littlest one crowing to the middle one, "Did you see me hold that pig?"

"Yes, but he almost got away," the middle one said. "I held mine all by myself."

"I held mine all by myself too—" the little one said, indignant.

"Girls! Shush," their older sister said. The excitement had left high color in her face, brightening her eyes. "I'm sorry if we created more difficulties for you, Master Good," she said.

"Not at all, miss," he said in his false jovial way, as if he were the neighborhood benefactor. "Now, we'd best be getting back to work, eh, boy? Time's a-wasting."

"Yes, sir." Will stole a glance at Miss Miller. She was looking at him with pity—he could not stand that. He had seen the way the littlest girl wrinkled her nose at him earlier. They thought him beneath them. He walked back to the barn and slammed the door behind him.

The barn's dark privacy was welcome, but in only a moment the door banged open. Master Good had followed him.

"What's that, boy? You're not showing a bit of temper, are you?" His voice was deceptively quiet.

Will's skin crawled, and he tried with all his might to blanch the anger from his face and substitute innocence. "No, sir. I'm sorry, sir." He wanted to retch, but he knew his master would have his hide at the slightest excuse.

"I'm pleased to hear it." Good crossed to the stall Will had been cleaning. "Still not finished here?"

"No, sir. I will be soon."

"What did you get from Miller about his techniques?"

"I just listened, sir. We only talked for a few minutes."

"You'll have to do better. You only have a few weeks."

"Yes, sir." Will knew he probably shouldn't say it, but he did anyway. "Sir, I may be able to copy some fitting techniques, but it won't be possible for me to learn his hand-tooling in that time."

Good pressed his lips together and went white around the

mouth. A lump of ice formed in Will's throat. Good paced past him. Then the world reeled and Will was down on his knees, vision blurred. He rolled to the ground, half-aware. The master had hit him with something. He didn't know what. A dull ache began on the side of his head. He knew it would be much worse in a minute.

Dimly he heard the master's voice. "Don't question me, boy. Miller said himself that your stitching was fine on that other saddle. But if you can't learn to tool the leather as well as he can, then you'll have to discover a way to make his work less attractive to his customer. Perhaps his billet straps are weak. Do you understand me?"

Will groaned. His eyes still would not focus, though the barn's spinning was slowing.

The barn door rattled as Good left. Will raised his fingers to the side of his head, where he could feel a huge lump already forming. A sharp sting revealed a break in the skin. His fingers were slick and red when he held them up close enough to focus on them.

He would live. Tom's head had bled worse than this when the master hit him with the poker two weeks ago. He thought vaguely that he would have to wash the blood off before dinner or he would get another thrashing.

But as the room slowed to a standstill, the ache grew and spread. He lay immobile on his side with his eyes closed, clutching his head in his hands as if to hold it together.

He thought he might like to die then. There was only pain, no joy in this miserable, dishonest life—there had been none for years. His brother would be ashamed of him, could he see him now, just as the Miller girls had been disgusted. That was why he had not written Johnny for a year, and his brother's letters had gradually ceased. Will did nothing of worth—he had no future without a reputation to start a business. He did not even have honor, but had turned into a cringing shadow ready to do what was necessary to get by.

Part of him wanted to kill his master, even if he would hang for it. But there was fear down deep inside him, ever since the first time the master had beaten him so badly. That was only a couple of weeks after his arrival in Pittsburgh. Will had sobbed and begged for mercy, his eyes swelling shut, his nose pouring blood, rib and fingers broken. It wasn't the pain, but the degradation of begging, his own weakness—as if the master had reached a skeletal hand down into Will's soul and closed on it like a vice so it would never be his own again. The memory claimed him—it showed him who he really was, who the master had shown him he was—a spineless beggar and a slave. A cloud of nausea filled him and he wished for nothingness.

He heard the barn door open and close. Now he had to get up. Master Good had no mercy.

But instead of Good's serpentine whisper, he heard a sharp intake of breath.

Light footsteps approached and cool fingers grazed his forehead.

For a moment, he remembered his mother and let himself fall back into a dream that she once again sat beside him. He could almost hear her soft humming and smell the honeysuckle that bloomed outside the window the last summer she had been at home, when she would tell stories and then sing him to sleep, half cradling him in her arms.

But the smell was not right—it was not honeysuckle, but instead the faintest fragrance of roses and warm skin.

"Can you open your eyes?" she whispered.

He cracked them open. It was Miss Miller, her pretty face pale with horror. He closed them again.

"Did your master do this?" Her voice quavered a little. He felt another gentle touch on his head. He couldn't bring himself to answer.

He heard a rustle as the sound of her footsteps moved away, then returned. Coolness touched the sting in his scalp. She was gently swabbing at the cut, holding something very cold on it. The throbbing eased a little. He moistened his dry lips so that he could speak.

"You must go." He kept his eyes closed, not wanting to see the disgust that must fill her at the sight of his bloody, filthy state. "It will be worse if he finds you."

"How can he do this?" she said. Then after a pause, "I have something for you. I will give it to you when you are better. Perhaps it will help you in some way."

"Go," he groaned, afraid Master Good might return at any moment. A tiny warm droplet fell on his cheek. *A tear.* A feather-touch brushed it away.

Then with another rustle she was gone, and he heard the door close.

He knew she was wrong and that nothing could help him. But the warmth of her tear lingered on his face and slipped down inside him to the dark, empty places, where it carried for a moment the honeysuckle smell of summer.

Eleven

ANN SLIPPED IN THE DOOR OF DR. LOFTIN'S HOME, grateful that the hallway was empty. Will's bloodied and sad face lingered in her mind's eye; it wrung her heart and forced tears to her eyes. She still clutched her handbag with Will's letters inside. They would have to wait for another day.

Hoping she could get to her room unnoticed, she hurried down the hallway into the front foyer. But as she passed the drawing room, Dr. Loftin's voice came through the open door.

"Miss Miller?"

She froze, arms crossed, head down to hide her dismay. She did not want to stop, but she could not be rude to her host.

"Is something wrong?" She heard the rustle of a newspaper, then his leather soles tapped toward her across the marble floor. She lifted her head to see him standing beside her, his brows knit together in concern, his wrinkles deepened around his eyes.

"Master Good is—" A sob rose in her throat and kept her from saying any more. She covered her face with her hands.

"What is it? What has happened?" The doctor's voice was soft. The comforting strength of his arm circled her shoulders, steadying her.

"Master Good is beating his apprentice. I just found him on the ground in the barn. He was barely conscious." She took the handkerchief he had produced for her, wiped her eyes, and dabbed at her nose.

The concern on his face gave way to surprise. His lips parted as if to ask a question, then he paused.

Her face warmed—of course the doctor wondered why she had been in the barn, but he was too much the gentleman to ask.

His face sagged in sorrow. "I suspected as much. But Will has never said anything. Nor do I think he has any recourse under the terms of his indenture."

"But there must be something we can do for him."

"I don't know that there is. It's a sad fact of indenture that some masters abuse their apprentices. The law turns as blind an eye as if it were a father beating his son. The cause is immaterial; Master Good can say what he wishes about the reason for it, and any judge will believe him."

"But he could kill him."

"Yes, and would probably get off scot-free for that also. Dead apprentices tell no tales."

"What about the other apprentice I saw with Will? Can't he be a witness?"

"He would face the same difficulty. A master's word carries more weight. And then Tom would no doubt face dire consequences of his own."

Then there was no way around it. Unless . . . "Can't you intervene, Doctor?"

"I've considered it, but from my observation of the man's temperament, I fear that he would deal with them even more harshly. I've chosen instead to do small things to alleviate their misery. And to pray fervently that they make it through the remaining years of their indenture whole in body."

"I can't accept it." Another sob threatened, but she wiped her nose again and took a deep breath. "I must think of some way to help."

"I hope you do." Dr. Loftin patted her shoulder. "I know it may be difficult under the circumstances, my dear, but we do have a dinner engagement to keep. We won't be able to help Good's apprentices tonight, so in the meantime, we should not be rude to our hosts. Perhaps something will occur to us by tomorrow."

She had forgotten that she should be dressing now for dinner with the Burbridges.

"Perhaps you should go look in on Susan and Mabel," the doctor said. "I will send Mary up to help you. She will bring you my late wife's gown."

"You're too kind, Doctor. I'll see to it that the girls are prepared." Mustering a weak smile, she balled the crumpled handkerchief in her fist and took a few steps to the foot of the stairs. "Have you seen my father?"

"I believe he's dressing already." With a slight bow, he withdrew to the drawing room and gently closed the doors. She ascended the stairs, deep in thought.

The gray-brown waters of the Allegheny lapped ahead of them as the Millers drove toward the bridge in the doctor's coach. All of the girls were muffled in capes and fur hats; the warming box beneath Ann's feet staved off the frosty bite of the air on her slippers. She sat stiffly beside her father, the blue-green satin of her borrowed dress spilling to the floor and encroaching upon Susan's knees. Dr. Loftin sat across from her father, and the two men conversed about the history of Pittsburgh. At least she herself did not have to make pleasant conversation. Her father's secrecy still disquieted her in his presence. Her little sisters chattered with one another about the width of the river.

As they left the cover of the bridge, a wintry gloom stole into the afternoon, hinting the approach of dusk. Ahead on the Pittsburgh wharf, hundreds of men crawled like rats from one skeletal boat hull to another, the sharp taps of their hammers echoing across the river. The hiss of furnaces and a low hum of engines rose from buildings all along the waterfront, as if the city breathed and its unseen heart beat somewhere below ground. Piles of coal tumbled into the edges of hills of white sand; raw riches of the earth heaped themselves in every spare yard of space. The line of glassworks and iron foundries stretched unbroken until the point of the city dropped away into the three rivers. And everywhere crept the musty smell of smoke that hung black against the somber sky.

The coach made its way through the streets. Ann was stunned by the number of wagons, horses, and pedestrians. She was glad Dr. Loftin had an expert driver as well as a coach to offer them. The doctor was himself an excellent amateur driver who enjoyed the pursuit and occasionally drove his own coach, but she felt safer with a real coachman at the reins. The heavy wagons headed west looked dangerous. They were so massive compared to the other conveyances on the road. If a driver misjudged his distance and hooked one of the fine coach wheels on a heavy wooden wagon wheel, it would splinter to bits. Their judicious driver kept them well clear of the wagons. It was more difficult to avoid the pedestrians, some of whom seemed driven by a fatal impulse to hurry as close to the coach as possible.

They moved away from the wharf. The products of factories disappeared, and the establishments of attorneys, tailors, and dressmakers appeared. A yellow brick church sat gracefully amidst a grove of trees.

"Ann, a castle!" Mabel pointed to another church. It was enormous, dark gray, with buttresses and spires. Susan gasped, and even Ann was impressed. She had never seen a building like this outside the pages of a book.

Her father looked out the coach window. "It's a church, girls. Trinity Church. Finished last year."

The coach slowed, turned into a narrow drive, and stopped. Ann slid the loop of her fur handbag over her elbow. She had brought a few essentials: a tiny hand mirror and comb, a handkerchief. But there was something else in her bag too. She had not wanted to leave Will's letters behind at the doctor's house. The crinkling of the paper when she touched the bag was like a talisman for the apprentice's welfare, reassuring her that she would somehow think of a way to help him.

Dr. Loftin opened the door and handed her out to the graveled drive. The Burbridge home was very large, as she had suspected it would be—a two-story red brick with imposing white columns. Evergreen hedges taller than a man were trimmed into neat lines and curves, forming a green wall circling half an acre around the home. Within this protective embrace, smaller evergreen bushes had been trained into tiered cones. Some were perfect spheres of solid dark green.

"Topiary," Dr. Loftin said in response to her expression of

wonder. "Not fashionable in Europe, perhaps, but pleasing to look upon." He turned back to help the little girls out of the coach.

"Good evening," a cheerful voice called out. Some yards from the coach, Allan Burbridge walked down the wide white steps of his home and came to greet Ann, bowing over her hand. When he looked up at her, his gray eyes were keen with interest. "I'm delighted you could come, Miss Miller."

"Your garden is lovely," Ann said.

"Thank you." He indicated the twigs protruding from heaped mounds along the walls of the home. "I wish you could see the roses, but they are asleep and cannot be awakened."

She smiled. "Like Briar Rose."

"You've read the Grimms' tales?"

"Yes, the new edition—the small book for children."

Susan came up beside Ann and took her gloved hand. "I love Briar Rose."

"She was beautiful and kind, like you and your sisters." Allan looked at Susan first, but then at Ann. She blushed.

She admitted that Allan was both intelligent and attractive. And it did not hurt that his thick wavy hair was neatly clipped, his broad shoulders clad in a fine black coat. But he was clearly not serious about this pursuit. He threw out flirtatious phrases with far too much aplomb and did not watch her closely in the way of a real suitor who would hang on his beloved's every response. And she might live in the country, but she was no milkmaid to heed the sweet whisperings of the lord of the manor. She did not realize she had smiled at her own thought until Allan smiled back.

"Shall we go in?" he said, offering her his arm. Dr. Loftin

took Susan's hand to be sure she would not slip on the steps, and Ann's father brought up the rear with Mabel.

A butler—a real butler—stood at the door and took their coats, Ann's handbag, and the leather portfolio her father carried with him when on business. The butler retreated back through a side door, presumably a coatroom. Ann composed herself so she would not look awed or silly, but it was hard not to marvel at the enormous foyer, the dark gold color of the walls, the high ceilings with white crown molding carved with Grecian leaves. Ahead through a wide double door frame, she could see blue and gold carpets and the dark, graceful curves of furniture made by masters. A chandelier shimmered with candles.

Her sisters' eyes were about to pop from their heads. Mabel let go of her father's hand and ran up to Susan, grabbing her arm. She jabbed Susan in the ribs as if to say "I told you so." Ann raised her eyebrows at Mabel, sending her a silent but familiar warning. Her littlest sister dimpled and left Susan alone to return to her father's side, contenting herself by gazing avidly in every direction.

"My family awaits us in the parlor," Allan said as he led Ann forward, his arm strong and steady under her fingertips. He bent his head and lowered his voice. "I'm afraid you're not our only guests tonight, though I dearly wish you were." His breath tickled her ear, sending a pleasant shiver through her. She should not allow him so close, but she did not know the polite way to tell him so.

She did not have to wonder for long at his meaning, for when they walked through the double door frame and turned into the oval parlor, she saw three very straight backs, two in satin and one in serge. The Holmeses.

Mrs. Holmes and Amelia descended upon them with the cries of predatory birds.

"Oh, Miss Miller, Mr. Miller! And the darling girls!" said Mrs. Holmes, swooping over in a cloud of heavy floral scent. Magnolia, of course.

"Ann, how wonderful that you could grace us with your presence!" Amelia poked out her chin toward Ann like a beak.

Ann was taken aback by the change in their demeanor—their false sweetness was almost as bad as their earlier snubbing, but at least it was less awkward. Perhaps the Holmeses had realized that if the Burbridges accepted the Millers, they would be best advised to follow suit.

Mr. Holmes shook Dr. Loftin's hand. "Good to see you again, Doctor." As Mr. Holmes extended his hand to her father, he wrinkled his nose toward his brows and made his startling, snuffling honk before saying, "And you, Mr. Miller."

Ann wanted to giggle at her father's alarmed expression, but he manfully took the hand offered to him. She snuck a glance at her little sisters. Thank goodness they were not laughing—yet. Susan and Mabel had dubbed Mr. Holmes "The Great Goose" in the privacy of their stateroom. Ann noticed that Mabel's hands were pressed together demurely in front of her, but her arms waved back and forth at the elbows, like wings; Susan's lips trembled. Ann laid her arms across each of her sisters' shoulders.

"I believe we may need to refresh ourselves after our coach ride," she said.

Louisa Burbridge, soft and demure in rose silk, came to her rescue. "Why of course. Come with me."

They left Ann's father and Dr. Loftin to make conversation,

while Louisa showed them to the back of the parlor. Ann led her sisters through a small door into a powder room, all white wood panels and gold trim, with a full-length mirror on a matching white stand. Ann did not have time to admire its beauty for long, as she had little sisters to admonish. They emerged suitably chastened, and Ann rested easier in her hope that perhaps they would avoid girlish mischief for the rest of the evening.

When they approached the group, Mrs. Burbridge welcomed Ann with a regal if somewhat tremulous sweep of her arm. "Miss Miller, we were just about to go in to dinner. Won't you accompany—"

But even as she indicated Allan, and he moved as if to offer his arm, Amelia Holmes fluttered between them and seized him by the elbow. "Why, thank you, Mr. Burbridge," she said.

Allan smiled at her, as a gentleman would, but the look he gave Ann over Amelia's shoulder was rueful. Dr. Loftin stepped up and offered Ann his arm with an air of amused sympathy, while Mr. Miller escorted Mrs. Burbridge. They all proceeded into the velvet-dark dining room with its rich, patterned wallpaper and softly glowing tapers.

They dined first on a creamy crab bisque, then little Cornish squabs, and finally a steaming succulent half pig, carved at the table by the manservant. Susan and Mabel were models of demure girlhood. Ann might even have begun to relax and enjoy herself, were it not for her creeping anxiety about the conversational cuts and parries of the Holmeses.

"How exquisite your gown is," Mrs. Holmes said to Ann. The Southern matriarch took a sip of wine and peeped over the rim of her glass. "I have been telling Amelia for weeks that fashions earlier in the decade were much more attractive than what

Paris is offering us now. And now you prove it for me beyond a doubt." She sighed. "You see, Amelia. The higher waist is more becoming."

Ann's face burned. There was no chance that she would be able to retort; she had little experience with other women, and certainly not women like these, who could present a glass full of poison so it smelled as sweet as ambrosia.

"Miss Miller is indeed a vision tonight," Dr. Loftin said.

"Well said." Allan turned to Ann. "But, beautiful as the gown may be, I believe it is not the dress that transfixes us but the timeless beauty of the one who wears it." The corner of his mouth quirked. He lifted his glass in Ann's direction. "A toast to classical grace."

"Hear, hear," said the doctor. He and Allan grinned at each other and then at the company. Mr. Miller, Mrs. Burbridge, and even Mr. Holmes raised their glasses with genuine goodwill, but Amelia's mouth was pursed and sour.

Her mother also looked vexed before hiding it with an overly bright smile. "And perhaps a toast for your daughter, Philip?"

He honked. Even in her discomfort, Ann wanted to laugh. Mr. Holmes finished clearing his sinuses and lifted his glass once more. "To a radiant daughter, possessed of all the feminine virtues her mother could bestow upon her."

Now she thought Allan would really lose his composure, because his shoulders convulsed for a moment before he quickly changed the subject.

"Mr. Holmes, have you had any success in business here?"

"My runaway slave is apparently hiding somewhere here in town, as I suspected."

Mrs. Holmes gave her husband a disapproving look, but he appeared not to notice.

"In a part of town known as Arthursville, which is infested with free blacks who harbor fugitives."

"How do you know his whereabouts?" Ann's father asked mildly.

"Oh, I have my means." Mr. Holmes waved at his glass, and the silent servant stepped forward to pour him more wine. Mr. Holmes watched the ruby liquid trickle into the glass with satisfaction.

"And it was worth it to you to travel all this way?" Her father surprised her with his persistence.

"It's the principle of it, you see." Mr. Holmes had lifted his glass, but thumped it down on the table so the wine trembled in it.

Did the man not see Mrs. Burbridge frowning?

"When my other slaves see one escape, they are emboldened to try the same thing themselves. Consequently, it is of great importance to bring runaways back and make an example of them."

Ann disguised a shudder, wondering what such an example entailed.

"I do not have to do it myself, of course," Mr. Holmes said. "There are men for hire who will bring back fugitives. But a planter of my acquaintance suspects that my slave ran away with one of *his* slave women, and I feel some responsibility to ensure that my friend's stolen property is returned too." Mr. Holmes patted his lips with a lace-edged napkin. "The best of it is that we have laid a little wager."

"Indeed?" Dr. Loftin's face was neutral.

"Yes," said Mr. Holmes. "He has sent a hired man to find his fugitive, and I have come to find them myself. If I find them first, my friend owes me his best thoroughbred mare. Should his hired man find them first, I owe him a year's supply of port. And that's a goodly amount of port, I assure you." He laughed gustily and then honked again. "Well, I must excuse myself for a moment." He pushed back his chair and got unsteadily to his feet.

Mrs. Holmes murmured something and rose to follow her husband. Ann had no doubt that Mr. Holmes was about to be read a lecture on the mingling of wine and politics.

As the Holmeses exited toward the parlor, Mrs. Burbridge spoke into the vacuum. "Tell us about your ministry, Mr. Miller. You must gather so many stories, riding about as you do."

The company embraced the new topic with evident relief, and when Mr. Holmes returned, he did not attempt to raise the subject of his fugitive again.

The rest of the dinner passed in more cheerful conversation, with only an occasional acerbic glance from Amelia. Allan was charming and attentive, and as he escorted Ann out into the hallway, he asked if he could take her to see some of the sights of the city soon. She agreed, grateful that the Holmeses were far enough behind to miss this exchange.

"Then I will see you this week?" he said.

"Yes." She smiled. "I have no pressing engagements."

"I'm a lucky man." He pressed her hand and turned to take her coat from the butler, who stood behind him.

"Your bag, miss." The butler spoke with a hint of an Irish brogue. He held her fur bag in one hand and the leather portfolio in the other. She took both and handed the leather case to her father.

"Why, thank you, Ann," he said. She was touched to see that he appreciated even this small gesture of help. But she shook off the tender feeling, remembering his harshness the day before. She could not trust him.

They set off in the coach. The girls were tired now, and they all rode in silence. Ann reflected on Allan's attention, smiling to herself. He was very entertaining. She smoothed her skirt and laid her handbag on the seat. It crinkled with the sound of dry paper.

The letters. The memory of the apprentice returned, along with a rush of guilt. *I have been prancing about enjoying myself and eating fine food, while he lies injured in a freezing barn.*

She must give the letters to him as soon as she could. But she could not afford to give Master Good any reason for suspicion. She would have to wait and watch for her first opportunity.

Twelve

MISS MILLER HAD BEEN AVOIDING HIM ALL WEEK. Will was sure of it. He had glimpsed her several days before, as she stood at one of the upstairs windows of the doctor's home, gazing out at the Goods' home with a preoccupied look. When she noticed him watching her from below, she started and stepped back, dropping the curtain into place over the window. He had not seen her since then.

He stood by Dr. Loftin's pig enclosure, where the pigs were now eating their morning meal. Perhaps she might come out to talk to him if he stood here long enough. But the longer he stayed, the more likely it was that Master Good would see him. And there was no sign of Miss Miller yet, not even a twitch of the curtains.

He clucked to the pigs, savoring this stolen moment of peace. Lucy raised her head, sniffing his hand with a moist, grain-flecked nose, then went back to her meal. The little piglets grunted and squealed as they shouldered one another aside at the trough. He put his arm through the fence and stroked a piglet on her rough, warm back. She pointed her tiny snout at him for a moment, her little pink nostrils working, button eyes bright. Then she flicked her curly tail and skittered down to the other end of the trough.

The back door of the doctor's house opened. To his disappointment, it was Mr. Miller who emerged on the stoop, a bag slung over his shoulder. The saddler raised a hand in greeting. "Good morning," he called across the yard.

"Good morning to you, sir."

"Have you some time to assist me this morning, young man?" Mr. Miller asked, walking toward him over the gravel.

"Yes, sir."

Master Good had told him that he must drop all other duties if Mr. Miller asked for his help. He had been working for Mr. Miller every day now for a week. It was far more pleasant than his other tasks. But poor Tom was working twice as hard to keep up, and guilt nagged at Will as he watched the younger apprentice staggering back and forth on various errands of animal tending and wood gathering.

Mr. Miller reached Will, and they fell in step, headed for the work area in the Goods' barn.

Once they were inside and the door fastened against the cold, Mr. Miller laid out his tools on the workbench. Will admired the craftsmanship of the large awl, its sharp metal head set flush and solid in the wood handle. Years of fine work in Mr. Miller's hand had lent all his tools a subtle gleam, a patina of history. Compared to their graceful lines, their aged wood and bone, Master Good's newer tools were crude and gaudy, like children's toys.

The model O'Hara saddle rested on one of the wall racks. Now that the tree and padding for the new saddle were ready, Mr. Miller no longer needed the model saddle's measurements. Will had been cutting stirrup straps and billet straps yesterday, but the master saddler cut the saddle flaps in order to assure the correct curve. Now a smooth piece of leather lay over the saddle seat, ready to be stitched into place.

"Will, if you would be so good as to begin the pommel stitching, I will start the embossing for the flaps."

He could not believe that Mr. Miller would entrust him with such an important task. Pleasure rushed through him, carrying with it slight anxiety. He did not know if his hand would be steady, with his nerves drawn tight by the need for perfection. He was glad Mr. Miller had already cut the stitching channel, so all Will had to do was sink the stitches.

He picked up his two needles and the awl and seated himself on the stitching horse. Hole by hole, thread by thread, he pulled the smooth hide taut into the desired position. He grew a little dizzy and had to remind himself not to hold his breath for each stitch.

Will paused and straightened up for a brief rest, hands still resting on the pommel with the needles and awl. Mr. Miller was deep in concentration a few feet away at the work table, bending over the saddle flap with a half-moon blade. Will marveled at the deftness with which the master saddler wielded the knife, his wrist rotating smoothly, the blade perfectly vertical as it etched a design of fine petals into the damp leather. He carved with astonishing speed, first one perfect rose, then another.

Mr. Miller must have noticed Will's fascination out of the corner of his eye, for he smiled down at his work as he finished the lines of another flower. "Would you like to approach and observe?" he asked without looking up.

Will was chagrined to be caught lollygagging, as Master Good would call it. "Oh no, sir." Then he realized that his master would want him to observe as closely as possible. "Or perhaps just for a moment." He laid his needles on the saddle seat, careful to keep the threads straight. Rising and swinging his leg over the bench, he crossed to where Mr. Miller still bent over his work.

"It's very fine, Mr. Miller." He said it with wonder, still absorbed by the sight of the knife flitting across the surface with such accuracy.

"Thank you, Will. The result of many years of apprenticeship under a demanding master." For the first time, the saddler lifted his knife away from the leather, turning his head to look Will in the face. "Not as demanding as yours, perhaps."

Will shifted his gaze, looking back at the saddle flap. Miss Miller must have told her father what had happened. It was humiliating, and yet part of him was relieved that someone, anyone, knew of his master's true nature.

He would say nothing. Mr. Miller seemed a decent man, but Will did not know if the saddler might repeat anything he said to Master Good.

The saddler laid his knife aside. He stroked his chin with one hand, then picked up the beveller and wooden hammer, scanning the floral design closely as if checking for any minor flaw. "My wife was particularly fond of this pattern."

"Was, sir? Is she no longer living?" Will would not usually ask such a question, but the camaraderie of their shared craft put him at his ease with the saddler, who was so different from his own master. Perhaps he had gone too far, even so.

But Mr. Miller did not seem offended, only a little sad. "Lost in childbirth with Mabel, my youngest."

"I'm sorry, sir."

"Mmm." The saddler applied the beveller to one of his fine cuts and began a series of small taps with the hammer. A delicate channel emerged in the flower pattern, bringing the line into relief so that it was more visible. "My two youngest don't even remember her. It's my eldest daughter who has borne the burden of her mother's passing, for some nine years now. I fear she has taken it too hard and will lose her youth in raising her sisters."

At this mention of Miss Miller, who had occupied his thoughts so prominently in recent days, Will was shy. He did not wish to say anything of her. But as he watched Mr. Miller bevel the pattern, his thoughts drifted on. Miss Miller had lost her mother years ago, just as he had. But he had lost his mother piece by piece, in a long wait punctuated only by letters written in a hand that grew gradually weaker and more unsteady. Unlike him, Miss Miller had lost her mother suddenly, in one shocking day.

He wondered if she still thought of her mother as often as he did—if she too remembered the softness of her mother's embrace, or the way her mother's eyes squinted at the corners when she laughed. He imagined the saddler's daughter as she must have been then—a little girl, gradually realizing that her mother would never come back to her, the fragments of her heart crumbling and scattering with every passing day. But at least she still had her father.

He turned abruptly from the saddler's side and went back to the stitching horse with a lump in his throat.

Time blurred as Will continued his focused stitching, checking to be sure the positioning was correct, careful not to pierce the thread with his second needle. He had worked his way back to the cantle when Dr. Loftin opened the door of the shed.

"Samuel, the cook has some cold meats and cheese prepared if you wish to have them now." The doctor included Will with a nod. "Care to join us, Will?"

"I'd better not, sir."

The doctor did not persist. He probably knew Will's refusal was rooted in his apprehension about Master Good.

Mr. Miller stood, stretched his arms and back, and walked to the door, holding it open for Dr. Loftin.

But the doctor stayed where he was. "I'll be inside presently, Samuel. I have something to discuss with this young man."

When Mr. Miller was gone and the door closed again, Dr. Loftin continued. "I have some good tidings for you. Mrs. O'Hara has agreed that her foreman will give the poorhouse girl a position at the glassworks, on the Pittsburgh side of the river."

Will's heart lifted. "Thank you, Doctor! You won't have cause to regret it, sir! I know she will be a good worker."

The doctor smiled. "There is still one hurdle to be overcome. She must have somewhere to stay. And that charge, I leave to you. Go down by the waterfront to some of the boarding houses there. See if you can find one that will take her. Preferably one that is not possessed of too ill a repute."

"Yes, sir." Will colored, thinking of his earlier reference to bordellos. More than one bawdy house plied the trade near the Pittsburgh waterfront.

"Here." The doctor held out a small velvet bag. "I will support her first week of boarding myself, and she can repay me when she receives her wages."

"Thank you, sir." Will wanted to convey his gratitude, but he couldn't find anything eloquent to say. But the doctor seemed to sense his elation, and his face reflected a measure of Will's joy.

"I'll send you across the bridge on an errand for the Millers. I believe your master will agree to that. And when it is all arranged, I will have my driver bring you in the coach to get her."

Will nodded. He was confident that Master Good would agree to anything that would ingratiate Will with Mr. Miller.

By that afternoon Will had found the place. Down by the docks, only yards from where he usually picked up the oakum, an old brown building advertised for boarders with a crudely lettered sign hung on its door. It was not completely respectable, perhaps, but completely respectable places were few, and they would not agree to take a young woman on her own like Emmie. At least this one was clean and not adjacent to a tavern. In the city, one was never too far from a tavern, but it was ill advised for a young woman to walk past one if she could avoid it. Drunk men were dangerous.

The docks were not free of drunks either, but Emmie would be close to the factory at the water's edge. And because Will had to get the oakum every week, he would be able to stop by this boarding house to assure himself that she had come to no harm.

The toothless woman who rented him the room leered at him when he explained that he would be renting the room for a "woman friend."

"She is a decent girl," he said defensively.

"Of course she is." She cackled and scratched her cheek with a knowing look. Her bonnet was grubby, and he smelled the nutty pungency of gin. But beggars could not be choosers.

The woman took the money in the pouch. "She'll have the attic room, then," she said. "Starting tomorrow."

He clambered down the stairs and made his way back toward the bridge. His coat was still ragged, but he did not feel the cold, so warmed was he by the pleasure of helping Emmie. He could not wait to see her face when he told her that he had come to take her away from the poorhouse.

But that might be several days from now. Until then, he must be very careful around Master Good. He did not want another beating to ruin the plan.

Thirteen

ANN SLIPPED OUT THE BACK DOOR OF DR. LOFTIN'S home and into the purple dimness that veiled the house and yard before dawn. She gathered her coat tight round her shoulders. The chill gusts of wind took her breath away. She picked her way down the stoop and over to the doctor's barn, which was closed up tight. No matter. She did not need to go inside for this errand.

She skirted the barn, grateful for the thick, concealing gloom under its eaves. It was not respectable to skulk about a host's property like a thief, alone, before sunup. She would shrivel with shame should anyone see her before she found the apprentice. But she had been trying to deliver the letters for days without success. She had only seen him unaccompanied a few times. He seemed to be always at work for his master or her father. And she could not go speak with him on Master Good's property without raising eyebrows. She might risk her father's disapproval, but not Master Good's violent temper.

She reached the far back corner of the building and stopped, leaning against the rough wood to still her nerves. From her window she had seen the apprentice come out every morning to draw water from the Goods' pump, which was only yards away from where she stood now. She hoped he would not be long. Her heart raced and her throat dried out with fear of discovery.

She must calm herself. It might be half an hour before he emerged. She closed her eyes and began to pray, first for him, then for herself. But her thoughts were so jerky and scattered that she apologized to the Creator for her distraction and ended the prayer.

The Goods' kitchen door opened. Will came out with a bucket in one hand. His face was set, as if sheer concentration could make the walk bearable in that tattered coat.

She could not call out. What if Mistress Good was awake inside? She stepped just beyond the eaves and waved an arm. He did not notice, mouth pressed in a line, tangled dark hair hanging forward as he pumped the handle. She waved harder. No luck. She jumped and waved both arms. What an utter fool she must look. But it might be her only chance.

His head turned. He stopped and stared. She brought her arms to her sides. Did he not see that she wanted him to approach? She beckoned. With a furtive glance at the house, he walked to her, and she backed behind the corner so he would follow. Now they were concealed from the Goods' window.

She ignored the smell of the pigsty and stepped close so she could whisper. "Is your master or mistress awake?"

"Not yet. But any minute." He glanced back in the direction of the house.

"I told you I had something for you." She reached inside her coat and retrieved the bag from the inside pocket. "I know I must be quick." She was so nervous that her clumsy fingers could not untie the strings. "Here." She pushed it into his hands. "Open it."

He plucked at them and worked them loose.

She must explain before he saw the letters. "I found these in a barrel that your master sent to my father more than two years ago. I did not think they should be tossed out."

He pulled the papers out and unfolded them.

She watched his thin, strong features. No expression. Had he gone pale?

"Are they yours?"

He nodded once, without meeting her gaze. His Adam's apple moved in his neck, where he wore no scarf. He looked away, and in his silhouette she saw the quick flutter of his eyelids.

He was not angry then, but fighting a softer emotion. Her grief rose to meet his, threatening to overwhelm her. She swallowed hard. "Have I done right in bringing them to you?"

He nodded again. He folded them and leaned back against the barn, tilting his head back. For a moment, sorrow and longing poured across his face in place of the tears he did not shed. Then he took a shuddering breath. How could she help? She laid one hand on his arm.

He lowered his face back toward her. Their eyes met, and the intensity of their shared emotion vibrated between them. Her most private feelings were laid bare. There was a kind of comfort in it, even with the pain, but she could not stand its strangeness for long.

She lifted her hand and stepped back. "You must take the letters."

"I cannot keep them. If he finds them again, he will destroy them." The strain in his whisper told her what that would mean to him.

"But you must have them." She dug her nails in her hands. There had to be a solution. "Can I leave them with the doctor?"

"No." His face flushed darker.

"I am sure he would not read them."

"No."

The tint in the air lightened from purple to blue. Dawn was near. She must hurry. "What if I keep them for you until your indenture is finished?"

"That will be more than a year." His jaw tightened as if it stretched like an eternity in his mind.

"I will keep them safe," she said. "And you must write to me care of the postmaster in Rushville, Ohio, when you are free. Then I will send them to you, wherever you are."

He met her gaze again, his dark eyes turbulent.

A scraping noise from the Goods' kitchen made her jump. The light was increasing by the moment.

She held out her hands and he gave her the letters and the pouch. "Go," she murmured.

He turned and walked out into the yard again. She crept up to the corner so she could watch. Had Mistress Good seen? Even if she noticed Will's absence, she would not see Ann over here behind the barn. That was some reassurance. Will might claim any farm duty had taken him out of Mistress Good's sight.

Will grabbed the full bucket as if nothing were amiss and lugged it back toward the house with flexed arm.

The air was translucent now. The sun must have cleared the horizon to the east, and only the trees beyond the road held back the morning.

Across the yard, Will grasped the door handle and stepped in.

A dull silence reigned over the Good house, with only the occasional clatter of iron from the kitchen. Mistress Good must not have noticed anything amiss.

She made her way back toward the doctor's door, tentative, checking if the way was clear. No one accosted her, and she went in as silently as she had come out. Inside she paused, bracing one hand on the plaster wall and letting out a pent-up breath.

What she had done seemed so futile. Had there been any worth in showing him the letters, when he had to return to his place of imprisonment? She could do so little when they were all bound by a law so unjust.

She would go upstairs now and bury the letters in the bottom of her trunk. Her sentiments were disordered, like unfinished seams that frayed and unraveled with every additional touch. She wanted to put the whole matter away and clothe herself again in the neatness of life before she ever met the apprentice. Delivering the letters should have calmed her and removed her preoccupation with his plight. Instead, his refusal to take them had only agitated her further. Perhaps it was better not to understand or be understood if it led to such painful disruption of the spirit.

She spun away from the door and walked up the hall, shaking her skirts into perfect folds with a quick flip of the wrist. No matter how ragged and frayed she became inside, her exterior appearance would not reveal it.

Fourteen

ANN'S FATHER HELD HER BACK FROM THE EDGE OF the street as a carriage swerved uncomfortably close.

"Be careful," he said gently. "You must be especially vigilant here in the city. You will have the girls to look after while I am on my errand." He turned and walked ahead down the sidewalk.

She felt a frown gathering on her brow. He had gall to lecture her about protecting her sisters when his seedy brawl aboard the boat was so fresh in her memory. She was not the one gallivanting around town on business too secretive to be respectable.

Collecting herself, she followed him toward the girls and Allan Burbridge, where they stood by the glove and lace shop.

She was in no mood for a gay shopping trip, but they had agreed days before to let Allan escort them this morning to visit the Pittsburgh merchants. While she and the girls shopped, her father was going on an errand of some undisclosed nature. The less he disclosed, the more she suspected he was in some sort of trouble. He was acting like a guilty man.

"Miss Miller, will you join us?" Allan called from under the green awning of the glover's store.

When she approached, he touched his fingers to the brim

of his hat and bowed his head, then smiled as intimately as if the two of them stood alone on the street. "I have a surprise in mind for you," he said, removing his hat to reveal an appealing dishevelment of his thick brown hair. "So I will go in search of it while you visit the glover."

"That's intriguing." Ann's burdened heart lost some of its weight at the playfulness in his gray eyes.

"I hope so." He grinned. "Mr. Miller, have you business to attend?"

"Yes, I do. Thank you for escorting the girls." Mr. Miller pulled his watch from his pocket and checked the time. "We'll meet back here in two hours, then?"

"Yes, sir." The two men shook hands, and Ann's father departed down the busy street, dodging other pedestrians without breaking his stride.

Allan opened the door of the glover's store and held it for the girls, Ann bringing up the rear. When she reached the door, she felt a light touch on her shoulder. She looked at him in surprise. He leaned close to speak in a low voice, and as the warmth of his body traveled through the wintry air, she smelled masculine traces of soap and leather—such a foreign smell from the sweet little-girl scent of her sisters.

"Don't leave this shop until I come back for you," he said. "This city can be a most uncivil place, even on its most civilized streets."

She nodded and stepped forward into the perfumed air of the store. Her sisters were already peering into glass cases and sighing at the luxurious wares. They pounced on Ann, leading her around with such glee that one would have thought they themselves had fashioned each item.

When they had each chosen a pair of gloves and a hand-kerchief—the more economical selections, though still dainty—the amused proprietor gathered their purchases and began to wrap them. The girls were still finding new treasures around the store, but Ann had her fill of gloves. She let her gaze wander to the street outside the checkerboard frame of the window. So many people. One woman rushed past the window, clasping her bonnet to her head with one hand, while a big riverman sauntered by and spat into the street as if he had not a task in the world but to stroll and chew tobacco. Then there was the man leaning up against the side of the building across the way . . . watching her.

Him! The man with the beaver hat. She made a decision in an instant. "Stay here, girls. I'll be back shortly."

The shop bell clanged as she threw open the door and hurried out, keeping her eyes on the man. When he saw her, he started and strode away on the opposite side of the street.

She would make him tell her what business he had with her father. Finding a gap in the steady stream of traffic, she picked up her skirts and ran across the street after him. He vanished around a corner, but she marked the space where he had gone and followed as fast as she could.

She rounded the corner into a narrow alley. It was gloomy, even in the morning's gray light. A stench of garbage and human waste rose from unidentifiable heaps next to the walls. She was afraid some of them were human, but she had no time to investigate. The alley ahead of her was empty. Her fugitive must have turned the corner at the far end and escaped into the next street. She picked up her speed, the walls blurring past her as she panted for breath against the constriction of her stays. The man would not elude her, not if she had any say in the matter.

She passed several nooks in the side of the buildings and a doorway. Almost there.

Something pelted into her stomach with great force, stopping her cold. She bent double. Everything stood still in agony. Her lungs would not work. She could not breathe. An iron band completely circled her at the waist, lifting her off her feet. It dragged her sideways, into a doorway. It was so dark she could see nothing. A rough hand covered her mouth. Dizzy, she willed herself to take even one breath, but she felt her limbs weakening. She thought in a dim corner of her mind that she might die here. Her senses faded.

***

The coach rolled to a stop at the foot of the hill. Will opened the door and jumped to the ground without even using the step. "I'll be back soon," he called up to the driver.

The poorhouse squatted at the top of the long flights of wooden stairs, but this time Will climbed them with joy. He had come for Emmie. He had done at least one good deed.

When he knocked on the door, a new housekeeper answered. She was younger than the previous woman, but her face was hard as flint.

"Whadda you want?"

"I've come for Emmie Flynn. She has been offered a position and a place to stay."

The woman's beady eyes widened with surprise. "You don't hear that every day. Not at this house." She turned and yelled over her shoulder, "Emmie Flynn!"

In a minute, Emmie walked up next to her. If she grew

any thinner, she would be transparent. Her hair still trailed out of her bonnet and hung over her shoulders, like a little girl's. "What is it, Mrs. Drew?" Then she saw Will, and a question formed in her eyes.

"You have a position in the glass factory now, Emmie. And a place to live."

For the first time, her lips curved upward. Her smile was beautiful but fragile, like a drop of water standing on a petal, sure to fall with the slightest breeze. He wished he could set a glass dome around her to protect the beauty of that smile forever.

"Will you come with me?" he said.

She nodded slowly. "I'll get my things."

He could not believe it when he finally handed her into the coach, savoring the feel of her little hand in his. From the look on her face, she did not believe it either. She sat on the edge of the seat, placing her worn bag next to her and sitting very straight with her hands folded in her lap. She stared out the window. Her slender form vibrated with the motion of the coach over the rocky road. Will feared she might fall off the seat.

"You may as well make yourself comfortable," he said as kindly as he could. "It will be a few minutes until we get to the boarding house."

She pushed herself back against the seat, and after a moment, her tense shoulders relaxed. She continued to watch the scene unfolding past the coach window, rapt. "What is that building?" she asked.

Will could not see where she was pointing, so he moved from the seat opposite her to the one next to her. "A new whiskey distillery," he said. "It went up last year." At this, a thought struck him. "How long have you been in the almshouse?"

"Three years."

The awfulness of it brought silence as he visualized it. The tedium and the grind of the same painful work, blistering and tearing her hands day after day. For a thousand days.

"And what brought you there?" he asked.

"My mother. She couldn't provide for us by honest means, and couldn't bear for me to see her . . . provide by other means."

It took a moment, but Will caught her meaning. His face flamed. "What of your father?"

"I never knew him."

"I'm sorry." His heart went out to her. He took one of her hands, as he had once taken his sisters' before they grew ill. "It will be better now."

"I hope so." She held his gaze for a long moment. Her lips trembled and tears welled in her eyes.

Then he leaned forward, an inch at a time, and closing his eyes, gently brushed her lips with his own. For one timeless moment, he breathed in her nearness, her fragility.

What was he doing? He would compromise a girl whose mother had condemned her to three years of hard labor rather than sully her. Though instinct impelled him forward, he drew back and opened his eyes. Instead of the outraged scowl he expected, she regarded him with an odd blend of vulnerability and wariness.

"I'm sorry," he said, releasing her hand. "I don't intend any dishonor to you."

She lifted her own hand and touched the one he had withdrawn, where it lay between them. "It's all right."

He moved back to the seat opposite her, clumsily rearranging his legs so as to avoid touching her.

They arrived at the boarding house after a few minutes of uncomfortable silence. Will caught her looking at him, which shamed him further. She would think he had rescued her for low motives, and that could not be further from the truth.

Once outside, he reached up to take her hand again. "Be careful on the step."

She flashed him a grateful look.

The gap-toothed landlady leered at them as Will asked her for the key. At least she held her tongue.

It took a moment to work the rusty lock, but eventually Will was able to open the plank door and let Emmie in. She passed into the room, looking around for something. It was furnished with a small bed and thin coverlet, a rag rug, and a dresser with missing knobs.

"There's a candle and tinder in the dresser," Will said, guessing what she needed in the dim room. "Top drawer."

He had placed the candle there for her because the top drawer, at least, was still possessed of its knobs and thus easier to open. She retrieved the candle, set it in the rusty holder atop the chest of drawers, and struck the flint and steel into the tinder. The tiny light guttered and caught, sending shadows dancing around them. She lit the candles.

"I'm sorry it's not much." He wished he could have found a better coverlet or quilt. She might be cold. He crossed to the dresser and wrestled with the second drawer until it opened with a scrape. "But my friend the doctor did send a shawl and gloves. And some shoes. See?"

"It's a sight better than what I had," she said softly.

He straightened up, relieved.

She interlaced her fingers and dropped her gaze to the floor. "I owe you so much," she said. "Why did you help me?"

"Because you needed help. You didn't deserve that life. That's all. I swear." Then he flushed, fearing he had said too much.

She lifted her head, her cheekbones standing out in the candlelight, her eyes bright. "You're a good man." She stepped forward and took his larger hand between her two small ones. Lifting it before her face, she pressed his hand to her lips, closing her eyes in an expression of profound thankfulness.

He felt her breath and the warmth of her mouth, and desire to touch her overwhelmed him. As she lowered his hand but did not release her grip, he found his other hand moving to her shoulders as if pulled there by some invisible, irresistible force. Her shirt was rough, but her hair was soft. He entwined his fingers in it and slid his hand to the back of her neck. He gently pulled her close to him. She did not resist, and this time, when he kissed her, he did not stop.

Fifteen

ANN AWOKE TO THE SOUND OF LOW VOICES. HER mouth felt strange. There was something in it—cloth that bit into her cheeks and pressed on the back of her head. Panic swelled and her breathing quickened. She lay on her side. Her hands were numb, and when she tried to lift them, she found they were bound by a cord or rope—she couldn't tell which in the darkness. A solitary line of ghostly light glimmered at eye level a few feet from her. After a moment, she realized it was the gap between a door and the floor. There must be a lamp in the room beyond the door, and it was from that room that the voices issued.

"I did what I had to do. She was coming after me. She knew I was following them." The man's voice was slow and Southern, but overlaid with roughness like splintered wood. She didn't recognize it.

"You're a fool. Someone may have seen you." The second man spoke in a more cultured drawl.

"No one did. I caught her in the alley outside."

"And what do you propose we do with her now?"

"I say we send a note to her father telling him that we will return his daughter if he returns what belongs to you."

"And if he refuses?"

"We make him aware that he will never see her again."

"And what would we do with the girl?"

"Dump her in the river and make it look like one of the flatboat men got to her."

There was a pause. Ann struggled to absorb what they were saying, fighting her rising terror.

"That seems . . . extreme."

"It's the only way to keep her from talking. We need to do it whether he gives you your property or not. Kidnapping a woman'll get us hanged."

She comprehended painfully and slowly what they had said. It was difficult to hear clearly over the blood pounding in her ears.

"Then you might as well do it now," the more educated voice said, with a tinge of reluctance. "That way there won't be any risk of escape."

"All right."

"I shall leave, and then you can take her to the river." A chair scraped on the floor. There was a loud honking noise and a man cleared his throat.

She could not believe it. It had to be Mr. Holmes. No one else could make that noise. How could he calmly tell the other man to kill someone with whom he had just dined?

A door shut somewhere. Mr. Holmes must have gone. A heavy tread moved around the room. She heard some clinking and rummaging.

She closed her eyes and prayed. *Help me! Help me, please. Have mercy. Look down on me and cover me with your hand.*

The boots clumped to the far side of the door. Light washed

into the room as the door opened. Her nerves shrieked. A silhouette moved against the light. When he squatted next to her, she recognized the man who had always worn the beaver hat, though he was hatless now. His hair was thinning and fell in greasy strings over his forehead.

"Hey there, girlie," he said, an odd stillness in his eyes. "It's a shame I'm gonna have to make it look like a river man got to you." His hand slipped between the buttons of her dress. She jerked away and her gag slipped to the side. She screamed, but the man struck her hard across the face, stunning her. He laughed softly and pulled her skirt to her knees, then higher. She kicked at him, but he threw her on her back and knelt on her legs with crushing force. She prayed wordlessly as his face drew near, grotesque with lust and power. In horror, she turned her head aside, staring at the other room through the open door. She felt his hot onion-laced breath and his hands moving under her disarrayed petticoat.

Someone burst through the door of the far room. All she could see was a flash of blue and a raised pistol. The report deafened her—a smell of black powder blasted through the room. Then the heavy weight on her legs was gone, and she heard running feet. He must have gone the other way, for she heard a door slam against the wall behind her and daylight poured in where she lay.

"Devil take it! I missed!" It was Allan, holstering his pistol and kneeling hastily to pull her dress back into a semblance of decency. Even in the flood of relief, she closed her eyes in shame.

"Ann . . . Miss Miller. I'm so terribly sorry." He fumbled with the gag, and she felt it loosen and fall away. She gagged as he removed the wad of cloth from her mouth.

"Did he . . . ?" He stopped in midsentence, cradling her shoulders and lifting her to a sitting position. When she finally nerved herself to look at him, she saw that despite the concern in his eyes, his jaw was tight and he was pale with anger.

"No," she tried to say, but it came out as a croak, her dry mouth refusing to work.

He untied the rope around her wrists with swift, strong fingers, rubbing at the marks in her soft flesh to bring back the feeling.

"You sisters told me you had run away down the alley. Thank heaven I passed just at the right time."

"How did you know where I was?" she said faintly.

"I heard a noise." Red rushed into his pale cheeks. He must have heard her scream.

"Can you stand?" he asked.

"I don't know." She slowly pulled her legs under her and rose to a kneeling position, but when she tried to stand, her weak knees gave out and she stumbled. Immediately, his hand was under her elbow. "Let me help you." He murmured reassurances and held her by the waist, lifting her to her feet. She had begun to tremble violently, and her legs still would not work. Seeing her difficulty, he swept her up into his arms as lightly as if she were a little girl and carried her out into the daylight.

By the time they reached the street, Ann had regained enough strength to force herself to walk. Allan brought her to Susan and Mabel, safely stowed inside the coach where he must have left them. She remained quiet, afraid the girls might hear her voice shake if she spoke. Allan put on a good semblance of normalcy and sent the girls ahead with Jensen to the Burbridge home, while he and Ann stayed to wait for her father.

Eventually her father came into sight, strolling along the street. He scanned the area with confusion, obviously looking for the missing coach. Then he saw Ann and Allan and headed for where they stood.

"Mr. Miller, something has happened," Allan said, before he could greet them.

His eyebrows shot up in alarm nearly to the brim of his hat. "To Susan? Mabel?"

"No, they're on their way to my parents' home. It's Ann who was attacked."

Ann leaned on Allan's arm while he explained, skirting the worst part with roundabout words. Her father's face pulled taut with dismay. Anger nibbled at the edges of her shock. How would he explain whatever he had done to cause this? She was surprised to see tears come into her father's eyes. *Tears of guilt.* Her heart hardened with every passing moment. And Allan hadn't even told him the part he didn't know—that it was her father's fault.

Her father stumbled over words of apology and embraced her. She heard him sniff. He turned away to wipe his face with a handkerchief. When he faced them again, he was more composed. "We should get you back to the doctor's house, Ann. You must rest."

She felt dislocated, as if she were watching herself from some other place. She grasped for anything that would root her back in the present, back in her body. She seized her anger and held on to it for her very life. "I want to know why," she said bitterly.

He looked at her in surprise. "What do you mean?"

"You've done something. You've taken something you shouldn't have." Her voice rose and her eyes grew wet. "You're responsible for what happened, and I deserve an explanation." Tears ran down her face. Allan tendered her his handkerchief and put his other arm around her shoulders as if to hold her shaking body together. The thought flitted through her mind that on any other day she would be humiliated to behave in such a way.

"He said you had taken something, and that they were going to pretend to ransom me to get their property back. But they were going to kill me anyway. And Mr. Holmes was with him."

The mention of Mr. Holmes froze both her father and Allan in shocked silence. Then Allan murmured, "We will find these men and call them to account. I give you my word."

"I am more sorry than I can say," her father said, bowing his head, "for having brought this on you."

She remained in stony silence, except for her jerky breathing. Allan did not seem at all put out or surprised by her loss of temper. But then, he had seen what had happened.

"I will show you why this has occurred," her father said. "And, Mr. Burbridge, as you are now inextricably concerned in the matter, you may see as well." He turned to the street and hailed a passing hackney cart. It pulled up, and he pressed a coin in the gnarled hand of the driver. "Arthursville, please," he said.

Allan helped her up into the cart, and the two men seated themselves.

"It will all be clear in a few minutes," her father said, pulling his muffler closer and adjusting his hat in the cold breeze of their passage. "I don't excuse myself for placing you in harm's way, but perhaps it will help you to know why."

The hackney cart moved at a brisk trot through the streets, turning several corners until they were in a quieter area of genteel homes. Ann's father instructed the driver to pull up at a two-story red-brick home, in the Georgian style. When they all dismounted from the cart and stood on the doorstep, he rapped with the large iron knocker.

A distinguished black man opened the door. He was dressed too well to be a servant, and his whiskers were close-trimmed like a gentleman's. "Samuel," he said, smiling. "An unexpected pleasure to see you again so soon! Did you forget something?"

"No," her father said. "This is my eldest daughter. She has suffered a terrible fright and abuse on my account. I feel it is time to share the truth with her." He addressed Ann. "This is Mr. Enoch Washington." Then her father acknowledged Allan with a nod in his direction. "And, Mr. Washington, this is Mr. Allan Burbridge. I owe him a great deal for his intercession today on my daughter's behalf."

Mr. Washington's face grew grave. He opened the door for them. "Come in."

He led them through the house, which was nicely furnished and still smelled faintly of fresh plaster. It must be quite new, this house. Ann did not know what to think. This had not been what she expected to see or hear from her father, and her anger and hurt still bubbled below the surface like a pot waiting to boil over. Yet the little part of her mind that remained capable of rational thought registered the enterprise of this free black man, who had built such a life for himself in a world where his people were often despised.

They followed him up the stairs to the second floor, where he pulled a little cord that hung from the ceiling. A trap door opened down from a hinge.

"It's me, Enoch," he said. "Come down."

A ladder appeared over the edge of the attic, and Mr. Washington grabbed its lower rungs to set it into place. A man's shoes stepped out above their heads, moving slowly backward down the top rungs. His trousers were plain, with worn patches, and as he descended, Ann saw from the back that his shirt was homespun and rolled at the sleeves. He wore a woolen vest and cap. Above him, a woman moved onto the ladder, the thin drape of her skirt covering her limbs, though the men averted their eyes nonetheless.

When the man stepped off the ladder to the floor and turned to face them, Ann had to stifle a gasp. His coffee-colored forehead bore a cruel, puckered scar in the shape of a circle bisected by a cross. One ear was nothing but a ragged hole in his head, the tissue missing. The woman who moved to his side behind him had the same disfiguring scar and had also lost an ear, though her black hair was braided loosely over it in the attempt to hide it. They regarded their visitors with calm dignity and an edge of wariness.

Ann's father turned to her and said, "I would like you to meet John and Clara, lately of Tennessee, who have now chosen the surname Simon. Mr. Washington and I are assisting them as they go to their freedom. They are the so-called 'stolen property.'"

Sixteen

THE O'HARA SADDLE WAS COMPLETE. IT SAT ON THE rack in the workshop, pommel gleaming. Embossed on the saddle flaps were scores of roses, each perfect, each carved by the master's own hand. Will was sure that even someone who knew nothing of saddlery would gaze in awe at Mr. Miller's work. The O'Hara saddle was no longer a product of craft but instead a work of art, lovely beyond price.

The door of the shop opened; Tom peeped around the door, then entered with an empty slop pail in hand. "Have you seen the master?" he asked in a low voice.

"Not since last evening," Will said.

Tom's tense face relaxed. He brushed his dark hair back out of his eyes and set down his pail. "What a beauty!" he said, stepping to the saddle rack and tracing the roses with the tip of his finger. "No wonder the master's beside himself."

Will winced. After his final, shaky attempts to copy the leather tooling, Master Good had ranted for half an hour. Spittle flew from his mouth as he told Will to sabotage the saddle by this evening, or live to regret it. The thought made Will sick.

"Are you going to do it?" Tom asked, lifting the flap to look at the billet straps.

"I don't know." Will turned to the work table and fiddled with the arrangement of the awls and scrapers.

"You must." Tom's eyes were worried under his tangle of dark hair. "You can't help who the master is. It's not your fault."

Will finished lining up the tools and stared at them in mute misery. "It's wrong."

"The master will have your hide if you don't. He may even kill you. Then what would I do? And what would happen to that girl you're helping?"

An added wave of guilt swept over Will. He thought of Emmie's soft warmth, the forbidden sweetness of her skin, his inability to control his desire to touch her. He knew what was virtue and what was sin. For hours after he left her, he had searched in vain for excuses for dishonoring her, fulfilling his own burning need in defiance of heavenly law. The thought of it stirred his desire again, sickening him even further. He must be truly a creature of the devil, to use her so. She had been willing, but the bed sheets had given undeniable evidence that she had been pure before he touched her.

His sin turned his insides to hot pitch. It spread through his body just like his desire, searing everything it touched. This must be how it felt to lose one's soul. Perhaps his soul was gone already. What point was there in taking a stand about the O'Hara saddle? Compared to what he had already done, sabotage was almost trivial.

He turned to look at Tom over his shoulder. "Leave me alone."

Tom's shoulders hunched. He snatched up his pail and slammed the barn door on his way out.

After a moment, Will reached for the round-bladed knife. He wiped it on his pants and held it up to the light. It was very sharp—keen enough to cut invisibly.

He walked over to the saddle and laid his hand in the seat, admiring again the smooth richness of the leather. He could not believe that he was about to ruin this beautiful work. He would have to slice halfway through the underside of one of the billet straps—just enough so that the girth would hold when it was tightened, but give way under the stress of a ride. He tried not to think of what would happen to the lady when the girth gave way. It was not his choice. He was his master's servant, and halfway to the devil.

He lifted the heavy saddle flap and knelt down next to it. Holding the flap open with his shoulder, he pulled the billet out in his left hand. He hesitated, the blade bright, poised against the leather. He repositioned it to just the right angle . . .

The door swung open. He jumped up and back from the saddle. Mr. Miller, of all people. Will went cold, then hot. He had not moved fast enough. Mr. Miller would have seen him kneeling by the saddle. And the round knife was in full view, clutched in his right hand. He lowered it to his side.

Mr. Miller's forehead wrinkled. For a moment, they both stood in silence.

"What are you doing, Will?" he asked.

At that moment, Will would rather have slit his own throat than stand before Mr. Miller. But the saddler must have sensed something of the sort, because he walked to Will and gently removed the knife from his nerveless fingers. Will gave it up without a struggle, his face averted. He did not want to see the hurt and rage in Mr. Miller's eyes.

"You were going to damage the saddle." It was not a question. Will braced himself for the blow he knew must follow. But Mr. Miller stayed motionless at Will's side.

"I didn't cut it yet," Will whispered.

"Your master ordered it?" the saddler asked.

Will did not know what to say. Master Good would deny it. There were laws about criminal apprentices. Will had heard of indentures extended. When Mr. Miller told the judge what Will had done, would they bind him to Master Good for another five years? He would rather die.

"He ordered it. I did not have a choice," he said at last.

Mr. Miller turned away. Now Will was sure that he would go first to Dr. Loftin, and then to the law.

The master saddler removed his hat and laid it on the worktable, his shoulders very straight in his gray coat. He paused, looking out the tiny box window above the table. "What course of action would you recommend I take, son?" His voice was tight, his words clipped.

"I—I don't know, sir."

"Your master will no doubt use you terribly if he finds you have not carried out his orders."

Unable to admit to his plight aloud, Will nodded.

"Should I turn to the law?"

His heart pounding, Will looked away, steeling himself for the inevitable.

"I think not. No crime has been committed here," Mr. Miller said.

Will's knees went weak with relief. He braced himself with one hand on the stitching horse so it would not show.

"I will not punish you for your master's sins, though I'd

dearly love to make your master answer for them. Instead, I'll immediately take the saddle with me to the doctor's house. You may tell your master you fulfilled his order. He will have no way of knowing whether the saddle is intact or not."

"Thank you, sir." His voice came out hoarse. He did not deserve this generosity.

"But I must tell you something, son." Mr. Miller walked back to stand right in front of Will. Something about his scrutiny made Will feel exposed in all his weakness. He hung his head and looked at the straw-littered floor.

"I've seen something of bondage and cruel masters," the master saddler said. He spoke quietly. "And I've seen enough of you to know you have a good heart."

At this, Will's heart stung him, as if in reproach. The sting moved to his throat and his eyes. "My heart's not as good as you think, sir."

There was silence for a moment. "We've all done things we regret, son."

Will felt his lips tremble and he bit them hard.

"I can't say I've walked in your shoes, Will. But I know men older and stronger than you who have crumbled in evil hands."

Will felt a light touch on his shoulder. His breath caught and he struggled against the upwelling of pain.

The saddler's words were slow, as if he wrestled to shape his thought. "What hurt those men most was when they saw the evil in themselves. They went into the darkness and couldn't find their way out. They thought they had no choice."

Mr. Miller squeezed Will's shoulder. "Look at me, son."

Will looked up, embarrassed at the tears that filled his eyes and spilled over.

The saddler's face was full of compassion. "You have a choice, no matter how it seems. There is a light that shines for those sitting in darkness and those in the shadow of death."

The words sank like fresh rain into his parched heart. *For those sitting in darkness.* He felt as if a tiny pinpoint of light appeared then, at his very center, where nothing had glimmered for so long. The relief was so great that he had to close his eyes, the tears still trickling down.

Mr. Miller sighed. "I would to heaven there was some way I could stay and help you with your present troubles. But I must go back."

Will opened his eyes again. He wiped his face on his sleeve and struggled against the lump in his throat. "Yes, sir."

Mr. Miller stayed put for a moment as if lost in thought, then his eyes focused on Will again. "I would like you to do something for me."

Will would refuse him nothing at this moment.

"I need a message taken across the river, and I would like you to carry it."

"Yes, sir."

"I believe the errand may do you some good. You may take the doctor's coach, and I will secure Master Good's permission."

Mr. Miller lifted the saddle and slid one arm through the gullet. "I'll go put this away safely, then I'll speak to your master. Meet the coachman in front of the doctor's house in half an hour."

"I'll be there, sir."

Mr. Miller picked up his hat in his free hand, then headed for the door. But he paused as he passed Will, his eyes once again full of perception so deep it was not quite earthly.

"No one can take your soul, son," he said. "Souls can be given, but they can never be taken."

Will held the letter in his pocket as the coach wound its way through the streets of Pittsburgh. He did not know what Mr. Miller had told his master. He did not much care. He was too grateful for the reprieve from punishment, for the luxury of a long coach ride, a respite from his labor. He had not dared wear his gloves for fear the master would see them, but the coach was a sight more comfortable than the outside, thanks to the foot warmer.

I should be clapped in irons, but instead Mr. Miller helps me. His throat clenched and he swallowed.

The coach pulled up in front of a two-story brick home. Will climbed out and walked to the door, which was white save for an iron knocker. He rapped three times, and after a minute a well-dressed, dark-skinned man came to the door. He raised his eyebrows in inquiry.

"I have a message for you, Mr. Washington." Will assumed this man must be the one Mr. Miller had described as a "black gentleman."

"Thank you," the man said. He took the paper from Will's outstretched hand, pulled a pair of spectacles from his pocket, and read it silently. Will wondered what it said.

Mr. Washington looked up from the note and eyed Will. "Come in, young man."

"I can't stay long," Will said. Too long an absence and Master Good might guess something was amiss.

"Mr. Miller has written to me here. He has arranged with your master for you to stay for a half hour or so without trouble."

Mr. Miller had mentioned Will in his note? Perplexed, Will followed Mr. Washington, who was already several steps down the hall. They reached the end of the hallway and emerged into a kitchen.

"Wait here, please," Mr. Washington said. A slender brown-skinned woman in an apron straightened up in front of the hearth. "Who is this, Enoch?" She had an open, pleasant face. The dress under her apron was fine, with a velvet collar. The lady of the house.

"A friend, my dear," Mr. Washington said. "Young man, this is Mrs. Washington, my wife. Have a seat."

Will obeyed, taking the indicated place on the kitchen bench.

"Grace, if you wouldn't mind scraping up something for him to eat, I'm sure he would not refuse." He exited into the hall again.

"Looks like you haven't seen a good meal in a while." Mrs. Washington opened the pantry and produced a plate with dried beef and two biscuits. The biscuits were soft and fresh. Will ate the first one in two or three gulps, but slowed down to savor every mouthful of the second. He had not tasted anything this good since his days at the Quaker farmhouse. He drank deeply from the glass of water she set beside him. The beef took some chewing but tasted delicious.

While he ate, Mrs. Washington put a kettle on the hook and stoked the fire. When his hostess wasn't looking, Will hid the last piece of biscuit and some jerky in his pocket for Tom. He wished he could also take him a cup of hot tea like the one Mrs. Washington set at his left hand.

Mr. Washington came back. He nodded approvingly at his wife when he saw Will with the tea and an empty plate. But Will was distracted by the others who walked into the kitchen after him.

The man and woman were dressed in farm clothes, though theirs were much cleaner than Will's. They each had a ragged hole where an ear should have been, a scar of a brand seared into their brown foreheads. Will tried not to show his shock.

The man sat down across from Will at the table. "I'm John Simon. This is my wife, Clara." She took a seat on the bench beside her husband.

"Hello." Will didn't know what else to say.

"Mr. Miller has done us much good," Clara said. Her plain face was calm beneath its scars. "He wants us to tell you our story." Will focused only on her bright eyes to keep from looking at the cross-and-circle scar above them.

Their hostess set down cups of tea for them and withdrew. Mr. Washington considered them for a moment, then followed his wife.

John Simon spoke first. "Mr. Miller wrote to say you have a hard master."

"Yes." Will found he could say it aloud to them.

"Our master was a hard man too," Clara said.

"And a drunk," John added. "I was born a slave, and so was Clara. We grew up working in the fields next to each other. We both loved the Lord, and we sang and we prayed together at night when we could sneak the time. One thing led to another, and we figured one day we should get married. So we did and life was hard, but we had each other." He gave her a faint smile, and she returned it.

"But our master was a gambler and a drunk. One day at cards he gambled away one of his slaves to another planter. That man, Mr. Holmes, he got his pick of us. He needed another house slave to clean his house, so he picked Clara."

A flicker of pain went across his wife's face, and she looked down at the table.

John cleared his throat. "I hollered at it, but it wasn't no use. The overseer knocked me down and they took me away. Then they took her away. And Mr. Holmes lived a good way off."

Determination hardened his face so Will could almost see him, on the plantation, as he must have gazed into the distance that had robbed him of his wife.

"I wasn't going to let Clara go. God put us together, and no man would pull us apart. So I went after her. The first time the master caught me, he whipped me 'til I couldn't stand. The second time, he cut off my ear."

Will repressed a shudder.

"Then he had Mr. Holmes cut off hers and send it in a box, to show me. He knew that would hurt me worse than anything he could do to me."

How could he remain so calm? John was like a mountain, quiet and unmoved even after a thunderstorm.

"But I didn't give up." John looked at Clara again. "I went for her one more time, and we ran for the North. We made it to Kentucky before the slave catchers got us in the woods." Their locked gazes spoke of a terrible memory, and John fell silent.

Clara spoke up in a soft voice. "They took us back and

branded our heads, in front of the other slaves. The master told us we needed a cross on our heads to remind us that if we loved the Lord so much, we needed to remember the Bible says slaves must obey their masters. And now we couldn't go anywhere, because we would be marked wherever we went."

John turned back to Will. "That was Mr. Holmes's idea, and my master agreed to it. He told me Jesus was going to betray us to everyone who met us, with his sign on our heads, because Jesus is a white man and we're nothing but slaves to him. But I knew my master was a liar." He leaned forward and put both hands flat on the table. "I told Clara before they took me away again that the sign of Jesus would be a blessing on our heads and a curse on theirs who tried to twist his name and his words. I told her we would escape under his sign."

Clara put her hand on top of one of his, and he turned his palm up to intertwine their fingers.

"And that was what came to pass," he said. "God sent messengers and angels to us. First one man helped us to Kentucky, then another to West Virginia. There we met Mr. Miller, who made a way for us to get here."

John looked at his wife as if to invite her to add anything he had forgotten. He took a sip of his tea. Clara nodded.

Will could not find anything to say. There was no answer to such a story, or to the visible signs of their suffering. Only respect.

"Thank you." He shook John's hand and stood up. John stood up with him. Will hoped that the scarred man and woman would see his sympathy in his face, as he could not find a way to speak it aloud.

"God go with you." Clara remained seated but smiled at him gently. He was staggered by the strange juxtaposition of her smile with the marks of her torture. That smile welled from a source untouched by any cruelty the world could inflict.

On the carriage ride home, Will's thoughts whirled together so he could not separate one from another, and he looked out the window in a half daze. With one fingertip, he absently traced a figure on the seat cushion next to him: a circle, bisected by a cross.

Seventeen

Dueling is a sin in the eyes of God," Ann's father said.

"With all respect, Mr. Miller, I believe God sometimes calls us to right wrongs," Allan replied.

Snow flurried around the figures of Allan and Ann's father. Wrapped in dark cloaks, their hats pulled low over their brows, they stood a few feet away from the road where their coach waited. The solitary hillside was already thick with snow—a white silence that swallowed their words, deadening their voices in the winter air.

Ann watched them surreptitiously from the carriage window. Allan would not be pleased if he knew that Ann had come along this morning. She pulled her cape tighter against the cold; her stomach roiled. Should she try to intervene now, before Mr. Holmes arrived?

Her father shifted the pistol case from one hand to the other. "God does not call us to sin in his name, Mr. Burbridge. And taking a man's life is a sin."

"The responsibility for the challenge is mine. I only asked

you to serve as my second. But it's too late for you to change your mind, in any case. Holmes will arrive shortly."

"I only agreed to be your second in hope of dissuading you."

"It's a matter of Miss Miller's honor. Surely you cannot deny what has happened. It cannot go unpunished."

Ann could keep silent no longer. She pushed open the coach door and jumped out, calling out to Allan as her boots hit the snow. "Don't do it, please!"

Allan turned away from her father and stared in shock. "Miss Miller! What in the name of—?" He walked toward her through the shallow drifts. "You have no business here. What possessed your father to bring you?"

"He did not wish to. I begged him to let me come. I hoped I might be able to reason with you, if he failed."

"You should get back in the coach and leave. Your father and I will handle this." He placed his hand gently under her elbow as if to escort her back.

"No, Allan." She pulled away and looked up in his face, willing him to truly hear her. "I do not want you to do this. You should not risk so much."

"I can't let it pass. I saw it. Holmes must pay for his part in what happened."

"But I only heard him, I didn't see him! What if I am mistaken?"

"If you were mistaken, he would not have agreed to my challenge."

She hesitated. "But I am the one wronged, and I'm asking you to drop the matter. For my sake, and for your family's sake. Please."

He was unmoved. "No gentleman could witness a stain on your honor and refrain from defending you. When another man of rank is responsible, he must answer for it."

"Is it my honor that concerns you, or your own?"

"Both." He blinked away the flakes that had caught on his eyelashes, blown even under his hat brim by the swirls of wind. "You know as well as I that were this matter to come before the law, your name would be forever ruined. I will not allow it." He grew more impassioned, his voice rising as he clipped off each word. "Nor will I permit such base behavior to go unpunished. The code of honor was developed for just such a wrong as this. There is no other answer."

She fell silent. The tension in his face subsided.

"Now, go sit in the coach and wait," Allan said. "You should not see Holmes. And you mustn't witness this." He lowered his voice to a murmur. "I cannot believe your father brought you here."

"I won't faint away at the sight of Mr. Holmes." But tendrils of dread sprouted inside her as she thought of what might happen. "I will stay here, Allan."

He tilted his head and took a quick breath as if to argue with her further.

A jingle of harness and a thump of hooves drew their attention to the road. Just topping the hill was the Holmes's hired coach. The coachman pulled up with a flourish, the two gray horses blowing steam in the frosty air.

When Mr. Holmes stepped out of the coach door, Allan left Ann standing by the coach and went back to where her father stood. Another man followed Mr. Holmes out into the snow beside the road.

The flurries were now so thick that they scattered Ann's view of the men into whirling fragments. Beyond those four dark figures, the snow pressed in so close that the men seemed to stand in white nothingness. She was grateful for the snow; perhaps Holmes would not notice her standing against the coach wheel, if she kept very still.

"You requested pistols," Allan said to Mr. Holmes.

Mr. Holmes nodded curtly, indicating with one hand his second, who carried a pistol case just like the one Ann's father bore. The second knelt in the snow and unlatched the box.

"You know, Burbridge, you're being a hotheaded young fool," Mr. Holmes drawled, then sniffed in his honking way. Ann's skin crawled.

"All you have to do is apologize for defending this . . . thief"—he looked at Ann's father, who had also knelt to open his case of pistols—"and Miller must tell me where he's keeping my property. Then, young man, all will be forgotten, and you can return unharmed to your family."

Allan crouched and retrieved one of the pistols. He stood, pointing it away from the group, raised the hammer with his thumb, then let it down again. "Holmes, you are well aware this is not a matter of stolen property. You have permitted a young lady to be outraged. I give you this last opportunity to apologize for it, and to turn over your accomplice to us. Or you may ready your pistol."

"I will confess nothing of the sort, nor will I apologize to thieves and the friends of thieves," Holmes said, checking his own weapon. An unpleasant smirk pulled his mouth crooked. "But my offer still stands. And I must warn you, I'm an excellent shot."

Ann's father stood, the pistol box at his feet. "Do not persist in this course, Mr. Holmes. Your stolen property, as you put it, is not this young man's fault. He knew nothing of it before your man took my daughter. If you need to address your grievance, address it to me."

"Very noble of you, Mr. Miller. But I won't agree to it. For though you might throw away your own life, I do not think you will let this young man go to his death to protect a couple of runaway slaves. So tell me where they are, or I proceed against Mr. Burbridge."

Ann's father did not hesitate. "I am certain that if I did know the whereabouts of the persons you seek, divulging them to you would be as good as a death sentence for them. So I will not weigh the value of one life against another. Mr. Burbridge must make his own decision."

"I am decided," Allan said. "And since you will not repent of what you have done, we will proceed."

Ann squeezed her gloved hands into fists under her crossed arms. Her knees were unsteady under her cape, and she braced herself against the coach. *Lord, Lord, please. Please preserve Allan. Misdirect their shots. Bring it all to an end without bloodshed.*

Her father and the other second went through the business of checking the weapons, loading them, and supplying one each to the duelists. Allan and Mr. Holmes moved away from their seconds; the snow blew thicker about them until they were hazy silhouettes. They stood back to back, pistols raised, Allan's young straight figure contrasting with Mr. Holmes's portly one.

"Ten paces," the other second called. "At my count!"

Ann clamped a hand over her own mouth.

"One . . . two . . . three . . . four . . . five . . ."

The figures drifted apart like shrouded specters. Ann stopped breathing.

"Six . . . seven . . . eight . . . nine . . . ten."

The pistols erupted, puffs of black smoke against the white.

Both figures staggered backward and fell. Ann rushed out into the snow, picking up her skirts as she ran, freezing wetness pouring over the tops of her boots. Her father ran a few yards ahead of her. He reached Allan and knelt beside him as Ann ran up.

A bright red splotch of blood marked the snow. Allan grimaced as Ann's father pulled him up and braced him in a sitting position. Then he caught Ann's eye and tried to turn it into a smile. "Just a touch," he said. "Not as good a shot as he claimed."

Ann's father pulled his coat away from Allan's breast to look at the wound; the young man gritted his teeth and stopped talking.

The blood on his white shirt was very high on the shoulder, though its vivid color still sickened and frightened her. She knelt next to him amid the folds of her blue dress.

"I'm sorry, Allan," she whispered, laying her hand on his ashen face. "I should never have run after the man in the hat. Please forgive me."

Though he was pale with pain, his gray eyes were free of the burden they had held since the attack. "You did nothing wrong. And I will live. It's a flesh wound, though it stings like the—"

"He's correct," her father said, gently easing Allan's coat back into place. "The ball passed clean through, Mr. Burbridge. As long as you keep it dressed properly, you'll be good as new in a few weeks." He stood and looked across the white hill to where

Mr. Holmes's second crouched over him. "Your opponent, however, does not appear to have come off so lightly."

Ann saw that Mr. Holmes had not risen, nor even sat up.

Oh no. Let me not be the cause of murder. She staggered to her feet again.

Her father grabbed her arm. "What are you doing?"

"I must see. I must help." She was incoherent, her tongue disconnected from her thoughts. She pulled free and stumbled through the snow toward the fallen man.

"Ann!" Behind her, her father's strained call heralded his pursuit. He was hampered by the snow and could not catch her as she reached her goal and stopped, almost falling in the drifts.

Mr. Holmes's second bent over him. The Southern man's face was almost as white as the snow he lay in, but his lips were grayish-blue. He moaned—an awful sound, like a dying animal in a trap, guttural and thick. All around him the snow was marked with spatters of scarlet, but near the middle of his trunk, there was a large circle of red pooling around him where his thrashing had packed the snow firm.

She had stopped a few feet away in horror. Her father continued past her and knelt next to Mr. Holmes as he had next to Allan. He took his limp hand. "Philip Holmes, I pray that God will have mercy on your soul, as I pray he will have mercy on all of us here today."

Mr. Holmes gasped for breath, then said in fits and starts, "I want none of your prayers, Miller. Rot in hell, all of you."

The man who had served as his second whispered something in her father's ear.

"Certainly," her father responded. The other man took Mr. Holmes by the shoulders, and her father lifted him by the feet, and they carried him to his coach. All the way, Ann could hear the man doing his best to revile in foul language her father and Allan, though his curses were broken by his cries of pain. There was silence after they put him inside the coach. Her father remained leaning inside for a minute. She heard a rattling noise.

She gazed at the circle of red against the white ground, so like the pure white of linen. The spreading blot, so like the color of her mother's vanishing life. Her vision blurred and a roaring in her ears blew her off balance. She fell forward, her arms plunging up to the elbows in the snow. Inches from her face, it seemed that two pools of scarlet joined in past and present, a stain seeping over her entire field of vision.

A hand touched her shoulder. "Ann." Her father's concerned face bent down to her sight level. He helped her sit up. "Breathe. Don't look at the blood." She did as he said, turning her head back toward Allan and the coach.

"There, your color is a little better now," her father said. "Let's attend to Allan and get him home." He assisted her to stand, and they made their slow way back to where the younger man lay.

Her father crouched down next to him and looked back at Ann. "Are you well enough to help me?" She knelt again beside them, unsure of how to proceed. Perhaps she should take one of Allan's arms.

"Mr. Holmes is dead," her father said to the younger man.

An expression of satisfaction crossed Allan's face. There was something terrible in it, to see a good man rejoice in killing.

She thought of mercy, and Amelia Holmes, and how she would have felt were it Allan or her father lying there. Nausea crawled through her. Would Amelia wake up at night sobbing, as Ann had after her mother's death? Would Amelia see Mr. Holmes in her dreams?

Ann's mother had given her own blood to bring new life into the world. A life given for a life. Mabel's new little soul had shown through her deep-blue infant eyes as Ann held her and wept. As God took away, he gave, both death and birth in blood.

But when men took away, there was only death. Here there was no sacrifice, and no beginning. There was only damnation, as men made themselves into little gods who wrenched away breath with metal and black powder. And this murder had been done in her name.

At the taking of a human life, there was some impalpable change in the air. She trembled, knowing that the all-seeing gaze of the Almighty fell upon them as they crouched over the telltale red patches in the snow.

Two days brought no respite from the constant return of the bloody scene to her mind. Ann could only hope that when they left the city tomorrow, as her father had announced, the haunting of her imagination would cease.

But first, courtesy required that she and her father stop by the Burbridges' home.

Louisa and Mrs. Burbridge received them with a kindness that shamed her. She hoped Allan had spared them the details of her sordid attack, but they must know something of it, or they would not be so forgiving. Or perhaps he had told them nothing at all. That would be more like him.

She dreaded seeing Allan. Mr. Holmes's terrible last curse

had followed her since the morning he died. It had to be a sin, as her father had said, for Allan to take a life in that way, no matter the cause. Allan must feel the burden as well, and even more heavily than she.

But he seemed quite cheerful, considering. He lay in bed, propped up against a few pillows, a book on the table beside him. A maid poked her head in the room while they were there, but when she saw visitors, she withdrew. Ann's father sat on the far side of the room and paged tactfully through a newspaper.

"So you will leave me, then?" Allan's eyes were bright with teasing. "To languish in my boredom while you taste the delights of Rushville society?"

"The delights of Rushville society include tending to cows, horses, and pigs." She folded her hands in her lap. No matter her inner state, she must be light and respond to his wit in kind. "You are welcome to join me in my social rounds, provided you have appropriate attire. A pitchfork is mandatory."

He chuckled. "Don't tempt me. I just might jump aboard a steamboat in a few months."

She felt herself growing warm and looked for another topic. "Are you certain, Allan, that the Holmeses will not seek legal remedy? I thought they threatened to call down the law on you."

"No fear of that." Allan relaxed, resting his head back against the headboard. "The law would ignore them, first of all. Matters of honor are usually kept quiet. But I also informed them as decently as I could of what had led to the duel. They do not want those circumstances made public."

Those circumstances, in part of Ann's making, had deprived the Holmes women forever of a husband and father. Guilt robbed her of words for a moment. She adjusted her bag in her lap. "But they are already gone?"

"Yes, they left yesterday." *Thank heaven.* She would not be able to bear encountering them on the return steamboat voyage.

After a few more entreaties from Allan that Ann return to see him, they took their leave of the Burbridges. The doctor's coach took them on another somber, quiet ride through the streets of Pittsburgh. When they arrived back at the doctor's house, there was nothing left but the last of the packing.

She folded clothing and stowed it in the small trunk. Her sisters were in the library with Dr. Loftin, enjoying their last opportunity for his company. He had grown quite fond of reading to them.

"Ann!" her father called from downstairs. She stood up, stretched her stiff back as well as she could in her stays, and walked out of the bedroom to the landing.

"Yes, Father?"

"I'm finishing some legal matters with the doctor. Will you take a message for me?"

"To whom?"

"Will, the apprentice." She would have liked to refuse but had no good reason. She could hardly tell her father she felt awkward around the apprentice since their secret meeting.

"Certainly." She walked down to meet her father at the foot of the stairs, and he handed her a sealed letter.

"There's another letter inside this one," he said. "Tell Will to read the outside letter and use the address I've enclosed to deliver the one inside."

"Very well."

"It's to our friends in Arthursville. We have good news. The man in the beaver hat—his name is Jack Rumkin—has apparently fled the city."

That was only partly good news to her. She wondered where he had gone.

As if reading her thoughts, her father added, "That will be wonderful for John and Clara. They can leave the city unnoticed and head north."

That was some comfort. The memory of their branded and mutilated faces made her sad. They deserved their freedom.

"That is good news," she said. She turned to the coat hook, donned her cape, and paused at the back door. "I'll be back shortly."

"Thank you. And tell him not to forget what we spoke of."

Strange. But she would pass it on.

When she walked out the back door, she heard Lucy the pig snorting uneasily in her pen. The doctor had said over breakfast that he put the pigs inside because the almanac forecasted more snow today. Ann called softly to Lucy, but the pig did not come over to sniff her hand as she usually did. The piglets squealed and trotted back and forth; Lucy grunted and swung her head toward the gray sky. It must be the weather making them restless.

Will stood out by the pump behind the Goods' house, filling a bucket. He seemed taken aback at the sight of Ann.

"Excuse me," she said. He stopped working the handle and stared at her. She approached gingerly, extending the letter toward him. "This is from my father. He would like you to deliver the letter inside it, as a favor. We are leaving now."

His stricken look was quickly hidden, but not before it struck an answering pain in her.

"I will do Mr. Miller any favor," he said shortly, taking the letter. "You're leaving?"

"Yes." She didn't know what else to say. "My father said not to forget what he spoke of."

"Tell your father I thank him. For everything."

"I will," she said faintly. She spun on her heel and nearly ran toward the doctor's house.

Will might not survive his apprenticeship whole—Master Good might scar him somehow, as John and Clara's master had mutilated them. If his master continued to beat him so savagely about the head, Will might not even retain his reason. How could she leave him to such a fate, having done nothing to truly help? Guilty tears came to her eyes, but she turned her head and let the wind blow them away. If she could not help him, she must forget his plight, for her own peace of mind. It was all too likely she would never see him again.

Eighteen

LUCY HAD ESCAPED THROUGH THE FENCE AGAIN. Will watched her nosing around the edge of the line of trees that began twenty yards from the barn. That section of the woods was all Master Good's land. The master would be livid—his hidden fury increased with each successive pig invasion.

"Tom, let's get Lucy back to the doctor's." Will dropped a log back onto the wood pile.

Tom laid his axe down on top of the old tree trunk. "It'll be hard to get the piglets without the master hearing. They're noisy."

The piglets were wandering around behind their mother, little more than small blobs in the murky half-light that preceded sunrise. "We have to try. It'll be better if the master doesn't see them. He may not be awake yet."

"All right." Tom started toward the closest of the piglets. It trotted away toward its mother and the tree line.

The back door of the master's house flew open with a clatter. At the sight of Master Good standing in the doorway, Will stopped in his tracks. Tom moved back to the wood pile and picked up his axe, and Will also began to chop again as if he had not noticed the pigs. The master's temper would be worse if he could claim that the pigs were distracting his apprentices from their work.

The master cut across the yard, not too near them, but instead went past the barn toward the trees. He had something in his hand, but in the dimness it was hard to make out. Will kept his gaze lowered as he picked a new piece of firewood from the pile. The master was passing closest now, only about ten yards away. Sneaking a glance at him, Will saw that he was staring at the apprentices, as if defying them to speak.

Will drew in a sharp breath. That dark object in the master's hand was a pistol.

Tom had noticed it too—he turned wide eyes to Will, his face pale.

Will turned back to Master Good. The master's eyes were noticeably light and deadly even in the gloom, his lips clamped together as if he forcibly contained a stream of invective. But Lucy had disappeared from sight among the trees, and he turned to follow her, quickening his pace until his figure also melted into the gloom of the woods.

Will dropped his axe and ran for the doctor's gate. If Dr. Loftin met Master Good in the grove, the master would not dare—

A pistol shot cracked through the morning air, leaving a wake of ominous, deep silence.

Will faltered and stopped. What now?

"*Psst.*" Tom called to him from to the wood pile. "Stay here. You can't get mixed up in it now."

He reluctantly returned. "But if I get the doctor, he might still be a witness."

"It won't matter. If the master has a brain in his head, he'll leave through the far side of the woods. There won't be anything to witness."

"I need to go see what he did."

"You know what he did. What if he's still in there?"

"I don't care." Will brushed past Tom and headed for the woods. He slowed as he passed through the trees, peering hard for any sign of movement. There. A few small shapes milling around near a tangled bush. The piglets.

He stepped over fallen branches and frozen dead leaves, his heart thudding. The dawn was coming, turning everything a paler gray. Master Good did not appear to be here. Perhaps Tom was right and he had left through the far side, where the trees opened out onto the road some way past the Loftin home.

A piglet skittered ahead of him. He followed it around the large bush and stopped short.

Lucy's motionless body sprawled on the hard ground, her legs limp and dangling. Two of her piglets sniffed at her belly. One made a whining noise he had never heard from a pig.

He knelt beside Lucy. "Don't be afraid," he said to the piglets, which jumped back. "I won't hurt you." He extended his knuckles to one of them. It approached and sniffed his hand, then bumped Lucy with its little nose.

Lucy's once-bright eyes were fixed and dull, like black marbles. A trickle of blood ran from a hole in her forehead. Master Good must have called her and shot her point-blank.

Will stroked her fuzzy head and her round cheek. His heart was heavy and dull. What a sickening waste. Lucy had been a good mother to her little piglets. He ran his hand over her side as if he could comfort her. The piglet still whined next to her, rooting under her neck as if to wake her up.

He wiped his eyes with cold knuckles and stood up.

When he came out of the woods, Tom was still splitting wood.

"He killed Lucy," Will said. His blood pounded and his breath came fast. He picked up his axe and vented his wrath on a piece of wood. Splinters flew up past his face, stinging his cheeks. He chopped even harder.

"Where is he?"

"Gone. He must have slipped through the other way, like you said."

"He knows we saw him. What do you think he'll do?" Tom hefted his axe and flipped a log over.

A motion by the doctor's house caught Will's attention. The doctor himself walked across the yard toward them and lifted the gate latch to let himself through.

"Is everything all right?" Dr. Loftin called from a few yards away. "I heard a shot." He closed the distance to the woodpile in a few strides. His forehead creased in concern, his white hair rumpled on top.

Will rested his axe head on the ground and looked at Tom. No help there, for Tom's mouth was half open and he was even more at a loss than Will. Will's heart pained him as he met the doctor's worried green eyes. "It's Lucy."

"Where is she?" The doctor turned slowly to scan the yard and woods as if to conjure his Lucy into sight. "What happened?"

Will's mind blurred as he tried to consider what to say, how much to tell or not to tell. "She's in there." He pointed to the woods. "See where the piglet is coming out? About thirty paces in." At the doctor's confused expression, he dropped the axe and started for the trees. "I'll show you."

The silence between them grew oppressive as they entered

the shadowy copse. When they reached the bush with the piglets milling around it, Will stopped and indicated it to the doctor. "Behind there."

He did not want to see Dr. Loftin's reaction, so he pivoted and walked quickly away. Nonetheless, he heard the doctor's choked cry of shock. A lump came to his throat. He hurried back to the woodpile and attacked the logs again with fervor. From the corner of his eye, he saw Tom watching him with trepidation, flinching as the chips and splinters sprayed up. Will ignored him.

After a few minutes the doctor came out of the woods, his shoulders drooping, his white head bowed. Dr. Loftin made his way toward them, and Will saw that the doctor's eyes were moist.

"Young men, this is a very serious matter," he said. "Is your master at home?"

Will shook his head.

"I suspect you know who shot Lucy." The doctor's voice shook, whether from anger or sorrow, Will couldn't tell. But then his tone became firmer. "It's a base act. And I'm quite sure neither of you is responsible. But I'm afraid I will have to ask you to do something for me. I will need you to witness to a judge."

Tom went sheet-white, and Will was sure he must look the same, as a frisson of fear traveled down his neck.

The doctor looked at Will. "Don't say anything, now. Before you say a word, I want you to think about the consequences. You know better than I what they may be. I don't want you suffering on my behalf." A muscle tightened and firmed the line of his jaw. "But I don't want the devil to have free rein either. Someone has to stand against cruelty, eventually, or it will continue." He cleared his throat. "So think carefully, both of you. The decision will be yours."

The image of John Simon, branded but resolute, flew through Will's mind. "I'll witness for you, sir," he said.

"Take time to consider first, Will."

"I'll do it, sir. I don't need time."

The doctor ran his hand through his mussed hair and sighed. "I'll be indebted to you, young man. I take this harder than I should, perhaps . . ." He trailed off and brushed past them, shoulders curved, headed for his home.

They continued to chop wood until the wheelbarrow was full of kindling. Tom was pensive and silent. That suited Will, as he was also in no mood for talk.

As night fell and time for sleep neared, Master Good still had not returned. Mistress Good was surly and ordered Will and Tom out of the house after another meager meal. Will led the way to the barn, and once in the saddle shop, he raked the pile of straw from the corner. They always piled it closer to the coal firebox at night and slept there, huddled back-to-back to keep from freezing as the temperatures dropped.

"Will, are you really going to speak against the master?" Tom's voice was hushed, though Will felt it vibrate through his back as they lay there in the darkness.

"Yes. I've had enough. What's the worst he can do?"

"Kill you." Tom sounded unhappy.

"I don't think he will. And besides, I don't think my life means much."

"It means something to me."

"It's worthless if I can't be decent or honest." Will heard a rustling in the straw, and Tom's back moved away from his. He turned his head to see that Tom was sitting up, facing him.

"But all you have to do is wait another year."

"I can't wait."

Tom leaned down, whispering urgently. "I don't think I can witness. I can't do it."

Will pushed himself up on one elbow. "You have to make your own choice. I can't decide for you."

"I want to stand up with you, but I'm afraid I won't be able when the master's standing there watching. He makes me lose my nerve."

Will burrowed down into the straw with a sinking feeling. "I don't want to talk about it anymore. All I know is that I will not lie to a judge. Especially not to save the master's pride . . . or his purse."

"I'm sorry, Will. I'll do my best."

Will was quiet, wishing Mr. Miller were still there. The saddler would approve of what Will had decided to do. *But Mr. Miller and his daughter are gone.* He opened his eyes in the darkness. The straw prickled through his clothes, and even their two blankets together were too thin. *I will have to stand up alone before the judge.*

He still had Tom, but he and Tom were in the same miserable plight. Mr. Miller was different. Behind his quiet ordinariness was a cloud of something otherworldly. Will had seen it looming and billowing in his eyes, blowing through his words. Perhaps it was sent from God. Perhaps it would come to Will, if he prayed for help. He envisioned a cloud descending on him in the courtroom, protecting him from the master.

A cloud went with them by day . . . The voice of his father rumbled low in his memory; Will saw his brothers and his sister sitting in the firelight at his father's knee, the pages of the Bible ivory in the lamplight.

He had not thought so much of his family in a long time. It hurt too much—and yet, as their faces lingered in his mind's eye, a faint flicker of light within him grew steadier, spreading into dim recesses and long-forgotten dusty corners. He remembered his mother walking through the field toward him, holding his little brother. Johnny wrapped his arms around her, his dark curls tumbling over his fat cheeks, as he called Will's name in his baby voice. *I will write to Johnny, if the doctor will give me paper and ink.*

But what would he tell his brother? That he was still bound to a tyrant? That he had stained the honor of an innocent girl? The acrid smoke of burning pitch poured through him again. He gritted his teeth and fought back.

I will marry Emmie. If she'll have me. As soon as my indenture ends.

The smoke rolled back, a fringe of darkness on the edges of his consciousness, though he sensed it waiting there for its first opportunity to return. *You will not win*, he told it. *I will marry her and put things to right.*

Tom sighed and his body crunched the straw.

Will murmured to him without moving. "I'm going to marry Emmie."

"Now?"

"No. When I'm free from the master."

"Oh."

"I'm going to make right from the wrong I've done."

Tom's only response was a raspy breath. He was asleep.

The thought of Master Good's likely reaction was terrible—but, oddly, Will felt calm. When sleep came, it was as if he fell slowly and gently into the massive cloud that waited for him, endlessly patient, behind Mr. Miller's eyes.

Nineteen

IN THE NARROW CONFINES OF THE COACH, THERE WAS nowhere to hide.

"You remember what I told you, boys," Master Good said.

Will's palms were slick with cold perspiration. He laid his hands on his rough trouser legs to dry them without his master noticing.

"Yes, sir," Tom said.

"And you?" The master pinned Will with his unblinking stare.

"Yes, sir," Will said. Better to lie now than in the courtroom. He didn't like the sheepish expression Tom had been wearing. It promised no help from his testimony. At the thought of challenging the master alone, Will felt the walls of the coach press in on him.

The rattling of the coach slowed, then ceased as the driver pulled up. Master Good shoved open the door and climbed down, Tom following with obvious reluctance and Will bringing up the rear.

The courthouse was red brick and square, much like any other building from the city's earliest days. Will followed Tom through the white double doors. At the far end of the room, a massive mahogany desk stood on a raised dais. Against the white walls, the dark desk stood out like a tower, topped by the figure of the judge in his curled wig. He leaned over the gleaming wood to murmur to the bailiff, who stood beside him.

A number of other persons sat in chairs down below on the floor. Some of them engaged in conversation, others sat alone, waiting for their own cases.

Master Good led Tom and Will to three empty chairs against the far wall. He made the apprentices sit closest to the wall, and he sat next to them as if to keep them from bolting from the room.

Just as they were seated, the door opened again to reveal Dr. Loftin. He was dressed immaculately, not a wrinkle in his coat, not a hair out of place. But when he looked at Will, his brow was tense with worry and his green eyes shadowed.

I won't lie. But Master Good's physical presence just inches from his left arm made him ill. Between his rebellious stomach and his dry mouth, it would be very hard to speak at all.

His nausea grew worse with the passing minutes, as the judge rapped his gavel and delivered verdicts on two other cases.

"Dr. Robert Loftin and Master Jacob Good," the bailiff called.

The two men stood and walked to the clear area in front of the desk.

"Which of you brings the complaint?" The judge lifted his head wearily to examine them.

"I do, Your Honor," said the doctor, his hat in hand.

"And what is the nature of the complaint?"

"This man, Jacob Good, shot and killed a valuable brood sow belonging to me."

"Did you witness this act?"

"No, Your Honor. But these young men back here can witness to it. And I found the weapon a few yards from where I found Lu—the sow. It belongs to Jacob Good. With your permission, Your Honor, I will tender it to the bailiff." When the judge nodded, the doctor walked back to his chair, where he had left his medical bag. From its depths, he produced a black pistol. He offered it handle-first to the bailiff, who brought it back and laid it on the surface of the desk at the judge's left hand.

"Is this your pistol?" the judge asked Master Good.

"Yes, Your Honor. But I must tell you—"

The judge cut him off with a sharp rap of the gavel.

"You, young man." The judge pointed to Tom. "Approach. What is your name?"

Tom got to his feet, noticeably unsteady, and walked to the front, standing apart from the master. "Tom Reece, Your Honor." He looked very slight and young, tilting his head up to address the judge, his hair as unkempt as ever.

"And did you witness the killing of the sow?"

"Not exactly, sir."

"Don't beat around the bush! Explain yourself."

"Well—uh—the pig went into the woods, and then—I heard a shot."

The judge frowned. "And did you see anyone in the woods?"

"Tell him what you told me, boy," Master Good said. "Did you not see the apprentice Will Hanby go into the woods?"

Will's nerves went taut. He felt the blood draining from his veins, leaving him like a figure cast in plaster.

Tom was silent. Will couldn't see his face.

"Well? Speak, boy!" The judge's face flushed red against the whiteness of his wig.

"Yes, Your Honor. Will went into the woods after the pig."

Will found it hard to hear what else they were saying through the thick, dreamlike state that had overcome him—as if his ears had been stuffed with wool. It simply was not possible. Will had expected Tom to be silent, but not to betray him—and commit perjury. But Tom was indeed telling the judge that he believed Will had taken Master Good's pistol and killed the sow.

"And you? I presume you are this Will Hanby. What do you have to say for yourself?"

Will realized that the judge was addressing him, but his tongue was as leaden as his ears were stopped. He glanced to his left and noticed Dr. Loftin regarding him with eyes squinted in disbelief, mouth slightly open. Was that skepticism at Tom's story, or sudden doubt in Will?

If I defend myself, they will not believe me. And even if they did—if Dr. Loftin supported me—Tom would go to jail for perjury.

"Answer me, young man! Do you deny it?"

He still could not speak. Through his shock came sharp, painful pity for Tom, who was perfectly wretched standing there by himself. *You may turn me over to them, but I will not do the same to you, my brother.*

The doctor murmured to Will from where he stood. "Speak, if you are innocent!" He was clearly perturbed, his look urgent.

"You see, Will does not deny it, Your Honor." Beneath the mock chagrin of Master Good's tone, Will heard a note of triumph.

"You realize, Jacob Good, that you are responsible for the deeds of your apprentice."

"Yes, Your Honor."

"And you will pay due recompense to Dr. Loftin for the loss of his sow. What would that sum be, Doctor?"

"At least fifty dollars, Your Honor." Dr. Loftin looked back and forth from Will to his master, obviously baffled.

"Then you will pay that sum, Master Good?"

"Yes, Your Honor. And I believe the law allows me to add the value of that debt to the term of my apprentice's service. It will take an additional two years for his labor to earn out that sum."

"Two years? Would it not be closer to one?"

"Not when I subtract the cost of lodging and board, Your Honor. Plus the still-amateurish quality of his work."

"Very well. But there must be papers drawn up."

"I have them ready here, Your Honor."

He planned it all in advance. The papers at the ready, leaving the gun in the woods, threatening who knows what to Tom. But Will could not believe that the master had killed Lucy just to trap him into more years of misery. No, that had been a freakish fit of temper and envy. It was afterward that the master must have seen how to use it to his own advantage.

Master Good strode up to the desk and handed a piece of parchment to the bailiff. The judge took it, scrutinized it, and laid it down in front of him. With a dip of his quill and a few scratches, it was done.

But apparently Master Good was not finished.

"Now, Your Honor, I think it only neighborly that my apprentice admit to what he has done and tender his apology to the good doctor."

Will's spine stiffened. *I will not.* It was intolerable as it was. He would not add perjury to the list of his sins.

Master Good paced over until he was so close that Will could feel his hot breath on the side of his face and smell the tooth-rot. "Come now, boy! Do what's honorable. Apologize for the heartache and time you have cost the doctor." Though the master's tone was still oily, Will could see the hatred flaring cold in his eyes. There would be hell to pay if Will did not comply.

I will not. Will stared at him defiantly. After a long moment, Master Good spun away.

"You see what I have to contend with, Your Honor!"

"A rebellious apprentice is a sore trial." The judge looked bored, drawling his words. "You must teach him better character than that."

"You can be sure I will do my best, Your Honor."

"Pay the fine to the bailiff, who will count it and give it to the doctor. And clear the floor, if you please. There are others waiting."

Will saw a flush creeping up the back of the master's neck and ears as he placed the bills in the bailiff's hand. He knew who would pay for that rage.

As they left the courtroom, Tom still avoided Will's glance, though his head was down and he was even redder than the master.

No matter what, I would not change places with Tom at this moment.

On the journey back, they were all silent. Master Good buried his nose in a newspaper and Tom leaned his head against the side of the coach as if he were sleeping, but with the way his head bounced around, Will knew that he was shamming.

Too soon for Will, they arrived at the Good house.

"Tom, go attend to whatever Mistress Good may need."

Tom slunk off in the direction of the house.

"You follow me," the master said to Will.

Will obeyed and headed toward the barn behind him, but his muscles knotted and his thoughts raced. *He will beat me. Should I defend myself? What have I to lose?* His breath came fast, though he tried with all his might to appear calm and unsuspecting. *As soon as he strikes me, I will fight back.*

"Sit down," the master said, indicating the stitching bench. Will reluctantly complied. The master turned his back and walked to the table where he stored his tools. To Will's surprise, he picked up the dusty Bible that had sat there unopened ever since Will could remember. The master flipped through it, then held open a page and handed it to Will.

What's this? The master had never quoted scripture at Will before, never even mentioned the name of God. Will looked down at the page.

"Read chapter six, beginning at verse five." It was unfamiliar to find a chapter and verse. Will hadn't done so since he left the Quaker's farm. But eventually his finger found the place. He read aloud, with rising distaste that he struggled to disguise. "Servants, be obedient to them that are your masters according to the flesh, with fear and trembling—"

Stunning force struck him on the back of the head and he fell forward off the bench. His forehead struck the packed ground, and a roaring filled his ears. A thud against his gut—the pain robbed him of breath. Again. Again. Something snapped under the barrage of blows. Now the pain was constant and he faded in and out of awareness. There was a pause and something yanked at his arms—the master, removing his shirt. Stinging, slicing pain on his back—a whip. It went on endlessly. He was dimly aware of a warm wetness spreading under his groin. He had lost control of his bladder—he heard the master chuckle and the kicking began again. He tried to draw another breath, but the crushing agony in his side and gut would not let him. He was suffocating. His eyes were open, he thought, but he could not see—*God save me.*

Nothingness rose up and swallowed him.

Twenty

ONCE MORE SHE STOOD BY THE WHEEL OF THE CARRIAGE, *watching as Allan and Mr. Holmes raised their pistols. She opened her mouth to scream, but no sound would come. Mr. Holmes collapsed facedown on the white hillside. Then the snow began to move under her, though her feet remained still. Paralyzed, she glided toward Mr. Holmes.*

The man who had served as his second knelt beside him, head lowered. As Ann drew near him, he looked up. His face was ghastly green and his eyes shrunken into their sockets like a corpse. He shot to his feet and pointed an accusing finger at Ann. "Murderesssss!"

"No," she tried to say, but her mouth only worked silently. The corpse-man grinned.

"I will show you what you have done," he said. He extended a withered hand to Mr. Holmes and rolled him over on his back. The face contorted in death was not Mr. Holmes', but Will the apprentice's.

She awoke gasping, a child's whimper escaping from the vanishing edges of her sleep. It took awhile to slow her breathing. Her back and neck were coated in perspiration; she felt it turning cold as she lay gazing at the wood shingles above her.

Lord, forgive me. I should not have left without trying something else to help Will. Please have mercy on him and protect him from his master. I humbly ask in your Son's holy name. Amen.

Prayer was the only thing that brought her even the slightest peace after the nightmares.

She rose from bed, grabbed a woven blanket from its place on her hope chest, and toweled herself off. It wouldn't do to take a chill, not when the dampness of the spring thaw could turn any cold into a full-blown ague.

She slipped into her house shoes and wrapped herself in her coat to walk to the front room. Striking a match, she lit the hurricane lamp on the side table and closed its glass door to keep it alight. When she lifted it and cast its glow on the mantle, the filigreed hands of the clock revealed that it was already five o' clock in the morning. She might as well rise now as try to go back to sleep for another half hour. Such early wakings had been frequent since her return from Pittsburgh.

She went back to her room and dressed, first in an old flannel shirt of her father's that was faded, but still thick and warm. She pulled on the men's trousers she preferred for her dirtiest work on the farm, belting them at the waist with the string she kept just for that purpose. Two weeks of mucking stalls and milking had turned the refinements of city life into a distant memory. The peace and solitude of the farm was balm for the bruises the city had left on her conscience.

On her way past the girls' bedroom, she saw they were still fast asleep. By this time, her father was usually awake and dressed, going about his own share of the farm's chores. But of course, he had ridden out on his ministerial rounds soon after their return and had only been back for a day at a time between trips. She was always uneasy in his absence, but her former nightmares about her mother had been replaced by her recurring dream of the duel and the apprentice.

The best cure was hard work, and there was no shortage of it. Dawn had come by the time she finished with the horses and cows. She trudged back to the house to make breakfast for herself and the girls. Sure enough, when she came in the door, they were up, fully dressed and huddled by the hearth with their hands stretched out toward the fire.

"What are we doing today?" Mabel asked.

"Chores, silly," Susan responded before Ann could. "What do we always do?"

"Be kind, Susan. We'll eat first," Ann said. "It's too cold to go out without something warm in your bellies." Not to mention that she didn't mind cooking over the warmth of the hearth after her time outside.

"Then what?" Mabel asked.

"You two can churn some butter. I just milked." Ann poured some of the milk into the floury mixture she was stirring in a large wooden bowl. It took on a creamy texture.

She had just ladled some of the batter on an iron griddle propped over the flames when a knock came at the door. Startled, she fumbled with the big kitchen spoon and dropped it on the floor.

"Susan, rinse this off with the pitcher water. It's on the stand," she said in a low voice. Ann went to the door. "Who is it?"

"Eli," came the reply, muffled by the wooden barrier between them.

What on earth?

She flicked a glance at her sisters. Like a couple of bird

hounds, they pointed their little noses at her, their eyes bright with curiosity.

She had done her best to avoid Eli by staying out of town as much as possible. Part of her yearned to speak with him, but her time in Pittsburgh had disturbed her so much that she preferred solitude.

She unbarred the door. She smoothed her face into an expression of serene welcome, then took hold of the handle and pulled.

He was paler than she remembered, whether from nerves or from gloomy weather, she couldn't tell. But pallor suited him. With his high cheekbones and fair hair, he looked like a wandering angel forlornly seeking the way back to paradise.

"Hello." He gave her a tentative smile.

"Good morning." She wished the girls hadn't crowded up behind her elbows. Even more fervently, she wished she were not wearing trousers.

He didn't notice or, if he did, pretended to be oblivious. "You've been so elusive that I thought I had better ride out here to see if your return from Pittsburgh was merely a rumor."

"My father isn't home." She wanted him to stay—now that his presence tugged at her from only a few feet away—but that wouldn't be proper.

"I'm sorry to hear that." His eyes stayed on her for longer than they should.

She noticed the fullness of his lower lip. Hot blood suffused her face.

It was awful to know she must be noticeably reddening. No matter how calm she kept her expression, she could not control her color. But Eli seemed, if anything, encouraged.

"I'll be on my way then," he said. "But I wanted to ask you—would you like to ride with me to the Murdochs' tomorrow? They've invited all the young people to a bonfire to pop corn and sing. In the afternoon, around three." Now he had that telltale casual tone that bespoke real nervousness.

Ann became aware that her little sisters were greedily drinking in every word of the conversation. And she smelled something burning. "Susan, go take the pan off the fire. Use the rag, don't burn your hand. And, Mabel, go find your dolly. She must be hungry too."

"She already ate breakfast. She's sleeping now." Mabel didn't move, her little head cocked at a mischievous angle, her hair mussed.

"Go wake her up." Ann gave her an ill-disguised glare.

Even when the girls walked away, she hesitated.

"And Phoebe?" She finally got the words out, blushing again at her own directness. But she must know before she gave him an answer.

Now he was the one to drop his eyes. "We have agreed that we are good friends, no more." He met her gaze again. "Please say you'll come with me."

Her wariness melted at the humble appeal in his eyes. "Very well, then. My father will return later today. I'm sure he'll agree."

Eli's smile lit his whole face. "I'll be back tomorrow, then."

She smiled too. "Thank you."

"Good morning to you." He turned and walked away with a spring in his step.

She watched him go. *I like him very much. I wonder what Mama would think.*

The longing for her mother swept through her, sharper than the freezing air outside. She closed the door hard as if she could force the emptiness away. *My sisters are still so young. I don't know if I can consider leaving them.*

But perhaps Eli could come live here?

She could not picture that. She was sure Eli would not be happy as a farmer. As far as she knew, he had always wanted to study to be a doctor. And she could not go so far away as Cincinnati, not now or perhaps ever. Her sisters would need her as they became young women.

She sighed in frustration and walked back to the hearth. Susan had set the pan on the stone, very sensibly. Picking it up, Ann used the flat fork to pry the burnt cake off the griddle, scratching the flaky black remnants off the cast iron.

Susan moved to Ann's side as she reached for the mixing bowl and poured more batter. "Is Eli your sweetheart?"

"That's none of your concern."

Mabel jumped out of the back hallway, where she had apparently been hiding. "Prince Eli and Princess Ann!" she chanted, waving her arms.

Susan giggled.

Ann slapped the spoon back into the bowl, splashing batter on her forehead. The girls cackled. Even in her annoyance, Ann felt her mouth twitching. She gave in and laughed, wiping her face with the rag.

"Get out of my sight until I call you," she said. The girls scurried back down the hall. She heard them arguing about who would be the princess and who the prince.

Ann could not sort all this out. She would have to leave it to Providence.

At the thought of Providence, she felt a sharp twinge of guilt and prayed again that Will was all right in Pittsburgh. And that God would forgive her—and Allan—for the death of Mr. Holmes.

Twenty-One

IT WAS THREE DAYS BEFORE WILL COULD STAND again, and a week before he could walk more than a few steps at a time. Had it not been for Tom, who cared for him like a nursemaid, he did not think he would have survived the master's beating.

But Tom still would not look him in the eye. More than once in the past week, Will had awakened in the dead of night to the sound of Tom's stifled sobs. He was probably so remorseful he could not abide himself. But beneath Will's pity for his friend was a knife-sharp edge of anger. Let Tom feel the pain in his spirit as long as Will felt it in his body.

He set the pitchfork against the side of the stall and rested his elbows on the wooden door, breathing deeply to steady his still-weak legs. Of course, as soon as he could walk he had to work, though Tom was still taking on more than his share. When Will lifted the pitchfork, he could feel the stiff hardness of the scabs on his back. He moved with care so as not to tear them and start the bleeding again.

The barn door opened. Tom propped it with one elbow to let himself in, carrying in both hands a bowl that steamed in the cold. The smell of real beef made Will's mouth water. Mistress Good had been secretly sending Tom out with food since the day of the beating.

"She told me to tell you this is the last day for meat," Tom muttered, head hanging. "She said back to stew tomorrow."

Of course. She had not been feeding him out of compassion, he knew all too well, but out of concern for their source of labor. Tom had told him that the mistress had actually dared to berate the master for risking their investment—until the master put a stop to her talk with the back of his hand.

"Here," Tom said, holding out the bowl, which Will could now see was full of sliced meat and chunks of potato. He took it from Tom and walked away to sit on an old crate. He did not object when Tom picked up the pitchfork to finish the stall. If that was how he wanted to soothe his conscience, so be it.

He ate slowly, feeling the warmth in his belly and the strength returning to his limbs. By the time he had eaten half of it, Tom had pulled the wheelbarrow to the next stall.

"I need your help with something." Will set the bowl on the crate and stood up. He winced as his movement jarred the deep soreness in his muscles and pulled at his whip-scabs.

"What?" Tom forked dirty straw, face turned only to his work.

"Listen." Will walked up close beside Tom, who glanced at him.

Will's whisper was barely audible. "I'm going to leave."

Tom straightened up and looked him full in the face, his jaw slack with astonishment. Then he leaned close and whispered, "You're going to run away? When?"

"Tonight, while I still have some food to take with me."

He looked at the bowl sitting on the crate. The two remaining palm-sized pieces of meat would keep well in the cold.

"But where will you go?"

"Westward." He could not trust Tom with specifics. A friend who betrayed him once might do so again.

"But if the master catches you, he'll kill you."

"He'll kill me if I stay, next time I refuse him anything."

"Just don't refuse him."

Will pulled back from their close conference and regarded Tom steadily. Guilt surged in his friend's face.

"You're right," Tom muttered. "You should go."

"I need you to do something." Will leaned close again. "I can't leave Emmie with no explanation. I need her to know I plan to marry her. Carry that message from me. Tell her I'll come back for her as soon as I can earn my living."

"But how will I tell her? Where is she?"

"Ask Dr. Loftin to direct you, after I'm gone. He knows. It's a boarding house beside the docks, near where we pick up the oakum."

"But how will I get away from my work?"

"You'll manage." Will fought his rising temper. "You will probably be sent for the oakum after I am gone. It should be simple enough to find her."

"All right." A line of worry split Tom's forehead.

"If I make it to a safe place, I may be able to write, care of the doctor. You can take her my letters on your errands down there. It's the least you can do."

"Very well." Tom rubbed his dark hair away from his face with his elbow and picked up the pitchfork as he turned away.

Will turned his back too. He could be just as proud and

standoffish as Tom. It hurt that his traitorous friend would dismiss him so, even when Tom knew full well he might never return.

Picking up the bowl of meat, Will crossed to the wooden box that held dried corn. A rag hung on a nail above the box; he grabbed it and wrapped the meat in it. He lifted the heavy, hinged lid and laid the bundle on the bed of yellow kernels. He would retrieve it tonight.

He walked back toward Tom, who was still working feverishly in the last stall on the end. "I'll finish." He held out a hand for the pitchfork.

Tom handed it over, face averted, but from the dirty smears on his face, Will could tell he had wept. He wanted to put his arm around his younger friend and wish him goodbye, tell him he was sorry to leave him in this misery. Then the knife of anger inside him flashed out, cutting off the impulse, and he took the tool without comment. Tom picked up the empty bowl and left the barn without another word.

Will was thankful that, even after night had fallen, the water stood dark and liquid in the horses' water buckets, without the white skin of ice that had formed every night last week. If the freezes had not ended, he could never have lived through a night in the open.

He uncovered himself from where he had lain sleepless in the straw. At his motion, Tom turned over. In the dense darkness of the workshop, a glint of white told Will his friend's eyes were following him. Will moved quietly to the place where he had hidden the doctor's gloves and drew them on.

"Take my scarf," Tom whispered.

Will hesitated a moment, then took the tattered strip of wool from Tom's hand. Tom would live without it. Will might not.

Next to them in the barn, one of the horses nickered as the other blew out a snort and stamped its hooves. Will froze, barely breathing, until they quieted.

The barn door faced away from the house, but the workshop door faced toward it. Will would have to go through the barn. He paused as he opened the flimsy door between the two spaces, glancing back to where Tom lay. But further speech would be too great a risk; he went on with no goodbye.

He took the meat, put it in his coat pocket, and stepped to the barn door. Silence, except for the soft breathing noises of the horses. He cracked the door open. It was lighter outside, but not much, as the moon was only a bare sliver in the sky. No life stirred. A dark gray expanse of ground led to a black line of trees.

He slipped out into the yard. His heart battered against his chest, but he forced himself to keep to a hurried, silent walk. He was in no condition to run any distance. He breathed in, breathed out, not looking back, hoping to reach the relative safety of the tree line. At last he was enveloped by the woods. He turned to look behind him. No movement, no light. His heart still beat as fast as a bird's.

He set off through the trees, picking his way over brush and twigs. There was a semblance of a path to take him through to the road, but he strained to find it. His movements sounded unnaturally loud; he flinched every time he rustled a bush or snapped a twig underfoot.

The trees cleared and he emerged onto the road. Out here on the packed earth, he could walk without sound, but someone might see him. He poured his nerves into quickening his pace. Now there was nothing to do but walk. Over the bridge to Pittsburgh.

He would need to cross the two rivers by going through the city; he knew no other way. At least he could mingle with the wharf men, who could be counted upon to be up at all hours carousing in the dockside taverns. He wished he could see Emmie—he would pass very near her boarding house. But his master might raise a hue and cry at any time, and Will feared he would soon be pursued. He had to try to make it out of Pittsburgh as fast as he could walk.

When he set foot on the bridge, his nerves went taut. The two lanterns set to guide travelers over the bridge revealed the silhouette of a man on horseback. The hoofs of the horse rapped with a hollow sound on the wooden bridge. Will tried to look purposeful as he hurried forward.

The horseman drew to a halt in front of him.

"Where are you going at this hour, young man? You can't be up to any good."

The man's voice sounded old, and Will could make out a big nose even in the shadowy darkness.

"If you please, sir, I'm on the way to fetch the midwife for my mistress."

The man continued to block the way on his horse. "Not headed to a tavern or some other . . . den of iniquity?"

"No indeed, sir. My mistress is in a bad way." His agitation must have lent his lie an air of urgency, for the man rode his horse forward and past Will. "Off you go then," said the old man.

Will's shoulders remained tight with apprehension when he

stepped off the end of the bridge onto the Pittsburgh levee. Now he had to concentrate on navigating his way among passing groups of men. Some were talking boisterously, some staggering in the throes of strong drink, leaning on their companions. Will kept his brisk pace, though it made him stand out among the leisurely rivermen. The midwife excuse had worked once; he would use it again if necessary.

He passed building after building. Many were silent and dark, the merchants having retired to their upstairs living quarters. But here on the wharf, every fourth or fifth establishment was a tavern. He skirted the dim pools of light cast by their wall lanterns, favoring instead the darker shadows of the closed shops.

And then he had made it to the final obstacle. The barn-like end of the Monongahela Bridge jutted against the sky. The toll-keeper lived up there in a small apartment. The last time Will had crossed this bridge was in broad daylight, when Master Good brought him to Pittsburgh. Would the toll-keeper still take the toll at this hour of the night? Would he suspect that Will was a runaway?

But as Will drew near, no one opened the little window above the bridge. It was all silent, candles guttering in the lanterns hung from the bridge's tunnel-like walls.

Three men came out of a tavern just to Will's left. They were dressed better than the rivermen—older gentlemen out for a night's pleasure, no doubt. Will had drifted into the light cast by the door lamp of the tavern. He could see the men clearly; all three gray-haired, one big-jowled, one with spectacles.

The one with spectacles looked familiar, and Will met his gaze. In a split second, he remembered. The last time he saw that face, it was under a white, curled wig. It was the judge.

He looked away and kept walking, panic rising. He turned his steps to the bridge. When he passed into its shifting shadows, he breathed more easily. The judge had not recognized him, or surely he would have known that this apprentice from Allegheny City must be a runaway.

He continued to go as fast as he dared across the bridge. He was at the halfway point.

And then the cry went up behind him. "Stop! Runaway! Stop him!"

He ran for the other side of the bridge, his feet thudding against the wood. Behind him, his pursuers' footsteps sent a rapid drumbeat echoing down the tunnel. They were gaining on him. His lungs strained to take in enough breath. The lantern on the far end of the bridge created a circle of light like a halo on the riverbank. If he could just get past that light and disappear into the woods . . .

Fragments of curses and threats flew past him like bullets. He dared not look back when they were so close. He redoubled his efforts, legs scissoring as fast as they could, fists pumping. In a flash, he passed under the lantern and into the welcoming darkness.

The woods were too thin here. Even in the dark of night, there might not be enough brush to hide him. He cast about wildly for another route. The din on the bridge was growing louder; they would be upon him at any moment.

He jumped to the side of the bridge and slid down the bank, feet first, scrambling for purchase through loose rock. His palms stung as they skidded over the gravel, then his shoes plunged into a thin layer of mud and icy water. Pushing himself up to a half crouch, he crept into the total blackness under the bridge itself.

He felt his way up and wedged himself prone in the crevice where the bank met the underside of the bridge. Footsteps pounded inches over his head, half-deafening him as they passed.

"Which way?" a man yelled, voice strained.

"He can't have gone far!" another shouted.

"Check behind that house!" A different voice.

"You go over into these trees!"

Will had lost track of how many were shouting—four or five. He tried not to wheeze for breath and prayed they would not think to check the bridge.

The middle of his back stung as much as his abraded palms. He must have torn some of the scabs from the whip.

It seemed like half an hour before he heard their voices again.

"Fast as a rabbit! Blast it!"

"He kicked up his heels like the devil himself was behind him!"

Laughter.

Will laid his cheek on the dirt in the blackness. A few feet away, a slice of moonlight revealed broken, dead reeds where he had slid down the bank. He stared straight ahead, praying they would not notice the marks of his passage.

"Ain't much of a reward, anyhow."

"No, not for a starveling apprentice."

"And the master might be too cheap, besides."

The sound of someone clearing his throat and spitting. "The next round's on me."

There was a shout of approval.

"Aye, the game's up for tonight."

Their feet clunked overhead and back across to the Pittsburgh side.

He did not know how long he remained there, collapsed boneless against the hard pebbles.

At last he inched back down from the bridge, wincing at the pressure on his hands. He moved crab-like over the mud at the edge of the river toward the swath of moonlight. He peered up the bank. Empty and quiet. This side of the river was less traveled, less populated. There would be only a few dwellings to pass.

He would have to make it to the National Road. It would be a journey so long he did not know if he could do it, alone on foot as he was. In a few hours, Master Good would be sure to discover his absence and send out notices far and wide. He might even come in pursuit himself, on horseback. So Will had no choice but to walk without stopping.

But he was free. And he would remain free. His determination stormed through him, stronger than his weakened body. Moving his stiffened limbs, he pulled himself up the bank. Still no sign of life around the scattered dwellings.

He did not think he could find his way by the stars, and he had no way to defend himself from wild creatures deeper in the forest. There was no choice but to stay close to the dirt roads.

But he would not rest until he found the saddler and his daughter.

Twenty-Two

ANN HAD FINISHED CARING FOR THE ANIMALS AND was preparing supper when her father returned. She let him in; he was travel worn and his hair in need of a trim.

He crossed to the kitchen bench and sat down, leaning back and closing his eyes. After a moment, he fished in his vest pocket.

"I have a letter from Pittsburgh." Handing her the sealed parchment, he bent over and began to unlace one boot.

She glanced at the address. "But it's addressed to you."

"Will you read it to me?" he asked. "All I want is to remove my boots. They aren't yet broken in." He huffed with the effort of pulling off the first boot.

She broke the red seal and unfolded it. "It's from Enoch Washington."

"Yes, I recognized his hand." Dropping the boot on the floor, he set to work on the other.

"Dear Samuel," she read aloud. "I hope this letter finds you well and your farm prospering. I have had some unsettling news that I must share with you. The bounty hunter—" She stopped. *Jack Rumkin*, spelled the cramped, neat handwriting. The man in the beaver hat.

"Let me see." He father stopped working on his boot and held out his hand.

She shook her head. She would not give in to the fear that crept through her and made the letter quiver in her hand. She steadied it to read again. "The bounty hunter Jack Rumkin has been making inquiries in all the taverns about town. My contacts tell me that he is looking for the Simons, who have sheltered with me here since your departure." She swallowed and continued reading. "We had intended to send them on to Canada, but Clara fell ill and we thought it best to wait. Rumkin's efforts have been so assiduous that I fear that it will not be long until he finds a man who will barter information for liquor."

Her father had disposed of the other boot, and now he stood in his stocking feet and gently took the letter from her. "Bravely done. I'll read the rest." He was quiet, his head bent over the paper, then he looked up. "Enoch says he is sending the Simons here."

"Why?" Her question was soft, but her thoughts veered in several directions.

"He doesn't think Rumkin will expect them to come west. He will be watching for them along the northern road. But if they come this way, we can send them north, to a farmer Enoch knows in Mount Vernon."

"But what if—" She hated the catch in her voice. "What if Rumkin follows them here?"

"I will take care of Rumkin."

The flatness of her father's reply made her uneasy. Would he kill the bounty hunter if he saw him? Surely not. He had been as upset by the death of Mr. Holmes as Ann herself.

But her next thought was too unsettling to speak aloud. *What if he comes here and you are not at home?*

She turned away to hide her disquiet and walked to the hearth. If Mr. Washington had chosen this course, she could not argue. He must know the ways of the bounty hunters better than she did, and she could not advocate some other route that might condemn the Simons to recapture. Back in Tennessee, their punishment would be dire beyond her will to imagine. Their enraged former master would hold them responsible for the death of Mr. Holmes.

She forced herself to think of something else. "Eli Bowen came by."

"Indeed?"

"He wants me to go with him to a party tomorrow. A bonfire at the Murdoch place, for the young people."

"That seems pleasant." He sounded surprised. "Would you like to go?"

"I suppose."

"Then of course you may."

Thank heaven he had asked no further questions about Eli.

His expression was nonchalant as he removed plates from the hutch and set them on the table. "Where are the girls?" he asked at last.

"Playing in their room."

"I'll call them to dinner."

After he walked to the back, it was only a minute before the girls came tumbling out of the hallway. Mabel talked without pause for breath about a wild panther in the woods, and Susan occasionally added a detail to the story.

"Its eyes glowed like fire! And it was black."

"I don't think we have panthers in these parts, girls," their father said, his mouth quirking.

"It was a panther, it was!" Mabel said.

"Perhaps it was a very large turkey." Her father always spoke with the greatest seriousness when he was teasing them.

The debate on the features of panthers and turkeys began in earnest, and Ann spooned potatoes and ham onto the plates.

She did not mind dreaming a little of Eli, as the good-natured wrangling continued. Their earlier courtship now took on the golden cast of a more innocent time. Perhaps she could take his hand and walk right back into that time. There would be no ugliness and no cruelty. It would be just Eli, Ann, and endless talk of wonderful books in their own private world. It would be a perfect union, unmarked by the trouble and sin that ruined everything else.

When Eli arrived to escort her to the bonfire, everything promised to be just as she had imagined. They rode beside each other, she sidesaddle on Bayberry, he on his bay gelding. Even their horses were perfectly suited. She had to guard against looking at him too long or too frequently; it was hard not to admire the strong, fine cut of his cheekbones, the lean but poised lines of his figure on horseback. The pleasure she took in his company was the same as ever and left her in an elevated mood as if she stood before a painting by one of the masters. She was slightly awed that such a man was actually beside her.

As they arrived at the Murdochs' farm, the dark smoke of the bonfire was already rising in the clearing behind the barn. It was still cold and gray, but the orange fire crackled merrily in the center of a circle of young people who sat on makeshift benches formed from hewn logs. James Murdoch noticed them ride up and came to help with their horses.

Eli supported Ann by the hand and steadied her at the waist as she cleared her skirts from the pommel and slid down. He stood very close and a thrill rippled up her arms from where their gloved hands touched as she remembered the feel of his ungloved hand. She pulled away and took his elbow instead.

He led her over to the fire, and they greeted some of the others they knew—their old schoolmates, their faces rosy with the heat. As they made their way to a free log, Ann saw over the wavering heat of the fire that David Crawford sat with Phoebe Vanderlick only a few yards away.

Ann dreaded the moment when Phoebe would look around and see them. She had no love for Phoebe, but she would not wish on her the pain of losing a cherished suitor.

After a while, the black curls bobbed and Phoebe's dark eyes flicked in their direction.

The hardness of Phoebe's stare made it clear that the girl was no more fond of Ann than ever. And probably less, given the circumstances. Phoebe presented her back to Ann and Eli and engaged in animated conversation with David, who gave them a perfunctory wave over her head.

James and his mother emerged from the house with mugs of cider. When Mrs. Murdoch, large and genial, handed Ann and Eli their mugs, Ann cradled hers in both hands, inhaling the sweet-smelling steam.

"Did you enjoy your time in Pittsburgh?" Eli's question was low and intimate.

"Most of it. The architecture and the music were wonderful."

"But there were some things that were less enjoyable?" He half smiled. He had always told her he liked her frankness.

"I wasn't enamored of the smoke," she said.

He grinned more broadly. "And the citizens?"

She fell silent. Will the apprentice came to her mind, as she had seen him last, skinny as a starved yearling and dressed in little more than rags. "Some of them are very piteous, and some are cruel."

He had stopped smiling. He must have sensed her sadness. "It's the way of the world, I'm afraid."

"I do not like it."

"Well, I am very glad that you are back. I did not know how much I would miss your sweet face." He took her hand unobtrusively, so the others would not see. "The heart went out of the town for me."

The flush in her face was not an effect of the fire, though she hoped it seemed so. She had nothing to say, but gazing at him was quite enough to occupy her attention. His eyes glinted a more crystalline blue in the firelight, the planes of his face sharpened in the shadow.

He looked down at the bare ground. "I must humbly beg your pardon for my treatment of you. I was hurt when you refused me. I did not want to wait. I behaved badly."

"Hush," she said gently. The logs hissed in the fire. "Let's not speak of it."

He set his mug down by his foot. "I have written something for you."

She was tongue-tied, both flattered and shy.

"Would you like to hear it?"

"Of course." She smiled.

He lowered his eyelids in concentration, then spoke quietly, looking into her eyes. "Shall I compare thee to a summer's day? Thou art more lovely, and more temperate."

She giggled.

"What's the matter?" he said innocently. "Don't you want me to tell you the rest? I worked very hard composing it." The way he bit his lip to keep from smiling gave him away.

"Oh, please do."

"Rough winds do shake the darling buds of May . . ." As he went on, the mirth that bubbled up in her brought something else—oddly, it was still romantic to have him recite those immortal words, looking at her as if he were composing them himself on the spur of the moment. He finished the sonnet and cocked his head, his eyes narrowing adorably. "What do you think?"

"Ravishing," she said. "And I wrote one for you."

"Out with it." He rested his hand on the log and leaned closer to her.

"Good nature and good sense must ever join—" she began.

He continued, "To err is human—"

"To forgive—"

"Divine." His last word breathed close to her ear. A shiver went down to her core; she closed her eyes.

"You always loved Pope," he said, still bent very close.

"He is so witty, one must love him or hate him." She opened her eyes and tilted her head up to meet his gaze.

"But I preferred Byron."

"I remember. You were the scandalous one. We certainly didn't hear Byron in school."

"But I only told you the virtuous poems."

"Such as?"

"Let me think a moment." In profile, his lips pursed as he thought. He was the kind of man who deserved to be sculpted. She wanted to touch him just to reassure herself that he was real flesh.

"Eternal spirit of the chainless mind . . ." he whispered again to her. She enjoyed his closeness, but something nagged at her about this poem.

"Brightest in dungeons, Liberty, thou art!"

Now she remembered. It was "The Prisoner of Chillon."

He went on, "And when thy sons to fetters are confined . . ."

Confined, imprisoned. Like Will Hanby. How could she laugh, spout poetry, and go courting, having left him to poverty and beatings, if not worse? She sat up straighter, wishing Eli would stop.

But he did not. "To fetters, and the damp vault's dayless gloom . . ."

Will's body sprawled in the gray gloom of Master Good's barn recurred to her like a slap in the face. She jumped up, murmuring that she was overheated, and walked away from the fire. She heard Eli a step behind her, then he caught up.

"I have offended you," he said. He laid a hand under her elbow and walked with her.

"No," she said. "An unpleasant memory. But it's no fault of yours." Smiling halfheartedly, she strolled with him in full view of the others, as if admiring the fire from a distance.

"Tell me what has disturbed you." His tone was pleading and the softness of his eyes almost dissolved her guard. But she remained silent, preferring to hold his arm and soak in the comfort of his presence. She did not know how he would respond to the story of Will. She did not intend to share it with him.

As she walked, the warmth of the fire dissipated from her clothing, and the cold of the afternoon seeped back in its place. When she remarked on the cold, Eli was happy to return to their seat by the fire and chat with the others. Ann stared into the leaping flames.

She had a fire to warm her on this cold day. But Will did not. She could not continue her life as if she never saw his plight. His lonely face had printed its image on her mind's eye, a constant reminder that her inaction had been no better for him, in the end, than cruelty.

Twenty-Three

WILL KNEW HE HAD COME MILES AND MILES. SOME time ago the sting of blisters had begun, but now his feet grew numb from the endless walking and cold.

The night was still dark, and the hard-packed road twisted narrow through the tall slender trees. He had seen no one since the bridge. No one else was fool enough to travel in near-darkness, when the world lay asleep.

He was so thirsty. He wished the patches of snow from a few weeks back had lingered, but then he probably would have frozen to death by now.

He thrust his hand into his pocket. The slices of beef were there, cold and hard. He fumbled one out and gnawed on it as he walked, as if he could draw moisture from it as well as sustenance. His mouth was dry. There was no water in him to wash down the food. He swallowed with difficulty and put the remainder back in his pocket.

He was growing dizzy, but he would not stop. He took out the beef again and bit off a piece to hold in his mouth. The flavor gave him something to focus on besides the effort of walking. He clenched his teeth and closed his eyes for a few steps, breathing every other stride. He had to stay conscious and moving.

But the dizziness was growing worse. The road lurched under him; he stumbled and fell to his knees. The sharp pain in his already lacerated palms cleared his head.

He stood up again and moved forward, but the road soon started swaying as it had before. He could not give up. He would keep moving. The edges of his vision darkened, making the night even dimmer. He concentrated on that pale ribbon of road stretching ahead, but his head drooped until he could only see his feet moving over the dirt and gravel.

The circle of blackness closed in on him; he fought, but it was no use. His feet slowed. His knees gave way. The hard road turned as soft and welcoming as a feather bed. His vision was only a pinprick, and then it winked out.

He coughed, choking, spluttering. He was on his back; he rolled to his side. Liquid sprayed from his mouth. He could breathe again. The sharp smell of whiskey penetrated his fog; it burned on his tongue.

He opened his eyes. It was still dark, though less so than before. Above him loomed the silhouette of a crouching man. It was over, then. Failure fell on him like a lead weight.

"You're in sorry shape, young'un," the man said. Will could not focus his eyes. The man was a stranger, just an indistinct shape against the starry sky.

"Someone's used you pretty ill, I'd say." The man whistled through his teeth. "When blood paints straight lines on back of a body's shirt, it's a pretty good guess how it got there."

Will stared dully ahead. Then his stripes must have reopened enough to bleed. At least enough to stain his dirty shirt. He couldn't feel much.

The man's big arm burrowed under Will's ribcage and hoisted him to his feet. Will's legs dangled; he was barely able to get his feet under him.

"The gods have smiled on you tonight," the man said almost under his breath, hauling Will a few paces across the road. Will lifted his head to see a wagon before him.

"I've tasted the sweetness of a good flogging myself, courtesy of the navy," the man said. "But since we're a ways from the sea, I know it ain't the navy that gave you yours. Get yourself up. Look lively."

He snagged a burly arm under Will's leg and pushed him over the sideboard of the wagon. Will was barely able to cushion his tumble with one arm.

He heard the man climbing up to the driver's seat. "A bad master, no doubt. So I won't ask your name, nor will I give you mine. It's better that way. Here you go."

Something thumped against Will's gut. He brought his hands down to it; it was a canteen. The idea of water revived him, and by great concentration he managed to raise himself on one arm. He unscrewed the cap with awkward fingers. Putting the neck to his lips, he drank the cool, sweet liquid in gulp after gulp. His hand shook.

"Don't you be wasting it now," the man said gruffly.

Will lowered the canteen and wiped his mouth on his sleeve. Fully conscious for the first time, he looked at the stranger. The man had a black beard like a pirate in a storybook. It bristled out over his huge chest. He wore an old brown vest; his arms were like hams bulging under plain shirt sleeves. No wonder he had been able to toss Will around like a rag doll.

"I'm going to the National Road," the pirate-man said. "Then to Brownsburgh."

"I need to go west, not east," Will said. "But I'd be obliged if you'd let me ride with you to the National Road."

"That I will," the man said. He turned around and picked up the reins, clucking and slapping them against the horse's back. The wagon lurched forward, and Will swayed back against the side.

"It'll take us a few hours," the man said over his shoulder. "If you're continuing on foot, you'd better sleep. There's a blanket under you."

Will felt the fuzzy roughness under his fingers. He shifted and pulled the wool blanket from beneath his legs.

"I can't thank you enough, sir," he said.

"You just joined the brotherhood of the whip," the man said. "Now you help some other poor bleeding blackguard when it's your turn."

"Yes, sir."

No one could have slept in the bumping wagon under normal circumstances, but Will's exhaustion was like nothing he had ever known. As soon as he lay on his side and pulled the blanket over him, he fell into a fitful doze.

A rough jolt against the side of the wagon awoke him. He sat up.

Some time had passed; the pale gold of dawn had come. In its light, he saw that dew lay on the grass under the trees. Dew, not frost. The wagon had stopped. Before them lay a much wider road, liberally packed with gravel. He saw a wooden post next to the wagon with a few numbers carved into it.

The big man turned around. "The National Road. You're sure you want to get out? I'm going this way." He pointed left. "It's a mite easier than walking."

"I need to go west." Will rubbed his eyes. "But I thank you." He pushed off the blanket and climbed off the back of the wagon, trying not to groan when his tortured feet hit the road.

"You remember now, brother," said the pirate-man. Nodding his head in farewell, he clucked to the horse and steered to the left. Will watched the wagon roll away for only a moment before setting out on stiff legs in the other direction.

Now that it was light, he had to be vigilant for the sound of other travelers around the bends in the road. A number of times he plunged into the woods, concealing himself while a horseman or coach passed. On one of those occasions, he found a little brook. Everyone knew not to drink from the rivers near Pittsburgh, but out here in the country the water smelled fresh where it trickled over its bed of pebbles. He savored its coolness.

The spring sunlight was weak. It was still too cold for his thin coat; he wrapped his arms over his chest as he trudged on. The sun moved higher in the sky. He kept on doggedly, though he had finished his meat hours before and his stomach protested. He had passed through the weakness and fatigue; now he continued as if some external force powered his legs, though they should not by rights have been able to support him. He was surprised by it.

But eventually, as the sun began to sink again over the trees, even this inexplicable surge of strength faded. The terrain had swelled into soft hills. The road ran between them as they rose on all sides, but even the slight slope in the road made him slow to a snail's pace.

He did not know if he should crawl into the woods to lie down and sleep in the growing dusk. He feared that he might not be able to get up again, with no food and his increasing fatigue. He kept walking, very slowly. It was getting dark. He could not continue much longer without food and rest. He could not tell if he shook from fatigue or cold.

He stepped off the road into the trees. He had to stop, he had no choice. His limbs refused to obey him now. He would have to sleep and pray that it did not get cold enough overnight to kill him. He looked around in vain for a warmer spot. Perhaps if he piled up leaves, there, next to the fallen tree. A quick vision of his rigid body rotting into the leaves should have made him shudder, but he was too tired.

He sat down on the log and waited to gather his strength so he could make a bed of leaves. A light glimmered then, through the trees, up the hill away from the road. It was not the flickering orange of a fire. It was a lantern, still and steady. The hill was quiet.

He stood up in a daze. The voice of his father echoed in his head. *I will lift my eyes up unto the hills, whence comes my help.*

He had to go to it. He knew then, with a certainty, that even if he survived the night, he would not be able to continue tomorrow without eating and drinking.

He made his way slowly up the hill. He fell once trying to climb over a fallen trunk. But when the trees opened out to a clearing that formed a bald spot on the hill's pate, he paused.

This was no friendly farmhouse. It was a mansion. Bigger even than Dr. Loftin's home. All white, with six immense fluted columns in a neat row across its many-windowed front. The light he had seen through the trees glowed in a window downstairs.

Will let out his breath as he lurked in the cover of the trees. How likely was it that the occupants of this house would shelter him or feed him? It was certain that no one who lived here would belong to the brotherhood of the whip. More likely the brotherhood of the whippers.

I will lift my eyes up unto the hills, whence comes my help.

He did not understand why he still heard the voice of his father. It was enough to make him break down and weep.

It makes no sense! he railed back at it. *No help will come from here.*

But an irrational impulse drove him forward out of the trees. *This is the action of a lunatic. Why would I walk up to their door and doom myself to capture?*

But he kept going.

He knocked on the door.

After a moment, it opened just a crack.

"What is it?" It was a woman's voice.

"Please, ma'am . . ." His voice caught. He did not know how to continue. Should he throw himself on his knees and beg for mercy?

The door opened wider. It was a woman in an elegant blue dress, her brown hair streaked with gray, her face round and kind. "Is something the matter?"

"Please, ma'am, I need help." And then to his horror, in his exhaustion and despair he was unable to keep back a sob. The rush of emotion unbalanced him, and he staggered against the wall.

Her kind face creased in dismay. She flung the door open and called behind her. "Henry!"

An elderly servant in red livery appeared in the hall. "Yes, Mrs. Crandall?" He looked in confusion at Will.

"Help this young man into the kitchen, if you please."

"Yes, ma'am."

The older man had a strong arm still, despite his white hair, and he brought Will over the doorsill, following his mistress.

It was like walking into paradise. The air smelled like flowers. It was warm, as he had not been warm in years. Rug after rug lay on the dark oak floor, soft beneath his tattered shoes.

The kitchen was even warmer, a huge fire blazing on the hearth. On one of the two large kitchen tables, there were two golden-brown, crispy chickens on a spit, lying on a metal tray.

The woman—Mrs. Crandall—immediately picked up a large carving knife and fork and began to slice meat from the breast. "Sit him down, Henry," she said, preoccupied.

When Henry assisted him to one of the kitchen benches, Will collapsed onto it. Before he could drop his head to the table, Mrs. Crandall slid a plate before him piled with the slices of chicken.

He looked up at her, still unable to believe it. She smiled and nodded.

He picked up one of the moist, tender slices in his dirty hand and began to eat. As he did so, she placed two thick chunks of bread onto the plate, and then a glass of milk beside his right hand. He drank.

When he had eaten enough to soothe the pain in his stomach, he looked up. She had seated herself at the other table, where she was ten feet away but still watching him.

"Thank you," he said.

"You're half-starved," she said softly. "And your shoes are in shreds."

"Yes, ma'am."

"And you've been . . . injured."

She must have seen the blood on his shirt as well.

"Yes, ma'am."

Her eyes told him she guessed everything. "I will leave you here with Henry, and when you have finished eating, he will assist you to bathe. He and our cook will heat the water for you."

"Yes, ma'am."

If entering the home had been like paradise, the simple bath was enough to start the angels singing. Henry and the Irish cook rolled in through the kitchen door a wooden laundry tub almost as broad as a wagon wheel. When the cook had set two kettles and a large stockpot on the hearth, she retired, leaving Henry alone with Will. Ordinarily Will would not have liked to undress before a stranger, but exhaustion had numbed him beyond a care for modesty. And the old man was very discreet as he held Will's arm and seated him gently in the enormous barrel.

He handed Will a chunk of soap and spoke in a voice scratchy as sandpaper. "Don't use it on your back, young man. The soap'll sting in those cuts."

The warm water splashed in around Will's shins. He sighed and leaned his head on his arms, which in turn rested on his bent knees. His mind drifted. He had not bathed in warm water since he was a boy in his mother's home.

When he summoned the strength to lather his chest, arms, and legs, the water turned brown. Without comment, Henry scooped out some of the dirty water with a pitcher and poured in more water until it ran clear off Will's skin.

The water cooled, and Will searched for his clothes, but they had disappeared while he was occupied in washing.

"Here you are." Henry held out a wide, soft piece of cloth, and Will wrapped it around himself as he attempted to stand. His balance failed, his knees rubbery, but Henry was at his elbow immediately to steady him. Will climbed over the scalloped edge of the tub, and Henry seated him back at the kitchen bench.

On the table beside Will lay a folded light-blue shirt and a brown pair of trousers. A pair of house slippers sat by his feet on the dark oaken floor.

Will donned the garments, his fingers clumsy with the small buttons. The fine weave of the trousers was unlike anything he had ever worn. And the slippers on his blistered feet—soft as goose down.

He toweled off his hair. When the inside of his arm brushed his chin, he found to his surprise that it was rough, as his father's face had once been when he shaved his beard and let it grow back. Had he not been so bleary with fatigue, he would have smiled ruefully. A promising time to become a man—when penniless, starving, and a fugitive.

He was clean, dressed, and dry. Henry led him out of the kitchen and up the wide curving stairs. Again Henry held his elbow while Will also leaned heavily on the mahogany banister to his right, lifting himself one step at a time. The stairs were almost beyond his power, but he was determined not to allow Henry to carry him like an infant—if the old man could even have done so. At last, Will attained the landing of the upstairs hall, and they crept down the lamp-lit hall to a side door.

The bedroom inside was unmistakably masculine. It was

spare, with hunting prints on the walls. The coverlet was dark green, the headboard of the bed simple but elegant.

"Mrs. Crandall bids you rest," Henry said. "If you need anything, do not hesitate to ring." He pointed to the bell cord beside the door. Then Henry withdrew, shutting the door quietly behind him.

In the cloudy softness of that bed, Will drifted off to welcome oblivion.

When he awoke, the dust motes floated in the sunlight that streamed through the window. He lay there watching them until he realized where he was.

He tried to sit up, but the aches of his body ripped a groan from his chest; he slumped back on his side, his head in the pillow.

A knock came at the door.

"Come in." How strange that he should be giving anyone permission to enter a wealthy man's bedroom.

Henry entered with measured tread and stood a few feet away to deliver a message. "Mrs. Crandall would be pleased if you would join her for breakfast." He left with the same stately step and closed the door behind him.

Will dressed, still unaccustomed to the fine clothing, and limped out of the bedroom to find Henry waiting for him at the top of the stairs. He followed the old man downstairs, past a vast oil painting of Christ on a mountaintop surrounded by crowds, across the marbled foyer, and into the kitchen.

"Good morning," Mrs. Crandall said. She sat in the light from the window, which colored her white morning bonnet with the pastel yellow of a spring flower.

"Good morning, ma'am." Will hobbled over to the other table, which had been laid with a plate of biscuits and even some preserved apples flecked with brown sugar.

"Please, eat." She stood up and walked over to seat herself across from him.

"What's your name?" she asked.

He swallowed a forkful of apple, which was so overwhelming in its sweet softness that he took a moment to answer. "Will." He did not want to give her his last name. It might cause her trouble later.

"Will, I would like to know where you are going. Do you have any family to help you?"

"No family, ma'am. But I'm hoping to find some friends."

"You've found one, at least." She smiled, her eyes crinkling in a face slightly faded from the bloom of youth, but all the kinder for it. "But I have not introduced myself. I'm Lavinia Crandall. My husband, Matthew, is a congressman, and he is away right now at the capitol. But had he been at home, he would have been first to insist that you stay with us."

"I can't thank you as you deserve, ma'am." Will looked at his plate. "To help a stranger as you have."

"No one could turn away someone in such straits as you were last night."

"I believe plenty would, ma'am." He broke apart the biscuit, which was still warm.

"Well, no one with a conscience would. Especially now that you are not quite so . . . fragrant." She laughed, her merriness making her look briefly like a girl of twenty.

Will smiled, but with some chagrin.

"I'm sorry." She grew more sober. "I know you cannot

help the condition in which you arrived. Of course I had to help you."

She went to the counter where she wrapped some leftover biscuit in a cloth. "And if others would not aid a stranger in such a state, the more shame on them." She set the top on the biscuit tin with a firm twist. "Where are you trying to go, Will?"

"Rushville. In Ohio, ma'am."

"That's quite some distance." She paused, then turned to face him. "And, in your condition, it seems you will need some help getting there."

Twenty-Four

THE GIRLS WERE SHOUTING FOR HER FROM OUTSIDE the house. Ann hurried to the kitchen window to see Mabel and Susan standing together, heads turned in the same direction. Susan pointed down the road and said a few words Ann couldn't make out. Someone must be coming. Taking off her apron, she walked out the kitchen door into the yard. She had to lift her skirts to step over the ruts of mud their own wagon had churned up.

"Ann, who is that?" Mabel asked, flyway hair in her face, hands on her hips as if questioning the right of any traveler to pass by.

Ann peered down the road at a coach drawn by two gray horses; it rocked and swayed over the bumps. She had never seen a private coach come down this way; she hoped it would not get stuck. Its narrow wheels did not look fit for the stresses of a country road.

The driver wisely pulled up in the road rather than brave the deeper mud of the yard. When he jumped down and removed his hat, she saw that it was Enoch Washington.

She patted her little sister on the back to get her attention. "Susan, go tell Father to come outside." Ann walked over to the coach.

"Welcome, Mr. Washington! We've been expecting you."

"Miss Miller," he said, smiling. His dignity did not desert him even here, far from his elegant Pittsburgh home. He was dressed in brown traveling clothes: coat, waistcoat, and hat, all less formal than his city attire. His coffee-colored skin had a grayish undertone—probably from fatigue—but his motions were brisk as he opened the door of the coach.

"We have arrived," he said. "You can come out."

John Simon stepped down into view from behind the coach door and helped his wife out. She leaned on his arm; she did not look well.

Ann's father walked out the front door then, bareheaded but wearing his frock coat.

"Welcome," he called to them. "Come inside; you've had a long journey."

"We certainly have," Mr. Washington said. The little party skirted the worst of the mud and followed Ann's father inside.

Her father showed their guests to the sitting room, pointing them to the comfortable green armchairs, then crouched at the hearth to stoke the fire. Ann put some water on for tea. With a few hushed words she banished Susan and Mabel to their bedroom.

"So the bounty hunter does not know where you are?" her father asked Mr. Washington, taking a seat on the straight-backed wooden chair closest to him.

"We hope we left town unnoticed. The coach was protection from prying eyes." Mr. Washington relaxed back in his seat. "We had to stop a few times in towns to refresh the horses, but very few townspeople saw John and Clara."

"We sure are grateful to you, Enoch, for taking us," John

said. "We couldn't go on the steamboat, not with these on us." John indicated his circle-and-cross-branded forehead. The scar reached almost down to the bridge of his nose. "I can't hide mine with a hat, not all the way."

"But he still wore his hat, and Clara pulled her bonnet down," Mr. Washington said to Ann's father.

Clara Simon remained silent, leaning against the wing of the chair.

"Are you unwell?" Ann asked. "Is there something I might do to help?"

"I'm feeling a little poorly, but I'll be better soon," Clara said, lifting her head.

"Don't be listening to her," John said. "She's had a bad fever since last night."

"It's nothing to worry you for," Clara said. "I get these chills every so often. And it's not catching."

"It's the marsh fever," John said.

"Malaria," Mr. Washington said. "From her time in New Orleans. We brought quinine with us to treat her, but it will be a week before she is fully recovered."

Ann's father considered Clara for a moment from his chair by the hearth. "I think you had better rest before you go on with your journey, Mrs. Simon."

"No, sir, I can go on. I'll be just fine," she said, but her head drooped again to the side of the chair.

"No, you mustn't," Ann's father said. "The next part of your journey will be more arduous. Mr. Washington will return to Pittsburgh with his coach, and I will have to take you to another man who will help you. At some point northward, you may have to go by foot."

"We don't want to burden you," John said.

"It's no burden. We wish to help," her father said.

The teakettle steamed on the stove; Ann walked back to prepare the tea. She brought the cups and saucers back into the sitting room on a tray.

"Out in the woods past our fields," her father was saying, "there is a one-room cabin I built when we first settled here. That would be the safest place. Even if someone came searching for you at our home, he would not find you out there in the woods."

Ann gave a teacup to Mr. Washington.

"And there is still a bed frame," her father added. "We can put the girls' mattress out there for you, and they can sleep with Ann."

"Oh no, Miss Miller, I can't take one of your beds," Clara said weakly as Ann set a teacup on the little table next to her.

"I won't take no for an answer," Ann said, smiling. "Sharing a bed for a week will bring back fond memories of when the girls were smaller. They always stole into my room halfway through the night."

She handed the last teacup and saucer to her father and seated herself on the other side of the hearth. She was glad the Simons were here, despite her lingering fear at the thought of Jack Rumkin pursuing them. Helping John and Clara soothed her wounded heart after her failure to help Will in Pittsburgh.

"I will help you set up there and get food and firewood, John," her father said. "You and Clara can have a little home of your own for as long as you need it."

John's eyes glistened with emotion; he did not say anything.

"It's very kind of you, Samuel," Mr. Washington said.

John recovered his composure. "Mr. Miller, you don't know how much it means to me and my wife."

"Call me Samuel, please." Ann's father stood up and walked to the hallway that led to the bedrooms. "Girls!" he called. "I need your assistance."

A bustle of activity began. Ann and the girls gathered food and supplies in baskets for the Simons while their father and John loaded the mattress in the wagon.

Ann placed a tin of dried beef in a basket and went back to the pantry to get some jars of apples. The younger girls had already set off for the cabin with their baskets, preferring to make an adventure of it rather than ride sedately in the wagon. Ann was alone with her thoughts as she packed the jars in rags to keep them from breaking against one another.

It was always possible that Jack Rumkin would find them. She pushed away the nauseating memory of his weight on her legs, trapping her. Her hand trembled as she reached for the box of salt on the shelf.

She would have to ask her father what they would do if he came after them. A loaded shotgun leaned in the corner behind the door—only a fool would live in this untamed state without a gun at the ready. She shuddered at the idea of staining her soul even more deeply with human blood. But she would do it, if she must. Even so, nothing promised that she or her father would be close enough to the house to get the gun in time.

She would just have to pray that Jack Rumkin never learned where the Simons had gone.

The heavy coach trundled down the road at a rapid clip. Will could not shake off his conviction that he was dreaming. He wore a coat that Mrs. Crandall had given to him with the insistence that her husband did not need it. She had also sent along an extra set of clothes and a few books to pass the time on the journey. On the occasions when the coach stopped for the driver and horses to rest, Will exchanged a few words with the coachman, but for the most part he read the books. One of them was about a man named Natty Bumpo. Will lost himself for hours in Cooper's dramatic tale of pioneers, settlers, and Indians.

Reading kept his mind occupied more fruitfully than contemplating the future. He did not know what else to do except to look for Mr. Miller. His only useful skills were in saddlery. But any saddler other than Mr. Miller would guess immediately that this wandering young man with nothing but his stitching skills to recommend him was a runaway apprentice. And most saddlers who needed apprentices already had them. He would have to rely on Mr. Miller's compassion for employment.

The daylight faded and his eyes grew tired. When the coach stopped and the driver came around to tell him they were in Rushville, his sense of unreality intensified. He disembarked from the coach, taking the knapsack that held the extra clothing.

"Mrs. Crandall told me you have friends here," the young ruddy-faced coachman said. "Where are they?"

"They live a little way out from town, off the main road," Will said. Mr. Miller had told him so while they worked together in Pittsburgh.

"Ah," the coachman said. "I'd take you, but the coach barely made it over this last road. A little more mud and we wouldn't make it back." The coachman extended his hand. "Good luck to you," he said.

Will shook it. "Thank you. And please give Mrs. Crandall my thanks, again."

"I will." The coachman climbed back to the driver's seat and turned the horses around.

As the coach rattled away, Will looked around him on Rushville's main street, such as it was. The whitewashed store in front of him displayed a sign that proclaimed it to be Sumner's General. It was growing late, but perhaps the storekeeper would give him directions. The sign on the door still read Open.

He walked in. A woman sat on a stool behind the counter, jotting something in a ledger. She looked up at the tinkle of the bell.

"Good evening! We are just about to close up. May I get you something?" She had a freckled face and a broad smile.

"Yes, ma'am. I mean, no, ma'am."

She chuckled. "Make up your mind now."

"I just need to know the way to Samuel Miller's farm."

"Are you a friend of the Millers?"

"Yes, ma'am." He felt it would be polite to explain more, but he didn't dare.

She gestured at the street outside. "Take this road past the town center. After about a mile or so through the trees, you'll see a big oak on the left that's been split in two by lightning. You can't miss it. It's huge." She made a circle with her arms. "Each trunk is this big, and it's split almost all the way to the ground."

Will nodded.

"Look to your right there and you'll see a smaller road through the trees—little more than a set of wagon tracks. You'll go down that road about another mile, and you'll see the Miller farm. You can't miss it; it's the first farm, and there aren't any others close by."

"Thank you, ma'am."

"You're welcome. But you'll need to hurry if you want any light to walk by."

He nodded again, but as he walked out the door he hid a wry smile. She did not know how accustomed he had grown to walking without light.

He moved up the road as rapidly as his blistered feet would tolerate; they still stung inside the sturdy boots Mrs. Crandall had given him. An oak was a landmark easy to miss, among all these other trees, especially in darkness. And the light was fading.

By the time he reached the split oak, it was almost dark, with just a trace of gloaming left to outline the tree trunks ahead of him. He followed the little road as she had instructed, as the stars came out overhead through the treetops.

After just a few minutes, he saw the farmhouse. It nestled between two hillocks, the glow of a fire faint through its front windows.

His chest clenched tight as he walked through the yard and headed for the front door. He could not believe he had made it this far. And if Mr. Miller would not take him, he did not know what else he could do. He reassured himself by recalling the sympathy in Mr. Miller's eyes when he spoke of the one who came to save people from darkness.

He took a deep breath and knocked.

Twenty-Five

A KNOCK CAME AT THE FRONT DOOR. ANN WAS DEEP in the pages of a novel by Mrs. Radcliffe. Her father would answer; he was out there reading to her sisters in the sitting room. The visitor was probably John Simon, who had been back to the house once already to collect a few small items after settling Clara in the little cabin.

The bar on the front door clunked, and a murmur of male voices seeped over the threshold of her bedroom. She hoped her father would not call for her help. Her candlelight time alone with her books was precious. Her reading gave her food for thought for the next day, keeping her mind alive through hours of repetitious chores.

"Ann." Her father raised his voice from its previous low rumbling so it carried clearly to her.

She sighed. Perhaps her father's request would be quick and she could return to her novel in just a minute or two. She marked her place in the book with one finger and clutched it to her bosom with one hand. With the other hand, she cleared her skirt from its tangles around her feet, then rose from her chair and brushed through her bedroom doorway.

There was enough light from the fire in the kitchen hearth

to guide her through the hallway. The shifting glow grew brighter as she emerged into the sitting room. Across the room, a lamp on the side table cast its whiter light down on the faces of Susan and Mabel where they sat at the foot of her father's empty armchair. The girls sat in total silence. Curious, this absence of chatter. They did not even glance at her. Instead, their attention was riveted on their father. He stood with another man, silhouetted against the flames that leapt behind the open hearth.

The visitor's back was to Ann. It was not John Simon, but a young man with dark hair, about her father's height. His blue shirt lay close over his shoulders, which were sharpened down to nothing but bone.

"We have an unexpected pleasure," her father said to her. The young man turned around.

Will Hanby.

He was different somehow. Neater. More civilized. His dark hair had been trimmed from its former wild tangle—now it waved thick but obedient above his brow and tapered to neat sideburns behind his cheekbones.

She was gripping her book so tightly that she must look like a scared rabbit. She scrutinized the spine of the book as if she had never seen it before, then laid it on the side table with the greatest care. She hoped that her eyes were not as wide and astonished as those of her sisters. It was not polite to remain silent for so long, but her social graces had hopped off down the rabbit trails and showed no signs of returning to her.

When she looked again at Will, his face was in shadow, unreadable. But he stepped toward her, and the lamplight rose up and caught his clear brown eyes.

He nodded and said, "Miss Miller," as any townsman would,

but his eyes could not conceal the same wild aloneness she remembered from before.

Only half civilized, then, despite appearances.

How should she address him? Mr. Hanby? No. She could not bring herself to speak to him as she would speak to Allan or another gentleman. It did not fit with the memory of his degradation and the strange intimacy of sponging the blood from his forehead as he lay on the barn floor.

"Good evening," she finally said. She was aware of the cold sound of it but blindly obeyed her protective instinct to raise a social barrier against his physical presence in her home.

His eyelids came down like shutters, his expression instantly aloof.

She did not know if she regretted that or not—she did not want to offend him, but the veiling of his gaze restored to her some sense of privacy.

"Pardon my daughter's discomposure, Will," her father said from behind him. "I'm sure you understand that your arrival comes as a shock."

"Yes, sir." As Will pivoted back toward her father, she realized a major improvement: Will no longer smelled of the pigsty. He had bathed.

Her father extended his hand to Will. "I agree to take you on as an apprentice."

Will grabbed her father's hand and shook it, his drawn face softening with relief.

Her father released his grip and put a hand on the young man's arm. "I cannot in good conscience turn you away, knowing the master you fled. We will just have to chance it, and pray that your master does not think to look for you here."

Ann could not believe her ears. Her mouth had fallen open like a fish out of water; she shut it with a snap.

"As long as you are aware, Will," her father added, "that there is not enough work in my saddlery to employ you fully. Are you willing to perform tasks around the farm as well?"

"I am familiar with the work, sir." Will smiled slightly. "And I have no objection to it, if I may work for a good master."

This was an unforeseen benefit. Help around the farm. She looked at Will's rangy frame with new appreciation. Skinny or not, he was a man, taller and probably stronger than she, even in his malnourished state. Her mountain of daily tasks might shrink to a more manageable size.

"Is he going to stay in our house?" Mabel said.

Heat flooded Ann's face. She swiveled to see Mabel jump to her feet as Susan tried without success to yank her back down by her skirt.

Her father's eyebrows rose, and he stared at the beams of the ceiling for a long moment.

"I had not thought of that. We cannot have you stay in the house, Will," he said. "Not with three girls here."

Ann occupied herself in retying Susan's hair ribbon. She did not want to know if Will's face was as scarlet as her own must be.

Her father cleared his throat. "But neither do I wish to consign you to another barn, without a real fire to warm you. The nights are still cold."

"I would manage, sir."

"No, I have another solution. We have guests who arrived earlier today who are staying in a cabin not far from here. The Simons, whom you met in Pittsburgh."

Will looked blank, then his eyes focused. "John and Clara?" he asked with a note of wonder.

"Indeed. I'm sure that given the circumstances, they would be amenable to your lodging with them. You would sleep in a blanket on the floor, but at least it would be warm next to the hearth."

"Yes, sir. That would be fine."

"And when they are ready to leave in a week or two, you may stay in the cabin by yourself."

"I'm grateful to you, sir."

"Then let me escort you out to the cabin before it grows even later. Ann, will you fetch a quilt?"

She retreated to the cedar chest and pulled their old red-and-white quilt from the pile of linens. It was faded, but clean. She skirted Will on the way back and handed the folded bundle to her father. With a quizzical glance at her, he passed it to Will and unhooked a lantern from the peg by the front door. He lit it and closed its glass hood.

"Shall we go?" he asked, taking his hat from the peg. "I'll be back shortly," he said to Ann before walking out.

Will followed, casting a last glance at her over his shoulder.

Even when the door shut behind him, she stayed rooted to the floor.

"The pig man!" Mabel said. "Why is he here?"

Ann wheeled on her and said more sharply than she intended, "That is ill-mannered!" She still did not know how to address him herself, but she had better instruct her sisters lest they adopt another teasing nickname. "You may call him Will," she said. Susan and Mabel were too young to worry about the propriety of using a man's given name.

Unabashed, Mabel flopped down on the braided rug next to Susan. "How long is he going to stay?" she asked Ann.

"I don't know."

"Will he do our chores?" Susan asked. "Father said he would have to help."

"No," Ann said. "He will do *my* chores." She laughed at the outraged scrunching of Mabel's pert nose.

While the girls wrangled about what Will would or would not do around the farm, Ann barred the door and came back to seat herself on her father's chair.

"Now, what was Father reading to you?" She picked up the Bible from the side table beneath the lamp and opened to the red ribbon that lay in the fold.

Will trailed Mr. Miller along the border of the field, which bristled with fine stubble from last year's crop.

"Ready to plow," Mr. Miller said, pointing to the hardened furrow.

Will knew nothing of plowing, as the Goods raised only livestock and a few garden vegetables in summer.

"Is it planting time?" he asked, hoisting his bag of extra clothing a little higher in his arms, where the quilt lay draped over it.

"We won't seed for a month yet, but an old farmer back in Pennsylvania once told me that early plowing brings a higher yield for corn."

"And how do you plow it?"

"With our mules. You'd be surprised how deftly two mules can work a plow."

"I'd like to see them, sir."

"Oh, you will have your chance."

They both chuckled.

"From the rear, sir?"

"To be sure."

"You'll have to teach me how to plow, Mr. Miller." Will hoped his new master would not be too disappointed that he lacked such a basic skill.

Mr. Miller stepped over the little rise in the earth between fields. "It's not difficult." His voice floated back to Will, reassuring.

They trudged over two more fields and reached the edge of the woods. Here the treetops blocked most of the moonlight. Will had to stick close to Mr. Miller's heels to find his way.

Soon the trees opened up into a small clearing, where the moonlight once again glistened on the moist grass. Scattered tree trunks testified to the labor that had produced this clearing. Will thought of the wide expanses of Mr. Miller's fields and wondered if he had cleared that land tree by tree with his own hands.

A log cabin sat in the clearing. Mr. Miller knocked on the plank door. It opened, and John Simon's good-natured face appeared in the lantern's luminous pool. The sight of the scar on his head struck Will with the force of a blow. That cross inside a circle had floated through his dreams in the week before he went to court with Master Good.

"Samuel, come in!" John said. "Did I forget something else?" He opened the door wide.

Will traipsed after Mr. Miller. Inside the tiny log-bound chamber, John's wife was lying in bed, propped up on a straw bolster.

She opened her eyes and raised her head, which gleamed at the temples with traces of perspiration. "Mr. Miller?"

Mr. Miller corralled Will with his arm and brought him forward. "This is Will Hanby, Clara. He came to see you at Enoch Washington's house. And, please, call me Samuel."

"Well, it sure is a surprise to see you here, Mr.—Will." She smiled. "Will." Despite the wrinkles and blotches etched on her cheeks by over forty years of sun and wind, her smile was natural and lovely.

He smiled back. "Likewise, Miss Clara." He balanced his armload again, as the quilt was sliding to the side.

"You can put that down over there by the chair." Clara barely lifted her hand from the bed to point.

He complied while Mr. Miller explained the situation to the Simons.

"You best stay with us, young man," Clara said.

"There's plenty of room in here," John said as he sat on the edge of Clara's bed and enfolded her hand in his.

"I'm much obliged." Will liked the Simons very much. Odd how he felt freer with ex-slaves than he did around Ann Miller, who seemed stiff and uncomfortable in his presence.

"I should be heading back," Mr. Miller said.

"Say good night to your sweet little girls for me," Clara said. "Maybe they can come for a visit tomorrow."

Mr. Miller took his leave, and Will spread out his borrowed quilt in front of the hearth, trying to compress himself into a corner to give the Simons some room. Clara was weak from the malaria relapse that Mr. Miller had spoken of—she could not continue talking much longer. But John exchanged a few more words with Will, his brown face even warmer in the firelight. He asked him about his escape and marveled at the kindness of Mrs. Crandall.

"Bless her soul. Just like Mr. Miller. They know what the Good Book says. 'For I was hungry, and you gave me meat; I was thirsty, and you gave me drink; I was a stranger, and you took me in.' Plenty of folk read it, but the Almighty bless the ones that do it."

Rolled on his side by the fire, Will murmured assent. He was unaccustomed to discussing religion, but John's profound gratitude touched a chord of similar feeling in him.

John glanced at Clara to make sure she was dozing again. "I thank the Lord every night for what he's done for us already, no matter what he has in store."

Will thought about it. The miracle of his escape bore a heavenly handprint that one would have to be a fool to ignore. His father would certainly have given all the credit to Providence, had he been in Will's place—he would credit heaven for the pirate-man and the brotherhood of the whip—for the seeming accident of stumbling to Mrs. Crandall's doorstep when he might have died alone beside the road.

"I will give thanks too," Will said.

John nodded, pulled the quilt over his wife, and lay back to close his eyes. The concentration on his face was not sleep—he was praying. Will averted his gaze, conscious of intruding.

Facing the hearth, he closed his own eyes so the dim firelight flickered red through his eyelids. He could be in Master Good's barn right now—or buried behind it. He was alive and free tonight only by the grace of heaven. As he went deep into that thought, he felt a palpable presence all around him—something vast and holy, listening and waiting. *Lord, thank you for delivering me. Thank you for your servants who took me in as a stranger and a beggar. I will live out my gratitude in service. I will do for others what they have done for me. I am your man now.* He opened his eyes and stared at the low ceiling, astounded and filled with peace as never before.

The intense feeling of presence subsided, as if someone standing next to him had just moved away but remained in the room. The fire burned so low on the hearth that only a few embers sparked in the darkness, the smell of hardwood rich in the air. He watched the glowing fragments for a long while.

Eventually he realized that he would have to relieve himself before sleeping. He clambered to his feet, still careful of his healing scabs and his sore bones.

He slipped out the door as quietly as he could. The night air was cold and pure; he walked out into the trees where he could not possibly be seen or heard.

A night animal screeched a few hundred yards away in the treetops. He jumped. An owl? He had to calm his nerves; he was as skittish as a colt.

As he fastened his trousers and turned back to the cabin, he stopped.

There, in the moonlit empty field beyond the trees, a shadow moved. A human shadow, flitting across the field like a wraith.

He watched it, paralyzed with anxious conjecture. It flowed toward the Miller home, but soon disappeared from his limited vantage point.

He had to know who it was. His coat lay back inside the cabin, but he did not want to disturb the Simons again, and if he did, he might lose the track of the shadow. He followed as softly as he could through the grove and out into the field.

Twenty-Six

ANN AWOKE.

It was quiet in her room. An odd quiet, as if the house held its breath. She did not know what had awakened her or why she lay still, afraid to move.

Tap tap tap.

At her window. Her heartbeat quickened. Should she open the shutter? One of the girls might have wandered out.

She pushed away her quilt and stood, shivering in her light cotton gown. The plank floor creaked under her feet as she tiptoed to the window.

A low whisper came from the other side. "Mr. Miller."

Someone had mistaken her window for her father's. One of their houseguests, she was sure, though she could not imagine what someone might want at this hour. She had better answer before the noise roused the girls. She hurried to her desk to light the small lamp, then carried it back to the window. Ignoring the flutter beneath her breastbone, she unlatched the shutter and opened it.

Will Hanby.

At the sight of her, his eyes widened. "I meant to wake your father."

"What is it?" She was glad that only her face was visible through the small window. It would never do to show herself in a nightgown. She pressed closer to the wall to be sure he could not see.

"There was someone outside your house just now, creeping around. I ran after him, but he made it to the woods and disappeared."

"What?"

From the gentle way he spoke, he seemed to understand that she was still sleep-befuddled. He repeated what he had just said while she tried to collect her thoughts.

"What did he look like?" she asked.

"I couldn't see—it was too dark."

"It could be Rumkin."

"Who?"

"A bounty hunter chasing the Simons."

"Or"—his eyes lowered—"it could be someone seeking me." The strong contours of his face gathered shadows in the wavering lamplight.

He looked up and met her gaze. They were only inches apart. She stood silent, unsure of what to do or say. She had never seen such deep but clear eyes as his. His lips were slightly parted; he took a quick breath as if to speak, but said nothing. The space was too close for words, yet something passed between them. She repressed a shiver and stepped back.

"You'll have to tell my father." She lifted her chin and summoned her dignity.

Horror! Stepping away had revealed her state of undress. She rushed forward to the cover of the wall.

He averted his face a moment too late and pulled away as if the window frame had become a hot griddle.

"The window to your left." She closed him away from her sight and latched the shutter. Then she collapsed to sit on the floor under the window, her flushed face buried in her hands.

She heard him renew his tapping on the next window. When her father responded, she could hear every word through the thin wood of her window shutter.

"Well, there's nothing we can do tonight," her father said. "Except keep watch. I'll remain awake here, and you do the same at the cabin. And take this."

A brief pause.

"Have you ever handled one?" her father asked.

"No, sir."

"Like this." She heard an unmistakable click.

"Then sight along the barrel, like so, and squeeze."

"Yes, sir."

"And take care."

Will's footsteps trailed away from the house into silence even as those of her father marked his passage out into the sitting room.

Her pulse did not slow its thready beat, even after she blew out the lamp and crawled back into bed. She breathed slowly. She must think of pleasant things to keep Rumkin's face out of her dreams.

She summoned the picture of Eli riding next to her, smiling. She imagined a clever, witty conversation, sentence by sentence. As slumber stole over her, she looked down at her horse and saw that she wore a flowing medieval gown that trailed over her sidesaddle. They rode on into the dream world.

―――――・◦・―――――

Will sat outside with the pistol across his lap, back propped against the cabin door. When his eyelids drooped, he stood and paced back and forth until his head cleared.

His run from Pittsburgh might attract a bounty hunter, if Master Good had posted a reward in newspapers. Master Good himself might even ride after him; Will would put nothing past that man. If someone had followed Will here, then his arrival had increased the risk that someone would discover the Simons.

He vowed silently that he would not be the cause of their recapture. He certainly would not fall asleep. Heaven itself would rise up against the treatment the Simons had received. But in this case, heaven appeared to have chosen Will. There was some design that he could not unravel woven into his meeting with the Millers.

Ann Miller was a beautiful girl. The way she had appeared at her window, hair down and disheveled from sleep, skin pure as a child's—it was pleasant to think on. And when she stepped away with nothing but a thin gown . . .

He pinched himself on the leg, hard, welcoming the pain. The pitch-black sense of sin rolled in again, smoky and familiar. Would he think of Ann as he had thought of Emmie, a naked body to touch? Shame doused his burning senses to dull ash. He should not think of Ann at all. By this time, he was probably engaged to Emmie, if she had accepted his proposal. And he had no reason to believe she would not. She had assured him of her affection with many tender caresses that day at the boarding house . . .

He pinched himself savagely again. It produced the desired effect.

He had to know if Emmie had promised herself to him. In the morning, he would ask Mr. Miller for postage for one letter.

If he addressed a letter to Emmie, in care of the glass factory, he did not know if it would reach her. But it was his only chance, for if he sent anything to Tom, it would be opened by Master Good.

A long night stretched ahead of him. He must not reflect on Emmie, nor his recent encounter with Ann, unless he wanted to greet the morning with legs pinched black-and-blue. Rising, he retained the pistol in one hand and opened the cabin door. The sound of soft breathing assured him that he had not disturbed the Simons. It was the work of a moment to retrieve the small Bible that Mr. Miller had loaned him.

But when he sat down again, he found the moonlight insufficient for reading. And he would not be so foolish as to light a lamp, not when any light would be spotted from a mile away. He laid the Bible down next to him and tried to scrape together in his mind the shreds of the passages his father had read to him so long ago. Will had even memorized some verses as his father taught him his letters.

The Lord is my Shepherd . . . Yea, though I walk through the valley of the shadow of death . . . He prepareth a table for me in the presence of mine enemies . . .

That was a good verse, a strong verse.

He prepareth a table for me in the presence of mine enemies . . .

He could say it over and over again to himself and not grow tired of it.

The stars faded and dawn sketched the treetops against the horizon. No further sign of a trespasser had materialized. He rubbed his face to clear the fog away. He would like to wrap himself in that quilt again and rest.

He cracked open the cabin door to find John already standing and dressed.

"A gun?" John asked quietly. "Did something happen last night?"

Will explained.

John's face grew grim. "Then we will both watch tomorrow. But for now, you get some sleep."

Will handed him the pistol, only too glad to comply.

When he awoke, the light coming in the window told him it was already afternoon. Clara was sitting up against her bolster.

"John's making us something to eat." She closed her eyes. She must be very weak still.

Will stood and straightened his twisted shirt. The pistol lay on the floor next to the bed. Mr. Miller might want it back—he did not know. He fetched it and walked out the door. A few yards away, John bent over a frying pan wedged over two stones with a small fire crackling beneath it.

"I must go speak to Mr. Miller." Will glanced at the ham and eggs sizzling in a delicious-smelling heap.

"Have some food first." John spooned some out onto a tin plate and handed Will a fork. "Mr. Miller was here this morning, but he didn't want to wake you."

"Did he see anyone last night?"

"If he did, he didn't say so. He's leaving to preach a funeral, a few hours' ride from here. He wants to talk to you."

Will swallowed his last few bites and headed across the fields.

When the farmhouse came into view, the yard was empty.

"Will." Mr. Miller stood framed in the open door of the barn. "I'm pleased to see you. Did John tell you I must depart for a day?"

"Yes, sir."

"I think it would be best to keep watch again tonight."

"We thought so too."

"I'll give John the shotgun, and you can keep that pistol. I shall charge you with watching over the girls in the house. You'll have to stay outside, but you can build a fire to keep warm. Over there." He pointed to a ring of stones behind the house. "But we don't want anyone to discover the cabin and the Simons. So John will keep the cabin dark for the night."

Mr. Miller disappeared into the barn, but emerged after a minute leading Bayberry, a saddle over his arm. "Most likely you saw a traveler, or even a youngster from one of the neighboring farms. There are a few wild ones about who have been known to roam when they should be abed. Should you see another tonight, call out a warning first."

"Yes, sir. I'm honored by your trust, Mr. Miller." Will stuck his hands in his trouser pockets, feeling useless. "Can I assist you?"

Mr. Miller ground-tied the mare and gently lifted the saddle over her withers, settling it on the pad. "No, I need no help, thank you. But you may assist Ann. She always has a great deal to do when I am gone."

"I'll do anything I can, sir."

"Help her care for the animals, if you would. That would leave her with the cooking and the care of her sisters." Mr. Miller dropped the girth down on the other side and reached under the mare's belly to pull it up to the billet straps.

"What do I feed the animals, sir?"

"Hay for the horses and cows, mostly slop for the pigs. The hay's in the loft. Ann will give you the slop from the kitchen. Perhaps she had better show you where we keep everything."

Will crossed his arms over his chest, ill at ease. Ann might scorn him as she had last night.

"Ann!" Mr. Miller called toward the house. He tested the girth. "I'm about to set off." Bracing his foot in the hanging stirrup, he hoisted himself into the saddle.

The kitchen door opened, and Ann came out in a dark-blue dress, a set of leather saddlebags in her arms. The younger girls came after her but lingered by the stoop, absorbed in some make-believe.

Ann handed the bags up to Mr. Miller. "Here, Father."

He thanked her and adjusted them behind his saddle.

She was pale, with faint shadows under her eyes. "When will you return?" She folded her hands in front of her, but Will noticed her knuckles were white from the pressure of her grip. She was distraught over something.

"Tomorrow afternoon or early evening." Mr. Miller's words were soft. "You'll fare well in my absence. Will is here to help you. You can teach him about the animals, and he'll keep watch tonight."

With a quick motion like a startled bird, she brushed her hair back from her brow. "Very well. Goodbye, Father."

"I will return soon. It's not far." Mr. Miller clucked to Bayberry and she walked away toward the road. "Goodbye, girls." He lifted one hand from the reins and waved. They called back to him in their little fluting voices.

Will watched Bayberry's swishing tail recede down the road.

"Come." Ann's tone was brusque. "I'll explain where we keep everything."

He followed her into the barn. Her trim and graceful carriage was more suited to a ballroom than a floor of packed earth.

"Pull some hay from there." She pointed to the loft.

He edged past her and mounted the ladder. "How much?"

"About three forkfuls, for now."

He picked up the pitchfork, threw down the hay, and climbed back to the floor.

When he stepped to the ground and turned, she was watching him with a bemused expression. Clearly flustered, she bent down and tried to get her small hands around the pile of hay at her feet. A few pieces of hay had floated into her hair.

He touched her elbow. "I will carry it."

Her full, dark lashes lowered for a moment. Then her lips curved—a tentative, tiny smile. "Thank you." He scooped up the hay easily with his longer arms, and she led the way out of the barn.

He liked her smile. He hefted the unwieldy armload, cheered by his body's returning strength. When they reached the cow byre, he threw the hay in to the black cow.

He trailed around the property after her, marking the storage and the cold cellar. He must treat her with respect. This was his new master's daughter—and he was probably already engaged to another.

"You don't have to care for the pigs," she said, a shadow flitting over her brow as she walked past the sty. Its familiar smell wrenched at him.

"I don't mind. Especially if I can wash up after."

Another little smile from her warmed him, and he smiled back with real merriment. Then she glanced away and dusted her skirt off, though it did not appear dusty. That made him smile even more at her unknowing back as she walked ahead of him toward the house. There was no harm in a little teasing.

Emmie, he reminded himself. But he would have to wait until Mr. Miller returned to write his letter. He certainly would never ask Ann for postage. Or perhaps he could write the letter now and post it upon Mr. Miller's return. He could ask Ann for ink and paper. That was a more respectable request.

"I believe that is everything." Ann stopped by the barn. The late afternoon sunlight brought rich and varied tones from her hair, which waved softly down her back and around her shoulders. He had not seen her wear it down before.

Her eyes turned opaque with thought. "I'm never at ease when my father is away." As soon as the words left her lips, she turned her face away as if she would like to take them back.

"I won't fall asleep tonight," he said. "You will be safe."

She nodded without saying more and left him standing there as she walked back to the house, her small shoulders very straight in her tailored dress.

He had left the pistol in the barn. Inside the barn door, he paused to let his vision adjust to the dimness. He picked up the pistol from the shelf where he had laid it, pulled back the hammer with his thumb, then released it gently. If anyone threatened Ann or her little sisters, he would not hesitate.

He must set off in search of firewood. Night would come soon.

Twenty-Seven

ANN'S LAMP GLOWED LONG PAST THE MIDNIGHT HOUR. Her father's absence had catapulted her to nervous wakefulness.

She propped one elbow on her desk and rested her cheek on her hand, absorbed in the Radcliffe novel. Not, perhaps, the wisest choice of reading for one who needed soothing. She had started it once before, but found herself unable to continue upon reading that the heroine, Emily, had lost her mother and was left with only her father. Now, a year later, having steeled herself to try it again, Ann sympathized with Emily so deeply that it was as if she lived inside Emily's skin and walked every step of her travels with her.

But on this page, Emily's father had fallen ill, which made Ann's uneasiness rise until her palms were moist.

Still, the father's words kept her glued to the story.

"One act of beneficence, one act of real usefulness, is worth all the abstract sentiment in the world."

She opened her diary and took her quill from its place on the desk, dipping it in the inkwell and copying the quotation. Through those words, Emily's world rose off the page and mingled with reality. Ann's abstract sentiment had done Will no good in Pittsburgh. But her father's act of benevolence in aiding the Simons had rippled beyond them and somehow, through Providence, had brought Will to their threshold.

Ann must be, like her father, a doer and not just an indulger in sentiment. It was a lesson that smarted as it sank deeper in her; she was not sure why. Perhaps she did not wish to give up all girlish sentiment. Eli understood that. There was still boyishness in his play with words. Would he be a man who acted in benevolence, who made himself useful to others in need? She did not know. He was not lacking in sentiment. But what would he do with his fine poetic feeling?

He still spoke of medical school, but he had delayed his plans two years since he first spoke of it. He told Ann that he had not felt any peace at the thought of going away without her. When he said such things, his intense gaze increased his otherworldly quality and left her stunned that such a man would think so highly of her. She had not dared to hope that he would ever speak to her in that way again.

He could not be far from proposing, and then she would have to decide what to do. It made her head ache. God had turned Eli's heart back to her, as she prayed for so many times. It was proof that the Lord must intend her to marry Eli. But she did not know how she would choose Eli over her sisters, or her sisters over him.

She put her quill away and closed the novel, finally weary. Stifling a yawn, she went to her window and peeped around the shutter she had left ajar.

Will sat in profile against the firelight, his head bent to a book—her father's Bible. She had seen it on a rock beside the fire when she brought Will his supper.

She must feel so close a kinship with the apprentice because of the strange accident of the letters, and because she had seen him sorely abused. That would explain why her heart went out to him and why she had been robbed of her power to speak when he first arrived at their home.

Yet, despite all his suffering, he had still tried to ease her burden today during her chores—to lift heavy things for her, to look after her needs.

When he was near, she did not feel moved to pity, as she once had. Instead, time grew slow and simultaneously wild, as if something unexpected was bound to happen, as if he had something to tell her and she him, but each waited on the other. Perhaps that sense of expectation was only in her imagination, a trick of the mind caused by sharing his mother's letters. In fact, she could now return the letters to his possession permanently. Perhaps doing so would dissolve their unusual secret and remove that oddness she felt in his presence.

She withdrew from the window and went to the loose floorboard over the hole where she kept her diary. Out of habit, she had hidden the letters there upon her return from Pittsburgh. Under the raised board, the little bag nestled against the bare ground. Now that Will sat only yards away instead of in the gloom of Master Good's barn, the letters seemed like a message of promise for his future. Ann pulled out the bag and stood to check her reflection in the glass before she headed outside.

She took her lamp and carried the bag of letters down the dark hallway and through the parlor. When she stepped outside, Will looked up quickly.

Now that his deep-set eyes were fixed on her, the same paralyzing shyness stole over her as on his arrival. Why had she thought it necessary to return these letters in the dark of night, when she would have to speak to him alone? At least the wavering firelight only reached one side of his face, leaving him in dancing shadows, so she did not have to read his expression.

She would keep it swift and practical. She marched up and held out the bag to him, where it dangled like a flag at the end of her stiff arm. "Here. These belong to you."

He took them slowly. "Thank you." If he wondered why she had come out after midnight to deliver them, he kept mercifully silent.

"Good night." She spun around and hurried back inside, cringing at her own awkwardness. Her ears were still tingling when she reached the refuge of her bedroom and closed the door. He would think her a mannerless eccentric.

At least her mortification had driven away some of her worry.

She assured herself twice that the shutter was completely closed before pulling her dress over her head, untying her stays, and stepping out of her petticoat. She hung the garments carefully in her wardrobe and donned her nightgown.

She should not be nervous. Her father thought there was no reason for alarm. And she was not alone; Will was here.

She blew out the lamp and climbed into her bed. She must not think of Will anymore if she wished to forget her foolishness and find any rest tonight.

She hoped the Simons were well at their cabin. Clara had seemed so ill yesterday.

Lord, please heal Clara and guard the Simons. Protect us all from evil men this night. Please help me to know why you have chosen Eli for me, and how I can marry him without leaving my sisters.

And calm my nerves and send me sleep. In your Son's holy name, I ask you these things. Amen.

———◆———

A stick cracked. Will's head jerked up. He could not tell how close or far away it was, though it came from the woods beyond the field.

It could be anything—a deer, a bobcat. But as he gazed at the indistinct trees, the hair rose on his arms.

There. Something moving, a blot of deeper darkness in the moon shadows.

He rose to his feet, gripping the pistol. But he saw and heard nothing more.

He could not stay here. He had to discover whether that was human or animal. He half ran into the field and over the bare furrows in the darkness.

When he reached the trees he paused, assaulted by the memory of his run across Master Good's yard to the woods.

Still no one in sight. He slipped through the grove, skirting knotty bushes, alert for any sign of motion. It must have been an animal. There was nothing to see.

He would go to the cabin and be certain that John was still awake, then get back to the house.

As he arrived on the border of the clearing, he froze. Thumps and thuds sounded from inside the cabin. The door was ajar, revealing faint light from a banked fire. John was nowhere to be seen.

He clutched the pistol and ran.

He kicked the door, throwing it back on its hinges. A man

leaned over the bed, tying Clara's hands. Her eyes were wide and terrified, her mouth stopped with a strip of cloth. John lay sprawled on the floor.

"Stop!" Will cocked the hammer and raised the pistol. The man arrested himself in mid-motion. He turned slowly to Will, hands in the air.

"Now, don't be getting' excited, boy." He wore a beaver hat low on his forehead. "I'm just claimin' some stolen property."

Will darted a glance at John, who was silent and motionless. "Get away from them."

"There ain't nowhere to go."

"Come out here."

The man grabbed something from the bed. Will ducked. A pistol blast deafened him, and the breeze of the shot puffed past his ear. He dodged behind the wall and dropped to the ground.

Complete silence in the vacuum left by the gun's report.

He waited. The bounty hunter would not kill John or Clara—they were good for a reward alive, not dead. But if Will went in there, the man would pick him off like a duck. Will would have to wait him out. He trained his pistol on the door and waited.

A blow to his head. The world spun. Someone from behind. Had he come out the window? A heavy body threw itself on top of him, hands at his throat. Will fought back, grabbing wrists, yanking against a vise-grip. The man was strong. Unable to break his grip, Will drove his knee as hard as he could into the man's midsection. He grunted and his grasp loosened. Will heaved him to the side and pounded at his jaw, but struck only a glancing blow. The man seized Will's hair and yanked his head to the ground, making him twist on his stomach to avoid a broken neck. A knee planted in the small of his back knocked the wind out of him.

"I'll be gone in an hour, boy," the man whispered. "My wagon's just down the road." A cold ring of metal touched Will's temple. He stiffened. *Lord, make it quick.*

A solid thud sounded above Will and the weight fell from his back. He rolled over and scrambled to his feet. Ann stood over the supine form of the bounty hunter, a thick log raised in both hands like a club. Her nightgown billowed in the slight breeze; her jaw was clenched, her eyes eerily vacant. She raised the log high over the man's head.

"No!" He did not want her to kill the man. She seemed driven by a force beyond her—a blind fury. He hardly recognized her, and she was not listening.

He launched himself up and pushed her. She stumbled sideways and fell, the log dropping from her hands. "Stay there!" he yelled.

The bounty hunter was already on his feet. On the ground the barrel of Will's pistol glinted, halfway between him and the other man.

Will dived for it. His hand just touched the handle as the other man grabbed the barrel. Grappling for it, both of them sprawled on the turf. Their hands became a straining knot of sinew. The man tried to turn the gun back toward Will and break his grip. Will's hands were slipping; the man rose to one knee, forcing Will on his back.

He had only one choice. Every muscle taxed to its limit, he moved his index finger to the trigger and pulled.

An ear-splitting boom. The impact of the shot spun the man half-around and threw him on his side a few yards away.

He staggered to his feet, clutching his bicep, his face slack with shock. Then he ran for the trees, hitching as he kept one hand to his wounded arm.

Will jumped up and ran after him. The man moved with surprising speed, crashing ahead through the brush. Will had to follow by sound alone, as the darkness pressed in and made every step a leap of faith. Something caught his foot; he went down like a felled tree, knocking the wind out of himself. When he scrambled up again, the sounds of the man were faint. He would not be able to catch him now.

Crestfallen, he retraced his steps to the cabin with more care. He hoped he had not hurt Ann when he pushed her; worry quickened his pace as he emerged into the clearing.

She was sitting up where she had fallen, her nightdress a pale pool against the black ground. As he approached, she lifted her head, tears streaking her face.

He hung his head. "Forgive me."

"No, you were right to stop me." She was as pale as her gown, her hair tangled. "I would have killed him."

"Still, I should never—"

"It was Rumkin. He tried to kill me once." Her face was stricken under its tear streaks. She blinked and then rubbed her eyes with the heels of her hands. "He escaped?" she asked.

"Yes."

She cast her eyes down, her white face tense.

"He won't be back tonight, not with a shot to the arm." Will stood. "I must see to John and Clara. I'll return shortly."

Upon entering the cabin, he found to his relief that Clara was sitting up in bed, untied. John perched next to her, his feet braced on the floor as he bent and rubbed the back of his head.

"Just a nasty bump." John spoke more slowly than usual, but seemed otherwise recovered. "I'm sorry. He must have snuck up quieter than a mouse and hit me with his pistol. I didn't sleep on the watch."

"At least you and Clara are safe for now."

"Praise God." John took Will's hand in both of his rough palms and shook it. "And thank you, brother."

"You have nothing to thank me for. He got away."

John's brow creased under its cross-shaped brand, but he pressed Will's hand once more before releasing it. "Still. If you hadn't come running, we'd be trussed up like turkeys in the back of a wagon."

"That's for sure," Clara said from where she lay on the bed.

Will glanced away and saw the shotgun standing in the corner. He retrieved it, feeling the reassuring weight of the stock. "We should all go to the main house, John, for the rest of the evening. Just to be cautious. You and I can sit by the fire outside."

"All right. And Clara can stay in the sitting room there?"

Will nodded.

The quilt lay on the floor by the hearth. Will picked it up and walked out of the cabin. A few feet away, Ann stood shivering, her arms wrapped around her blowing gown. "Here you are." He wrapped the quilt around her shoulders. "We will all go back to the house together."

Her lower lip trembled, but she swallowed and whispered, "Thank you."

She needed comfort. He knew he should not, but he put his arm around her shoulders.

To his amazement, she bowed her head and leaned in to his shoulder like a little girl. Her warm sweet smell rose up, making him want to pull her close and embrace her. He forced himself to stay very still. Then John came out of the cabin, and she jerked away.

"Miss Miller, are you all right?" John asked. The pistol was thrust through his belt and he supported Clara, who had mustered enough strength to walk.

"I'm well, John." Ann's voice was tight. "Let's go back. I woke at the sound of the pistol shot. If the girls woke too, they must be frantic."

John murmured to Clara. "Keep good hold of me." He turned to Ann again. "Come on, Miss. We'll be there in no time."

They all set off across the clearing, Will in the rear with the shotgun.

The men did not enter the house when they arrived. Ann took Clara's arm and helped her over the threshold. She murmured a good night and closed the front door behind them.

For the few hours of darkness that remained, John and Will sat by the fire. Every now and then, one would stoke the fire with the poker or add another log.

"Why don't you get some rest?" John asked at one point. "I can watch."

But after the fight, all Will's senses remained alert. "No, I cannot sleep. You should sleep instead."

John shook his head.

So they stayed there, backs propped to big logs.

"When Mr. Miller returns tomorrow, we will ask him what to do next," Will said.

"In case Rumkin comes back?"

"Yes."

John sighed. The silence was heavy, but after a few minutes

it became more meditative. John gazed at the fire, as if other sights painted the canvas of his memory.

The log on the fire cracked and sparked. Will's eyes drifted to the closed shutter of Ann's bedroom window.

He tried to conjure up Emmie's face to feel what he should feel for her.

But Ann's warm fragrance lingered and returned, all night long.

Twenty-Eight

SOMEONE WAS RIDING TOWARD THE HOUSE. IN THE afternoon light, Ann could see that his horse was a bay. Her father. She sighed and the tightness in her chest eased for the first time since he had left. But she would have to tell him about Rumkin. Would she tell her father about her own part in the attack?

Two hours earlier, Will had escorted the Simons back to the cabin, leaving her to keep a lookout with the shotgun.

"Even if Rumkin were able to come back—and he will not, with a bullet in his arm—," he had said, "he would not seek you out here. He would come to the cabin."

Though she knew it was true, since Will's departure she had been hard-pressed to hide her anxious watchfulness from the girls. She had brought a bucket of potatoes out and peeled them, cleaned the barn, fed the animals, and done any other chore that would keep her outside where she could see. And while she watched the road, one disbelieving thought rippled through her mind: *I would have killed him.* The same savagery that so horrified her in Allan Burbridge had crept into her own soul, so she would have beaten a man to death. She was worse than a beast, to witness a crime against heaven in the murder of Mr. Holmes and still be prepared to do the same.

The horse and rider drew nearer. But the man in the saddle was not her father—he was too tall and lean. When he doffed his hat to her from twenty yards away, blond hair shone in the sunlight.

It was Eli. Standing on the stoop, Ann clutched the kitchen door with one hand and touched the other to her forehead. She had completely forgotten about her plans to ride with Eli this afternoon.

He rode up, oblivious to her sinking heart, his eyes bright.

"Good afternoon!" he said. A relaxed and expert horseman, he held his hat easily across the pommel and reined in his bay gelding with one hand. He scrutinized her attire with evident surprise. "Are you . . . dressed for riding?"

"I must ask your pardon, Eli." She was sure she did not look presentable, having slept very little after the struggle. "I cannot go with you after all."

His smile disappeared. "Is something amiss? Have I offended?"

"No, no. I am so very sorry. I cannot discuss it." She pasted a smile to her lips.

He tilted his head, his blue eyes piercing. "I hope you will tell me if something is the matter. I will be glad to help."

"Really, everything is fine."

But everything was growing less fine by the moment, for across the field on the other side of Eli's horse, Will was walking quickly toward them. This would only complicate the matter. She wished he would turn around and go away.

"Where is your father?" Eli asked, still unaware of Will's approach.

"He should have been home by now." Distracted, Ann tried to keep her attention on Eli.

"Are you worried on his account?"

Will was only a few paces away. Eli's horse must have caught sight of him, for it spooked forward a few steps. Eli regained his balance quickly, his eyebrows shooting up as he noticed Will.

"And who is this?" he asked Ann without taking his eyes off Will. The apprentice's shirt was streaked with dirt and his hair tousled from his struggle the night before, in sharp contrast to Eli's impeccable white collar and navy coat.

"Perhaps I should ask who you are, as you are on the Millers' property." Will's face was drawn with fatigue, but he appeared taller and more substantial than she expected, even though he had to squint up at Eli on his horse.

"Oh, let me explain—" She had to save this situation. Will's brows were knit together and Eli's face as cold as marble. "Eli, this is Will Hanby, my father's new apprentice."

"I see." Eli gazed down at Will and turned back to her as if he did not see at all, his perfect eyebrows drawn into a flat line. "Is he staying here?" A faint dryness edged his question.

"Of course not," Will said. "I'm sleeping in the barn." A muscle twitched in his cheek, but otherwise he remained motionless.

"Ah." Eli sat equally still on his horse, matching Will's stare with the hauteur of a French nobleman dismissing a grubby revolutionary.

Trotting hoofbeats thudded down the road. Grateful for any distraction, she turned to look. This time it really was her father. Bayberry's trot accelerated to a canter as he closed the distance between them. But when he drew near, his expression visibly relaxed, and he slowed Bayberry to a walk again.

He guided the mare next to Eli's gelding and halted.

"Good afternoon, Mr. Bowen. You've met my apprentice, Will?" He looked from one young man to the other. Ann hoped that was not amusement that flickered across his face. She would be irked if her father found this situation comic.

She hurried to answer before Eli or Will could say anything further. "I am a featherbrain, Father. I was to ride with Eli today, but it completely slipped my mind. Now something has interfered with that plan." Her voice dwindled to awkward silence. No further explanation could be made in Eli's presence.

"Mr. Miller, I must speak with you," Will said. "It's a matter of some urgency."

Her father dismounted. "Pardon us, Mr. Bowen," he said, nodding to Eli. He took the reins over Bayberry's head and led her toward the barn. Will followed.

She marveled at their silent complicity. Consumed with his mission, Will seemed more a partner than an apprentice as the two men strode through the yard and went into the barn together.

But they had left her to manage Eli.

"It seems quite a melodrama is taking place at the Miller home," he said.

"Yes." She approached his horse and rested her hand on the bay's neck. "Something unusual has happened, but I'm not at liberty to discuss it. Please forgive me."

"I could never resist a plea like that." His face softened into a more familiar half smile, but it faded. "You didn't tell me your father had taken an apprentice."

"It was all very sudden. He only arrived two days ago."

"And he was already acquainted with your family? A cousin, perhaps? He seemed to believe he had the right to interrogate me."

"He's not a blood relation, but my father worked with him previously in Pittsburgh."

"A little rough around the edges, isn't he?"

"Yes." She did not wish to discuss Will with Eli, so she changed the subject. "May I accompany you down the road on your way back? I'm truly ashamed of my forgetfulness."

His expression lifted. "I would be delighted to have your company. But I won't ride while a lady walks." He dismounted smoothly to stand next to her. "So let us walk side by side."

He led his horse and they ambled down the road together.

"Perhaps you will come to tea soon with my mother and father. They have asked me several times if you will join us."

That made her nervous. Mrs. Bowen was quite the formidable townswoman: tall and fair-haired, like all the Bowens, and well known to be possessive of Eli and his brothers. Ann was certain Eli had never told his mother of his first impulsive proposal. But now that his courtship was public, Mrs. Bowen undoubtedly wished to investigate.

"I would be happy to visit your family."

Her agreement seemed to put him in good spirits, and he asked her about her reading. When they finished a light-hearted debate on the merits of Mrs. Radcliffe—she pro, he con—they were a good half mile from the house.

"I had better go back," Ann said.

Their conversation had been a pleasant diversion, but Rumkin rushed back into her mind with unpleasant force. What would her father advise them to do? They did not have much time.

Eli stopped his gelding in the road, then took her hand.

"I'll consult my mother about the best day for a teatime visit." He stroked the back of her hand lightly with his thumb.

With a quiet goodbye, they parted and he mounted again. As he rode off, he tipped his hat with the air of roguish artifice that always made her giggle.

As she walked back up the road, she had time to reflect on his invitation. If the Bowens wished to meet with her, they must be willing to consider her as a potential bride for their son. Assuming she passed muster, a proposal might not be far off. She sighed. She could not think any further on that today. One dilemma at a time.

⸺ ● ⸺

"Rumkin was here?" Mr. Miller asked. He stopped in his tracks just inside the front door of the barn.

"He came to the cabin. He tried to take John and Clara, but I shot him in the arm, and he ran off." Will made his explanation as matter-of-fact as he could.

Mr. Miller's tanned face turned grayish, then reddened. He turned away and hung his hat on the hook with slow deliberation.

Will had never seen the saddler like this. "Do you think he will return?"

"Not until he recovers, or retains an accomplice. That will take some time."

"What are we to do if he does?"

Mr. Miller did not respond for a minute. He paced over to the window, then back. "We'll have to get John and Clara safely north. He will not return if he discovers they are no longer here.

And he mustn't ever come back, not if we wish to preserve Ann's peace of mind."

Will remembered Ann's tear-streaked face of the previous night, her reference to Rumkin's attempt to kill her. He dared not ask what circumstances had led to that attempt, or why a young lady would lose her temper so completely as to rush to the brink of murder. Better not to know, or he might face the same temptation. For now, he must concentrate on the task at hand. "Clara is still unwell. How will she travel?" he asked.

"I know two families who may be willing to help them go north. They live near Blendon Township, about four days drive northwest." Mr. Miller removed his coat. "The Lawrences, or else the Westerfields. The Westerfields own a good bit of land out there, but in this case, I'd go to the Lawrences first."

"You will escort the Simons?" Will asked. "Perhaps I should go with them instead, so you can stay with Ann. She is very unsettled."

"I believe you and I will both need to escort the Simons." Mr. Miller rubbed the back of his neck as if to massage away saddle-stiffness. "It would be too great a risk for one of us alone with the Simons, in a wagon too slow to outrun pursuit."

"Pursuit from Rumkin?"

"No. From outlaws and robbers along Zane's Trace, and even more on the Lancaster Road."

"But what will Ann do?"

"I will send her to the Sumners with her sisters until we return. That will remove them from any danger and ease her mind."

Will hesitated. He would follow his new master anywhere, especially in this cause, but one more doubt remained. "What if Rumkin calls the law on us?"

"Rumkin won't want anything to do with the law. He's too close to the noose himself."

"Yes, sir." He did not know quite what Mr. Miller meant by that, but he must trust his master's decision.

"On our way out of Rushville," Mr. Miller said, "I will not conceal John and Clara. Rumkin will be certain to hear that they have left town. I don't think he will be able to pursue us anytime soon, given his injury."

So Will would travel with Mr. Miller for at least a week. He anticipated the adventure and the chance to begin serving others, as he had vowed to heaven. But he also felt a trace of chagrin that he would not see Ann for some time. And that blond milksop, Eli, would certainly be very attentive to her.

He had no business entertaining such thoughts. He had better write that letter and send it to Emmie.

"Mr. Miller . . ."

"Yes?"

Will dropped his eyes. He did not like to ask directly for help. "I need to write a letter."

"Of course. There's paper in my desk. When you are finished, give me the letter, and I'll post it at Sumner's store on our way out of town."

"Thank you, sir."

The front door burst open.

"Father!" Mabel ran through the doorway and jumped to embrace Mr. Miller. He circled her with one arm, his usual air of reserve softening for a moment. Susan entered more sedately and untied her bonnet strings.

"Girls, have you been behaving yourselves?" Mr. Miller asked.

"Yes," Mabel chirped.

Susan gave her a skeptical look. "We went to see Clara at the cabin," she told her father. "She seems better. I made her some broth."

"Good girl. Now I need you to pack some food for the Simons. They will be leaving today. We'll need traveling food like jerky."

"I thought Clara was too ill to travel," Susan said.

"She isn't well enough to walk, but I'm revising our plan. Will and I will take them by wagon northward. So, Mabel, I also need you to go to the barn and fill one of the big saddlebags with corn for the mules."

"Don't worry, Father. We'll take good care of everything while you're away." Susan put on a very adult expression of dutifulness.

"You will not be here. You girls will go with Ann to the Sumners. I'm sure two of the Murdoch boys will be pleased to earn some wages by caring for the farm again for a week."

"We'll be in town for a week?" Mabel said. "I can't wait to see Hattie!"

Susan appeared equally excited as she opened the pantry and began rummaging through the shelves, pulling out items. Mabel poured out a stream of chatter advising Susan what she should or should not pack.

"Mabel, the corn," Mr. Miller said.

She scurried out the door, loose hair flying every which way.

Mr. Miller beckoned Will out the open front door and spoke in a low voice as Mabel ran across the yard out of earshot. "They don't know about Rumkin, do they?"

"No, sir."

"Good. Now if you would please go tell the Simons about

our plans, I'll prepare the wagon. We'll get a good night's sleep and leave tomorrow morning."

As Will crossed the yard to the fields, he saw Ann's slight blue-clad figure twenty yards down the road. She was headed toward him.

He wanted to wait for her, but that might not be wise. She would be shy after the events of the previous night. Feeling awkward himself, he lifted one hand to acknowledge her and kept walking.

To his surprise, she waved at him and smiled. He would do a great deal to see her smile at him so again. A great deal.

And that was why it would be wise for him to leave town for a while.

Twenty-Nine

SETTING OFF IN A PARTY OF SEVEN PEOPLE MADE THE two miles to Main Street feel like a pilgrimage. Will walked after the wagon as it squelched through a thin layer of April mud and gravel. Mr. Miller drove the mules while Susan and Mabel sat just behind him in the wagon bed. Separated from the girls by a pile of hay, Clara and John sat against the tailgate.

In the clouded gray light of the morning, the girls' silky dresses contrasted with the homespun clothes of the Simons, and even more so with the coarse ropes binding the couple's wrists. Will hated to see John and Clara bound, even though he knew it was all a sham and Mr. Miller had tied the ropes too loosely to hold them.

He averted his eyes from the disturbing sight. Rushville's center was small, consisting of only ten or twelve buildings clustered along the narrow street. Will read each sign as he trudged past: a doctor, a blacksmith, and a dry goods store. The only brick building had a beautifully lettered sign proclaiming it the Dodson Hotel.

The mules' heads bobbed and their strong legs moved like pistons, flinging up soupy scree.

"Whoa." Mr. Miller set his shoulders back and reined them to a stop.

They had arrived at the general store where Will had first asked for directions. It seemed an age ago.

"May we go in, Father?" Susan asked from her perch in the back of the wagon.

"Wait for Ann, please." Mr. Miller jumped down to the street and tethered the horses to the hitching post. As he finished his knot, Ann rode up behind them on Bayberry, her blue skirt draped in a graceful arc down the mare's side.

Mr. Miller walked up beside her stirrup. "Hold Bayberry's head, if you would," he said to Will.

Will approached and took hold of the leathery straps under the mare's chin. He wasn't sure he had ever seen a woman dismount from a sidesaddle, but it must be a complicated operation. He turned discreetly away, looking at the storefront. In the dim reflection of the store window, he saw Mr. Miller brace Ann by the hand while she extricated herself from the saddle horns, which involved much rearranging of the skirt. Finally, Ann turned sideways on the mare's back and slipped down as if sliding down a mountain into her father's steadying arms.

Now he could look at Ann without the risk of seeing something he ought not. Though he had already seen her in her nightdress. His face flushed hot as he pictured filmy cotton in place of the elaborate embroidery twining down the back of her riding coat.

As Mr. Miller started back toward the wagon, Ann paused beside the mare and looked directly over her right shoulder at Will. He was sure she wanted to say something, but she only met his gaze silently. Her brown eyes were large and fringed with beautiful dark lashes, her skin so smooth and pure she reminded him of a cameo. No, not a cameo, cold and perfect, but instead warm—he had held her in his arms and felt her breath on his neck. Almost undone by that thought, he could not think of anything to say. After a long moment she broke their mutual gaze and walked after her father. Will patted Bayberry's neck while his scattered reason reassembled itself.

In the wagon Mabel gathered her skirts, then hopped over the side, briefly revealing her lacy petticoat. That earned her a soft scold from Susan, who waited demurely for her father to assist her. When they were both on the ground, Ann took their hands and headed for the store. The Simons remained sitting—Clara leaning her head on John's shoulder. John sat very still in his bonds, his eyes following the others in their activities.

"Will, watch them while I go in with the girls." Mr. Miller's businesslike tone kept up the charade. He had said that, until they reached Lancaster, the safest course was to pretend that he and Will were taking John and Clara to the river to send them back to captivity.

"Mr. Miller." Will found the folded parchment letter in his pocket and extended it to the saddler. He took it with a nod, then followed his daughters under the porch and through the door of Sumner's.

Will held the mare and wished they would hurry. Once they left Rushville and headed down Zane's Trace, he and Mr. Miller could at least speak to John and Clara in a normal fashion.

Soon Mr. Miller came out of the store with a quiet, burly man whom he introduced as Mr. Sumner. The man took Bayberry's reins from Will; the mare would be staying with the girls, boarded in the Sumners' barn.

Mr. Sumner glanced at the bound wrists of the Simons as he led the mare away. What had Mr. Miller told him? The truth, or the false story?

"Come on, Will." Mr. Miller climbed up to his seat, and Will hoisted himself into the wagon bed. With a cluck to the mules and a slap of the reins, the saddler drove down Main Street and out of town.

Once they were out on Zane's Trace and away from prying eyes, Will relaxed his guard. He might as well take what pleasure he could in the journey, thanking Providence that he was alive and free in the countryside, for today, at least.

Though it was cloudy, it was not too cold. The mules trotted along, up and down gentle slopes that did not tax them too greatly in their harness. They would make good time, if the road stayed this fair and broad the whole way.

The musty smell of late winter had blown away, and the air quickened with the promise of new life. The bare branches of the trees were no longer gray, but had reddened or greened to prepare the way for what was to come. Little leaf-knobs sprouted on twigs, and yellow catkins hung bright against the creamy bark of the birches. It was that moment of early spring like the pause when a fiddler has lifted his bow and holds it over the strings, ready to call forth the music.

"A penny for your thoughts," Mr. Miller said over his shoulder.

"None worth mentioning, sir."

"Would you like to learn to drive the mules?"

"Yes, sir."

"Then I'll teach you when we're a little farther along the road." He twisted a little farther in his seat. "John, how are you faring?"

"Fine, sir." John seemed to be contemplating the trees as well. His face was peaceful. Will did not know how a man could be hunted like a beast and forced to masquerade as a captive, yet still preserve such calm in his soul. Clara sat with equal composure at his side, looking rested, her eyes alert. Her bound hand was clasped in one of John's bigger hands.

"We will stop in Lancaster tonight," Mr. Miller said to them. "It's a town on my circuit, and I know the people well. We can depend on one of the brothers there to shelter us and help us with provisions."

"Is he an abolitionist?" John asked.

"We all are," Mr. Miller said.

That intrigued Will. He leaned forward. "If you don't mind my asking, sir, who's 'we'?"

"The United Brethren."

"A church?"

"Yes. Well—a group of like-minded people. I suppose you could call us a church, though most of us don't meet in church buildings."

"And they pay you to preach to them?"

"'Pay' is a strong word." Mr. Miller smiled. "But I started riding the circuit unpaid, and so anything they choose to give me is a gift beyond my expectations."

"Is that why you aren't a full-time preacher?" Will's parents had been Methodists; he knew the Methodists had full-time circuit riders. He vaguely recalled a circuit preacher who used to visit his family in Beallsville.

"The United Brethren are an upstart group—we only formed a few decades ago. So all our circuit preachers ride out of sheer love of spreading the gospel. We must support our families with other work. Most are farmers."

"How do they choose them? The preachers, I mean."

"We choose ourselves. Thus the quality of preaching varies widely." Mr. Miller chuckled.

"I never heard of these United Brethren before we ran away," Clara said. "But now we've met a few, on the road with Mr. Washington. And what foreign talk are they saying to each other, Mr. Samuel? I heard them in the kitchen when we were at one house."

Mr. Miller swiveled around. "German." He turned his attention back to the mules. "They started as a German-speaking group, but now they're beginning to prefer English. That's easier for me, as my German is not what it once was."

"You speak German?" Will said in wonder.

"Ja voll." Mr. Miller gave Will a humorous glance with a raised eyebrow. "My family name was not Miller, originally. When my grandfather first came to Pennsylvania, we were the Muellers."

Will knew a handful of words in German, because Pennsylvania was full of German emigrants who said *wilkommen* and *ja*. But he had never even suspected Mr. Miller might be German. Will's own grandparents had been English, and faced with an English name like Miller, well, he had drawn the wrong conclusion.

"That's how I learned my craft," Mr. Miller said. "Germans have always made good saddles. My father taught me as his father before him."

"Was your father one of the United Brethren?" Will asked.

"No, he was Reformed."

Will did not know what that meant, but he did not want to stop Mr. Miller's story.

"I heard a man named William Otterbein preach when I was a young man. He spoke of a personal faith, an indwelling of the Lord in one's life. I had not known that idea before. That day, it seemed to me that I had found true faith. Faith with the power to transform." Mr. Miller's eyes clouded as if he saw something Will did not, leaving Will as awed as he had been when he first saw that gaze in Master Good's barn.

Indwelling. Will thought of the strange presence he had felt in the cabin the night before last as he stared into the fire. *Yes, I believe that.*

A flicker of motion in the distance drew Will's attention to the road ahead. Mr. Miller watched too, falling silent.

"Well," the saddler said at last, as the moving dots on the road ahead resolved into a couple of mounted men. "It seems our first encounter is imminent. Act as naturally as you can. Let's talk of farming for a space, until they pass."

"Perhaps you can tell me how you plow and what you will be planting this spring."

"Excellent. To begin with, we'll allow the farthest field to lie fallow." Mr. Miller went on in more detail, though Will had difficulty keeping his mind on the conversation. He forced himself to pay attention so he could respond.

The horses drew nearer: forty yards, thirty. The two men wore buckskin and weathered hats, their long beards ropy like the manes of wild horses.

"Hullo!" Mr. Miller called, lifting a hand.

They lifted their hands in return. Friendly enough, thus far.

Will lowered his elbow so it touched the butt of the pistol at his belt. They had four pistols now, including the ones the bounty hunter had left behind. Mr. Miller wore one at his waist and one under his coat. John had the fourth hidden in the hay beneath him.

The men were abreast of them. Will's palms were clammy. He tried to appear casual as Mr. Miller pulled the wagon to a stop. "On your way east, brothers?"

"Yes, indeedy," the taller of the two said. His voice sounded cheerful, but he did not smile. The shorter man stared at them hard. Will thought his eyes lingered on the visible pistols.

"We're headed to the city to take these slaves down to the river." Mr. Miller said it jovially. It shocked Will to hear him speak that way.

"Runaways?" The taller one peered at them.

"The worst kind," Mr. Miller said. "Dumb enough to do it twice." His bark of laughter was mirthless, its strangeness making Will's skin crawl.

"Ugly as sin too." The short man guffawed.

Will strove to keep his face blank.

"Well, we'd best be getting on," the tall man said. He spurred his horse forward; it tossed its head and the whites of its eyes flashed. The short man followed.

"So the corn will go in around mid-May . . ." Mr. Miller continued loudly just where he had left off. He clucked to the mules and the wagon lurched forward again.

"Ever planted corn, son?"

"No, sir."

"Well, you'll learn. It doesn't take a great deal of know-how.

The plowing, on the other hand, takes a bit of practice. If you plow too quickly . . ." Mr. Miller went on for a good ten minutes, though Will did not absorb a word of what he was saying. Eventually, the men topped the hill on the horizon behind them and disappeared.

Will exchanged relieved glances with John and Clara. He saw John take Clara's hand again. He must have released it when the men rode by. Probably wise.

Will turned back to Mr. Miller. "They're gone, sir."

Mr. Miller stopped his monologue. "Then I no longer have to weary your ears." He smiled. "Farming is best learned on the farm, not on the road. But it provides a great deal of fodder for conversation, when necessary."

"They didn't question the story."

"Most men we meet probably won't, if I play the ignorant villain well enough." A look of disgust passed over the saddler's face. "And they'll leave us alone if we have pistols in plain sight. Robbers prefer to attack unarmed fools, or men riding alone."

"Do you think those men were robbers, Mr. Samuel?" Clara asked.

"We'll never know. And that's the way we should keep it."

"Amen," John said.

The wagon rolled onward.

Birds flitted through the still-transparent treetops. As the sun rose higher in the sky, Will spied numerous squirrels, even some wild turkeys through the tree trunks a few yards from the road. A hedgehog trundled along in the tall grass of the brake; Will remembered the one he had kept as a pet, at the Quaker farmer's house long ago. He had liked its quivering nose and the metallic feel of its thick mat of spines.

More travelers approached and passed by them: a few other wagons, a coach, riders. The worst were the men on horseback who overtook them from behind, usually at a canter. Will kept his fingers poised near the handle of the pistol whenever he heard the tattoo of hoofbeats.

They had to pause every so often to give the mules some water.

"Not too much," Mr. Miller warned. "Or they'll colic."

Will took his turn driving and learned "Gee" and "Haw," though Mr. Miller said those commands were more useful for plowing than for ordinary driving.

By around noon the woods thinned out and fields appeared. Farm houses squatted in the middle of stubbly rectangles of earth.

"Almost there." Mr. Miller turned around in his seat. "Just keep up our charade until I give the word. We have friends ahead, but there's no telling who else might be watching."

The wagon rolled up another small hill, the mules blowing harder as they leaned into their yoke, their ears twitching back at the sound of their master's chirrup of encouragement.

As the wagon crested the hill, a red brick building came into view.

In its two-story facade, eight large windows framed a white door recessed in the brick. A large yellow sign hung above the portico, swinging in the spring breeze. It read "Shupp's Tavern" in black thick-painted letters. A double chimney towered at each end of the oak-shingled roof.

Instead of driving up to the front door, Mr. Miller laid the reins across the mules' backs, calling "Gee!" The wagon veered right down the gravel path beside the inn.

Will sat alert, trying to see in every direction at once. But the stable yard they entered was empty, and the inn was quiet.

Mr. Miller pulled up the wagon; the mules snorted and lowered their heads.

The back door of the inn opened and a big man ambled out, one hand raised in greeting. Dark hair sprang over his brow; his face was ruddy and full.

"Mueller! Welcome, brother." His deep voice carried across to them like a battlefield drum. "I was not expecting you, but my heart is glad to see you!" The man's speech had a foreign rhythm, musical to Will's ears.

"I have some prisoners with me," Mr. Miller said. "Do you have guests at the tavern?"

The big man stopped in mid-stride and took in the scarred faces of the Simons. "Not yet. They will come at twilight."

"Good." Mr. Miller handed the reins of the wagon to Will, who climbed up in the driver's seat as Mr. Miller jumped down and shook the big man's hand.

Will heard them exchanging a few low words in German. Then Mr. Miller walked to the back of the wagon, bringing his friend with him and addressing Will and the Simons together. "This is Mr. Friedrich Shupp. Friedrich, I must introduce you to my friends, John and Clara Simon. You may remove your bonds now." As John wriggled his hands out of the loose ropes and helped Clara with hers, Mr. Miller raised a hand in Will's direction. "This is my apprentice, Will."

Mr. Shupp gave Will an appraising look, then walked over and shook John's newly freed hand. He steadied Clara as she climbed shakily out of the wagon. "You are unwell, sister?"

"Yes, sir, but I'm getting better."

"Come in and have a cup of tea with my wife." He waved in the direction of the inn.

John and Clara walked toward the house hand in hand. Mr. Shupp clapped Mr. Miller on the shoulder.

"Let's go in and talk," he said in a low voice. "Are you headed for Blendon Township?"

How did the man know? Had Mr. Miller made this journey before?

"We are," Mr. Miller said.

"Then I must tell you some news." The man raised his voice again. "But I am the rudest of hosts! Come along, Wilhelm!" He chuckled as he turned to Will. "A good German name. Now come inside and let's get some food into you before any nosy strangers arrive."

"I must put away the mules," Mr. Miller said.

"I'll do it, sir," Will said.

Mr. Shupp spoke up. "No, let my boy do it. He needs the practice. Fritz!"

A rawboned youth shambled out of the dim stable entrance. "*Ja*, Father?" He was tall like Mr. Shupp, but gangly as if he had not yet learned to direct his long limbs properly. "Shall I unhitch them?"

"Yes, son. But keep their straps on, in case our guests should need to leave in a hurry."

Will imagined why that might happen and fervently hoped it would not. The young man led the mules away, bringing the wagon out of sight behind the barn.

When Will followed the older men in through the back door of the inn, he found John and Clara already seated at a long table. A middle-aged woman as dark-haired and fat-cheeked as

Mr. Shupp smiled as she bustled over to Mr. Miller. "So good to see you, Brother Samuel!" Her speech was more heavily accented than her husband's. She took Mr. Miller's hat and coat.

"And you, Greta. This is my apprentice, Will. Will, Mrs. Shupp."

"Good afternoon, Will." She helped him out of his coat. He did not think anyone had done that for him since he last saw his mother. He saw her face in his mind, as she had knelt before him helping him pull his arms from his small sleeves. He ducked his head, hoping Mrs. Shupp would not notice his sudden emotion.

But she was too busy to see, and she whirled away to hang their coats on the end of a long row of hooks on the wall. Then she whisked her portly apron-covered form over to the rough-hewn table, where a breadbox sat along with some cutlery and a salt shaker. Will and Mr. Miller sat down with the Simons. In a trice, she had served them all thick slices of bread, plunking down a small crock of sweet butter between them. John ate with relish, Clara with the impaired appetite of the convalescent. Soon the kettle steamed on the hearth, and Mrs. Shupp brought over a mug for each of them. "Spicewood tea." She said it with pleasure as she set them on the long, beveled planks of the tabletop.

Aptly named, Will discovered, as an herbal smell rose warm in his face. The tea was sweet, with a bracing tart aftertaste like rhubarb.

As they ate, Mrs. Shupp kept the conversation light, about the weather and their journey.

"And where are Frieda and Maria? And Paul?" Mr. Miller asked.

"They are all at their uncle's house for the afternoon. They have instructions to be back by dusk for their chores," Mrs. Shupp said.

"And Mr. and Mrs. Kruse?"

"She is still a little under the weather, but I know she would love to see you if you can spare the time."

"Perhaps on the return trip."

While they exchanged more news about folk whom Will assumed must be members of the church, Mr. Shupp turned away and squeezed his big shoulders through the door that led to the public parlor. After he disappeared around the corner, Will could see a fire banked low on the hearth and a number of large chairs pulled round. The furniture was as immaculate and new as the inn. The Shupps must host a large number of travelers from Zane's Trace, with all the westward travel these days.

Mr. Shupp came back into the kitchen, a roll of ivory paper in one hand. He seated himself heavily in the chair at the head of the table next to Will.

"I hate to be the bearer of bad tidings," he said. "But you may have more difficulty passing through to Blendon than you might have expected."

"Oh?" Mr. Miller's head lifted and he set down the tea he had been nursing.

"Yes." Mr. Shupp's wide mouth went flat. "You see, I recognized you, Mr. John and Ms. Clara."

He separated one of the pieces of paper from his roll and unfurled it flat upon the table, turning it toward them. Unease stirred in Will as he scanned the crude drawing and read the text:

Stop the Runaway.

RANAWAY from Mrs. Philip Holmes of Nashville,
Tennessee, a negro man named

JOHN,

Formerly owned by the late Mr. Holmes. He is around forty
years old, of a dark-brown complexion. He is marked with a
cross-and-circle brand on the forehead; he is well built and
is about five feet eight inches in height. He may be traveling
in the company of a slave woman with an identical brand
whom he claims as his wife. Anyone taking up this negro
and lodging him in jail or delivering him to his rightful
owner shall be well compensated.

The drawing was a ridiculous caricature with huge lips and white eyes, but the brand stood out on the cartoonish forehead.

"How did you get this?" Mr. Miller's voice had an edge, though Will knew it was not directed at Mr. Shupp.

"You know the bounty hunters are always after me to look at these fugitive notices and tell them if I have spotted any of them. I take them on the excuse that I will watch for runaways, but I keep the notices hidden in my desk." Mr. Shupp set his elbows on the table and interlaced his fingers in concentration. "A man came by with this one about a week ago."

"Did he wear a beaver hat?" Mr. Miller asked.

John, Clara, and Will were all quiet. No one moved.

"I do not recall," Mr. Shupp said. "Greta had taken his hat by the time I met him, and he was gone early in the morning."

Mrs. Shupp paused by the stove. "I cannot remember either. I'm sorry."

Mr. Miller addressed John. "Let us hope it was Rumkin, as we can be fairly sure he will be incapacitated for a few days."

"I think so, Mr. Samuel." John's eyes were worried. "But it still means someone might recognize our brands."

"Then we will cover them. Your hat will be pulled so low as to invite suspicion, perhaps, but better that than instant discovery by someone who has seen the drawing."

"And I'll wear my bonnet." Clara appeared unperturbed, as if her illness had wrapped her in a protective haze.

"It is an additional concern, Friedrich, but not insurmountable." Mr. Miller rubbed his own upper arm. He was probably aching from the hours of driving, though he had said nothing to Will.

Will was relieved to hear a proposed solution. "We only have two more days on the road, isn't that right, Mr. Miller?"

"Yes, son."

"And the Lancaster Road—is it as busy as the Trace?"

"Not quite. But our greatest risk will be when we turn onto the National Road toward Columbus." Mr. Miller's gaze was far away, as if he sorted solutions in his head.

"And there's no other route?"

"Not by wagon. And Clara cannot travel by foot, or even by horseback for any distance." Mr. Miller picked up his tea again. "We will simply have to cover the brand and hope for the best."

Will nodded.

But Mr. Shupp removed his arms from the table and sat up

straighter, a half head taller than any of them. "There is one more concern." He unrolled the second piece of paper.

Will took in a sharp breath. There was his own face, staring back at him, a fair likeness instead of the other foolish sketch of John.

REWARD
RUNAWAY

Absconded on Saturday evening the 28th, WILL HANBY, an apprentice to Master Jacob Good, saddler of Pittsburgh. The said WILL HANBY is eighteen years of age, about five feet ten inches in height, fair complexion, black hair, and a sullen countenance. Whoever will apprehend the said Apprentice and return him to his Master shall receive a substantial Reward on application to the said JACOB GOOD. And whoever harbors the said Apprentice after this public notice will be prosecuted according to the Law.

Will's throat constricted.

"And this came from the same bounty hunter?" Mr. Miller's tone was hopeful.

"No, this was another one. It came while I was out. Greta took it, knowing my wishes."

"I do not remember what he looked like," Greta said from the hearth, where she was stirring a pot of broth that sent a rich chicken smell through the kitchen. "I'm sorry, Brother Samuel."

Mr. Miller sighed. "It's not your fault, Sister."

Will cleared his throat to get his words past the tightness.

"Perhaps it would be better if you went on without me. I will endanger you further."

"Nonsense." Mr. Miller was brusque, and his face creased in tense lines. "We need as many armed men as we can muster, and that includes you."

When the papers were rolled back up, Mr. Miller and Mr. Shupp tried to continue as if nothing were amiss, but Mr. Miller crossed his arms too frequently and more than once paused too long before responding as if his thoughts were elsewhere.

Eventually Mrs. Shupp showed them to a room way up in the garret, where Will and the Simons could sleep on straw ticks on the floor. Mr. Miller would sleep in a more public place, where he could watch the travelers who arrived.

"Until then," he told Will, "I will spend some time visiting my brethren here."

"Yes, sir."

"And we will leave well before dawn, under cover of darkness. So if you and John and Clara can sleep this evening, that would be wise."

"I'll try, sir." But Will knew that would be impossible. The sight of Master Good's name, ugly and stark, had shaken him beyond any chance of rest. Will's time in the air and light could not last. A shadow pursued him and would not relent until it took him back.

Thirty

ELI'S MOTHER REGARDED ANN WITH WINTRY EYES. "We have appreciated the opportunity to converse with you today, Miss Miller." Mrs. Bowen's white-blond hair coiled around her head like a crown. Her husband stood beside her in the foyer, as dour as he had remained through the parlor formalities with the tiny cakes and silver tea set.

Eli opened the door and invited Ann to precede him out.

"Good afternoon," his father said, bringing his total number of words for the teatime to at least ten.

"Good afternoon," Ann replied. The door closed, and Ann let out a pent-up breath into the fading light of the early evening.

It had not been the most comfortable tea she had ever attended.

When she and Eli had progressed a little way down the road, he offered his arm. She took it without comment.

"My parents are not easy to come to know. But they are good people."

"Yes, I'm sure they are." She pitied his subdued manner. He was not to blame for their stiff manners, nor for his mother's pointed questions about Ann's fitness to be a doctor's wife.

"You know I don't plan to settle in Rushville. I will not be tied to my mother's apron strings."

She smiled, but said nothing. The trees stood thick along this part of Main Street, their budding branches intertwined like the arms of dancers. The Bowens' farm lay a mile to the east of the town center, and so it was only a short walk back to the Sumners' home and store.

"I do have to leave for medical school soon," Eli said. "My parents are beginning to think me a malingerer." He grinned and pressed her hand where it lay on his arm.

"If you would not lie on their fainting couch and quote poetry all day long, they might not be so eager for you to leave."

He laughed, sounding relaxed and merry for the first time that evening. "Yes, that is just how I spend my days there. And then I tell them that all my poems are for Miss Miller. They find that especially endearing."

She giggled, glancing sidelong at his profile when she thought he was not looking at her. But he was, and his gaze intensified.

"Do let's be serious for a moment." He gently stopped her in the road. "I have dared to hope that perhaps things have changed between us since I last asked you to marry me. I want to ask you once more."

He pulled her closer to him and tilted his face down toward her, so she looked up at him. Her heart thudded; she wanted those perfectly curved lips to touch hers, but she stood on the balls of her feet as if she could still run away.

"Won't you marry me, Ann? And come with me to Cincinnati? We won't have a great deal for a few years, but we could live with my brother on his farm there until I am a doctor. I have already written to him."

She hesitated. She should explain about her sisters—but then he might offer some compelling argument, might tell her father that she would not marry because of her sisters. And then her father might offer more arguments, or insist that she leave. She did not want anyone else to make this choice, or even to know of it.

"And once I start a practice, you will lack for nothing. Just imagine the life we might lead there. You would have a housemaid, a cook, even a nanny if you wish. Never again would there be an evening when you did not have the time to read. In fact, we would host literary salons right there in our own parlor. Cincinnati is becoming an oasis of culture. I know how to make you happy, my love."

His endearment sent a shiver across her shoulders.

"Doesn't that sound divine?" he asked with a light in his eyes.

"Yes," she said. But there was something not quite right in it. Was that the life she wanted? She stepped back and retained his hand, so as not to seem cold. If only she asked the correct question, she would find some revelation that would allow her to share his easy assurance in the future.

"Would that be enough, Eli? Would you enjoy being a doctor?"

"I would enjoy it because its material advantages would allow me to pursue my passions." He led her with him to walk slowly down the road.

"But will you find rewards in the work itself?"

"A profession is a profession. It must be either medicine or law to make the living I want for my family. And the law is so dry, and it sometimes leads to politics." He made a face.

She laughed. "Is it so terrible to involve yourself in the business of our country?"

"It is worthy work for some, perhaps, but not for me. You and I and others like us inherit another responsibility."

"And what is that?"

"The pursuit of beauty and refinement. Life must not be a dull monotony, and we who are capable of caring for the beautiful things in life must do so, or they will be lost to everyone."

"You make it sound very honorable."

"It is."

"And it also just happens to be pleasurable." She looked at him sidelong, teasing.

"For us, yes. God has suited each of us to our calling, if not always to our livelihood."

"It sounds too ideal to be true. That life could be pleasant and happy at all times, full of leisure and entertainment, and yet we would be fulfilling a high purpose?"

He stepped ahead and pivoted to face her. She could not arrest her step and plowed into his waistcoat. He set gentle hands on her shoulders to keep her close and looked deep in her eyes. "It is true, for me and for you. Not for all. But it is true. As true as my love for you."

His almost-beautiful face so close and intent on her erased all other thought.

"Marry me." He whispered it and bent nearer. His lips touched hers, feathery-light, but then more firmly when she did not protest. He slid his hands around her back and pulled back just enough to murmur again, "Say you will." He kissed her again. She responded, her senses melting into his closeness, the softness of his lips.

Then he stopped, as if mastering himself with an effort. "No, don't say anything." He slid his hands down to her elbows and held her there, still close. "Just consider it from your heart. I will speak to your father when he returns, as I should have two years ago. And I will ask you for an answer in a week."

She nodded. A week's reprieve, to choose between Eli and her sisters. Clearly she could not bring them to stay on his brother's farm in Cincinnati. It would be one or the other, Eli or the girls. She struggled to keep her face from betraying her distress. She must have succeeded, for he smiled again.

"We had better get you to the Sumners. They will be watching my every move in your father's absence."

Normally she would have issued some tart reply, but the tingling still on her lips had made her vague and dreamy.

He offered his arm again and they walked together, as if their closeness had said all that could be said and anything else would be a mere formality. And perhaps it would.

Thirty-One

IT WAS DARK, SO DARK ON THE LANCASTER ROAD. Even Mr. Miller slept, lying in the back of the wagon with John and Clara, while Will drove on. The mules had rested in the daylight hours and were fresh again. They should soon come upon the National Road.

The gibbous moon floated above trees that filtered its light to a faint milky sheen on the road ahead. Will strained his eyes but could make out no details in the formless mass of forest to either side of them. The jingling of the harness and the mules' plodding feet on the dirt echoed in his ears like the din of a whole army. But there was nothing to be done about it. It was jarring only because the night was so silent.

If he thought too long about the posted bills for runaways, he could raise the hair on his own arms. He had done so more than once in the day of travel since they left Mr. Shupp's tavern. So he would not.

Mr. Miller had counseled him yesterday to rest in the power and protection of the Lord. At that, John and Clara had nodded as if they understood something. Their calm did not make any earthly sense, as they were probably not even as strong as Will himself and would fare worse should it come to a physical contest with abductors or robbers. Yet all three of the older folk seemed less anxious than Will.

Because they do not know Master Good as I do.

But he knew that was not true. The peace of the Simons and Mr. Miller was part of the presence that had come to Will in the cabin. He could not feel the presence now. But he could see it in them: in the calm luminosity of Clara's glance at her husband, in the even tones of Mr. Miller and John as they prepared for sleep an hour ago.

He wanted to serve. He had vowed himself to the Lord. Would he also be granted this strength that he saw in the others—the assurance of the presence?

Show yourself to me, Lord. Speak to me.

He was aware of the audacity of his request, but his weariness emboldened him.

Tell me what you wish me to do! I want to be certain, like the others.

In an instant, the night sky became more vast, the vault of heaven opened to limitlessness. Will felt himself miniscule in the sight of something that was everywhere and moving through him, as if he broke apart and mingled with it. His breath came in short, staggered puffs. Who was he, to have asked for an audience with Eternity? At the same time, he felt acceptance such as he had never known, as if these fragments that made him were revealed in all their brokenness and inadequacy . . . and he was fully loved. He would never be alone again.

Tears started to his eyes. He bowed his head and closed his eyelids and the drops leaked out, warm on his cheeks in the cool night air. He blinked and looked up again at the hazy stars ahead, though he knew it did not matter if he looked or not. But he lifted his face and let the tears run down in praise of this Great Being and its love.

Tell me what to do, and I will do it. Anything.

And something came—not exactly a voice, but a rolling in his consciousness that carried him like a wave far out beyond his own comprehension.

Then serve. Follow. You are a stranger. Go where you must go to serve. Break the chains of the captives. I will show you.

The immanence condensed and resolved to a kind of glittering thread inside him, so that he felt himself back in his whole breathing body. He was left with a certainty: *Go where you must go.*

He pondered it. Such a mysterious thought really should not bring him this quiet confidence, and yet he reveled in the last promise: *I will show you.*

He did not understand, but he knew he would, eventually.

A rustling behind him made him look over his shoulder. Mr. Miller was sitting up, watching him with keen interest. Will was abashed.

"Have you been talking to the Lord, son?" Mr. Miller's face was just a blur in the darkness.

"I suppose . . . yes, sir."

"I thought so." The saddler's voice was gentle. "And has he been speaking to you?"

It seemed too personal and precious a thing to share, yet he could not forget that he owed it all to this man who had shown him God in his eyes. He would not refuse him an answer. "Yes, sir."

Mr. Miller did not pursue it, though Will thought he saw him smile.

"Would you like me to drive, son?"

"Yes, sir, if you're not too weary."

Mr. Miller stood up, bracing his legs against the bumps of the wagon. Will handed him the reins and they switched positions.

After a while Will heard Mr. Miller humming under his breath. It was a pleasant sound. There had not been much singing under Master Good. Mr. Miller's song drifted back to him, barely audible.

> *A stranger and a pilgrim I*
> *With thy command, O Lord comply*
> *I go where thou dost send*
> *My high commission I obey*
> *The toils and dangers of the way*
> *Shall all in lasting comforts end . . .*

Now the back of Will's neck prickled, and shivers raced down his arms. This would be how the Lord showed himself, then. Through the words and deeds of others, he would confirm his will. The Lord had not walked away and left the world swimming in its own darkness. He was here at work. He had brought Will to this place and this godly man for his own purpose, and Will had simply to pay attention.

The wondrous calm that fell over him then was like a warm

blanket that lulled him to sleep, his head nodding down toward the hay . . .

Mr. Miller's shout snapped him awake. The wagon lurched and the mules began to canter, then gallop. With sleep-bleared vision, Will saw a dark form on horseback burst through the brush on the side of the road. Will fumbled for his holster, seeing at the edge of his vision that John was scrabbling under the hay for the other pistol.

Mr. Miller was too busy driving the mules as fast as he could, probably faster than was safe on the unpredictable road surface. As Will brought up his pistol, another horseman erupted from the opposite side.

Crack!

The pistol jerked back in Will's hand, the smell of sulfur filling his nostrils. There would not be time to reload; he reached for the holster at Mr. Miller's side and yanked out the gun.

Crack!

On the heels of the ear-splitting sound, John's gun went off too, sending a double boom. At the same time, a flash went off behind them, and a ball whistled close overhead.

One of the horses shied, another reared. Will heard one of the men yelling to the other as they fell back; perhaps he had been hit.

"Blast that no-good apprentice!"

Will's fingers went cold with shock around the pistol handle. Not robbers or slave-catchers. Bounty hunters, for him. He sat down on the floor of the wagon, where John had already thrown himself to pound paper and ball into the mouth of the pistol.

The men receded farther down the road as the wagon continued its pell-mell flight. He saw one of the men drop to the road. The other man's horse was tossing its head and squealing; one of their shots must have hit it. He did not like to wound an innocent animal, but when human lives were in the balance . . .

Mr. Miller leaned forward and urged the mules on at a dead run until they were far from their assailants, then pulled the mules back to a canter. Will followed John's lead and reloaded, but the men did not reappear.

"I cannot run them any more without breaking their wind," Mr. Miller called back to Will. He eased them down to a trot.

Will slid his pistol back into its holster, craning his neck to see back down the road. Still empty.

"They were after me, sir. They said 'the apprentice.'"

Mr. Miller did not turn all the way around, but Will saw his shoulders stiffen in surprise. "You're certain?"

"He did say that, Mr. Samuel," Clara said from the back, where she had dared sit up again.

"Well, highwaymen are highwaymen, whether their prize is gold or flesh." Mr. Miller sounded dismissive, but Will thought he detected concern beneath his nonchalance.

None of them could sleep after that. The Lancaster Road met the National Road, and they turned west as the morning extended fingers of pink light behind them over the trees. John and Will both sat upright, each watching one side of the road with unfailing vigilance.

Even with his eyes glued to the tree line, Will's mind would not remain still.

You said you would show me, Lord. Make it clear to me. I am risking them by my presence here. And if bounty hunters follow me,

I will bring danger to the Millers, even if we deliver the Simons to safety. So where must I go?

Ann's face and figure drifted through his thoughts, her softness, the depth of intelligence in her eyes that Emmie's flat prettiness could never match. But he had a duty to fulfill. And he could never place Ann in jeopardy.

Then, reluctantly, he began to understand.

Thirty-Two

PULL UP HERE, WILL." MR. MILLER INDICATED A place in the road indistinguishable from any other spot in the miles of tree-lined road they had traveled that day. Then he pointed to a tree a few feet back in the woods. "See that arrow?" Now that he pointed it out, the whitewashed triangle high on the trunk of the maple jumped out at Will like a beacon.

"Whoa!" Will called to the mules, drawing back the harness reins between his fingers until he could feel the bits in their mouths on the end of the line. At his gentle pressure, they plodded to a halt. They needed no encouragement to rest; four days of travel had taken their toll.

Mr. Miller turned his head toward John and Clara, who sat in their usual position, backs to the side of the wagon, close enough to touch one another. "We have almost arrived." Mr. Miller clambered over the side of the wagon and dropped to the ground as he spoke. "We will walk through the woods the back way to let Old Lawrence know we're here. His house is that way." He pointed off past the trees in the direction of the arrow.

"Why the back way?" Will asked.

"Well, we could get there by following this road. But

Blendon Tavern is just past the next curve. It's a rough place, and too likely to be busy."

"And full of bounty hunters?" John asked.

"Precisely. Will, you must stay here with the wagon. John and Clara, come sit off here in the trees a way, in case anyone passes."

The spring sunlight was bright this afternoon, lighting every hillock of the road, but the shadow of the trees was more forgiving. John helped Clara out of the wagon, and they hurried into the woods. They seated themselves at the foot of a great black oak, where the massive ripples of its trunk enfolded them like wings. When they were still, Will could hardly tell they were there. So much the better.

Mr. Miller had followed them into the sheltering trees. He turned back to Will, raised one hand, and slipped farther into the woods and out of sight.

It was hard to believe the journey was almost over, at least for the Simons. Freeing the reins, Will climbed out of his seat and walked around to the mules' heads. If anyone should pass, he must pretend to be occupied. He could not just sit in the road like a halfwit. He would act as if he were checking the harness.

Minutes passed. When he glanced into the woods, he could see the outline of their heads against the base of the oak. He peered down the road. Empty. He breathed a prayer of gratitude. They were so close. He felt cold perspiration under his arms and swabbed at it with his shirt, annoyed, trying to keep his eyes on the road.

A rustle in the trees startled him. To his relief, Mr. Miller came into view, picking his way through the undergrowth.

Behind him walked two young men about Will's age. One was fair, the other dark. As they neared, Will saw that the first one had the high color of the Dutch: red in his fair hair, a rosy tint over his pronounced cheekbones. The dark youth was shorter, his square face open and honest, his shoulders powerful.

"Will." Mr. Miller indicated the fairer young man. "This is Peter Westerfield. And his friend is Teddy Lawrence."

The brown-haired one nodded at Will. "Our thanks to you for bringing them so far." He crossed to where Will stood holding one of the mules by the bridle and held out his hand.

Will took it with pleasure. He liked the glint in this young man's eyes; it spoke of a youth familiar with hardship but unbowed by it. There was something about this Teddy Lawrence that made Will want to sit down and talk.

But there was no time. Peter Westerfield came over and shook hands as well, his demeanor more guarded and evaluating than Teddy's.

Mr. Miller spoke up from the shelter of the trees. "Gentlemen, here are our guests, John and Clara Simon."

During the business of greetings, the Simons had walked up behind Mr. Miller. Teddy and Peter introduced themselves and shook hands with the same courtesy they had given Will. He liked them for it.

"Well then," Mr. Miller said, "it appears we have reached our parting." He took off his hat and took John's hand himself. Will noticed that the saddler's chin was suspiciously firm, in the way of men who hide deep feeling. After a few murmured words that Will could not make out, he clapped John on the shoulder and took Clara's hand. Then he turned on his heel and walked back to Will, taking the reins from him to hold the mules.

"Go and wish them Godspeed," he said. Will thought Mr. Miller's eyes glistened, but the saddler turned away to rebuckle the mule's cheek strap.

Will walked over to where the Simons stood.

"Thank you, young man." John extended his hand, but then pulled Will into a clumsy half embrace. His voice thickened with emotion. "Thank you for doing the Lord's work."

"Yes, indeed," Clara said. She patted Will's arm as her husband loosed his grip and stepped back. "Will Hanby, I think you're gonna be a powerful warrior for the Lord someday." She gave him that smile of pure loveliness once more, her weathered face alight. He ducked his head.

When he looked up, they had turned away. Teddy Lawrence had taken Clara's arm, and Peter Westerfield led them back the way they had come through the woods. Their backs receded, Clara's plain skirt bunching as she gathered it to clear the twigs and budding bushes. John helped her from the other side. They were a brave little band of four.

And a cloud went with them by day, and a pillar of fire by night. The voice of Will's father murmured in his memory once more, and he had to rub his eyes hard. He thought his father would be gladdened by the sight of this man and woman walking away to their freedom. Evil men had intended to break their spirits with the seared circle-and-cross in their flesh, but John and Clara wore it as a sign of salvation. Their journey to freedom was the Lord's work. In their upright backs, Will read his future. He would see as many fugitives as he could walk away from him, just like this.

The saddler had already resumed the driving seat. "No time to waste, Will. Let's be getting back."

Will hoisted himself over the wagon side, and Mr. Miller slapped the reins on the mules' backs. "Gee!"

They whirled around and took up a brisk trot, back through the endless lines of trees, over one gentle slope and another.

It was some time before Mr. Miller or Will spoke. The wagon rattled and bumped; the mules sighed. Their silence was almost reverent. Mr. Miller must be as deep in thought about the Simons as Will was himself.

After a while, though, it became a companionable quiet. Since Mr. Miller had asked him about his conversation with heaven, or whatever one might call that singular experience, Will had felt complete ease in his presence. Once a man had seen you weeping before God, there was little left to hide. Mr. Miller seemed to understand and accept whatever had happened to Will as a matter of course. Will could only conclude the saddler had undergone something of the same nature. Perhaps more than once.

As the distance opened between their wagon and Blendon Corners, Will's thoughts returned to their constant fixation. The weight of it was too much for him. He had to tell Mr. Miller.

"Sir?"

"Yes?"

"I've been thinking . . ." He stopped, unsure of how to tell him. "Since the bounty hunters came after me . . ."

"What is it, son?" Mr. Miller seemed alert now, even though Will could only see him in profile.

"I don't think I can stay with you."

Mr. Miller kept his eyes on the mules, transferring the reins to one hand. "And why is that?"

"I will always be a danger to you and your family, sir. As long as Master Good has a legal claim on me, you will be subject to the law. Not to mention any bounty hunters who might come to the farm. I can't allow that to happen."

Mr. Miller leaned back and rubbed his temples with his free hand. "Where will you go?"

"Back to Pittsburgh, sir. I can't run from my old master any longer. If I do not serve out my term, I will never be free of him. After I finish my apprenticeship, I hope you will accept me back in your employ."

"Don't be a fool." Mr. Miller's tone was sharp. "Jacob Good almost killed you even before you ran away. You would not last a week in that household."

"I will have to take my chances."

A deep frown folded lines around Mr. Miller's mouth. "I will not accept this. It would be throwing your life away. Would you have counseled John and Clara to return to their masters?"

"But they had no end to their slavery, sir. If I can just survive until my indenture runs its course—"

"You will not survive!" Mr. Miller's vehemence surprised Will. The saddler was usually so controlled. Now the older man sighed and moderated his tone. "I am sure of it, son."

"But what choice do I have?"

Mr. Miller rubbed the reins between his thumbs and fingers, as if the motion would spur his thought.

"I have a proposition." Mr. Miller looked straight ahead at the mules. "Your labor will be of great value to me over the next three or four years, Will. If you work the farm with me, I will not have to hire any field hands from among my neighbors' sons. You could easily earn out the cost of your apprenticeship to Master Good."

Mr. Miller glanced at him and must have detected his lack of comprehension.

"So I suggest we return to Pittsburgh and offer to compensate your master for the value of your lost labor. I will pay him for you, and you will repay me by your help on the farm."

"You would come with me to Pittsburgh, sir?" Will could not believe the saddler would undertake the journey again.

"I believe it will be necessary. Jacob Good would need to have the money in hand to agree to sign a paper releasing you. And he cannot be trusted if I am not there to watch the proceedings."

"Sir, I am very grateful for your offer. But I can't accept such generosity. You have already—"

"Accept it. I insist. You are correct, I believe, in thinking that you will be a fugitive as long as Jacob Good lives. And that could be two decades. My solution is the only answer."

"I can't let you go to such pain and expense on my behalf." A twinge went through Will at his next thought, and he spoke it without thinking. "You must rue the day you met me."

Mr. Miller turned all the way around, letting the mules pick their way by themselves. His eyebrows lifted as he looked at Will for a long moment. "Not at all, son. Not at all."

Will shifted sideways to look at the trees, unsettled by a churning mass of feeling he could not sort out. For years, no one had cared for him as Mr. Miller seemed to. He did not deserve it; it humbled him.

"Consider this, son. I am your new master, by your choice and by mine. You no longer have sovereignty over yourself. I do. And my decision is that, if you must do this, we will go together to Pittsburgh and I will settle your accounts. Jacob Good is a lover of money. He will be satisfied with the full payoff of your indenture, with perhaps a slight interest payment for his wounded ego." Mr. Miller's tone turned dry with his last words, and his mouth quirked up at one side.

There was nothing to say. Mr. Miller was right. Will owed him everything, and the saddler's decision must be honored.

"Yes, sir." Will sat back against the side of the wagon. It was back to Pittsburgh, and back to Emmie. Mingled with his sense of peace at the idea of facing Master Good and buying his freedom was a twist of rue. He wondered what Mr. Miller would say when he found out that Will must bring a wife back with him to the farm. He might be relieved at having even more help. Emmie would be delighted to assist Ann with farm chores in the clean country air, after her imprisonment in the city's filth and smoke.

Will dreaded even more what Ann would think of Emmie. But he had made his bed, as the old wives said, and now he would have to lie in it.

Thirty-Three

ANN COULD NOT BELIEVE SHE HAD PROMISED TO GIVE Eli an answer today. Would he seek her here at the Sumners even though her father had not yet returned?

Her chair scraped as she moved it a few inches closer to the window. Even the sunlight pouring into the parlor did not suffice for the needlework on her lap. The hem of Susan's dress had to be let out, but her mind drifted too often back to Eli while the needle slipped in and out of the fabric. She was no closer to a decision on marrying him than she had been a week ago.

The Sumners' parlor sat behind their storefront, separated from it by a thin wall and a curtain over the doorway. Ann could hear the friendly voices of customers as they came and went. Their conversation reassured her that no bounty hunters could approach, not with all these people here. For the first time since her mother's death, Ann felt comfortable in her father's absence.

Of course, if she married Eli, she would leave the farm and embark upon a whole new life in which she had no one to look after but herself and her husband. The freedom of that vision was heady; after he started a medical practice, she would keep a small house with no animals—except horses, for pleasure.

Compared to the farm's endless chores, it would be like entering the aristocracy. She would be able to read for two hours a night, if she wished. And yet she could not stop the nagging voice of love and conscience that told her not to leave her sisters.

"Ann." Mrs. Sumner's voice preceded her, but then she pulled aside the curtain, her freckled face beaming. "Your father is here."

Ann's spirits soared. They could go home to the farm with her father and Will. Despite the past week's respite from her arduous chores, she loved being home best.

When she followed Mrs. Sumner through the curtained doorway, her father was standing on the other side of the counter, his shirt rumpled, his collar open.

"My girl." He opened his arms and she ran around the end of the counter and into his embrace. He had not called her his girl in a long while. It warmed her all through.

When she let go, he held her at arm's length and smiled. "You look well."

"Did you deliver the Simons?"

"We have sent them on their way." The peace with which he said it assured her that the journey had been a success. "Pack your things, and let's be off. I could do with a good scrub and my own bed."

It took only a few minutes to gather their bags and make their goodbyes to Mrs. Sumner, with many a word of thanks.

"Ann helped me immensely, Mr. Miller. It was no trouble at all." Mrs. Sumner smiled at Ann as she and her father exited to the street with a *ping* of the store bell. Susan and Mabel tripped after them, asking her father three or four questions at once. He laughed and told them to bide their time.

A brisk breeze stirred the curls on Ann's neck. The wagon stood outside in the mellow afternoon light, Will the apprentice in the driver's seat. He looked at her as she came out from the shelter of the porch. He seemed different to her, older. His face had a golden tint under his dark hair; his unfastened collar revealed a neck tanned by days of driving. That must be it. It was the sunlight on his skin that had transformed him so. The beaten apprentice had vanished, his starved frame replaced by broadening shoulders and the musculature of a young man in good health.

He turned away, fiddling with the reins. Was he not glad to see her?

Mr. Sumner shambled bear-like out of the barn, leading Bayberry. "Don't forget your horse, Miller."

Her father chuckled and shook his friend's hand, then took the mare's reins. Never one to waste words, Mr. Sumner nodded farewell and walked back into his store.

"Would you like to ride in the wagon with the girls, Ann?" Her father did not move from the mare's side. "I can take Bayberry, if you wish."

She nodded, sensing that perhaps it was her father who wished to ride, after so many days on the road with the mules. He lifted himself into the saddle and turned Bayberry's head toward home.

Will clucked to the mules and they lurched to the yoke, the wagon creeping forward until they picked up their pace to a brisk walk. They knew that home was near.

Her father rode yards ahead of the wagon on Bayberry. She sat next to Will, who drove with what seemed the ease of long practice. Behind them the girls looked over the back of the wagon and commented on whatever it was they could see in their wake.

"So the Simons are safe." She kept her voice soft when she spoke to Will to avoid attracting the attention of the girls.

"Yes." A look of satisfaction lit the side of his face she could see.

"And was the journey hard?"

"It had moments of . . ." He searched for words. "Trial."

"And Mr. Lawrence took the Simons?"

"I only saw his son and a friend. But they seemed to know what they were about." Now his mouth curved into a faint smile, though he did not look at her.

"You are glad you did it?"

He did not reply. She feared she had pried into his feelings. But with his eyes on the mules' backs, he spoke. "Yes. I would do it again. I *will* do it again."

"It is dangerous work." She could not dismiss a trickle of dismay, the same feeling that went through her each time her father rode away from the farm. Did they not worry they might be injured, imprisoned, or otherwise kept from those who needed them?

"Nothing worth doing will be easy." He flicked his eyes at her, and she saw something flaring in their depths before he turned back to face the road.

"What do you mean?"

Now he clamped his mouth shut and did not answer. She was too curious of his exact meaning to be put off.

"What won't be easy?"

Reluctantly, he replied, "Serving those who need help." She could not see his eyes, but the tightness in his voice told her that his heart was full.

She watched him for a moment before turning to look at her

sisters. From the corner of her eye, she could see the curve of his shoulder as he adjusted the reins and sat up straighter.

So he did intend to help fugitives, as her father did. How strong his sense of mercy must be, to survive such abuse and scorn as his former master had heaped on him and still want to ease the sufferings of others. Her sympathy rushed out to him like an invisible cord connecting them, even as they sat three feet apart. She was sure that he must feel it as well.

"Hullo! Mr. Miller!" A call came from behind the curve they had just rounded. Hoofbeats pattered out of sight, then grew louder as a horse came into sight around the trees.

Eli.

He cantered up behind them, then trotted up by Ann at the side of the wagon.

"Good afternoon, Miss Miller." He reined the gelding to a walk and tipped his hat to Ann. "Girls." When he did the same for Susan and Mabel, Mabel giggled with hero worship in her eyes and clutched her sister's elbow.

Will glanced back at Eli, but neither of the young men addressed each other.

"I wondered if you might like to ride this afternoon." Eli looked down at Ann, a smile rounding his high cheekbones into boyish appeal. "Will you come with me?"

"I don't know if my father will need me at home—"

"Then I will ask him." He grinned and spurred his gelding to a brisk trot. When he reached Bayberry and Mr. Miller, he slowed again to a walk. Their hats bobbed as they spoke words Ann could not catch. After a minute or two, both men halted in the road.

"Whoa!" Will called, reining in the mules. As the wagon

rolled to a halt, her father dismounted and led Bayberry back to the wagon.

"Mr. Bowen would like to ride with you, so I told him it would be best if you went now for a short ride and then joined us in half an hour at the house."

"Father, don't you need me to help put the house in order?" She adjusted the lay of her skirt on the wagon boards to avoid Eli's gaze.

"We will manage. I don't want to disappoint a young man who rode in such haste to catch you." Her father's face remained straight, though his tone was arch.

Will seemed to be ignoring the whole business from the driver's seat.

"Very well." She stood. Her father maneuvered Bayberry close to the wagon, and as carefully as she could, she sat backward on the saddle and turned to hook her right leg over the pommel, skirt and all. Modesty preserved, she gathered the reins and clucked to Bayberry, squeezing with her left leg where it hung down by the girth. The mare swung into a walk, and Ann urged her toward Eli's gelding.

"We'll move on ahead, Mr. Miller." Eli tipped his hat to her father, then looked over at Ann. "Shall we canter?"

She nodded. Eli's gelding took off up the road, its silver shoes flashing. Herd instinct prompted Bayberry to follow. After a few bouncing strides of trot, the mare broke into a smooth canter. Gripping both horns with her legs, Ann gave the mare some rein without allowing her to open into a gallop.

They left the wagon far behind, and then Eli turned up the road that led along the top of the valley. Below them sunlight glanced from the surface of the creek so it sparkled like a diamond necklace winding through the trees in the river bottom. Eli slowed to a trot, then to a walk. Ann cued Bayberry to slow as well, as the steep bank was too close for a fast pace here. The breeze was picking up; it stirred her hair and even chilled her a little through the thin fabric of her blue bodice.

"You look beautiful." Eli turned toward her. "Your hair turns the richest color in the light."

She stared straight ahead between Bayberry's ears, abashed by his intense regard.

"Did you enjoy your stay with the Sumners?" he asked.

"Yes, very much." A diffusion in the light made her look up. The clouds rolled swiftly across the sky, white fluffy mounds running ahead of gray storm clouds that threatened to swallow them from the south. This did not look promising.

Eli had followed her upward glance and was watching the clouds himself. "This blasted weather. One can never count on it."

The horses walked with spring in their steps; horses always knew when rain was on the way. Bayberry danced sideways as a low-hanging branch blew toward Ann. She swayed in the saddle but tightened her knee grip and kept her seat.

Eli's brow wrinkled. "Does Bayberry shy often?"

"Hardly ever, but the winds bother her sometimes."

"Let's dismount, then. I can't have you falling from a wild mustang." He swung his leg back over the saddle and dropped lightly to the ground. His shiny Hessian boots made his legs look very strong in their close-fitting trousers.

He tied his gelding's reins to a sapling by the path. This was not standard practice, tying reins, as a horse could snap them or injure its head, but she knew Eli needed his hands free to help her.

He walked back and took hold of Bayberry's head with one hand. "Can you extricate yourself?"

She unhooked her knee and dismounted. Her skirt caught on the leaping horn and made a ripping noise before it gave way and dropped her into Eli's arms.

He did not release her right away. Instead he lowered his head and gently kissed her. Her head swam and she wanted to lean into his kiss, but she pulled back. He would not think well of her. Women were not to allow too much liberty to their suitors, and she had already allowed him to kiss her once before.

She steadied her breathing and made a show of looking at the back of her skirt. Thank goodness there was no visible tear. It must have been her petticoat that ripped.

"Shall we walk them back?" Eli extended Bayberry's reins to her, and she took them. As she did so he caught her hand in his and held it.

"I can't wait any longer." He took off his hat, threw it to one side, and knelt in the path, charming her with his lack of care for his pristine trousers. "Will you be my bride, Ann Miller? You're the most beautiful girl I know, both outside and in. I love you with a passion." He searched her face and jumped to his feet, reaching for her and crushing her to him. Her breath left her as she felt his warmth and unfamiliar masculine body through their clothing. He kissed her urgently, depriving her of the ability to think.

Lightning flashed over the trees and a thunderclap echoed it. The reins jerked in her hand, which was now wound around Eli's side. In a second, she had lost her grip. She tore herself away from Eli as Bayberry half-reared, presented her haunches to them, and bolted back down the path toward home. The gelding jerked his head so the leather reins strained, then snapped. He staggered back and pivoted on his hocks to gallop after the mare.

Ann saw her dismay mirrored on Eli's face. Not only would they risk losing their mounts, but the gelding's snapped reins would make it obvious that they had dismounted and tied their horses. People might assume the worst.

A droplet touched Ann's hand, then another. She saw them falling like tiny needles in the increasing gloom. As they stood gazing at the receding horses, the rain came in earnest. In the downpour, Eli ran for his hat and returned to grab her hand and head for home. A true spring drenching. His fine-boned face was slick with rain, and her hair was totally soaked, hanging in wet tendrils on her neck, one damp lock plastered down the side of her face.

"How can we go back like this?" She stopped.

"Engaged," he said. He gently pulled her toward him. Her indignation vanished at the sheer romance of being there in the rain with him, the water running down her neck into her sodden dress, pouring down Eli's face as he bent his head and sheltered her as best he could. He whispered right in her ear. "Marry me, please, Ann."

She wanted to say yes and be done with the decision. But an insistent prodding from her more rational self would not let her. "I can't think," she said in a louder voice. "This is no time to answer a proposal." She turned and marched down the road, trying vainly to shield her face from the rain. She heard the splash of his footsteps as he followed. He would have to wait, like it or not. She was not the heroine of a Gothic romance; she would not answer while she was swept away by storms, without and within.

Now they would have to hope her father would trust that

no compromise had taken place, despite unseemly appearances. She hurried on into the rain.

———◆———

"What I fail to understand," her father said, "is why you did not accept his proposal."

Eli was gone, having left for home as soon as he deposited Ann on her doorstep. He had apologized to her father, assuring him, red-faced, that she had "come to no harm."

She stood in her wringing wet clothes, her skirt dripping and forming an arc of water in front of her toes. "How did you know he proposed?" She avoided his question with her own.

"He told me, on the road before the two of you rode off together. I assumed you would have told me had you accepted. So why did you not?"

Ann saw half of Mabel's face peeping around the corner of the hallway where it opened on the parlor. "Mabel, go to your room." The little eye and nose disappeared.

She wrung out her sleeves where they hung from her wrists, limp with water. "Father, I did not think I was in the proper frame of mind to consider it."

Turning to the cedar chest, her father plucked the folded old quilt from atop it and shook it out, wrapping it around her shoulders. "You know I regret the pain he caused you," he said. "But it seems he still appeals to you as a suitor. I will give you my blessing, if you are certain he is a good man and the kind of man to whom you wish to yoke your future. I encourage you to accept him, if your estimation and affection for him remain strong and true."

She reached for the edges of the quilt to keep it in place and sat down by the hearth. "I'm considering it, Father." She hunched under the quilt and let the fire warm her right side. Why was it so difficult to be certain?

"I have some news for you." He moved across the rag rug and sat beside her on the other corner of the stone hearth. "I'm going back to Pittsburgh in a few days."

She waited for the shock to wear off so she could speak again. "Why?"

"Will does not feel he can stay here as long as Master Good is searching for him. I agree with him. So we have determined to go back to Pittsburgh and pay off his indenture."

She said nothing, the possibilities whirling in her head. Master Good was capable of anything. "I'm coming with you."

"Ann." His tone was exasperated. "We have just been through a very long journey. It is too expensive and too arduous for you girls to travel back with us."

She did not like it, but there was only one solution. "Then they can stay with Mrs. Sumner again, and I will come with you." She did not know why she was afraid to stay behind this time. She knew everything would be fine at the Sumners. But the thought of watching Will and her father ride away without her was completely unacceptable.

"Then I will strike an even harder bargain with you for this journey," her father said. "If I allow you to come with us, you must accept that young man's proposal without delay when we return. Provided that you want him, of course. You must make a decision that will give you a future. You cannot stay on the farm forever—you would be throwing away your happiness. I won't allow it."

Brilliant! She would now be able to put off her answer to Eli even further. Perhaps some solution for her sisters would come to her. She would gain at least an extra three weeks. It was a godsend.

"Agreed," she said with only a trace of guilt. She would explain it to Eli. She would tell him she was sure she cared for him, but she needed to make sure her father had an apprentice if she were to even consider leaving the farm. Thus, she needed to see Will's case settled. And she felt she owed it to the apprentice to lend her support, given what she knew of his former master.

As she thought through her explanation, it all made sense to her. *That* was why she wanted so desperately to go with them.

Thirty-Four

SHE THUMPED THE MAN'S HEAD WITH THE LOG. HE *fell soundlessly into the snow, facedown. There was no visible mark upon him, but a scarlet circle bled outward into the whiteness like a diabolical halo. She looked up, still clutching the log. Her mother stood in front of her, and her face grew old at an impossible rate, furrows dragging her skin downward, her hair graying to a silver mist.*

"I'm sorry," she said. Her mother turned and shuffled away through the snow.

"Don't go!" Ann called after her, her voice thick with tears.

She dropped the log and stood. A pain in her hands made her turn them palm upward. They were smeared with blood, which dripped down through her fingers and fell like crimson rain into the snow below her.

She opened her eyes. Her hands were curled toward her in the bed, her legs drawn up under the covers as if she huddled for protection. Leaden sadness pressed her down, making her limbs heavy and useless, as if she were not in control of her body but only an observer trapped deep inside it.

She took a breath and broke the dream's spell, finding herself once more capable of motion. She pushed herself up to a sitting position. The sadness remained, but she was accustomed to it after so many nights of similar dreams. She would go to her pre-dawn chores and work hard, and the hollow inside her would fill up with the business of the morning. They were to depart for Pittsburgh in only four days. There was still much to prepare in order to leave the farm in the care of the Murdochs.

She pulled on her work dress. With Will on the farm, she could no longer work in men's trousers, no matter how convenient it might be. She wrapped herself in her coat and walked down the hallway in the darkness to exit the house. Her family was sleeping, as they did not have to rise until dawn. If only she did not wake so early. She would be glad for an extra hour of sleep, but her spirit did not accept rest after such violent imaginary upheavals.

The barn was quiet. She grabbed a pitchfork from the wall, but it was too dim to see the floor inside the stalls. She retrieved the lantern and lit it with the flint, steel, and tinderbox on the shelf inside the door. She brought the lantern to the center of the barn and hung it from the long ceiling hook to prepare for her work.

Armed again with the pitchfork, she slid back the bolt on Bayberry's stall and opened it. The stall was clean. That was odd. And Bayberry was munching hay. The cows had already been fed as well. Her father was still asleep, so it must have been Will. How early had he risen? Perhaps he had gone back to bed in the cabin after his work. She smiled. It was good to have help. Now she could see to her other tasks. Yesterday's hard rain had left the ground moist and soft. It would be a perfect time to plant the beans and peas in the kitchen garden.

With a quick puff she blew out the lantern. She left the animals to their morning meal and picked up a hoe from the collection of tools on her way out. She carried it across the yard, but let it fall in the dark soil outside the kitchen and continued up the stoop.

Inside the kitchen, the seeds for the spring planting were safe in a few bottles on the top shelf of the hutch. She fetched two bottles and pulled out the corks that kept the seeds dry. With one in each hand, she descended the stairs again and set them carefully by the foundation of the house before picking up the hoe again.

She opened the little gate of the small picket fence that enclosed the kitchen garden. With free-roaming pigs all over the woods and fields, a barrier had to protect the garden's delicacies from their greedy snouts.

She raised the hoe and plunged it into the ground. The iron bit deep into the soil with each blow, turning over the flat surface into chunks of sod that would accept the seed readily. The usual hard labor of hoeing was not quite as arduous after the rain. And there was just enough early light here in the open air to allow her to see her work.

She had turned over half a row. Her stiff arms warmed and her breathing quickened, sending new blood coursing through her sleep-dulled body. Now she was truly awake, though she could have wished for a little more strength. Hoeing on an empty stomach was not ideal, but she did not want to breakfast without her family. She would finish two rows of beans and two of peas, and then go make preparations for the morning meal.

She lifted the hoe. *Thunk.* She lifted it again.

"Would you like some help?"

She started. Behind her, Will approached, carrying a load of small sticks. He walked past her to deposit his collection by the kitchen stoop.

"Yes, I would be glad of some assistance," she said. No need to ask where he had been. He must have been gathering kindling in the woods after finishing his work in the barn.

He came in through the gate behind her. Ann stood the hoe on its end and poked the handle toward him.

He took it and hefted it in one hand. "How long would you like the rows? To the end of the fence?"

"Yes, please. I will come after you and seed."

He shrugged out of the coat that Mr. Miller had given him and folded it over the white fence. Beneath it, he wore a shirt and suspenders. She was glad to see it, for if he could wear straps over his back, his wounds had completely healed.

He began to move down the row, his shoulders rolling under the shirt with the rise and fall of the hoe. He was much quicker than she at the work, making it look effortless. She knelt in his wake and began to pour seeds in her palm, shoving them two at a time into the rich loam. They were blessed indeed here in Ohio. She had heard other farmers say before that the land here was like a Garden of Eden. Even the least competent gardener had simply to shove seeds into the ground and up they sprang, watered and nurtured by God's own hand in the perfect balance of rain and a temperate climate. Once the frost had passed, of course.

Bent from the waist, she followed Will. She was practiced in this work. Between the two of them, they would finish soon.

He ended the row and turned back toward her where she had just pressed the soil down over the seeds. She still had a few more to plant on the row. He waited patiently, probably as aware as she that whacking the soil right beside her would fling up clods in her face. She continued her work, kneeling down.

A flash of her mother's image recurred to her again from the dream. Her conscience would not leave her alone.

"You look burdened," he said. "Is it the upcoming journey? I do not want to add to your cares."

"No." She rubbed a stray lock of hair back with her sleeve so she would not streak mud across her forehead.

She had not told anyone about the nightmares. But thinking about her mother walking away from her in her mind's eye made her chest hurt. Perhaps Will had the same kinds of visions when he should be sleeping peacefully. If anyone could understand, he might.

"The journey is not troubling me." She dropped more seeds in the churned ground. "It is simply that I have disturbing dreams. They are hard to forget."

His look grew more intent. "About the bounty hunter?"

"In some ways." She found it too painful to admit her mother's presence in her dreams, even though he might have similar visions. But having admitted the cause of her trouble, the urge to be understood drove her onward. "I dreamed that you did not stop me, and I killed the bounty hunter." She did not stop in her work, moving two feet on to the end of the row, dumping another small handful of seeds into her palm from the bottle.

His silence forced her to look up when she had planted the final two.

"I dream as well. Sometimes it is unpleasant." For a moment his face seemed to lose the health and color he had gained since his arrival and returned to a hint of drawn, sharp pallor.

She rose to her feet.

"Have you told your father that it still troubles you?" he asked.

She shook her head.

"He told me something that has helped me." Will averted his eyes, as if shy on the verge of such a confidence.

"What is that?"

"That seeing the evil in ourselves is the worst trial we ever face."

She let the words sink in. Yes, there was evil in her, in the desire to take revenge, to crush the life from a human soul and personally send Rumkin to his final judgment for what he had done to her. Her unwilling twinge of pleasure at the thought released an answering flood of self-hatred. "I do not like it." Her voice was loaded with repulsion.

"Neither do I. But I have accepted it. As your father told me, we are not sinless. And if we think we are, we will become proud and harsh."

Had this depth of spirit opened up in Will merely because of her father's counsel? It could not have. Humans did not create the capacity of a soul. It must have been there all along, God's gift in him, waiting only to be liberated.

She must not become tearful in front of him. Thank goodness he shifted back to the new row in the ground and began to turn it over, allowing her to gather herself and steady her hands to her task.

They worked on in silence, the wet soil giving to the pressure of her hands like clay. The light grew and pinkened, reminding her of the last time she and Will had met on the brink of dawn.

By the time they finished, the skyline was rose-gold over the trees and fields.

She tucked the seed bottle under her arm and watched the bright edge of the sun clear the tree line.

"Weeping may endure for a night, but joy cometh in the morning," she said to herself.

Footsteps told her that Will had walked up alongside her.

When he had given her his letters for safekeeping, she would never have imagined they would stand here only six weeks later, under such different circumstances, watching the sun rise again.

"Is there anything fairer than morning?" she murmured, not expecting an answer.

He was quiet for a moment. "I can think of three things."

She looked at him in surprise. "You can?"

He met her gaze. "Freedom."

She smiled. "And?"

"Heaven."

"Well, yes. But that's hardly a fair comparison." She teased him to lighten the seriousness of his expression. "And the third?"

He had bowed his head over the handle of the hoe. He looked up sideways and met her gaze. He said nothing.

Just as her cheeks began to burn, he turned and lifted the hoe in his hand. He walked toward the barn.

Why had he refused to answer and given her such a curious look? She took a few quick steps to the wall of the house, bent to retrieve her second seed bottle, and rushed back up the stoop into the kitchen. Her father's apprentice might have improved himself tremendously since coming to their home, but he still lacked social graces.

Breakfast had to be made. Her flustered annoyance made her snatch the poker and stir the banked fire in the hearth so hard that sparks flew up the chimney.

Thirty-Five

WILL LOOKED OUT THE STAGECOACH WINDOW AT THE
streets of Cincinnati, grateful for an excuse not to stare at Ann
sitting across from him, a hat tied in a graceful bow under her
firm little chin. She sat next to her father, reading a book that
she held in one hand while the saddler read a newspaper.

The discovery that Ann was accompanying them to Pittsburgh
had taken Will by surprise. Why would she go to the trouble?
Surely she would prefer to stay with Mr. Milksop, though that
blond dandy was not nearly good enough for her.

He had thought far too often of Eli Bowen in the past few
days, and never with pleasure. He had to gain control of the jeal-
ousy that rampaged through him like a herd of wild pigs. Like the
demon-possessed pigs in the Bible, in fact. He wished he could send
them into the lake, as the Lord had. He would reread that story
later. Since coming to Mr. Miller's farm three weeks ago, he had
spent every quiet moment studying the Bible, often by firelight.
He had already read through all of the New Testament and was
halfway through the Old, though he had skipped Deuteronomy
and Leviticus. They did not seem as important to the great story
he was following. He would read them some other time.

The driver of the stage coach yelled and the coach swerved. Will wondered what hapless person they had just avoided. As they rattled along the streets, the noise of their passage joined the din of scores of cart and coach wheels and the yells of boys hawking papers and what-have-you from the sides of the road. The familiar odors of the city intruded again—smoke, though not as strong and acrid as in Pittsburgh, a sickly smell of rot from the riverfront, and the mingled foulness of a hundred other types of refuse that flew into the streets every day from homes. A shudder crept over him as he remembered Pittsburgh.

They pulled up at the stagecoach station, which was a tavern. As Mr. Miller and then Will stepped down to the street, hostlers ran out past them and began to unharness the horses. Will turned back to hand Ann down from the coach, telling himself that the feel of her gloved hand in his did not delight him, but knowing he was a liar. She smiled at him, her cheek dimpling. Then she held a little nosegay of pink blooms to her face. He did not blame her. He would do the same if he were a woman and had some way to keep the stench away without looking unmanly.

The driver threw down their bags, which were minimal, just one large case per person. Will hefted his own and Ann's while Mr. Miller grabbed his own and led them without delay down the wharf. "The packet will leave soon," he said over his shoulder.

The steamboat *Emissary* was moored at the dock. Ann and her father did not seem impressed by it, proceeding to the packet office matter-of-factly, but Will could not take his eyes off the huge vessel as he followed the Millers.

In minutes, Mr. Miller had purchased tickets. They hurried up the gangplank, where it looked as if the rest of the passengers had already boarded and were moving around the decks.

Mr. Miller beckoned Will to come with him toward the bow while Ann headed for the stern like a seasoned traveler.

After Will had marveled at the maritime neatness of their two-bunk stateroom, the boat shuddered to life under their feet, and clanging bells announced its departure. Will and Mr. Miller walked to the stern, where they found Ann leaning against the railing, watching the dock as they drifted away from it. She appeared to be deep in thought and only smiled halfheartedly when Mr. Miller broke her reverie with a comment on the spectators waving farewell.

They stood there watching for a few minutes, Ann between Will and her father. As they pulled away from the city, the trees by the river spread great clouds of pink and white blossoms along the banks. Their ethereal lightness made him want to hold Ann's hand.

"It's a magnificent sight," he said.

"Yes." She seemed drawn in by the beauty around them as well. It was like a fairyland, steaming up the river between forests of pink and white, the blossoms quivering with the slightest wind.

"Do you like traveling by steam?" He wanted to speak with her, on any subject at all.

"Oh yes." She still seemed distracted. She looked down, removing her gloves one finger at a time and stowing them in her small handbag. "Our previous journey was very eventful."

"In what way?"

She closed her handbag with a sharp pull at its strings. "Many ways." She turned and leaned forward to speak to Mr. Miller. "I think I shall retire until dinner, Father."

The saddler took his daughter's hand and pressed it. "Of

course." Will wondered what had happened on that previous trip. Mr. Miller was solicitous, and Ann disturbed.

She walked around the end of the ladies' cabin, her perfect carriage not disturbed by the motion of the floor beneath her.

Mr. Miller and Will passed the time at the rail in pleasant conversation about the boat and the people on it. Then the conversation turned to Scripture and some of the strange stories in Genesis that Will had read recently. He was so absorbed by Mr. Miller's explanations that dusk crept up before he knew it.

"Well, we had better dress for dinner." Mr. Miller stepped back and touched his hat as a lady passed in an amber-colored dress bedecked with feathers.

"Yes, sir." Will followed the saddler back to the stateroom, where they unpacked their cases. There was an empty wooden bowl on a small fixed shelf between the bunks. Mr. Miller took it, left for two or three minutes, and returned with water in the bowl. He produced a bar of soap from his case and shaved quickly and precisely. Will followed him, drying his face with the small white towel that was a little dingy, but serviceable.

Mr. Miller had loaned Will an evening coat and collar to wear for meals on the boat. To his surprise, the saddler also produced a second hat from a hatbox in his case. It was not as tall as Mr. Miller's top hat, but its blackness gleamed in the cabin light. Will took it from Mr. Miller's hands, careful not to bend the brim.

Mr. Miller opened the door and stepped over the maritime sill. He fit his own hat to his head, then turned back to watch as Will navigated the step and donned his hat.

"Excellent," Mr. Miller said. The saddler looked Will up and down. "Indistinguishable from any other cabin passenger, son."

Will's confidence surged and he took a deep breath. Mr. Miller led the way to the ladies' cabin to wait for Ann.

* * *

Ann pushed a hairpin into place to trap a loose wave that always liked to come down at inopportune times. She would not be late to dinner this time, now that she had no little girls to chatter and ask questions and lose their stockings. She missed her sisters already. It had been hard to leave them with Mrs. Sumner. She had never left them, not since her mother died. It was more painful than she had expected, and she found herself having to pray down the worry.

She fastened the last of the long row of buttons on the wine-red dress. It was presentable—as well made and flattering as the dresses the other ladies had worn the last time. Retying the bow of her hat, she tried to use her hand mirror to examine herself by holding it far away and then close, and then far away. The cabin lamp was too dim for her to see well.

She put the mirror in her handbag and stepped out of her state-room. Her father had told her to meet him at the door to the ladies' salon, and so she headed sternward. After a few yards of curving deck, she spotted her father, looking very gallant in his evening coat. Behind him stood someone else in evening coat and hat.

She blinked twice in the twilight. The handsome young man in the evening coat was Will. She had noticed, of course, that the marks of his abuse had faded. But she had not expected that his evening attire would transform her view of him in quite this way, allowing her to see him as if she had never known that starved, beaten person who had once lived at Master Good's house.

Mr. Miller looked at Will with paternal pride. "Why don't you escort my daughter to dinner? You should learn how to do these things."

Will stepped to her side and offered his arm as if it were second nature.

"Very good, son!" Mr. Miller chuckled. She thought Will flushed slightly under his tan, but could not be sure in the uncertain light from the wall sconce next to him.

She put her arm through his, remembering when she had last done so on this boat with Allan Burbridge. She was disconcerted that Will did not suffer at all in comparison to Allan. In fact, Will's darker hair and his eyes shadowed by his hat brim reminded her of some smoldering hero in one of her novels. She smiled to herself at the ridiculousness of her thoughts. Yet it was always pleasant to walk to dinner on the arm of a well-dressed young man.

He was silent as they followed her father. His arm was steady and he matched his pace to hers, which slowed his longer stride. She was also quiet, trying to accustom herself to this new Will.

When they reached the dining room, the lamplight was ambient and golden as the guests milled about, talking to one another. They had only just crossed the sill when a knot of three young ladies of varying heights broke apart and reassembled itself around the newcomers.

"Good evening!" The tallest extended a hand to Will. He took it and bowed, removing his hat. Had her father been coaching him in etiquette? Admiration mingled with amusement as she watched him greet each young woman with quiet good manners. She had arrived at the ball on the arm of a transformed prince, as if she had walked into a story she would read to her sisters from the Grimms' tales. And yet—her heart softened as she thought it—who could be more deserving than this young man who had proven himself kind and brave on several occasions? Those were the very qualities that graced the ordinary youths in the tales and set them above their enemies.

She was not surprised that the young ladies in the room were drawn to him like so many brightly colored moths. His hint of reserve made him, if anything, more interesting to them.

"And do you follow a trade?"

"He is my partner in saddlery and on the farm," Mr. Miller interjected from the side, his eyes glinting. Her father seemed to take muted glee in watching his protégé's entrance to the dining room.

These girls did not seem a bit deterred that Will was a craftsman.

"Oh, how fascinating," the girl in bright blue piped. The taller one in amber next to her gave her a subtle look of disgust. Ann wondered if any of them would speak to her at some point, or if they would go on cooing solely at her escort.

"And what takes you to Pittsburgh?"

Ann was sure this question would flummox him, but just then the captain entered in the same navy brass-buttoned coat he had worn before. They all moved to their seats at the table. Ann had to restrain her smile at the sight of the girls jostling each other with apparent nonchalance as they strove to sit next to Will. The girl in amber won, and the one in blue had to be content with moving to the seat across from them. The girl in green was less aggressive and took the seat next to the girl in amber with a crestfallen air. When the captain bid them be seated, Mr. Miller surveyed the seating arrangement with ill-concealed mischief. Ann had never seen him enjoy himself so in company.

The same horde of covered dishes overran the table. Will reached for one and removed the lid.

"Would you like some roast?' he asked her.

"Yes, please." She smiled at him, and he answered with a slow, warm smile as he looked into her eyes. He picked up his fork without looking back at the dish and gazed at her the whole while as he speared a slice of roast beef and transferred it to her plate. Then he took one for himself.

She chuckled, and he grinned more broadly.

"That's quite a skill," she said, relieved that he had finally looked away at her laugh. His unbroken regard was comical, but stirring somehow.

"I have a strong instinct for finding food. It came in handy more than once." His gaze turned a little more serious, though his tone was still light. She wanted to touch his hand to show him her understanding, but that would be too forward. Instead, she touched another dish.

"Very well then. What do you think is in this one?"

He knit his brows together in mock concentration. "Beans."

She peeked inside, then lifted off the lid. "How did you know?"

They both grinned.

The girl in amber spoke around his shoulder. "You must have great mental ability. Are you a spiritualist?"

He turned to answer. "No, miss."

"I've seen spiritualists in Philadelphia tell the number of a card plucked from a hat."

She said something else that was frivolous, and Will answered politely. Ann could tell that he was not very interested in the girl's flirtatious remarks, but he could not escape her direct questions. A little flame of annoyance lit in Ann's heart.

While Will's head was turned away, she looked across at her father. He was watching her with a knowing look. She looked back defiantly and raised her eyebrows as if to ask him what he intended by that. He smirked and picked up his knife and fork to busy himself cutting his meat.

"Don't you think so, Miss Miller?" Will turned back to her with a visible effort to redirect his attention away from the other girl.

"Why . . . yes." She could tell that he knew she had not heard the subject of their discussion.

Will picked up the pitcher of lemonade in front of them and refreshed her glass. Before he could continue the conversation, however, the girl in amber broke in again.

For the rest of the meal, Ann fumed in silence at being deprived of Will's company. It was simply rude of that girl, that was all. No man could have extricated himself from her, though Will made several attempts. Ann made conversation with her father instead, though she thought he could tell that her heart wasn't in it. She redoubled her efforts to sound interested and cheerful.

She was glad when the captain stood up, bowed to the company, and left. With a quick "pardon" to the girl in amber, Will turned to Ann. "Are you finished?"

"Yes."

"Shall we go?" He stood and she rose with him. At the disappointed look on the girl's face, he said, "It was a pleasure meeting you, miss."

Ann realized he did not remember the girl's name. That made her happy. But she was being petty.

Mr. Miller excused himself to the company and came round to join them.

"Perhaps we should take a walk on deck. It's much warmer than it was on our last journey."

Will agreed. They all left the dining room and stepped into the darkness and the river breeze. After only a few steps astern, however, Mr. Miller clapped his hand to his head. "I have forgotten my hat," he said.

Ann looked at him askance.

"Don't wait for me." He left them and walked back to the dining room.

Will offered her his arm again and they walked on. The lamps flickered beneath their glass panes. They walked all the way to the stern railing that overlooked the engine deck. The men down there were less rowdy than the first crew had been. They still played cards and drew swigs from long-necked bottles, but with only a low hum of talk and an occasional laugh.

Away from the deck lamps, they could see the sky more clearly. Scattered clouds made dark blots against the stars.

Ann felt Will move and noticed that he had removed his hat with his right hand. He set it on the crate to his right by the rail, but he did not move the arm she was holding. She liked his closeness and chose to keep her hand tucked around his elbow.

"Do you ever wish you could change the past?" His hair lifted in the light breeze from the ship's passage.

"Many times." She thought of her mother. Then his. "What would you change?"

"What happened to my parents."

Her heart pained her at the loneliness that echoed in his flat statement, even though she had known what he would say.

"You also lost your mother," he said.

"Yes."

"It must have been hard to become a mother to your sisters."

"Not as hard as it would have been to lose both my parents." She pressed his arm with a gentle hand.

"If my parents had lived, so many things would not have happened. I would never have gone to Master Good's."

"That's true."

"But I also would never have met your father. Or you." He looked at her, his eyes even darker out here.

"I don't think my father and I are such great prizes."

"Perhaps not." He smiled.

She smiled back but affected an injured tone. "You're supposed to say we are pearls beyond price."

"Then you are. You are." Beneath his humor was an affection and gentleness that made her want to put her arms around him and soothe away all the misery he had endured.

"But in all seriousness, I can never repay what your father has done for me."

She wondered at that, but held her tongue, sensing that he needed her to listen, not speak.

"He has opened the gates of heaven—" His low voice caught and he cleared his throat and turned his head away. "I will never be the same."

She inched closer to him and interlaced her arm through his. He turned back to her and smiled, his face both familiar and new to her. The wildness was gone, replaced by peace.

They stood at the railing for some time, side by side, with silent understanding.

Thirty-Six

MR. MILLER HAD TOLD WILL THAT THE FAMILY hosting them in Pittsburgh was well-to-do, but Will was unprepared for the magnificence of the curved driveway, or the vast lawn ornamented with dark evergreens trimmed in classical symmetry. The coach rolled away behind them, leaving Will, Ann, and her father standing next to their small pile of baggage. Will stared up at the columned mansion from the base of its wide white stairs.

"They are expecting us?" Ann asked her father.

"I sent a letter two days ahead of our departure, so I trust they know by now."

"I do hope they won't mind."

"I'm sure Mrs. Burbridge will be pleased to help us. And we had little choice. It would be unwise to stay with Dr. Loftin, under the circumstances." Mr. Miller hefted one of the large traveling cases and started up the stairs. Will took the other two cases and followed the saddler and Ann to the door. He felt conspicuous enough as it was, with all the time and trouble the Millers had taken on his account. He would rather lurk in the background at this grand place, carrying bags and calling no attention to himself.

At the tap of the polished brass knocker, the door opened to reveal a middle-aged man in a black coat and stiff white collar. "Mr. Miller," he said, crisp and clear in his Irish brogue. "Miss Miller." He bowed and ushered them into a high-ceilinged foyer. "Mrs. Burbridge awaits you in the parlor. May I take your hats? And please leave your bags; I will take them up for you."

Following Mr. Miller's example, Will set down the cases and doffed his hat to give to the butler. Ann took a moment to untie the wide bow beneath her chin and lift her larger, more delicate hat from the loose curls atop her head. The butler balanced all three hats in his hands and retreated into the small anteroom to the side of the front foyer.

Mr. Miller offered Ann his arm and led her through the foyer. Will marveled at the elaborate carved paneling that gave way at waist height to dark-gold walls. He had never seen moldings of the sort that adorned the ceiling of the foyer and led the eye to the wide parlor doorway ahead. As they walked through into the vast blue and gold room, he noticed that the room took the shape of an oval, its dark mahogany furniture sitting on rounded feet in graceful clusters, upholstered in blue crushed velvet and gold brocade. Will looked down to make sure his boots were clean before he stepped on the Oriental rug.

"Welcome, Samuel!" An elderly lady rose from the chaise longue at the far end of the room. At the same time, a young man and woman stood from the chairs flanking her. For a moment, they looked as if they posed for a formal portrait, in their sumptuous, tasteful garb.

The young woman broke the frieze and hurried to Ann. "We were so glad to receive your letter." She embraced Ann.

The old woman had followed her and stood beside her to

address the saddler. "And, Mr. Miller, of course you and yours are always welcome in our home."

Mr. Miller took the hand the old woman offered. "My deepest thanks." He stepped aside to gesture toward Will. "Will, this is Miss Louisa Burbridge and her grandmother, Mrs. Lewis Burbridge. Ladies, this is the apprentice I mentioned, Will Hanby. I'm here to settle his case."

"So unfortunate, the way some of these masters abuse their apprentices," the old woman said. Will's neck warmed, but there was only sympathy in her age-cracked voice. She approached, her stiff dark skirt advancing in slow measures, a foot at a time over the thick rug. "You will always have our support, young man."

He ducked his head, unsure of how to respond.

The young man had lingered back by the chairs, but now he walked up beside his grandmother, a curious look on his patrician face. He went to Ann and took her hand, bowing over it. "Miss Miller." There was no mistaking the intent look in his gray eyes as he looked up at her, and indeed she was dainty and beautiful in her red dress. Will turned away in disgust, pretending to examine the pianoforte in the corner. Would these fellows never leave her alone?

Mr. Miller spoke up immediately. "And this is Mr. Allan Burbridge, a good friend to our family."

What did that mean? Did this man also have some claim on Ann's heart? Will forced a civil look to his face as Burbridge straightened up and finally turned his attention from Ann to Will.

"A pleasure to meet you." Though his words were polite, his careful gaze assessed Will from head to foot. Then, as if dismissing Will from further notice, he leaned toward Mr. Miller and shook his hand. "Welcome. Was the journey arduous?"

Behind Burbridge's back, Ann crossed her arms over her bodice and shot Will a surreptitious glance. He did not want her sympathy and looked away. Clearly he was not of sufficient station for Burbridge to shake his hand. Will would not give the rich young man the satisfaction of seeing his snub hit home.

After more pleasantries, during which Will acquainted himself with the contents of a curio cabinet, he heard Burbridge telling the Millers that his sister would show them to their rooms.

Mr. Miller headed for the stairs after Miss Burbridge, tall and slim and blond in her mauve silk, then paused and turned back to his hostess. "Mrs. Burbridge, might I trouble you once more for the use of your coach in a half hour?"

"So soon? Do you not wish to refresh yourself, take tea, perhaps?" The elderly woman cocked her gray head.

"That's very kind, but it would be best if I went directly to Master Good with my proposal. A great weight will be lifted from all of us when that contract is bought out."

"And I will go with you, sir." Will would not let Mr. Miller do his business for him, cowering in some far-off hiding place under Ann's watch. He would face Master Good himself.

Mr. Miller raised his eyebrows as if to object, but after regarding Will for a moment, he nodded once. "Very well."

In the rush of satisfaction that followed, it took Will a moment to see that Ann's face had blanched as white as the marble stairs behind her. She turned and hurried up after Louisa.

After a splash of cold water from a bowl on the washstand and a perfunctory wipe with a towel, Will rejoined Mr. Miller at the foot of the grand staircase that dwarfed even the one he had seen in Dr. Loftin's home.

Mr. Miller and Mrs. Burbridge exchanged some thoughts on a minister whose name Will did not know. The butler came in to tell them that the coach awaited them outside.

"We should return in no more than an hour or two." Mr. Miller took Mrs. Burbridge's hand and bade her farewell with a courtly half bow from the waist.

The Burbidges' black town coach with blue liveried driver was only a few steps from the door across the crunching gravel. The butler moved ahead of them with the understated grace of long service and clicked open the coach door. After they had stepped up and found themselves facing one another, the butler closed the door behind them. "And a good day to you, gentlemen," he said.

It took only a few minutes to reach the end of the Burbridges' drive and emerge onto the Pittsburgh street, which grew more congested as they drove toward the Allegheny bridge. Will recognized the ramshackle outline of Emmie's boarding house as they whisked by. He was ashamed that his palms were clammy.

"I feel myself to be a coward," he muttered, clenching his fists.

"Why?" Mr. Miller raised his head from the papers he was examining and directed a keen look at him from under his hat brim. "Because you fear your former master?"

Will remained silent, battling the waves of fear and anger. He would be a man, not a cringing boy.

"You would not be in your right mind if you did not fear him." Mr. Miller's voice remained calm. "But I trust that his greed will win him over to our proposal. It would not be in his self-interest to refuse it." He glanced down at the papers again.

Will took the small Bible from where Mr. Miller had laid it

on the seat. Only the word of God himself could uphold him and steel his nerve through the next hour. He turned to the Psalms.

When the coach pulled up, Mr. Miller slid the papers back into his satchel and buckled it. "Be of stout heart now," he said to Will, and stooped to exit the coach.

When Will stepped down, he was unprepared to see Dr. Loftin's white, neat house. Mr. Miller headed for the blue front door, but Will had to take a deep breath before he followed. The memory of following a different man to this same door years ago, unwittingly signing himself over to the devil—or at least his loyal henchman—was too much. He rubbed a hand over his face and walked after Mr. Miller.

The maid let them in—all was exactly as it had been that fateful day, except that Mr. Miller stood beside him instead of Master Good. Even the painting on the wall was still the same: the dark valley lit here and there by rays breaking through banks of cloud overhead.

The double doors of the adjoining room opened, and Dr. Loftin walked into the foyer. A wide smile spread across his face. "Samuel! This is a pleasant surprise. But what on earth brings you back—" He halted, mouth open, as he spotted Will standing back by the front door. He regained his pose. "I assume you do not come as a bounty hunter, Samuel. I know you too well for that."

"No. I've come to buy out Will's indenture. And I need you to witness the agreement."

Dr. Loftin crossed to Will with a slow step and stood close. He spoke in a hushed voice. "You did not kill Lucy. Tell me you did not."

"No, Doctor."

The worry lines on the doctor's forehead eased. "I knew it. But why did you not say so before the judge?"

"I would not have Tom thrown in prison for perjury."

"A shame Tom did not show equal loyalty to you. No wonder he has seemed so down at the mouth this past month." The doctor raised his hands and clapped them on the sides of Will's shoulders. "But I'm very glad to see you, Will. And overjoyed that you have found a good master."

"I've brought the money with me," Mr. Miller said. "A goodly sum, far more than the indenture is worth."

"A wise strategy," the doctor said.

"Then let us summon Master Good." Mr. Miller hefted the satchel in one hand with a grim look and set it on the small table against the wall.

"I will go for him." Dr. Loftin headed for the back hallway. "We'll give him an unexpected delight today." The sardonic tone of his voice was unmistakable as it floated back over his shoulder.

After the back door closed with a thud, the house was so quiet Will could hear the clock ticking in the parlor. *Fear not evil men . . . they will wither as the grass . . .*

The back door thumped again, and he heard the false jovial voice that made the hair of his neck prickle. "Yes, my good doctor, but what's all the mystery about? You have me quite at a loss."

Master Good walked out of the back hall and into the foyer and stopped dead in his tracks. His light blue eyes remained on Will for a long moment, then returned to Mr. Miller.

"What is the meaning of this?" He took a lightning step toward Will, then coiled back on himself like a snake and turned to the saddler. "Master Miller? You have brought me my runaway?"

"In a manner of speaking." Mr. Miller's voice was as stiff as Master Good's was sinuous. "I have come to buy out Will Hanby's indenture." He turned and drew the papers from the satchel, thrusting them toward Master Good at arm's length. "Two years, plus the two added by the court. I offer you ample compensation for his remaining obligation."

Master Good accepted the papers and scanned them. His face twitched and he read on avidly. They had not been mistaken. The man was eaten alive by his greed. Mingled repulsion and relief flooded through Will, but he could not take his eyes off the black-haired man.

Master Good scanned each page. He continued looking at the first page for some time, even though Will was sure he had taken twice the time he needed to read it.

The light blue eyes flicked up again, directly at Will.

"And you think," the master said slowly, "that I would accept any sum of money, after the pains this reprobate has put me to?"

He crumpled the pages in his hand. "No. I will accept no offer of yours, Miller. You lured my apprentice away and harbored him somewhere, making you his accomplice!" His voice had risen to a choking shout, his face was twisted. "I'll haul you before the judge along with him and make you pay the fine."

Will's empty shock began to give way like a dam crumbling at the edges.

Master Good jerked his gaze back to Will. "And as for you, you son of a worthless whore—"

Will hurled himself across the room into Good, throwing him against the wall. Something fell with the sound of breaking glass, but Will fastened his hands on Good's throat and squeezed. The man's eyes began to pop. Blows from the side landed on Will's brow bone and jaw. He felt no pain. Only overwhelming passion to hang on until he squeezed the life from his tormentor.

He was wrenched backward, a cry of frustration torn out of him at the same time as his fingers slipped off Good's throat.

Mr. Miller's voice seeped through the fog of anger and pain. "Will! Will! I won't see you go to prison for murder!"

Dr. Loftin seized Will's other arm, yelling, "Stop!"

Will came back to his senses, his breathing ragged, his eyes unblinking on Good, who had staggered forward, his fingers curled and his knees flexed as if he would spring back at Will.

"Stand off, Jacob!" Dr. Loftin stood between Will and his former master, breaking their view of each other.

After a moment of tense silence, Master Good edged around to where Will could see his furious glare. "When I have you before the judge again," he rasped, "I'll own you for the rest of your days." He spun on his heel and stormed out the back hall, one hand to his bruised throat. The door slammed.

Dr. Loftin stood immobile, facing the back hall. Mr. Miller released Will's arm and sat heavily in the chair under the painting.

"I misjudged." He leaned back against the wall and closed his eyes, his face weary, as if he had aged ten years in the past three minutes. "Forgive me."

Dr. Loftin turned to him. "We all misjudged, Samuel. Jacob is beyond all reason."

Will crossed to Mr. Miller and slumped on the floor beside his chair, his back to the wall. The saddler did not turn to him, but Will felt a hand on his shoulder.

They remained that way, in heavy silence, until Dr. Loftin escorted them out to the coach.

"I had almost given up hope." Allan grinned and moved a chair immediately adjacent to hers, where she sat with a book in her lap. "You didn't write."

"I'm sorry." She smiled at him, though her thoughts were far away. Despite the enticing selection of books at the Burbridges' home, she had read the first line of this one at least ten times without absorbing it.

"Were you too busy to even think of me?" he asked.

"In a sense."

"Is some Rushville beau chasing you?" His question was light as he fell back into their old banter.

"And if one were?"

"I would have to hunt him down." He grinned, but a wolfish quality gave her pause. *This man killed for me.* She wished herself with her father and Will rather than alone here with Allan and the memory of the duel.

"I have difficulty . . ." She stopped. "I have been troubled by what happened here."

"Of course you have." He picked up her hand in his and pressed it lightly. "Any woman would. It's no disgrace. Your honor is unquestioned."

Honor. What honor is there in murder? He did not understand. She could not explain without insulting his courage in the duel, which had been the only way he knew to respond to what he had seen.

"Have you thought of me, in our separation?" He was teasing again but retained his hold on her hand.

Without answering, she withdrew from his grasp and stood. She paced before the cold hearth. "You did not shake hands with my father's apprentice."

He paused. "No, I did not. Should I have?"

She touched the frame of a tiny landscape painting as if it fascinated her. "I thought you were a democrat."

"I am. Except when I am jealous."

She turned in surprise. He was grinning at her.

"Surely you jest." His ridiculous suggestion provoked her to smile back at him.

"He is a man, apprentice or not. And he has seen you every day for weeks. That alone would have me raving with envy." He was too witty to be sincere. "And then, of course, he venerates the very ground you walk on."

Her laugh was short. "He is my father's apprentice, Allan." She must change this uncomfortable subject. "There is someone else in Rushville. He has proposed."

"And will you accept?"

"I don't know."

"What are his merits? Tell me." He challenged her with a tilt of his head. "Then I will tell you if you should marry him."

She could not help but chuckle. "In your unbiased view."

"Of course." He ducked his head in mock humility.

"He is intelligent."

"How intelligent?"

"I don't know!" She put her hands on her waist in mock exasperation.

"As intelligent as I?"

She smiled with him. "Perhaps."

"As intelligent as your father's apprentice?"

"Don't bring him into this. We are having a serious conversation." Unsettled, she began her pacing again.

"Then tell me about your suitor, without making me drag every detail from you."

"He is handsome. He is a gentleman. He loves poetry."

"Ah." There was a world of condescension in Allan's sigh.

"What?"

"Oh, nothing."

"What?" She whirled on him now, both curious and irritated.

"He is one of *those*."

"Just because he loves poetry?"

"Because you mention it."

"Lord Byron loved poetry," she said.

"And would he have made a good husband?"

"You don't know Eli."

"But I know you."

She fell silent. Did he? Did he know her well enough to judge whether she should marry Eli?

He rose from his chair and walked to her, standing behind her and bending down to whisper in her ear. "I will tell you this . . ."

She shivered at his breath on her neck.

"From your description, I fear this handsome poet less than your apprentice."

She eased away, annoyed. "You presume too much."

"I intend to." He looked at her sidelong with his gray eyes, still smiling. He did amuse her so, even when he transgressed.

But the memory of murder hung in the air around him.

A knock came at the front door, beyond their line of sight. Ann heard the butler's polite mumble. After a moment, her father and Will walked into the parlor.

They were not happy.

"He has refused my offer," her father said. "I believe he will have the bounty hunters here for Will posthaste."

"Then we must leave," she said.

"No," Will said. "I won't run again. I'll leave it to the court."

"But the court has already decided against you!" Ann's voice rose. She had crossed to within a foot of him in her agitation, staring up at his resolute face.

"I'll leave it in God's hands."

"Don't do that, man." Even Allan seemed unsettled, untangling his limbs and rising from his chair. "You can't just throw your life away in the hope that some divine power will rescue you. It will not."

"It is not some nameless divine power." Will met Allan's gaze, his dark eyes shadowed. "It is the Lord who parted the Red Sea and brought the Israelites out of Egypt."

"If you choose to throw away your life on the hope of primitive tales and miracles, I can't dissuade you." Allan stalked away, shoving his hands into his trouser pockets for emphasis.

His skepticism shocked her, but she did not agree with Will's decision any more than he did. She pleaded with him softly. "But the Lord helps those who help themselves, Will." He seemed as unmoved by her words as he was by Allan's.

Her father spoke up. "Both of you hold your peace and let him make his decision."

Her stomach in knots, she raced for the stairs, afraid she would lose control of herself if she stayed. She heard her father talking to Will in a low voice as she turned on the landing and continued her flight, clutching her skirts with white knuckles.

Once down the hall and in the privacy of the bedroom, she began to pace again. Then she fished the Bible out of her traveling case and held it to her chest as if it could take away the fear. She knelt down beside the bed, not caring if she wrinkled her dress, and prayed with her face pressed into the quilt.

Some time later a knock came at the front door.

She jumped up and hurried out of her room again, almost tripping down the stairs in her haste. Allan and her father were exchanging words with some rough-looking men who had seized Will's arms and were hustling him out of the parlor. He went quietly, his head held high.

She rushed through the room after them, wanting to scream. Her father, just as distressed as she, placed a hand on her arm to stop her, but she made it into the foyer before he was able to arrest her completely.

Just before they dragged him through the front doorway, Will wrestled around to look back. He glanced only at her, with calm reassurance in his eyes. She stepped forward with some wild idea of begging his captors for mercy, but her father's grip tightened and held her back.

The door closed.

A little sound escaped her. She stood still, like a child who has cut herself for the first time and stares in wonder at the red line, before the pain comes.

Her father folded her in his arms, and the pain came.

Thirty-Seven

A SOFT TAP CAME AT THE BEDROOM DOOR.

"Ann?" It was Louisa's voice.

She pushed herself up from the bed to sit on the edge, straightening her dress, brushing at her hair with her hands. "Come in."

Louisa peered around the edge of the door, her fair skin seeming even paler with uncertainty.

"It's all right." Though all was plainly not right, Ann could not hide away forever. She had already missed supper with the Burbridges the previous evening, knowing she was too distraught to make pleasant conversation.

"I'm sorry to disturb you." Louisa moved to the bed and sat down beside Ann.

"You could never disturb me." Ann smiled faintly.

Louisa folded her hands in her lap and turned her gray eyes to Ann. "I hate to see you so sad. Is there anything I can bring you? Anything at all?"

"No." A wild idea blazed through her. "Yes. A coach and driver."

"Would you like to go out? I believe that's a capital plan."

"I would like to go on a drive. To the jail."

Louisa went dead white. "Where?"

"Will you come with me?"

"To the jail?" Years of etiquette training could not keep the shock from Louisa's question.

"Please."

Louisa twisted her fingers together, the wisps of blond hair around her face adding to her air of maidenly distress.

"We would not be long. There must be guards—we would be safe."

"I will ask my grandmother about the coach. Meet me downstairs in a few minutes." Louisa slipped around the door again.

Ann scrambled to her wardrobe and pulled on her stockings, then shoved her feet into her short boots, buttoning them with fingers clumsy with impatience. She made a quick attempt to restore her tidiness in the glass of the vanity, then clunked downstairs once more to wait for the verdict.

She could tell by Louisa's light, quick step as she descended the stairs that Mrs. Burbridge had agreed. Louisa was animated by nervous excitement.

"Did you tell her why?" Ann was too curious not to ask.

"I merely said we wished to go out for a while."

That was a relief. Ann would not have wanted her new friend to lie on her behalf.

"The jail is not far from the wharf." Louisa spoke in a hushed tone. "I'll ask the driver to take us to a nearby street, and then he can pick us up at the same point."

Ann nodded and followed Louisa out, pausing only to retrieve her hat.

"Ann?" Her father's voice made her jump. He stood behind them in the foyer, having approached as silently as a cat.

"Yes, Father?"

"Where are you going?"

Louisa raised her voice above its usual level, sounding cheerful. "I thought I would take Ann out for a breath of fresh air, Mr. Miller. She has been penned up in her room for so long, I thought it would do her good."

"Oh yes, Miss Burbridge. Just the thing."

"Goodbye, then."

"Enjoy your drive." Mr. Miller walked back into the parlor.

Ann let out her breath and, tying the sash of her hat, walked out to the coach.

The sky was overcast, making the crowded buildings near the wharf seem even dirtier and duller.

"This way." Louisa started across the street, turning her head constantly to check for oncoming wagons. Puddles of mud threatened their dresses; if any water splashed up, Louisa's silk would never recover. Picking their way from one dry patch to another, they made it to the line of stores and taverns on the other side.

"It's on the next street." Louisa led her around the corner of a butcher's shop.

Ann followed her down a narrow alley. The rank, foul odor rising from piles of scraps and human waste brought bile to her throat, and she covered her mouth and nose with one hand. She kept a wary eye on the windows above. Mud puddles were bad enough, but chamber pots would be a horror.

She breathed easier when they emerged onto the next street. The buildings here were nondescript, large, like storehouses. A small, rough field lay to their left, and then beyond the field another building squatted, ugly and low. The double gate was faced with black, studded metal.

"The jail," Louisa said, pointing.

They walked to it, still forced to maneuver around the mud and refuse. Most of Pittsburgh's streets were not amenable to fashionable walkers, which is why the fashionable did not walk here.

A couple of burly men in open-necked shirts loitered across the street in the yard of one of the buildings. Conscious of their leering gazes and mutterings, Ann quickened her step. Louisa did likewise. The men chuckled.

At the post beside the gate was a small barred window. Ann approached it cautiously and leaned toward the bars. "Hello?"

A head popped up inches from her, causing her to jerk back. The man was scarred with old pox and missing his front teeth. "Whaddya want?" He spat tobacco juice to one side. Ann watched with repulsion as it ran down the wall next to countless similar stains.

"I'm here to see a prisoner."

"That ain't usual."

"They don't get visitors?"

"Not like you." The man guffawed. "But I suppose some do come through now and then."

"This one came in yesterday. His name is Will Hanby."

"I don't know their names, miss." He spoke with grudging respect. "But you can come in and look around. It ain't a proper jail like in Philly. It's small. You can't miss him, if he's in here. And the two of you can't do any harm." He shuffled to the back of the booth, and in a moment a loud series of scrapes and clanks announced the turn of the key in the gate. It creaked open a foot, then two.

"Go in, then." The guard jerked his head. Ann edged around him.

The guard locked the gate with a turn of the key after Louisa sidled by. "When you go out," he said, "just keep going. There's another guard in back. That's the way you go. In the front. Out the back."

A windowless hallway lit only by a few candle sconces turned at a sharp right angle a few yards ahead. The first cell held a misshapen bundle of rags sprawled on a cot. He smelled of strong spirits and groaned when they walked by. Ann shuddered.

When they rounded the first corner, she discovered that the jail was like a rat's maze, small as it was. Two cells on each side, then another sharp left in the corridor. Why they had built it this way, she did not know, but her nerves jangled every time they turned a corner. She was afraid of the people in the cells, though most stared at them without speaking. One jumped at them and reached through the bars; Louisa gasped and grabbed Ann's arm. The old man shrieked with glee and gibbered nonsense at them.

Another corner. A bearded man scratched himself where he slouched against the wall. "Hey, girlies." He followed his greeting with a stream of suggestions so vile that Ann and Louisa almost ran to the next bend in the hall. Louisa was shaking when they paused.

"I'm sorry," Ann said.

"Don't worry," Louisa said. "I won't faint."

As if to prove herself, she led the way down the hall. The first cell was empty. The second held a familiar form. Will lay on the wooden shelf that passed for a bed, his eyes closed.

With a sympathetic look, Louisa motioned silently to Ann to go speak to him. She pointed to herself and pantomimed going around the corner, then promptly did so.

Ann inched closer to the barred cell. "Will." She did not want the other prisoners to hear her and start a racket—or worse, a commentary.

He blinked. He sat up.

"Ann!"

She laid a finger to her lips.

He jumped up and strode to the bars, grasping them as he spoke in a low voice. "What are you doing here? Are you here alone?" His whisper contained a hint of outrage.

"No, Louisa came with me. She's waiting for me."

"Still, this is no place for you." His hair was unkempt and a faint shadow darkened his jaw line.

"I had to see you."

He did not move, his dark eyes locked on her.

She dropped her gaze, confused. She leaned close and whispered, "Was I right to visit you?"

"Yes." He moved closer and extended one hand through the bars, palm up. She was too surprised to move for a moment, but he plainly wanted to take her hand. She laid it in his.

"Thank you." He closed his fingers around her hand. As she felt the warmth of his touch, it struck her with terrible force that he was behind bars—that after the judge spoke, he would in all likelihood be legally bound to Master Good for the rest of his life. Her lip trembled and she swallowed hard, pressing her hand into his. He gently pulled her toward him. They stood, almost touching, save for the bars. Her eyes filled.

Footsteps echoed back in the direction of the other cells.

The groans and cries of the prisoners announced the passage of another. "I must go," she whispered.

He released her hand with reluctance.

Ann turned and pattered around the corner. Louisa waited a few steps ahead in the hall.

Ann hurried up and murmured in her ear, "Someone's coming." She heard footsteps behind them, so close that they must be at Will's cell. She and Louisa froze.

A female voice she did not recognize called Will's name.

"Emmie!" His shock traveled even around the corner. "How did you know I was here?"

"Tom found out from your old master. He told me." It was a young voice, uneducated but sweet.

"Did you get my letter?" Will's voice carried clearly through the stone corridor.

Ann did not want to eavesdrop, though she was mortally curious. She started down the hall away from Will's cell, toward the back gate. Louisa kept pace at her elbow.

As they went, the echo of Will's voice faded, but before they turned the next corner, Ann heard him say one thing.

"Did you say that you would marry me?"

And the girl responded.

"Yes."

Thirty-Eight

THEY'RE TAKING YOU UP TO THE COURT TODAY." THE jailer sorted through the keys at his belt and selected one to shove in the lock of the cell door.

Once inside he held out a rope almost apologetically. "I'm gonna have to tie you. Put your hands in front of you."

Will obeyed while the man looped the rope around them in a complicated knot. The smell of the man's rotten teeth nauseated him; he had to turn his head. When the jailer finished, the knots were tight. Will would not able to slip them off, as John and Clara Simon had slipped from their mock bonds in Blendon Township.

The jailer took hold of the end of the rope and ushered Will out of the cell in front of him. When they came out of the prison gate, the afternoon light hurt his eyes; he squinted and shuffled along behind the jailer, half-blind for a minute or two.

The courthouse was only two streets away—still, Will kept his head down, mortified to be taken through the crowded streets at the end of a rope. Some rivermen jeered him as he went, raising their tankards as they sat on a bench outside a tavern.

A woman called out to him, "A fine piece of manflesh you

are! Come up here and I'll set you to rights!" The rivermen started a round of coarse jokes and offered to go in his place.

On the next street the crowd was more genteel, which was almost worse. Will's ears burned. Finally they walked up to the brick court building he recognized from his last visit there. The jailer pointed, and he stepped up the stoop and through the door.

The same assortment of citizens dotted the courtroom: mostly tradesmen, craftsmen, and the poor, for the rich did not get hauled before the law. The observers leaned against the walls or sat on benches, dwarfed by the mountainous judicial table at the end of the room.

A familiar face turned to him from one of the benches. Mr. Miller. There was Ann next to him, and Louisa Burbridge as well, holding her friend's hand. Ann was pale and her reddened eyes revealed that she had been weeping, though she was none the less beautiful for it. Her bruised look made him want to take her in his arms again and comfort her, as he had on her farm. But that would hardly work, with his wrists tied up like the legs of a pheasant.

Mr. Miller stood up and stepped around the feet and bodies of strangers until he made it to Will's side. "How are you faring, son?" The saddler's face was drawn and tense.

"Middling, sir." Will was not as starved and weak as he had been on his last appearance in this courtroom, but Mr. Miller's question stirred up the dread that had boiled inside him all morning.

He tried to stave it off with silent prayer. *Thou preparest a table for me in the presence of mine enemies . . .* His confidence wavered as an unbidden image came to him of Master Good with a poker in his hand, beating Tom. Then the memory of losing control of his bladder when Good beat him so savagely before his escape . . . and most of all the master's eyes, void of human compassion, brightening only at the pain and sorrow of others.

Thou preparest a table for me in the presence of mine enemies. The Lord is with me. He cast about inside himself for the presence that gave him hope. It was there, faint but steady.

The judge looked up behind his spectacles, his wig wavering next to his cheeks.

"Master Jacob Good."

Motion caught Will's eye; Master Good rose from behind a cluster of seated men. His mask-like face turned to the judge. "Here, Your Honor."

"You bring before me the case of a runaway apprentice?"

"Yes, Your Honor. One who was before this court not so long ago for killing a neighbor's pig." He pointed an accusing finger at Will. "Now his rebellious nature has led him to run away, causing me all kind of trouble and inconvenience. And one who should have returned him has instead harbored him, in defiance of the law."

"That is . . ." The judge scanned a paper on his table. "Mr. Samuel Miller?"

"Yes, Your Honor."

"And is Mr. Miller here?"

"I am, Your Honor." Mr. Miller strode to the front of the room to stand before the high bench.

"Do you deny this accusation, Mr. Miller?"

"In part, Your Honor. I wish to present the truth to you, not half-truths and outright lies."

The judge peered at Will where he stood bound beside the jailer. "I recognize the apprentice now. I saw him in the very act of running away, near the bridge. Bring him up here." He scowled as if he had not eaten to his satisfaction that morning. Will fought off a whisper of foreboding as he followed the jailer to the front of the room. He shifted his arms to try to bring some feeling back to his numb hands where they hung useless before him.

"And what, Mr. Miller, is your version of the truth?" The judge did not even look at the saddler.

"This man, Jacob Good, had beaten this young man to within a hairsbreadth of his life, which caused him to run away. And it was not the first time Jacob Good beat his apprentices." Mr. Miller grew more impassioned, addressing only the judge without acknowledging Master Good at all. "Nor did he feed them enough to even keep body and soul together."

"That is what the apprentice told you?"

"I know it to be true, Your Honor."

"Did you witness this beating, or this starving?"

"I witnessed the results, Your Honor. And Will bears the scars of a flogging that will be with him the rest of his days." The reference made Will's scars itch.

"So do many sailors. That does not excuse mutiny or absconding."

Mr. Miller fell silent.

Master Good smirked. "You see, Your Honor, this rival of mine attempts to undermine my business by stealing my apprentice and then besmirching my name."

The lines around the judge's mouth deepened.

What would Ann think of this slur against her father's character? Will looked over his shoulder at the young women. Ann's brown eyes were huge in her pale face.

"Mr. Miller," the judge said through his nose. "I see no evidence that your opinion is correct. You have broken the law based on the word of an apprentice who has already committed other criminal acts. Is this not the young man who killed your neighbor's pig, Master Good?"

"It is, Your Honor." Satisfaction oozed across Jacob Good's face.

Now Will's palms were sweating, and he closed his eyes and searched again for the holy presence to comfort him. But this time, he felt nothing.

Another voice whispered in his head. *The Lord did not help our Savior when he groaned on the cross—he died in agony, crying that his Father abandoned him.*

He bowed his head while his soul shrank within him.

Allan Burbridge was right. The powers of this world are stronger than the powers of heaven.

Behind him the door of the courtroom opened and closed.

"Your Honor, may I speak on this matter?" The baritone was familiar. Will swiveled far enough to see Dr. Loftin walk up beside him in an impeccable frock coat and collar, his white hair adding to his air of authority.

"You have some involvement with this case?" The judge lifted his bewigged head, adjusting his spectacles on his nose.

"I am the neighbor whose pig this young man was accused of killing."

"He did kill it." The judge corrected the doctor. "He did not deny it, and the other apprentice confirmed that he killed it, as I recall."

"I'm the other apprentice, Your Honor." A younger voice came from behind Will, and a familiar, thin youth with a mop of dark hair passed by Will's elbow and stood by Dr. Loftin. What on earth was Tom doing here?

"I lied about the pig, Your Honor." Tom's voice was strained.

"That is called perjury, boy," the judge snapped. "You know men go to jail for it?"

Tom's hands were shaking. He looked straight at Will, as if the sight of his former friend could keep him standing. "Yes, Your Honor. But the truth is that Will didn't kill the pig. Master Good killed it. He went into the woods before Will, and the gunshot went off while Will stood right next to me."

"And you saw this?" The expression on the judge's face wavered.

"Yes, sir. But Master Good threatened to kill us if we did not perjure ourselves. Then he almost beat Will to death afterward." The last words spilled out in a rush as if Tom were afraid the judge might cut him off.

If the judge did not believe Tom, they would both surely die at Master Good's hands. But if the devil could manifest himself in Jacob Good, the Lord had just walked into the courtroom in the starved body of Tom Reece. *A light shines for those sitting in darkness.* And the Lord did not always spare his children from pain and death, but he would make himself known, even in this world. Tom stared at Will, a question writ large in his tense face. Will held his gaze and nodded.

With a thump of his hand on his table, the judge snapped at Tom. "I should clap you in jail this minute." The judge pressed his lips together. "Except for the fact that your master apparently compelled you to perjury with every means at his disposal. And perjury is a most grievous offense against Justice herself." He glowered at Master Good. "What say you to this, Jacob Good?"

"It's all lies, Your Honor. They have cooked up some scheme between them." Master Good's voice grew ingratiating, his unnatural smile as broad as a crocodile's.

The judge was unmoved. "I now have the word of four men that you are a perjurer, a swine-killer, and a would-be murderer. This apprentice"—he indicated Tom—"is willing to go to prison for his testimony against you."

"I am a solid citizen, Your Honor, and a good Christian man!"

All of the buzz in the courtroom had ceased, and Master Good's words fell into the silence like a stone dropped in a deep well.

"I think not. And on account of you having suborned this young man to perjury, I hereby remand you to three years confinement by the State, followed by a year additional for killing the doctor's sow."

Master Good took a step back, visibly stricken.

The judge rapped his gavel, then waved it at Will. "Untie that young man. He has suffered enough at this man's hands. I hereby cancel his debt and his indenture, and that of the other apprentice too. And young man"—he raised his voice at Tom—"though perjury is a very serious offense, I am willing to grant clemency under your circumstances."

Tom's face lit up and Will was sure his own reflected the same joy. Mr. Miller and Dr. Loftin shook hands and slapped each other on the shoulder.

Almost as an afterthought, the judge added, "Tie up Jacob Good and take him to the holding cell."

Master Good jumped, looked around wildly, then pushed his way for the door. Mr. Miller stepped in Good's way and seized his upper arms. With a stream of oaths, Master Good jerked like a puppet in his attempt to free himself. But other men in the courtroom threw themselves upon Master Good, and he was soon facedown, struggling feebly against four captors. Flushed with their role in enforcing the law, the men jested and laughed, drowning out Good's muffled imprecations from a face squashed against the wood floor.

Will's jailer finished untying him and moved with his rope to the small cluster of men holding Good down. Soon Good was tied as Will had been only five minutes before. The jailer ushered the men back and hauled Good to his feet none too gently.

"I think you'll be a shade less pleasant than my last charge," the jailer said, and pushed Good toward the door.

Good's face contorted and he spat at the jailer.

Compelled by an impulse he didn't understand, Will followed after Good. At the door, his former master turned and looked him in the eye, his frozen stare malevolent.

Will spoke as if each word could penetrate the man's thick shell of ego and hatred. "The light shines in the darkness, and the darkness overcomes it not."

"You son of a whore!"

The jailer cut off Good's invective with an elbow to the gut. The black-haired man doubled over, gasping.

Good's insults did not provoke Will now, not even the mention of his mother. He watched as the jailer shoved a bent Jacob Good out the door. *No longer my master. Never again.*

Then he remembered Ann. When he turned to find her, she stood embracing her friend Louisa. The light from the window revealed the sheen of tears on Ann's face. She smiled self-consciously, lifting the handkerchief in her hands to blot her cheeks. But then something clouded her eyes, and she grew pensive. She turned her back to him and took Louisa's hand. With a quiet exchange of words, they began to move toward the door on the other side of the courtroom. He looked after them, mystified.

"Will." Someone touched his shoulder. Tom hung his head. "I hope you can forgive—"

"There is nothing to forgive." Now a lump hurt Will's throat. "You just saved my life at risk of your own." He and Tom pounded each other's backs, cleared their throats, and turned to stand side by side in an appropriately manly way, though Tom sniffed once.

"I should remind you," Tom said, gazing at the chaotic courtroom while the judge pounded for order and eventually threw up his hands and took a recess. "Someone is waiting and will be glad to hear your good news."

Emmie. His buoyant heart deflated.

"You have kept her informed of the news?"

"As well as I could."

"Thank you." He shook Tom's hand, wishing the other young man could eradicate that last trace of guilt from his countenance. Time would heal the wound, he hoped.

"I think you should go tell her yourself," Tom said.

"I suppose so." Will tried to sound enthusiastic. "I'm surprised she isn't here. She came to see me in jail, you know." His sinking sensation redoubled at the memory of her acceptance of his proposal.

"Perhaps she was too nervous." Tom looked unsure of himself, in this role as go-between. "Would you like me to come with you to see her?"

"Yes, if you are willing."

"Of course."

Will beckoned Tom to follow and found Mr. Miller. "Sir, I must fulfill an obligation. Will you wait half an hour for my return?"

The saddler looked curious but agreed.

Will set off ahead of Tom, hurrying down the courthouse steps. He must act now, before he could weaken from his duty.

It was maddening that she could not seem to stop her tears. Just when Ann thought they had run their course, a piercing thought would force out another. This unhinged state of joy and sorrow would drive her to an asylum should it continue much longer. Ann dabbed at the corners of her eyes before the moisture could become apparent. Louisa pretended not to notice, bending her head to the knitting in her lap.

Ann's father had sent them ahead to return to the Burbridges' while he waited for Will, who had gone on an errand.

After the judge's decision, the words that sent joy flooding through her like sunlight, Ann could think of only one kind of errand that would be so important as to take Will away immediately.

He has gone to see her.

She dabbed at one eye again, letting the moisture seep into a dry part of the handkerchief. She needed a common handkerchief, not this dainty, lace-edged piece of frippery. It was half-sodden already.

She was glad Allan was away from home, having gone on business out of town. If he saw her in this state, with his keen faculty of observation, he was sure to make some trenchant comment to her about Will.

And she could not bear to admit he had been right. Somehow, despite her conviction that she would marry Eli, she had lost her heart to the former pig-keeper, the runaway apprentice.

And now she knew why they called it losing one's heart. Inside her drifted a painful absence, where something of her had gone away. It was the same part of her that went out to Will as they stood together on the deck of the boat—the same pulse of living sympathy that had pulled her close to the bars of his jail cell. Never had she felt such complete oneness and peace of mind and heart with a man. She realized now that Allan and even Eli had always been to her exciting foreign forces that blew into her vicinity and then blew back out again, having stirred things up but leaving her unchanged by their departure.

The clock ticked in the hush of the parlor. She tried to read her Bible, but her eyes glanced over the page without taking it in.

Why had God brought about the circumstances that led to Eli's second proposal: his remaining in Rushville, his renewal of his courtship? It had all seemed to be a heavenly response to her prayers.

Maybe it was. Perhaps the Lord did want her to marry Eli, and it had been her own foolishness that led her to speak so intimately with another young man.

A chill sent her past the point of tears as she gazed sightlessly at the open pages, white in her lap against the red of her dress. She would have to marry Eli, if she wished to marry at all, because Will did not love her. He was to marry someone else.

At that blunt thought, a flicker of anger heated her cheeks.

She snapped shut the Bible, causing Louisa to look up in her direction with wide, gray eyes. Ashamed, Ann opened it again, as if it had been a fumble.

Why had Will spoken to her so tenderly, so confidentially, if he had made promises to another? She admired his compassion, his resolve to help others. The cruel circumstances of his past had not crushed or altered a character that, beneath the dirt and pain, was loving and selfless. Had he not realized that his actions might mislead her? Was he deliberately fickle—no, she could not believe that of him. He had not toyed with her affections. It had been an unfortunate accident of timing and proximity that she had come to know him well enough to discover his nature, the goodness that stole into her consciousness so quietly, and with results now so devastating.

A sting at her eyes again brought her kerchief up to hide them. He might bring the girl home with him. He might even be marrying her now. So the naïve fancies that refused to completely dissipate were only a torment to her—the realization that Will would live on the farm—that had she married him, she could have stayed with her sisters and also found a deep happiness of the sort she could not envision with Eli.

But now she would have to marry Eli, because she would not be able to stay on the farm if Will brought another young woman there as his wife.

It all struck her as a merciless jest of the kind that did not come from heaven. She had been tempted, all-unknowing, to long for what could never be hers. And in the fierceness of the longing, she begged silently for relief.

Thirty-Nine

THE BOARDING HOUSE STANK OF URINE. THE ROTTING timbers of its stairwell were damp and sprouted white lichen. Will mounted the stairs, guided only by the cracks of daylight that filtered through the decaying walls. At Emmie's door he paused to wait for Tom, who had to climb slowly in his poor state of health. When his friend stood behind him, Will knocked.

The plank door opened and Emmie peeped out, her narrow face suspicious at first.

"Oh!" She smiled, her crooked teeth marring an otherwise beautiful effect. "Come in."

She opened the door wide and backed up, one hand clutching at her skirt as if she did not know quite what to say or do.

"It's all right, Emmie." Will pretended lightness that did not match his leaden mood. He was grateful that the Lord had spared him today, but coming face-to-face with Emmie leached the color from his future. He had imagined too often his conversations with Ann, her intelligence, her gentleness, the two of them sharing a life in which faith was natural and life-giving. By comparison, Emmie's placid simplicity would leave him alone in their marriage, her world defined completely by food and clothing.

But he would never let Emmie know. He would do his best to be a loving husband, letting duty serve where commonality could not.

"You're free from him?" she asked.

"Yes, he has gone to prison for at least four years."

"Oh, la! That's music to my ears." Her smile was genuine, but her arm circled around Will's neck with the stiffness of a marionette in a play as she held her body away from his. He understood. It felt awkward to him as well.

"Both of you, free! Just imagine, after all he's done." She touched Tom's arm as if to share his relief too. That was Emmie, all quickness, body, and animal instinct.

He did her injustice. He must not begin this way. He would respect her and honor what she brought to the marriage. It was volition that made a marriage, and honoring one's promises.

"I would like you to come with me to the farm where I live now." He took her hand, making up for his mental criticism.

"Well, I see as how that would be nice." She kept her hand in his, not meeting his eyes. Perhaps she sensed his reluctance. He would be kinder, as kind as necessary.

"You will be happy there, I know it. The air is fresh, and the Millers are good people. You would not be as tired as you have been here." She had confided to him at the jail that her hours at the factory were so long that she had little time for anything else but sleep.

"Are there lots of flowers? And cheese, and milk, and chickens?" She gave him a tiny smile, her yellow hair framing her face and spilling out under her bonnet as it always had. He squeezed her hand. She was just like a little girl, in some ways.

"A chicken every Sunday."

Her smile widened, though it was still a little tremulous. It was only to be expected. For a girl who had seen nothing but tenement dwellings and the inside of a poorhouse, any change would be frightening.

"And, Emmie, Will can teach you to read." Tom stood by the door, shifting from one foot to another as if uncertain whether to stay or go. Will was just as happy that Tom remained. His presence delayed the necessity of more physical demonstrations of affection.

"You know how you told me you wanted to learn to read." Tom cracked his knuckles and looked at the floor. "I can't read, save my own name, but Will can read as good as any schoolteacher."

"I'll be pleased to teach you, if that's what you wish."

She withdrew her hand from his and crossed her arms, rubbing her dress sleeves. "Shall I pack up my things, then?"

Would he really have to introduce her to the Millers—to Ann—now? He steeled himself. Might as well do it sooner than later, for he would need to cherish her and learn to think of her as his wife without hesitation.

"I don't know if you will come stay with us this very day," he said, "because we are ourselves guests. But I would like you to meet the Millers." He managed to say it with complete sincerity. His heart would learn, if his manners preceded it. "Would you like to meet them now?"

"I suppose I would. You don't think they'll mind me coming back to their place with you?"

He pitied the self-consciousness that made her pick at her bodice.

"No. They will think you charming and kind."

Tom shuffled some more and fidgeted. "I guess I'd better be going."

For the first time, Tom's situation dawned on Will. "But where will you go, Tom?" No wonder Tom had come with him. What else could he do? Mistress Good would surely be devastated by the loss of her income represented by Master Good's imprisonment. And she would not even know her husband's whereabouts until Tom told her. Master Good had not even brought her to court, so certain was he of his victory.

"I suppose I'll go back and tell Mistress Good," Tom said, echoing Will's thoughts.

"No, you cannot do that." Will would have to think of some other solution. His conscience pained him—in a way, he had been the cause of Mistress Good's temporary widowhood. And, though he would not say it aloud, it might very well be her permanent widowhood, with the way disease and hard labor cut swaths through a prison population.

Will rubbed his forehead and sighed. "Come with us back to the courthouse, and we will ride to the Burbridges' house with Mr. Miller. I think Dr. Loftin will be there too, and we can seek his counsel about Mistress Good."

Tom agreed with noticeable relief. Will gave Emmie his arm, and they all went down the reeking stairs together.

"Mr. Miller, this is my bride-to-be, Emmie Flynn." Emmie made a little bob of a curtsy to the saddler, while retaining her tight grip on Will's arm.

Mr. Miller froze in the act of touching his hat brim, one foot still on the courthouse steps where he had come down to meet them. Slowly, he continued the gesture of courtesy with a nod of the head. "Miss Flynn. Happy news, indeed." His tone was wooden. Will cringed. He should have told Mr. Miller in private.

But the saddler was nothing if not a courteous man. "Will had not told us of the news. You will be coming to live with us, I hope?"

Will could have embraced him just then.

"I think so, sir." Emmie spoke in a mumble. Perhaps she was trying to hide her teeth. Will patted her arm.

"What I don't know, sir, is where Tom is going to go." Will glanced at his younger friend, who flushed.

"I want to stay here, Mr. Miller, sir, in Pittsburgh." Tom lifted his chin, a little defiant. "It's all the home I've got."

"Well, why don't you come with us, and we'll talk it over at more length." Mr. Miller turned back to the open door of the courthouse. "Doctor! The celebration will begin without you if you don't make haste."

Dr. Loftin shouldered his way through the crowd at the door, chuckling and donning his hat. "Patience, Samuel! Some of us have friends here, you know." He also inspected Emmie with curiosity, registering the fact that her hand lay on Will's arm. "Miss Flynn, I presume?"

The doctor had quite a memory. But perhaps when one gave money to help a person in need, it was easy to remember her name.

"Yes, Doctor. Thank you for all you've done for me, sir." Emmie dipped her head again.

"Not at all."

Mr. Miller waved to the coachman and turned to Dr.

Loftin. "They are coming with us to talk, Robert. We must figure out what Tom shall do for a living now, as he wishes to remain here."

"Well, I may be of some help with that. Come along then." Dr. Loftin shooed them toward the Burbridges' coach and then headed for his own, which stood waiting behind the larger one. "Tom, will you ride with me?"

Will wished the doctor had asked Emmie to ride with them as well, as Will would have loved the chance to explain to Mr. Miller, at least in part. He thought the saddler had a trace of a wounded look about him. Will should tell him what had led to this situation, without some of the shameful details.

But it was not to be, and the conversation on the ride to the Burbridge mansion was stilted. Will grew quieter as they neared their destination, leaving Mr. Miller to discuss the weather with Emmie.

Now he would have to face Ann. It seemed terrible. He prayed for the courage and judgment to behave as he should.

The butler took their things, including Emmie's ragged shawl and bonnet. Should he have brought her here? She looked painfully self-aware in her threadbare dress. Against the sumptuous colors of the walls and the plush pile of the rug under their feet, she might have been an urchin from any fairy tale who found herself by magic in the king's palace. He must support her. He held her arm and smiled down at her. She still looked mortified and reluctant, her thin face pinched.

Following the doctor and Mr. Miller, he brought Emmie down the hall. Tom stayed close, his eyes big, his mouth shut.

Then came the moment he feared. They rounded the doorway into the oval parlor.

Louisa sat at the far end of the parlor facing them. She stood up, her needlework falling from her lap into a little heap on the floor. Her mouth was slightly open, but she closed it and moved toward them with her customary grace. Ann had been sitting with her back to the door; at Louisa's motion, she twisted to look, and then after a pause, rose to her feet. Will could not take his eyes off her pallor, transfixed by the haunted look in her eyes.

"I am Louisa Burbridge." The young lady held out her hand to Emmie as if the orphan girl were from the finest family in Pittsburgh. "Welcome."

Emmie took her hand shyly. Will cringed at the dirt that streaked his fiancée's arm. At that moment, Ann reached the small group.

"Tom," she said. "I am so glad to see you." To Will's surprise, he saw tears gather in her eyes. She was more emotional than he would have expected. But she swallowed and seemed to regain her composure.

"Thank you, miss." Tom touched his forelock.

"Miss Burbridge," Will said, as neither Mr. Miller nor Dr. Loftin had spoken. "This is my fiancée, Miss Emmie Flynn."

"And you are so pretty," Louisa said. "Where has he been hiding you?" There was no hidden meaning in her tone, just soft compliment.

Emmie beamed before looking uncertain again.

When Louisa released Emmie's hand, Ann thrust her own out, less than gracefully. "Miss Flynn. Delighted to meet you."

Emmie took Ann's hand as well, clearly at sea in this

perfumed world. Ann was still very pale. Will felt stirrings of nausea. What had he done in arranging this painful encounter? He must get them all through it as quickly as he could.

"Miss Flynn has agreed to come back to the farm with us . . . when she is my wife." He forced it out.

Ann clasped her hands in front of her, tension wrinkling her dress across her collarbone. "How lovely. My congratulations."

There was heartbreak in the air, so solid that it could not be waved away by the best manners or the most open welcome Louisa could provide. Will knew he should stop looking at Ann, but immobility was all he could manage when what he really wanted was to bury his face in his hands.

Then Emmie began to sob.

Horrified, he ushered her to a chair. He had not dissembled well enough. She had seen the look that passed between Ann and Will. She must know.

Tears ran down her face, and she could not speak. Her shoulders heaved, she breathed in great gulps. He knelt beside her, offered her his handkerchief, and patted her hand, beyond hope. He had ruined everything, even this young girl's illusions. Mr. Miller and Dr. Loftin stood helpless in the way of widowers unaccustomed to women's tears.

"I'm sorry," Emmie sobbed, crumpling the handkerchief in a ball. "I can't do it. Not for nothing."

Will bowed his head.

"It's all right, Emmie," a low voice said behind him. Tom stepped up before the weeping girl and looked at the little knot of stunned observers. "I'll tell them."

He raised her to her feet, where she leaned against him as if otherwise her knees would give way.

"We couldn't bear to tell you, Will," Tom said. "Not after what you've been through. Not after what I'd done to you. But Emmie and me—well, we didn't mean to, but we love each other. I went to help her after you left, like you told me. Every time I picked up oakum. We were so sad, I guess we just comforted each other."

Will stood up. What was this?

"You can hit me if you want, Will. I mean, we can step outside." Tom tripped over his words. "I haven't been a good friend to you."

A burst of laughter threatened to erupt out of Will at any minute. He knew it was shock getting the better of him, but exhilaration swelled beneath it, far away, not yet real.

"Tom, no one could be a better friend than to do what you did for me in that courtroom." He struggled to sound subdued and regretful. "There is nothing I wouldn't sacrifice for you, not even the love of a wonderful girl."

He offered his hand and Tom shook it.

Emmie dared to peep around Tom's dirty sleeve. "You're not angry?"

"I am crushed, of course." He did not even know what he was babbling. How to preserve her feminine self-regard without showing his jubilation was a balancing act. He did not know if he could maintain it much longer.

Tom hung his head. "We'll leave you to think if this is what you really want. I'll let you have her, Will, if that's what you and Emmie think is right."

Will wrung his hand again.

The doctor cleared his throat. "I'll come with you, Tom. We have more to discuss about your application to the factory."

"Yes, sir."

When they had left the room, Will could not even look at the others. His head was spinning. He strode away down the hall, toward the back door that opened out on the yard and the barn. He had to be alone.

Forty

"WILL WISHES TO SPEAK WITH YOU." HER FATHER leaned his head around the door of the Burbridges' guest bedroom.

"I do not wish to speak to him." Ann's words were clipped as she sat at the desk with borrowed pen and paper. It was high time she wrote to her sisters.

"He has been waiting for some time."

"I am otherwise occupied, as you can see."

Her father gave her a knowing, disapproving look and withdrew. His footsteps trailed away down the wood of the upstairs hallway. But in a few minutes, she heard him returning. She sighed with exasperation and turned to face the door, ready for his reappearance and a lecture.

There was a light knock, and the half-open door creaked wider. Will stood in the doorway, his shoulders almost filling it. In his long dark coat and high collar, he could have passed for a well-born friend of Allan's.

"Come for a walk with me. Let me explain." He asked like a man, not pleading but with quiet urgency. His handsomeness infuriated her at that particular moment. What of it if his dark hair waved down just over the back of his collar?

"What do you mean?" She fixed him with a stare of mock innocence.

He looked contrite. "I would like to apologize and to explain. And I will not leave you alone until you allow me to do so."

She jabbed her quill back into the inkhorn and jumped to her feet. She probably looked like a jack-in-the-box, but in her temper she did not care. "Very well. As you insist, I suppose I must agree."

He offered her his arm, but she brushed ahead of him and stalked down the hallway without looking back.

He did not try to speak as they went down the stairs, though she was conscious of his watchful presence behind her. The butler emerged from his little anteroom—she did not know how he always spotted them so adeptly—and offered their hats.

"I won't take mine, thank you," Will said. "It's a fine day, and we'll just walk the grounds."

She would not be agreeable, not even to agree that it was a fine day and it might be pleasant to walk with the sun on her face and the breeze in her hair. She took her hat from the butler and tied it firmly under her chin. When the man opened the door for them, she sailed ahead and down the wide steps, across the drive, and onto the green lawn.

She was already surrounded by the cones and spheres of the topiary when a firm hand clasped her elbow. "You should go out for footraces. You'd give any man a run for his money."

She was forced to slow down as he drew her closer to his side and interlaced their arms, trapping her hand with his. His fingers were warm over hers. She glanced up at him, but the affection that lit his face disconcerted her. She turned to study the topiary they passed as if he were of little interest.

"You have every right to be angry with me."

She would admit nothing. "Why should I be angry?"

He paused. "Let's sit down. I would like to see your face."

She had been enjoying the fact that she could cut him out of her peripheral vision with the wide brim of her hat. The woman who designed this style of hat must have known that there were times when one just wanted a man out of sight.

Out beyond the hedge, beyond the road, the dogwoods and cherry trees blossomed in white and pink clouds. He led her that way without further comment. A few yards into the grove, there was a bench. It was late enough in the morning that the wood of the seat was dry. He released her and indicated the bench by opening his hand, inviting her to sit before him. She flounced down, as much as her stiff skirt would allow her to flounce.

He seated himself next to her, far closer than he should.

"Look at me." It was almost a whisper. She turned, compelled by curiosity, if nothing else. He was so close. The light streamed through the fragile petals of the dogwood above them, and the dappled light made his brown eyes even deeper, picking out points of bright amber from their depths.

"It's not a pretty story that I have for you, but the truth. I offered to marry Emmie Flynn because it was the only honorable thing to do."

She flinched as his words struck new pain from the wound she had tried to cover. She had suspected it, but his confession conjured the image of him kissing the other girl, holding her close—she took a deep breath and looked straight ahead, willing herself not to cry. She had done too much of that of late.

"Is she with child?" she asked.

"No," he said slowly. "But a man may owe a woman a proposal nonetheless." He sounded mortified. She felt rather than saw him stand up. Good, now he would leave.

To her shock, he knelt on the grass in front of her so his upturned face was only a little below hers. He took her limp hands from her lap and held them. "I am deeply sorry for wronging her, and for causing you pain. I am yours, Ann. I have been for months, with all my soul, as I never felt for Emmie. If I had married her, I would have spent the rest of my life trying not to think of you. Tell me you feel the same. I know I have hurt you, and I never want to hurt you again. I hope to have the rest of my life to make it up to you. Do you feel the same?"

The hurt welled up again. She wanted him to feel the pain he had caused her. She turned her face. "No, I do not."

He paused. The hurt was palpable. Guilt mixed with her agitation.

"I do not believe you," he said.

She looked back at him. He stood and raised her to her feet so they were standing closely, as only lovers would.

"May I remove your hat for you?" He pulled gently at the tie of her hat. When the bow gave way, he lifted it off her head and dropped it behind her. She stared up at him as if mesmerized.

She felt his arms encircle her. She stopped breathing. He drew her even closer, and she closed her eyes at the touch of his lips on hers. The union of spirit and body was so overwhelming she thought she would faint. She turned her face up to his kiss and breathed in the sweet warmth of his face. She wanted to be closer, as if the missing part of her had come home with the touch of his skin and the strong warmth of his body next to hers.

He drew back, and she opened her eyes. The blood rushed to her face, and she tried to drop her hands from where she had placed them on his shoulders. He grabbed them, holding them in place.

"You don't want to marry me?" He murmured it as if he could not believe it.

She could not lie while caught in the tender gaze of his dark eyes. "I do."

"You will?"

"I'll marry you." She smiled, and his answering smile was so joyful she thought it would light the whole grove. He kissed her again, making her so weak she held his arms to steady herself.

"You know I asked your father for his blessing."

"And he gave it, of course. The meddling matchmaker."

They both laughed.

"Let's walk for a while before we go back." Will took her hand and started down the path through the trees, and she walked at his side.

As they went, a gust in the breeze brought the petals drifting down around them in white and pink, feather touches on Ann's cheek and bright on Will's shoulders.

Forty-One

I WOULD PREFER YOU STAY HERE." WILL PRESSED ANN'S hand as they stood in front of the open gate of the jail.

He could tell from the determined expression on her lovely face that she wanted to object. "I would prefer to come in with you." She put her hands on her hips.

He smiled and paused, completely smitten even in the dank air that poured out from the jail. But then the seriousness of his errand came back to him. "You are certain?"

"Yes." She swished past him before he could say anything further. Mr. Miller stood a few feet inside the hallway, watching them with amused forbearance.

Will's mind returned to the present need with a shock like diving in cold water. He joined Mr. Miller. "We had better go see him."

The saddler nodded, growing sober. Will took Ann's arm to guide her down the twisting corridor. Some prisoners slumped in sullen silence. The madman asked them to bring his cloak and then screamed insults when they did not answer him.

They had come to the end, the very same cell that had held Will before. Will sent up a quick prayer. *Lord, help me.* He did not know if he would be able to do what he had come to do. He glanced at Ann. Her eyes were soft in the lamplight. She released his arm, as if she knew he must go alone to the bars.

His former master sat with his back to the side wall, gazing sightlessly at the opposite wall. His formerly smooth face was shadowed with stubble, his hair unkempt. A stench rose from the bucket in the corner.

"Jacob Good." Will would not ever call him master again.

He looked up. Where pride and malevolence had lived in his light stare, there was now only emptiness, like broken glass.

"They will be taking you to the state prison next week."

He regarded Will without speaking.

Mr. Miller stood beside Will, watching. He had already said that he would leave this conversation to Will, Jacob Good, and God.

"I have spoken to your wife," Will said. At that there was a flicker of something in Good's countenance. Disdain? Or hurt, impossible as that seemed.

"Dr. Loftin has pledged to help her sell the house and find gainful employment. And Tom will help her as long as she needs it."

Good blinked, as if a hand had passed before his face. Then his whole body twitched. Had he lost his wits?

Will took a deep breath. It was hard to say it, even though he had sought the words on his knees for hours the previous day.

"Jacob Good, I forgive you all the wrongs you have done me, because I have been first forgiven. And because the Lord gave his life for you as for me."

Will held a small Bible out through the bars. "I will pray for your soul as long as you walk this earth, that you will know forgiveness and mercy."

When Good remained motionless at the wall, Will bent over and slid the Bible under the door of the cell.

He looked back inquiringly at Mr. Miller, who nodded.

Will had said all that could be said. He stepped up to the bars one more time, unsure of what he felt as he regarded the broken figure that had once tormented him.

But as he turned away, Jacob Good's face glistened in the shifting light. Will walked a few steps, stunned as the realization dawned. His former master was weeping.

Ann said nothing, seeming conscious of the gravity of the moment. She put a gentle hand in Will's, and they followed her father quietly down the corridor.

The jailer opened the gate once more, and Ann moved into the morning light, which glowed on the lace of her white sleeve. She would not release Will's hand, but waited until he had come all the way through the gate to join her so she could take his arm again. He soaked in the comfort of her warm presence. He did not want to be parted from her either.

At the feel of the sunlight on his face, Will thought that Jacob Good would not see it for some time, if ever again. For the first time, real pity filled him for the wretchedness of his former master. *Lord, have mercy on him*, he prayed, and meant it.

With that prayer, it was as if the last ghostly shackle fell away from him, one that had been there so long he had forgotten its pressure.

He was free. There was no hatred left in him to bind him to his old master, only the inexplicable, all-encompassing love of God.

He turned to look at his beautiful fiancée. She sensed his gaze and turned to him, still serious, as if she understood everything.

He stopped and took her in her arms, heedless of Mr. Miller and anyone who passed by.

He knew that no one could deserve the grace and love that broke upon him now as a rain of blessing.

As he embraced his bride-to-be, the words he had read that morning came to him, and he gave them back as both praise and promise to the Lord.

I, the Lord, have called thee in righteousness
And I will hold thy hand, and keep thee
And give thee for a covenant for the peoples
For a light of the Gentiles
To open blind eyes
To bring out the prisoners from the prison
And them that sit in darkness out of the prison house.

Afterword

History and Fiction

WILLIAM HANBY AND ANN MILLER ARE REAL PEOPLE who lived in Ohio in the mid-nineteenth century, fell in love, married, and eventually had eight children. Their son Ben Hanby was a composer who wrote "Darling Nelly Gray," a wildly popular song that influenced antebellum American sentiment against slavery. The entire family worked on the Underground Railroad, harboring fugitives at their homes in Rushville and Westerville.

My novels about the Hanbys reflect historical fact, though the limited information available required me to imagine many elements of the world of the Hanbys. The Hanbys, the Millers, and Master Jacob Good bear their real names, but most supporting characters are fictional. In some cases, I have used names that suggest real citizens of that period, as in the Westerfield family, who eventually gave their name to the town of Westerville, Ohio. In actuality, that founding family's surname was Westervelt.

William Hanby really did indenture to a cruel master named Jacob Good. Master Good did shoot his neighbor's pig, then almost beat William to death for refusing to perjure himself in court. William escaped by night and fled forty miles on foot to West Virginia, where a congressman's wife sheltered him. Her life-saving hospitality inspired William to promise God that he would help other fugitives whenever he could.

Continuing to Ohio, William found a haven with another saddler, Samuel Miller, and fell in love with his daughter Ann Miller. William did eventually insist on returning to Jacob Good to pay off his indenture. Jacob Good refused his offer and attempted to re-enslave him through the courts. Master Good was unsuccessful and William went free.

Ann and William married, and William went on to run his own saddlery and work as a circuit minister for the United Brethren Church. William Hanby was also a founder of Otterbein College, which appears in the second novel of the series.

I changed a few significant historical details as I wrote *Fairer than Morning*. William Hanby actually indentured under Master Good in the town of Beallsville, Pennsylvania, not far from Pittsburgh. I could not resist the opportunity to show my readers the real conditions of an industrial city in 1826; accordingly, I relocated Will's indenture to Pittsburgh itself. I have also taken poetic license with details about parents and siblings of both Will Hanby and Ann Miller. Finally, there is no evidence that the Millers met Will Hanby in Pittsburgh before he arrived at their home in Ohio—but wouldn't it be romantic if they had?

The facts behind this series come from *Choose You This Day*, a biography of William and Ben Hanby written by Dacia Custer Shoemaker and published by the Westerville Historical Society in 1983.

Acknowledgments

My heartfelt thanks go to my husband and daughter, who shared my time with good grace and who always believed in "Mommy's book."

I am honored to work with my editor, Ami McConnell, and all the gifted folks at Thomas Nelson, as well as my freelance editor Lisa Bergren. Both Ami and Lisa gave wonderful suggestions that encouraged me and improved the novel.

My agent, Rachelle Gardner, first saw the potential in my work and supported me through the submission process for many long months.

I could not have written these novels without expert feedback from fellow writers Lorena Hughes, Barbara Leachman, Dave Slade, Gwen Stewart, and Nathan James.

My beta readers Rachel Padilla, Bonnie Bassham, Angie Drobnic Holan, and Laura Johnson gave me fresh perspective with their insightful responses to my manuscripts.

My sister, Kathryn, and her husband, Josh, made me laugh many times with their witty wisdom about writing and publishing.

My parents were my first teachers and passed on their love of learning.

I am grateful to Bill and Harriet Merriman of the Westerville Historical Society, who assisted me beyond the call of duty with helpful information. Special thanks to Pam Allen and her husband, Jim, who manage the Hanby House and who are a fount of knowledge and generosity on all things Hanby related.

Many thanks also go to Carolyn and Lowell Fisher of Rushville, who kindly supplied details about their town and gave me a tour.

My community of writer-friends in ACFW and online shared the ups and downs of writing life, which means more than I can express here. Thanks especially to Allison Pittman and my Wordserve buddies.

Thanks to the faculty and students of LSMSA '88–'90, who will always be like family to me. And thanks also to the other true friends who have stuck with me through thick and thin.

Most of all, thanks to the original Author, who gives me hope and a future.

Reading Group Guide

1) Ann's journey by steamboat to Pittsburgh provides the opportunity for reflection and change, as travel often will. Why does Ann's first trip to the city change her?

2) How does Mr. Miller influence Will Hanby? Have you ever known someone like Mr. Miller, who has stepped into a parental role for a young person unrelated by blood?

3) Jacob Good behaves in ways that are shocking, by normal standards of decency. What do you think motivates him in his relationships to others?

4) After Ann reads *The Mysteries of Udolpho*, she reconsiders her attitude toward sentiment and benevolent acts. Do you think some novels can either benefit or harm the way people think? Why or why not? And if so, can you think of examples?

5) Where is Will spiritually at the beginning of the novel? How and why does he change by the end of the novel?

6) Will's trials could have left him a broken person, but instead he chooses to help others in similar abusive situations. Do

you know anyone who has turned pain into a desire for serving others?

7) How does the environment (weather, countryside, cityscape) reflect what is happening in the story?

8) Why does it take Ann so long to understand her emotions toward Will?

9) Will spends much of the novel repenting his behavior with Emmie Flynn. Why do you think he crossed his own moral boundaries and did something he later regretted?

10) Dueling was controversial in the nineteenth century. Gentlemen felt it was necessary to defend their honor, but many spoke out from the pulpit against the practice. Do you think there could be a legitimate reason for a duel in 1826?

11) In the afterword, the author describes which parts of the novel are factual and which have been fictionalized. What is the difference between a historical account and historical fiction? What are the advantages and disadvantages of fictionalizing history?

The saddler's legacy continues in

SWEETER THAN Birdsong

AVAILABLE
FEBRUARY 2012

About the Author

ROSSLYN ELLIOTT GREW UP IN A MILITARY FAMILY and relocated so often that she attended nine schools before her high school graduation. With the help of excellent teachers, she qualified to attend Yale University, where she earned a BA in English and theater. She worked in business and as a schoolteacher before returning to study at Emory University, where she earned a PhD in English in 2006. Her study of American literature and history inspired her to pursue her lifelong dream of writing fiction. She lives in the Southwest, where she homeschools her daughter and teaches in children's ministry.